LORDS OF THE SITH

By Paul S. Kemp

Star Wars
Star Wars: Crosscurrent
Star Wars: Riptide
Star Wars: The Old Republic: Deceived
Star Wars: Lords of the Sith

The Sembia Series
The Halls of Stormweather
Shadow's Witness

The Erevis Cale Trilogy
Twilight Falling
Dawn of Night
Midnight's Mask

The Twilight War
Shadowbred
Shadowstorm
Shadowrealm

Anthologies and Collections
Ephemera
Realms of Shadow
Realms of Dragons
Realms of War
Sails and Sorcery
Horrors Beyond II
Worlds of Their Own
Eldritch Horrors: Dark Tales

The Tales of Egil and Nix
The Hammer and the Blade
A Discourse in Steel

STAR WARS®

LORDS OF THE SITH

PAUL S. KEMP

DEL REY • NEW YORK

Star Wars: Lords of the Sith is a work of fiction. Names, places, and incidents either are products of the author's imagination or are used fictitiously. Any resemblance to actual events, locales, or persons, living or dead, is entirely coincidental.

2016 Del Rey Mass Market Edition

Published in the United States by Del Rey, an imprint of Random House, a division of Random House LLC, a Penguin Random House Company, New York.

DEL REY and the HOUSE colophon are registered trademarks of Random House LLC.

Originally published in hardcover in the United States by Del Rey, an imprint of Random House, a division of Random House LLC, in 2015.

This book contains the short story "Orientation," which was originally published in *Star Wars Insider Magazine* #157.

ISBN 978-0-345-51145-4
ebook ISBN 978-0-345-54985-3

Printed in the United States of America

randomhousebooks.com

9 8 7 6 5 4 3 2 1

Del Rey mass market edition: February 2016

For Jen, Riordan, Roarke, Lady D, and Sloane.
Love you all.

THE DEL REY
STAR WARS
TIMELINE

ACKNOWLEDGMENTS

I wrote this book during the most trying period of my adult life. It wouldn't have been possible without Shelly Shapiro. Shelly, my thanks for your patience.

A long time ago in a galaxy far, far away. . . .

LORDS OF THE SITH

Eight years after the Clone Wars ravaged the galaxy, the Republic is no more and the Empire is ascendant. The man who rules as Emperor is secretly a Sith Lord, and with his powerful apprentice, Darth Vader, and all the resources of his vast Imperial war machine, he has placed the galaxy solidly under his heel.

Dissent has been crushed, and freedom is a memory, all in the name of peace and order. But here and there pockets of resistance are beginning to kindle and burn, none hotter than the Free Ryloth movement led by Cham Syndulla.

Now, after many small-scale strikes against the Imperial forces controlling their world, Cham and his fellow freedom fighters take their chance to strike a fatal blow against the Empire and plunge it into chaos by targeting its very heart: Emperor Palpatine and Darth Vader. . . .

CHAPTER ONE

VADER COMPLETED HIS MEDITATION AND OPENED his eyes. His pale, flame-savaged face stared back at him from out of the reflective black transparisteel of his pressurized meditation chamber. Without the neural connection to his armor, he was conscious of the stumps of his legs, the ruin of his arms, the perpetual pain in his flesh. He welcomed it. Pain fed his hate, and hate fed his strength. Once, as a Jedi, he had meditated to find peace. Now he meditated to sharpen the edges of his anger.

He stared at his reflection a long time. His injuries had deformed his body, left it broken, but they'd perfected his spirit, strengthening his connection to the Force. Suffering had birthed insight.

An automated metal arm held the armor's helmet and faceplate over his head, a doom soon to descend. The eyes of the faceplate, which intimidated so many, were no peer to his unmasked eyes. From within a sea of scars, his gaze simmered with controlled, harnessed fury. The secondary respirator, still attached to him, *always* attached to him, masked the ruins of his mouth, and the sound of his breathing echoed off the walls.

Drawing on the Force, he activated the automated arm. It descended and the helmet and faceplate wrapped his head in metal and plasteel, the shell in which he existed. He welcomed the spikes of pain when the helmet's neural needles stabbed into the flesh of his skull and the base of his spine, unifying his body, mind, and armor to form an interconnected unit.

When man and machine were one, he no longer felt the absence of his legs or arms, the pain of his flesh, but the hate remained, and the rage still burned. Those, he never relinquished, and he never felt more connected to the Force than when his fury burned.

With an effort of will, he commanded the onboard computer to link the primary respirator to the secondary, and to seal the helmet at the neck, encasing him fully. He was home.

Once, he'd found the armor hateful, foreign, but now he knew better. He realized that he'd always been fated to wear it, just as the Jedi had always been fated to betray their principles. He'd always been fated to face Obi-Wan and fail on Mustafar—and in failing, learn.

The armor separated him from the galaxy, from everyone, made him singular, freed him from the needs of the flesh, the concerns of the body that once had plagued him, and allowed him to focus solely on his relationship to the Force.

It terrified others, he knew, and that pleased him. Their terror was a tool he used to accomplish his ends. Yoda once had told him that fear led to hate and hate to suffering. But Yoda had been wrong. Fear was a tool used by the strong to cow the weak. Hate was the font of true strength. Suffering was not the result of the rule of the strong over the weak, *order was*. By its very existence, the Force mandated the rule of the strong over the weak; the Force mandated order. The Jedi had never seen that, and so they'd misunderstood the Force and been destroyed. But Vader's Master saw it. Vader saw it. And so they were strong. And so they ruled.

He rose, his breathing loud in his ears, loud in the chamber, his image huge and dark on the reflective wall.

A wave of his gauntleted hand and a mental command rendered the walls of his ovate meditation chamber transparent instead of reflective. The chamber sat in the center of his private quarters aboard the *Perilous*. He looked out and up through the large viewport that opened out onto the galaxy and its numberless worlds and stars.

It was his duty to rule them all. He saw that now. It was the manifest will of the Force. Existence without proper rule was chaos, disorder, suboptimal. The Force—invisible but ubiquitous—bent toward order and was the tool through which order could and must be imposed, but not through harmony, not through peaceful coexistence. That had been the approach of the Jedi, a foolish, failed approach that only fomented more disorder. Vader and his Master imposed order the only way it could be imposed, the way the Force required that it be imposed, through conquest, by forcing the disorder to submit to the order, by bending the weak to the will of the strong.

The history of Jedi influence in the galaxy was a history of disorder and the sporadic wars disorder bred. The history of the Empire would be one of enforced peace, of imposed order.

A pending transmission caused the intercom to chime. He activated it and a hologram of the aquiline-faced, gray-haired commander of the *Perilous*, Captain Luitt, formed before him.

"Lord Vader, there's been an incident at the Yaga Minor shipyards."

"What kind of incident, Captain?"

The lights from the bridge computers blinked or didn't as dictated by the pulse of the ship and the gestures of the ragtag skeleton crew of freedom fighters who staffed the stations. Cham stood behind the helm and looked alternately from the viewscreen to the scanner as he mentally recited the words he'd long ago etched on the stone of his mind so that he could, as needed, read them and be reminded:

Not a terrorist, but a freedom fighter. Not a terrorist, but a freedom fighter.

Cham had fought for his people and Ryloth for almost a standard decade. He'd fought for a free Ryloth when the Republic had tried to annex it, and he fought now for a free Ryloth against the Empire that was trying to strip it bare.

A free Ryloth.

The phrase, the concept, was the polestar around which his existence would forever turn.

Because Ryloth was not free.

As Cham had feared back during the Clone Wars, one well-intentioned occupier of Ryloth had given way to another, less well-intentioned occupier, and a Republic had, through the alchemy of ambition, been transformed into an Empire.

An Imperial protectorate, they called Ryloth. On Imperial star charts Cham's homeworld was listed as "free and independent," but the words could only be used that way with irony, else meaning was turned on its head.

Because Ryloth was not free.

Orn Free Taa, Ryloth's obese representative to the

lickspittle, ceremonial Imperial Senate, validated the otherwise absurd Imperial claims through his treasonous acquiescence to them. But then Ryloth had no shortage of Imperial collaborators, or those willing to lay supine before stormtroopers.

And so . . . Ryloth was not free.

But it would be one day. Cham would see to it. Over the years, he'd recruited and trained hundreds of like-minded people, most but not all of them Twi'leks. He'd cultivated friendly contacts and informants across Ryloth's system, established hidden bases, hoarded matériel. Over the years, he'd planned and executed raid after raid against the Imperials, cautious and precise raids, true, but effective, nevertheless. Dozens of dead Imperials gave mute testimony to the growing effectiveness of the Free Ryloth movement.

Not a terrorist, but a freedom fighter.

He put a reassuring hand on the shoulder of the helm, felt the tension in the clenched muscles of her shoulder. Like most of the crew, like Cham, she was a Twi'lek, and Cham doubted she'd ever flown anything larger than a little gorge hopper, certainly nothing like the armed freighter she steered now.

"Just hold her steady, helm," Cham said. "We won't need anything fancy out of you."

Standing behind Cham, Isval added, "We hope."

The helm exhaled and nodded. Her lekku, the twin head-tails that extended down from the back of her head to her shoulders, relaxed slightly to signify relief. "Aye, sir. Nothing fancy."

Isval stepped beside Cham, her eyes on the viewscreen.

"Where are they?" she grumbled, the darkening blue of her skin and the agitated squirm of her lekku a reflection of her irritation. "It's been days and no word."

Isval always grumbled. She was perpetually restless, a wanderer trapped in a cage only she could see, pacing the confines over and over, forever testing the strength of the bars. She reminded him of his daughter, Hera, whom he missed deeply when he allowed himself such moments. Cham valued Isval's need for constant motion, for constant action. They were the perfect counterpoints to each other: her rash, him deliberate; her practical, him principled.

"Peace, Isval," he said softly. He'd often said the same thing to Hera.

He held his hands, sweaty with stress despite his calm tone, clasped behind his back. He eyed the bridge data display. Almost time. "They're not late, not yet. And if they'd failed, we'd have had word by now."

Her retort came fast. "If they'd succeeded, we'd have had word by now, too. Wouldn't we?"

Cham shook his head, his lekku swaying. "No, not necessarily. They'd run silent. Pok knows better than to risk comm chatter. He'd need to skim a gas giant to refuel, too. And he might have needed to shake pursuit. They had a lot of space to cover."

"He would've sent word, though, something," she insisted. "They could have blown up the ship during the hijack attempt. They could all be dead. Or worse."

She said the words too loudly, and the heads of several of the crew came up from their work, looks of concern on their faces.

"They could, but they're not." He put his hand on her shoulder. "Peace, Isval. Peace."

She grimaced and swallowed hard, as if trying to rid herself of a bad taste. She pulled away from him and started to pace anew. "Peace. There's peace only for the dead."

Cham smiled. "Then let's stick with war for at least a bit longer, eh?"

His words stopped her in her pacing and elicited one of her half smiles, and a half smile was as close as Isval ever got to the real thing. He had only a vague idea of what had been done to her when she'd been enslaved, but he had a firm sense that it must have been awful. She'd come a long way.

"Back to it, people," he ordered. "Stay sharp."

Silence soon filled all the empty space on the bridge. Hope hung suspended in the quiet—fragile, brittle, ready to be shattered with the wrong word. The relentless gravity of waiting drew eyes constantly to the data display that showed the time. But still nothing.

Cham had stashed the freighter in the rings of one of the system's gas giants. Metal ore in the rock chunks that made up the rings would hide the ship from any scans.

"Helm, take us above the plane of the rings," Cham said.

Even in an off-the-chart system, it was a risk to put the freighter outside the shelter of the planet's rings. The ship's credentials wouldn't hold up to a full Imperial query, and Imperial probes and scouts were everywhere, as the Emperor tried to firm up his grip on the galaxy and quell any hot spots. If they were noticed they'd have to run.

"Magnify screen when we're clear."

Even magnified, the screen would show far less than long-range sensors, but Cham needed to see for himself, not stare at readouts.

Isval paced beside him.

The ship shifted up, out of the bands of ice and rock, and the magnified image on the screen showed the outer system, where a single, distant planetoid of uninhabited rock orbited the system's dim star, and countless stars beyond blinked in the dark. A nebula light-years away to starboard painted a slice of space the color of blood.

Cham stared at the screen as if he could pull his comrades through hyperspace by sheer force of will. Assuming they'd even been able to jump. The whole operation had been a huge risk, but Cham had thought it worthwhile to secure more heavy weapons and force the Empire to divert some resources away from Ryloth. Too, he'd wanted to make a stronger statement, send an unmistakable message that at least some of the Twi'leks of Ryloth would not quietly accept Imperial rule. He'd wanted to be the spark that started a fire across the galaxy.

"Come on, Pok," he whispered, the involuntary twitch of his lekku betraying his stress. He'd known Pok for years and called him friend.

Isval muttered under her breath, a steady flood of Twi'lek expletives.

Cham watched the data display as the appointed time arrived and passed, taking the hopes of the crew with it. Heavy sighs and slack lekku all around.

"Patience, people," Cham said softly. "We wait. We keep waiting until we know."

"We wait," Isval affirmed with a nod. She paced the deck, staring at the viewscreen as if daring it to keep showing her something she didn't want to see.

The moments stretched. The crew shifted in their seats, shared surreptitious looks of disappointment. Cham had to work to unclench his jaw.

The engineer on scan duty broke the spell.

"I've got something!" she said.

Cham and Isval fairly sprinted over to the scanner. All eyes watched them.

"It's a ship," the engineer said.

A satisfied, relieved rustle moved through the bridge crew. Cham could almost hear the smiles. He eyed the readout.

"That's an Imperial transport," he said.

"That's *our* Imperial transport," Isval said.

A few members of the bridge crew gave a muted cheer.

"Stay on station, people," Cham said, but he could not shake his grin.

"Coming through now," the engineer said. "It's them, sir. It's them! They're hailing us."

"On speaker," Cham said. "Meanwhile, alert the off-load team. We'll want to get those weapons aboard and destroy that ship as soon as—"

A crackle of static and then Pok's strained voice. "Get clear of here right now! Just go!"

"Pok?" Cham said, as the crew's elation shifted to concern. "Pok, what is it?"

"It's Vader, Cham. Get out of here now! We thought we'd lost the pursuit. We've been jumping through systems to throw them off. I'd thought we'd lost them, but they're still on us! Go, Cham!"

The engineer looked up at Cham, her lavender skin flushing to dark blue at the cheeks. "There are more ships coming out of hyperspace, sir. More than a dozen, all small." Her voice tightened as she said, "V-wings probably. Maybe interceptors."

Cham and Isval cursed as one.

"Get on station, people!" Cham ordered.

Vader's customized Eta-interceptor led the starfighter squadron as the star-lined tunnel of hyperspace gave way to the black of ordinary space. A quick scan allowed him to locate the hijacked weapons transport, which they'd been pursuing through several systems as it tried to work its way out to the Rim. The squadron disengaged from their hyperspace rings.

The heavily armed transport showed slight blaster damage along the aft hull near the three engines, behind the bloated center of the cargo bay.

"Attack formation," Vader ordered, and the pilots in the rest of the squad acknowledged the command and fell into formation.

Concerned that the hijackers might have dropped out of hyperspace to lure the squadron into an ambush, he ran a quick scan of the entire system. The interceptor's sensor array was not the most sensitive, but it showed only a pair of huge, ringed gas giants, each with a score or more of moons, an asteroid belt between the planets and the system's star, and a few planetoids at the outside of the system. Otherwise, the system was an uninhabited backwater.

"Scans show no other ships in the system," Vader said.

"Confirmed," the squadron commander replied.

The voice of one of the pilots carried over the comm: "They're powering up for another jump, Lord Vader."

"Follow my lead," Vader ordered, and accelerated to attack speed. "Do not allow them to jump again."

The V-wings and Vader's interceptor were far faster and more maneuverable than the transport and closed on it rapidly, devouring the space between. Vader did not bother consulting his instrumentation. He fell into the Force, flying by feel, as he always did.

Even before the interceptor and the V-wings closed to within blaster range, one of the freighter's engines burped a gout of blue flame and burned out. The hijackers had overtaxed the transport in their escape attempt.

"I want the shields down and the remaining two engines disabled," Vader said. Disabling the engines would prevent another hyperspace jump. "Do *not* destroy that ship."

The heavier armaments of the transport had a longer range than the interceptor and V-wings' blasters and opened up before the starfighters got within blaster range.

"Weapons are hot, go evasive," said the squadron leader as the transport's automated gun turrets filled the space between the ships with green lines. The starfighter squadron veered apart, twisting and diving.

Vader felt as much as saw the transport's blasters. He cut left, then hard right, then dived a few degrees down, still closing on the transport. One of the V-wings to his left caught a green line. Its wing fragmented and it went spinning and flaming off into the system.

The larger, crewed, swivel-mounted gun bubbles on either side of the transport's midline swung around and opened fire, fat pulses of red plasma.

"Widen your spacing," the squadron commander said over the comm. "Spacing!"

A burst of red plasma caught one of the V-wings squarely and vaporized it.

"Focus your fire on the aft shields," Vader said, his interceptor wheeling and spinning, sliding between the red and the green, until he was within range. He fired and his blasters sent twin beams of plasma into the aft shields. He angled the shot to maximize deflection. He did not want to pierce them and damage the ship, just drain them and bring them down.

The rest of the squadron did the same, hitting the transport from multiple angles. The transport bucked under the onslaught, the shields flaring under the energy load and visibly weakening with each shot. The entire squad overtook and passed the freighter, the green and red shots of its weapons chasing them along.

"Maintain spacing, stay evasive, and swing around for another pass," the squadron commander ordered. "Split squadron and come underneath."

The squadron's ships peeled right and left, circling back and down, and set themselves on another intercept vector. Vader decelerated enough to fall back to the rear.

"Bring the shields down on this pass, Commander," he said. "I have something in mind."

Pok had left the channel open so Cham and his crew could hear the activity aboard the hijacked freighter's bridge—Pok barking orders, someone calling the attack vectors of the V-wings, the boom of blasterfire on shields.

"Pok!" Cham said. "We can help!"

"No!" Pok said. "We're already down one engine. We can't power up yet, and there's a Star Destroyer somewhere behind these V-wings. There's nothing you can do for us, Cham." To one of his crew, Pok shouted, "Get the hyperdrive back online!"

An explosion sent a crackle of static and a scream of feedback along the channel.

"Shields at ten percent," someone on Pok's bridge called out.

"Hyperdrive still nonoperational," said someone else.

Isval grabbed Cham by the arm, hard enough for it to hurt. She spoke in a low, harsh voice. "We have to help them."

But Cham didn't see how they could. If he left the

shelter of the rings, the V-wings or interceptors or whatever they were would pick them up on scan, and Cham had no illusions about the ability of his helm or his ship should they be discovered.

"No," Cham said to the helm. "Stay put."

Vader watched the transport go hard to port, taking an angle that would allow both of the midline weapons bubbles to fire on the approaching starfighters. As soon as they entered the transport's range, the automated turrets and gun bubbles opened fire, filling space with beams of superheated plasma. The V-wings swooped and twisted and dodged, spiraling through the net of green and red energy.

Vader, lingering behind, piloted his ship between the bolts, above them, below them. A third V-wing caught a shot from a gun turret and exploded, debris peppering Vader's cockpit canopy as he flew through the flames.

When the V-wings got within range, they opened fire and the freighter's shields fell almost immediately.

"Shields down, Lord Vader," the squadron leader reported.

"I'll take the engines," Vader said. "Destroy the turrets and the starboard-side midline gun bubble."

The pilots of his squadron, selected for their piloting excellence and a demonstrated record of kills, did exactly as he'd ordered. Small explosions lit up the hull, and the gun emplacements disappeared in flowers of fire. The transport shook from the impact as the V-wings swooped past it, up, and started to circle back around.

Meanwhile Vader veered to his left and down, locked onto the engines, and fired, once, twice. Explosions rocked the transport aft, and chunks of both engines spun off into space. Secondary explosions rocked the vessel, but it otherwise remained intact. Vader slowed still more, trailing the transport.

"She's running on inertia now, sir," said the squadron commander. "When the *Perilous* arrives, she can tractor the transport into one of her bays."

"I have no intention of leaving the hijackers aboard the ship that long," Vader said. He knew the hijackers would try to blow the ship, and there were enough weapons in the cargo bay to do just that. "I'm going to board her."

"Sir, the docking clamp on that ship is too damaged, and there's no landing bay," said the squadron commander.

"I am aware of that, Commander," Vader said.

The sole remaining gun bubble—operated by one of the hijackers—swung around and opened fire on Vader's ship. Still using the Force to guide him, Vader slung his ship side to side, up and down, staying just ahead of the blasterfire as he headed straight for the bubble. He could see the gunner inside the transparent canopy, feel his presence, insignificant and small, through the web of the Force.

"Sir . . . ," the commander said as the V-wing squadron circled back around, but Vader did not acknowledge him.

Vader hit a switch and depressurized the interceptor's cockpit, his armor shielding him from the vacuum. Then, as he neared the transport's midline, still swinging his ship left and right to dodge the incoming fire, he selected a spot on the transport adjacent to the gun bubble and, using the Force, took a firm mental hold on it.

His interceptor streaked toward the gun bubble, aimed directly at it. Content with the trajectory, he unstrapped himself, overrode the interceptor's safeties, threw open the cockpit hatch, and ejected into space.

Immediately he was spinning in the zero-g, the ship and stars alternating positions with rapidity. Yet he kept his mental hold on the air-lock handle, and his armor, sealed and pressurized, sustained him in the vacuum. The respirator was loud in his ears.

His ship slammed into the gun bubble and the transport, the inability of the vacuum to transmit sound causing the collision to occur in eerie silence. Fire flared for a moment, but only a moment before the vacuum extinguished it. Chunks of debris exploded outward into space and the transport lurched.

A great boom sounded through the connection. Alarms wailed, and Pok's bridge exploded in a cacophony of competing conversations.

"Pok, what just happened?" Cham asked. "Are you all right?"

"We had a collision. We're all right. Get me status on the damage," Pok said to someone on his bridge. "Get someone over there now."

"Sir! Sir!" the squadron commander called, his voice frantic in Vader's helmet comm. "Lord Vader! What's happening, sir?"

Vader's voice was calm. "I'm docking with the transport, Commander."

Using the Force, Vader stopped his rotation and reeled himself in toward the large, jagged, smoking hole his interceptor had torn in the transport's hull. Loose hoses and electrical lines dangled from the edges of the opening, leaking gases and shooting sparks into space. A portion of his ship's wing had survived the impact and was lodged in the bulkhead. The rest had been vaporized on impact.

Vader pulled himself through the destruction until he stood in the remains of a depressurized corridor. Chunks of metal and electronics littered the torn deck, the whole of it smoking from the heat of impact. The V-wings buzzed past the transport, visible through the hole in the bulkhead.

"Sir?" said the squadron commander.

"All is under control, Commander," Vader said.

Several members of the fighter squadron whispered awed oaths into their comms.

"Maintain comm discipline," the squadron leader barked, though Vader could hear the disbelief in his tone, too. "My lord . . . there are dozens of hijackers aboard that transport."

"Not for much longer, Commander," Vader said. "You are on escort duty now. I will notify you if anything else is required."

A pause, then, "Of course, sir."

The transport's automatic safeties had sealed off the corridor with a blast door, but he knew the codes to override them. He strode through the ruin and entered the code. The huge door slid open, and pressurized air from the hall beyond poured out with a hiss. He stepped through and resealed the door behind him. A few more taps on a wall comp and he'd repressurized the hall. The shrill sound of the transport's hull-breach alarm wailed from wall speakers.

A hatch on the far side of the hall slid open to reveal a purple-skinned Twi'lek man in makeshift armor. Seeing Vader, the Twi'lek's head-tails twitched, his eyes widened in surprise, and he grabbed for the blaster at his belt. By the time the Twi'lek had the blaster drawn and the trigger pulled, Vader had his lightsaber in hand and ignited. He deflected the blaster shot into the wall, raised his off hand, and with it reached out with the Force. He made a pincer motion with his two fingers, using the Force to squeeze closed the Twi'lek's trachea.

The Twi'lek pawed frantically at his throat as Vader's power lifted him off the deck, but to his credit he held on to his weapon, and gagging, dying, he managed to aim and fire his blaster at Vader again and again. Vader simply held his grip on the alien's throat while casually deflecting the blasts into the bulkhead with his lightsaber. Then, not wanting to waste time, he moved his raised hand left and then right, using the Force to smash the Twi'lek into the bulkhead. The impacts shattered bone, and Vader let the body fall to the deck. A voice carried over a comlink on the Twi'lek's belt.

"Tymo! Tymo! What is going on there? Do you copy? Can you hear me?"

Vader deactivated his lightsaber, picked up the comlink, opened the channel, and let the sound of his respirator carry over the connection.

"Who is that?"

Vader answered only with his breathing.

"Tymo, is that you? Are you all right?"

"I'm coming for you now," Vader said.

He crushed the communicator in his fist, reignited his lightsaber, stepped over the dead Twi'lek, and strode into the corridor beyond.

CHAPTER TWO

CHAM AND ISVAL SHARED A LOOK OF ALARM. They'd heard the communication through the open channel. They knew the sound of the respirator.

"Was that . . . ?" Isval asked.

"Vader," Cham said. "Had to be. Pok?"

"I agree," Pok said. "That had to be Vader."

They knew Vader by reputation.

Silence weighed heavy on the bridge.

"What do we know?" Cham asked Isval in a whisper.

She shook her head, her lekku squirming in agitation. "Not much. Second- and thirdhand stories. I've heard that the regular officers hate him, but the Stormtrooper Corps almost worships him."

"How did he get aboard Pok's ship?"

Isval shrugged. She wasn't pacing. A bad sign. "They say he can do things no being should be able to do. Everyone is terrified of him. This is bad, Cham."

"I know." Cham's eyes followed hers to the viewscreen. They couldn't see the hijacked freighter, of course, but Cham could imagine it in his mind's eye. And now he imagined Vader aboard it.

"Situation, Pok."

For a moment, Pok didn't answer. Perhaps his attention was on something else, then, "Engines are dead, Cham. Weapons are destroyed. We're . . . boarded somehow. You heard."

"How'd he board?" Cham asked. "Is he alone?"

"I don't know," Pok said, then to someone on the bridge, he added, "I need that information now," then, "Cham, there are twenty-six of us here. We can fight. Make them pay, at least."

"Pok . . . ," Cham began, but Pok spared him the need to say it.

"Don't worry. We won't be taken. My crew knew the risks when they volunteered for this. Unfortunately I can't self-destruct with the engines offline, but I've got a team of my best on the way to the cargo hold. We can use the weapons there as a fail-safe . . . What? Hold, Cham." Some background chatter that Cham could not make out, then Pok's voice: "Well, raise them. Raise them right now."

A pause, then someone in the background said, "They're not responding, Pok."

Cham muted the comm and said to his engineer, "Keep us hidden and tell me instantly if any of those V-wings so much as heads in our direction."

Cham knew V-wings had little in the way of long-distance sensors, but he had moved the freighter to the edge of the rings. Even the V-wings would pick it up if they got close enough.

"Yes, sir," the engineer said. "They look like they're holding formation around the weapons transport."

"We can't just let him kill himself," Isval said to Cham, her voice tense. "Let's get out there and help them. We can fight our way out."

"They're dead in space," Cham said, and instantly regretted his choice of words.

"Cham—"

Cham ignored her and unmuted the connection. "Pok?"

Pok cleared his throat. His bridge was quiet. "I've lost the team I sent to the hold, Cham. I don't know what . . . they're not answering their comms. Vader must have intercepted them."

Cham clenched a fist but kept his calm. "Understood."

Isval spoke through clenched teeth, slow for emphasis. "We should help them."

Cham muted the connection and whirled on her, the thread of his patience finally snapping.

"Help them how, Isval? They're without engines and surrounded! Even if we could destroy every V-wing, and you know we can't, it would take time to get them from their ship to ours. There's a Star Destroyer on the way, and some . . . man is aboard who managed single-handedly to wipe out a group of Pok's best people!"

She held her ground in the face of his outburst. The rest of the crew buried their faces in their stations.

"Vader's not a man," she said tightly. "Not from what I've heard."

"Yes, he is," Cham said, loud enough for the entire bridge crew to hear him. "He has to be. But there's nothing we can do to help that won't end with all of us dead, too. Pok knows it; they all know it. And we all know it." He sagged and looked back at the viewscreen. "We don't like it, but we all know it."

Pok's voice came over the comm. "Cham is right, everyone. We knew the risks. We took them willingly."

Cham cursed. He thought he'd muted the connection. "Pok, I'm sorry." Emotion choked his voice. "I thought . . ."

"I know," Pok said, and chuckled—actually chuckled. "Is that Isval over there?"

"It is, Pok," she said.

"Still blowing in like a sandstorm, I see," Pok said. "That's good. I'm glad we got to say good-bye. You keep Cham on course, all right? He's too damn principled for his own good."

"It doesn't have to be good-bye," Isval said, and stared at Cham.

"It does and it is. We'll see if we can't kill this Vader first, though. I've got an ambush set up . . ."

Someone on Pok's bridge crew said, "Blasterfire in the main corridor off the bridge, sir."

For a moment no one spoke on either bridge. Long moments passed. Then there was some talk on Pok's bridge in the background. Cham could not make it out.

"Situation?" Pok asked someone in his bridge crew.

"No one is answering the comm," came the reply.

"How can— There were eight men waiting for him! What is going on out there?"

"Bridge lift is coming up!" another member of Pok's crew said.

Pok spoke into the comm, his breathing audible over the connection, as if he was leaning in close. "Cham, we'll kill Vader and blow the ship. No one will get taken alive."

"Pok . . . ," Cham began.

"It's been an honor," Pok said. "Keep up the fight. All of you."

Someone on Pok's bridge shouted, "For a free Ryloth!" and the rest of the bridge crew echoed the cry.

Isval was gripping Cham's arm so hard his hand was growing numb. He stared at the open comm as if it held some secret meaning, some hidden thing he could discern that would save Pok and everyone else. But there was nothing.

The rest of his crew sat in silence at their stations, heads down, listening.

"It's opening!" said someone on Pok's bridge.

A burst of blasterfire carried across the connection, but only for a moment before falling silent.

"There's no one," said a voice. "The lift's empty."

"Check it," Pok ordered. "He's still aboard somewhere—"

A sizzle and hum sounded, shouts, a thump, repeated blasterfire, a prolonged thrum, rising and falling, a series of shouts and screams.

"Pok!" Isval cried. "Pok!"

Cham cursed.

"What's happening over there?" Isval asked. "What's that sound?"

The rising thrum dredged memories from the back of Cham's mind.

"It's a lightsaber," he said. The sound of the blade had been seared into his head during the Clone Wars, when Jedi had wielded them: Jedi doing things, like Vader, that no ordinary being could do. But there were no more Jedi and there was no more Republic. There was only Vader, and the Empire.

Another thump, then another. More alarmed shouts. Only two or three blasters were firing, and in the relative quiet another sound came over the comm: breathing, loud, as though amplified through a speaker or respirator. Vader's breathing.

"What is that? Is that Vader?" Isval asked, her own breath coming rapidly. Cham hurriedly muted the connection on his end.

More shouts, the crash of something heavy, and still the hum of the lightsaber, rising and falling.

"For Ryloth!" Pok shouted, and the sound of rapid blasterfire filled the comm.

The hum of the lightsaber rose and fell, and Cham imagined Vader deflecting the blaster shots with the blade. He'd seen it before. Abruptly the shots stopped. A strangled gasp came over the comm: Pok, choking.

"He's strangling him!" Isval said.

The choking went on for seconds that felt like hours, Vader's amplified breathing the counterpoint to Pok's dying gasps. Cham knew he should cut the connection, but he couldn't. Cutting it would feel like abandoning Pok a second time.

"Tell me what I want to know," said a deep voice, Vader's voice. "And your death will be easier."

They heard a pained gasp and a deep inhalation, followed by Pok cursing Vader in Twi'leki.

"Very well," Vader said.

Pok gagged again, gasped, and went silent. Then a thump sounded, something heavy but soft falling to the deck.

Isval screamed a curse. Cham's heart was a hammer on his ribs, but he said nothing. There was nothing to be said. The only sound was Vader's breathing carrying over the comm.

"Cut it off, Cham!" Isval said.

Cham stared at the comm, open but muted on Cham's end. Vader's breathing grew louder, as if he had picked up the comm to study it or hold it close to his face. The breathing. The breathing.

"Cut it, Cham!" Isval said.

Cham realized he was holding his breath. He seemed unable to breathe.

There was only Vader's respiration, regular as a pendulum. Loud. Ominous.

Cham finally got ahold of himself and exhaled,

thinking of Pok, the awful gasps that had been the last sounds his friend had made.

"Your allies are dead," Vader said, and the words made Cham wince.

Isval slammed her hand on the comm, cutting it short.

Silence.

"Cham, we should go," she said. "Right now."

But Cham knew it was already too late. If they tried to flee the system now, they'd end up exactly as had Pok and his crew: pursued, caught, and executed.

When he made no reply, Isval said to the helm, "Take us out of here."

That brought Cham around. "Belay that!" To Isval, he said softly, "It's too late for that. They'll see us."

"The V-wings are spreading out, sir," the engineer reported. "They look like they're starting a sweep. Another ship is coming into the system. A Star Destroyer."

The air went out of everyone all at once. All eyes fell on Cham. They were waiting for orders, waiting for salvation. Pok was gone, the spell was broken, and Cham did not hesitate.

"Take us deep in the rings. Make us a rock, helm. Minimal life support. Take everything else down. We float."

"If we go dark, we won't be able to run if they detect us," Isval said. "By the time we get the engines back online—"

"There's no running, Isval," Cham said matter-of-factly. "We hide or we die. Do it, helm."

The helm nodded and did as she was ordered. The ship descended deep into the rings, and the viewscreen filled with pockmarked, irregular blocks of ice and stone, all spinning and whirling.

"Power us down," Cham ordered.

"Aye, sir," the engineer said, and the bridge lights and viewscreen went dark.

Dim auxiliary lights cast the bridge in a faint orange glow. The shadowed faces of the crew looked at one another, at the ceiling, the bulkheads.

Bits of ice and rock ticked against the hull. With life support at minimum, the temperature started to drop quickly. But it wouldn't get life threatening, merely uncomfortable.

Cham was more worried about the ship taking a high-speed impact from one of the larger rocks or ice chunks. The hull could take a beating, but it wasn't impregnable, and if the ship started bouncing around in the rings, he'd have no choice but to fire up the engines.

"Steady now, people," he said.

Some of the crew bowed their heads; others stared at the blank viewscreen. The tension was worse than the cold. Within a few minutes Cham could see his breath in the air. He tried not to shiver. He walked from crewperson to crewperson, touching shoulders, backs, whispering for them to be at ease. He eventually circled back to Isval and spoke to her quietly.

"I should've cut that comm sooner. I put us at risk."

Isval did him the credit of not denying his error. "Let's hope you get a chance to do so again."

"That was . . . hard to hear."

"Yes," she said.

"This is the last time we hide from Vader," Cham told her.

She looked him full in the face and nodded agreement.

An impact shook the ship and the crew exclaimed as one. The helm nearly lost her seat, but used her instrument panel to stay at her station. There were no follow-up impacts.

"That was just a rock," Isval said. "Steady, people. If that Star Destroyer picks us up, it'll be over before we feel anything."

"That ought to cheer them," Cham said, and Isval gave him one of her half smiles, or maybe a quarter smile.

They sat in silence for a long while, hope rising with each passing minute. Soon the crew was breathing easily again.

"I think that's long enough," said Cham. "Power us up, helm."

Despite the time that had passed, the crew grew palpably tense as the systems came back online. If any Imperial ships were nearby and scanning, the freighter would light up on their sensors immediately. The lights and viewscreen returned, the engines engaged, and they headed up out of the rings. In moments the rings gave way to the black of the system.

"Nothing on sensors," the engineer said.

The viewscreen showed an empty system. The V-wings were gone, the Star Destroyer, Pok and his crew. All gone, as if it had never happened.

"Take us back to Ryloth," Cham ordered.

He fell in beside Isval as the ship moved out of the gravity well of the gas giant and powered up its hyperdrive. "No more half measures," he said. "We stay smart, but we think bigger."

Isval locked on to the first half of his statement and echoed it back at him. "No more half measures. Aye that, sir."

The points of stars turned to lines and the black of space surrendered to the blue of hyperspace.

Vader stood behind his Master's throne in the dimly lit receiving room on Coruscant. The steady rhythm of the respirator marked the passage of the minutes. Two members of the Royal Guard, covered head-to-toe in the blood-red armor indicative of their order, flanked the door. Each held a stun pole at station. Vader knew that each of their crimson capes hid a heavy blaster pistol, a vibroblade, and various other weaponry. Huge windows opened out onto the Coruscant skyline, countless ships buzzing past the glass, metal, and concrete spires of the megacity. The sun threw its last light over the horizon, washing the terrain in orange and red.

The Emperor sat on the throne in silence, seemingly lost in thought. But Vader, standing behind the throne, knew better. His Master was never lost in thought. The Emperor's thinking ranged over time and distance in a way not even Vader fully understood, allowing him to anticipate and plan for contingencies that others did not recognize. Vader hoped to learn the technique one day, provided he didn't kill his Master first.

Soon after destroying the Jedi, the Emperor had told Vader that he would one day be tempted to kill him. He'd said that the relationship between Sith apprentice and Master was symbiotic but in a delicate balance. An apprentice owed his Master loyalty. A Master owed his apprentice knowledge and must show only strength. But the obligations were reciprocal and contingent. Should either fail in his obligation, it was the duty of the other to destroy him. The Force required it.

Since before the Clone Wars, Vader's Master had never shown anything but strength, and so Vader intended to show nothing but loyalty. In that way, their mutual rule was secure.

Perhaps Vader would attempt to kill his Master one day. Sith apprentices ordinarily did. They must, if they were trained well. An apprentice was unquestioningly loyal until the moment he wasn't. Both Master and apprentice knew this.

"But our relationship is different, Master," Vader had said then.

"Perhaps," his Master had said. "Perhaps."

Or maybe self-delusion was part of the training a Master instilled in an apprentice.

"Your thoughts are troubled, my friend," the Emperor said, his voice loud in the quiet. The Emperor often referred to him as a friend, and perhaps they were friends, in some sense, though Vader saw purpose in the use of the term. He thought his Master used a term he might use with a peer to emphasize that Master and apprentice were not, in fact, peers.

"No, my Master. Not troubled."

The Emperor chuckled, the sound coming out a cackle. " 'Troubled' perhaps misstates the matter. Your thoughts are on violence."

He turned in his throne to glance back at Vader, and his eyes burned out of the shadowed recesses of his hood.

"You ponder the nature of strength, do you not?"

Vader never lied to his Master. And he understood that his Master asked questions only with great forethought, so that the answer revealed more than the words. "I do."

The Emperor turned away, showing his back to Vader, itself a calculated gesture. "Share your thoughts, my apprentice."

Vader did not hesitate. "I was thinking of the lessons you once taught me about the relationship of a Sith Master to his apprentice."

"And?" his Master asked.

Vader dropped to a knee and bowed his head. "And I perceive strength all around me, my Master."

"Good," the Emperor said. "Very good."

The moment having passed, Vader rose and stood station behind his Master.

Together they waited for the arrival of Orn Free Taa, the puppet delegate from Ryloth. Vader did not know the purpose of the audience. His Master told him only what he needed to know.

Before long the two members of the Royal Guard, no doubt alerted to the senator's imminent arrival via their helmet comlinks, moved to open the double doors. But before they could, the Emperor gestured with his finger and pulled the doors open with the Force. The light from the chamber beyond backlit the wide silhouette of the corpulent Twi'lek senator. He stood there a moment as if pinioned by the Emperor's eyes, or perhaps he merely needed to work up the nerve to enter.

"Come in, Senator," the Emperor said, in the voice he used when attempting to disarm something small and weak and easily frightened.

"Of course, of course," Taa said, waddling into the room. He eyed the guards sidelong as he passed and slowed for a moment when the doors audibly closed behind him.

When he stood before the throne in his embroidered robes, he gave as much of a bow as his girth allowed.

"Emperor Palpatine," he said. Sweat glistened on his wrinkled blue skin, and his gaze danced nervously between Vader and the Emperor. His wheezes were so loud, they nearly matched the sounds of Vader's respirator.

"How do you fare, my friend?" the Emperor asked.

"Very well," Taa said between breaths, then quickly added, "Very well. But not *so* well, my Emperor. Because I know the spice production on Ryloth has slowed considerably due to . . . some unfortunate events, but—"

"By 'unfortunate events,'" the Emperor said, leaning forward in his throne, "do you mean the terrorist attacks of the Free Ryloth movement?"

Taa sniffed and licked his sharpened teeth, a nervous habit. His lekku squirmed. "Yes, my Emperor. They are misled zealots and put all of my people at risk with their recklessness. But—" He paused to catch his breath before continuing. "—between the Twi'lek security forces and the Imperial troops answering to Moff Mors, I believe matters are well in hand and that production will soon be back to full capacity."

"Alas," said the Emperor, "I do not share your optimism, Senator. Nor your high opinion of Moff Mors."

Taa looked like he had been punched. His skin darkened. He blinked, gulped, took a half step back. "But surely—"

"Because I do not think matters are 'well in hand,' I have made a decision."

Taa's eyes birthed fear, went to Vader, back to the Emperor. "My lord . . ."

"And it is this: Lord Vader and I will accompany you on an official visit to Ryloth. There we'll investigate matters for ourselves. I will notify Moff Mors that we are coming."

Taa sagged with relief. "I . . . don't know what to say."

"You need say nothing," the Emperor said. "The decision is made. The planning for the journey is already 'well in hand.'"

"Of course." Taa looked down as he adjusted the folds of his robes around his belly. "But *me* return to

Ryloth? Perhaps I can be of more service to you here, my Emperor?"

"I think not," said the Emperor. "Your presence there will be invaluable. I believe it's time the people of Ryloth were made to feel, truly feel, a part of the Empire. Do you not agree?"

"Oh, of course, of course," Taa said, his chins bouncing.

"You still look unconvinced, my old friend."

Taa shook his head so hard his fleshy ear flaps spread like wings. "No, no. It's just . . ." His voice fell to a murmur. "It's just that it's . . . rather unpleasant there."

"I'm sure you'll manage, Senator," the Emperor said, his voice carrying the full weight of his contempt. "We'll all make the journey together, aboard the *Perilous*."

Taa looked up, his wide face crinkled with concerns and excuses, but he seemed to think better of voicing them.

"You are dismissed, Senator," the Emperor said.

"My Emperor," Taa said with a bow. "Lord Vader."

Once the doors were closed behind him, the Emperor said to Vader, "Give me your impressions of the senator, my friend."

"He is fearful of you, as he should be, but he is not as timid as he seems. He will do as he's asked in order to preserve what power and privileges he still retains, but he will do no more than what he's asked. And he will do it all with an eye first to his own interests, then to his people, and then to the Empire."

"Hmm. Would you say then that he is . . . loyal?"

"Viewed through those constraints, yes, I'd consider him loyal."

"Viewed through those constraints, yes. I concur

with your assessment. And so I conclude that Orn
Free Taa is no traitor to the Empire."

"You suspected him of treachery?"

"Either him or a member of his staff. He seemed an
unlikely candidate, but one never knows. Someone is
providing the terrorists of the so-called Free Ryloth
movement with knowledge of what transpires here.
The hijacking you thwarted was indicative of that.
The treason must originate in Taa's staff."

Vader should have seen the Emperor's purpose. As
usual, the Emperor's thinking was one step ahead of
his.

"And that's why we'll travel to Ryloth?" Vader
asked. "To act as bait? Why take that risk, when I
could simply kill Taa and his entire staff? That would
eliminate the traitor."

The Emperor shook his head and stood. The moment he rose, the Royal Guardsmen hurried from
their station at the door to flank him. Vader fell in
with them as they started walking toward the chamber doors. The sun cast its final rays over the Corsus-
cant skyline, throwing the room into deeper darkness.

"But that would not eliminate the roots of the
treachery," his Master said. "Nor would it reveal the
scope of the treason, which I suspect reaches well beyond the senator's staff."

"I see," Vader said. "Then I should go alone.
There's no reason to put you at risk."

"But there is," said the Emperor. "We must tear dis-
loyalty out by the roots, expose it, and there let it
wither and die where all can see."

"An example to make the point."

"Yes. An example for the rest of the Empire."

"A needful one," Vader said. Since the consolida-
tion of the Republic into the new Galactic Empire,
pockets of chaos had appeared here and there. Most

of the former Republic accepted the Empire without complaint, but there were many bands of resistance fighters and Separatist remnants lurking around the galaxy. The Free Ryloth movement was one of the more capable and notorious.

"Indeed," said the Emperor. "And that lesson is one that *I* must administer. Besides, old friend, it has been too long since we've traveled together. Inform Moff Mors that Orn Free Taa is returning to Ryloth for a state visit and that he will be traveling aboard the *Perilous*. She should not be informed, at least not yet, that we will be accompanying the senator."

"Yes, my Master."

"You have been to Ryloth before, have you not, Lord Vader?"

The question dredged memories of war from the depths of Vader's mind.

"Long ago, Master. Before I learned wisdom."

"Of course."

CHAPTER THREE

CHAM SAT ALONE IN HIS DIMLY LIT QUARTERS IN one of the many underground staging camps from which he conducted his guerrilla war against the Empire. He had several such bases secreted around Ryloth. He'd spent years building his forces, cultivating his network, caching ships and weapons, laying the foundation for a major blow, and now, seemingly, an opportunity had come, more than he could have hoped for. Far more.

He was sweating.

He stared at the decoded message he held in his hand. Even after decryption the message was obscure.

OFT en route w/1 and 2. Transport 1SD. 10 dys.

He deciphered it again, ensuring he had the right of it.

Orn Free Taa was returning to Ryloth. He would be accompanied by Emperor Palpatine and Lord Vader. They were coming via Star Destroyer in ten days.

He was reading it right; it just didn't make any sense. He smelled a trap.

He raised Isval on his comlink. He needed her take. She came promptly, a question in her eyes, and he showed her the decrypted message. She licked her lips as she read, then looked up at the wall, thinking.

"Not possible, right?" he asked her.

"When did this come in?"

"An hour ago, via the usual channels."

"Trustworthy?" she asked.

"The source? Yes, but that doesn't mean he wasn't misled."

"Right," she said. A vein pulsed in her forehead. She'd had it ever since they'd heard Vader kill Pok in the hijack that had gone wrong. She handed the paper back to him. Her lekku swayed with irritation. "It's wrong or it's a trap. Has to be."

Cham crumpled the paper, burned it in the flame of the candle on his desk. "I thought so, too. But what if it's not? It's an opportunity."

She sniffed, paced the floor of his room, shaking her head, her hands on the twin blasters she wore at her belt. "The Star Destroyer makes sense if they were coming. The *Perilous* is Vader's flagship but . . . *why* would they be coming? That's where this falls apart. And Vader *and* the Emperor coming to the Outer Rim? The only time they're ever in one place is on Coruscant. The 'why' is the trouble here. We need a why."

Cham stared at the candle flame, thinking of Pok. "I don't know. To make an example of Mors, maybe? A show of force? Our attacks *have* slowed spice production to a trickle."

The Empire used spice—refined ryll, harvested from the countless mines that made Ryloth porous—and its derivatives for countless purposes, particularly in the Imperial science and medical corps.

"Maybe they're coming to replace Mors?" Isval said. "With Dray, maybe?"

"That'd be useful, but . . ." Cham shook his head.

"No. If Mors goes down, Belkor Dray will go with her. He doesn't see that, but there's no way he stands if Mors falls."

Isval was warming to her theorizing. "Bring more stormtroopers? They've got a bunch of conscripts and enlistees here now. Nubs looking for adventure, but not true soldiers. Maybe bring more troops, elite troops, and lock down Ryloth and spice production?"

"Maybe, but one Star Destroyer? For the Emperor and Vader?"

"It's a Star Destroyer, Cham! Think about what you're saying."

"Yes, but . . ."

"I'd wager the fleet is spread pretty thin across the galaxy," Isval said. She'd stopped pacing and now stared at the wall, white knuckles clenched around her hope for an opportunity to strike a telling blow. "Or maybe the Emperor is worried that a big fleet presence would send the wrong message. Make it look like he was afraid of the piddling freedom fighters of Ryloth."

"I need you to be the voice of reason here, Isval. I'm leaning too heavy in one direction."

"Yeah, but maybe you're right to do that," Isval said. "Maybe you're overthinking this, Cham. When has our intelligence been wrong? There could be a dozen reasons we can't see, and if we spend all our time trying to find them an opportunity could slip past us."

"And you're underthinking it. These are clever men. If they're luring us into an overreach . . ."

"Even clever men make mistakes," she said, returning to her habitual pacing. "And they have no idea of the forces at our disposal, Cham. We've been acting like a tiny band of terrorists for years—"

"Freedom fighters," Cham corrected her.

"Freedom fighters. But we have ships, hundreds of soldiers, heavy weapons. This is the Emperor and Vader and Taa. *Vader*, Cham. Think of what he did to Pok."

Cham had recurring nightmares about Pok and always woke gasping, certain he was being choked. "I don't need a reminder, Isval. But we're fighting first for a free Ryloth, not to topple the Empire."

Isval stopped pacing and stared at him. "How are they not the same thing?"

"What?"

"They're the same thing, Cham. We want a free Ryloth, then we need a toppled Empire. Or at least a weakened one. We need fires blazing all over the galaxy. Then maybe, *maybe*, they'll leave us alone."

Cham didn't agree, but it didn't matter. Taking out Vader and the Emperor would send the message Cham was keen to send: Ryloth is too costly to occupy, spice or no spice.

"All right," he said. "Let's start planning and put the cells on alert. But don't do anything yet, Isval. I mean that. No extra chatter. Let's see if we hear from Belkor. If he tells me Vader and Palpatine are coming, then I'll know they're baiting us."

"How's that?"

"Belkor would never give us a shot at Vader and the Emperor unless he was told to. He's ambitious, but he's not suicidal."

Isval nodded. "Makes sense."

"Well, then, go get started. I'll let you know if I hear from Belkor."

Isval nodded, gave him a half smile, and bolted out of the room as if running a race against the fear that Cham might change his mind.

Cham sat at his desk after she'd left, planning how

he'd break things to Belkor. The Imperial officer was in for a rude surprise.

As was his custom, Belkor Dray used the shuttle flight from Ryloth to its largest moon to square away his thinking and don the mask he wore when facing Moff Mors. He sat alone in the expansive passenger compartment and tried on the various expressions he'd wear to conceal the contempt he felt for her.

"Approaching the moon now, Colonel," the pilot said over the comm.

"Let the Moff know we're on approach, Fruun," Belkor responded.

"Aye, sir."

Fruun was one of Belkor's men, one of the hundreds whose loyalty he'd bought through favors or secured through blackmail. Moff Mors—lazy, sloppy Delion Mors—left the running of Ryloth's occupation to Belkor, and Belkor had not been idle. He'd filled several Imperial units with commanders whose first loyalty was not to Mors, or even to the Empire, but to him, and the soldiers would do exactly as their commanders told them. The stormtroopers were a problem, of course, but there weren't very many members of the corps on Ryloth. In essence, Belkor had a shadow force at his disposal, and he'd call on it when the time was right.

"Moff Belkor Dray," he said, trying out the title the same way he'd tried on false expressions. Not colonel. Not general. *Moff.*

One day.

Mors would be easy to discredit, but Belkor needed to do it in a way that reflected well on himself. He had plans in the works to do just that.

"Setting down, sir," Fruun said.

Belkor stood up straight and checked his uniform: clean and pressed, with creases that could cut meat. Shoes shined. Insignia of rank at exact regulation distance from the edge of his collar. He removed his hat, smoothed his hair into place, and put the hat back on.

Belkor took an interest in the small things, the details others missed. The practice kept him from getting sloppy. And he carried far too many secrets to allow himself any room for sloppiness.

The shuttle alit on the outdoor landing pad, and Belkor pressed a button to open the door. He wrinkled his nose at the verdurous, humid air. Trees forty meters high stood sentinel around the pad. The arm-thick, ubiquitous vines so prevalent on the moon hung like a thousand nooses from the trees' thick limbs. Screeches and howls from the native fauna punctuated the air. The towering jungle canopy blocked his view of Mors's well-appointed command center, which had been built by Twi'lek forced labor.

A young junior officer—Belkor had forgotten his name—and three stormtroopers waited on the pad. They saluted, rather sloppily in the case of the officer, as Belkor descended the ramp. Belkor returned the gesture with crispness.

"The Moff was unable to greet you personally," the junior officer said.

Because she is in a spice haze, Belkor thought but didn't say. *Or engaged with her Twi'lek slaves.*

"I'll walk you to her."

Because she is too lazy to walk this far herself, Belkor thought, but he said only, "Very good, Lieutenant."

A trio of V-wings on patrol cruised low overhead, the telltale in-atmosphere buzz of their engines temporarily quieting the cacophony of the native animals.

The moon's humidity had exacted a toll of sweat by the time Belkor and his escort reached the climate-controlled confines of Mors's luxurious command center—more akin to a noble's villa on Naboo than an Imperial installation. Belkor's sweat-stained uniform fouled his mood, and he barely returned the salutes of the stormtrooper sentries on guard outside the villa's main doors.

Vast windows looked out on the rolling viridian waves of the jungle. Rounded edges, burnished wood tables, and overstuffed chairs, divans, and lounges seemed to be everywhere, the whole of it giving the impression of softness, which fit Mors's personality precisely. The stone "sculptures" so favored by Twi'leks—chunks of rock naturally carved by Ryloth's winds, as Belkor understood it—stood here and there on tables. Twi'lek servants moved like pale-green ghosts through the rooms. Mors chose only Twi'leks with pale-green skin for her household servants—the Moff refused to call them slaves, though none could leave.

"Their skin goes well with the surrounding trees," she had once said to Belkor.

The stormtroopers in the escort peeled off and took station at their interior watch posts while the junior officer led Belkor toward the villa's open-air central courtyard, where Mors seemed to spend all her time while Belkor did all the work planetside.

The courtyard was covered in a retractable clear dome to allow in ambient light. At the moment, the dome was fully retracted and hundreds of the brightly colored, hand-sized native insects common to the top of the jungle's trees flitted about in the air.

A walking path meandered through colorful flowers, bushes, and dwarf versions of the native trees. Belkor found Mors, looking as overstuffed and soft as the villa's furnishings, seated on a bench near a fountain in the center of the courtyard, leaning into a conversation with a Hutt. The Hutt's three-meter-long sluglike body, covered in wrinkled, leathery skin, convulsed in something that might have been laughter. It took Belkor a great deal of effort to keep the disgust from his face. He filed the presence of the Hutt away in the cabinet of his mind, intending to look into travel records later. Implicating Mors in a conspiracy with the Hutts, who were engaged in any number of criminal enterprises, would give him another tool to discredit the Moff.

Mors held up a finger to forestall Belkor's advance while she concluded her business with the Hutt. Watching the exchange, Belkor was struck by the similarities between the two. Both woman and alien looked like overfilled sausages, only Mors was wrapped in a wrinkled uniform rather than leathery skin. Her watery eyes and vaguely slack expression showed that she was in a spice haze. The Hutt's watery eyes and slack expression showed that he was, in fact, a typical specimen of his kind.

"Who is that?" Belkor asked his escort softly.

"Nashi the Hutt, an envoy from Jabba."

Neither of the names meant anything to Belkor, but he filed them away, too. "What does the Empire have to do with the Hutts?" he asked.

To that, the officer said nothing. Belkor did not press. Meanwhile, Hutt and human shared a belly laugh—the Hutt's tone unexpectedly high-pitched—and Mors gestured for Belkor and his officer escort to approach.

"Come, Belkor!" Mors said, then, to the officer, "Lieutenant, please see that Nashi is returned to his ship. Oh, and see to it that he's given three cases of Theenwine."

"Yes, ma'am," said the officer.

Nashi turned his serpentine body fully around to face Belkor. Before Belkor could speak, the creature belched a cloud of stink, the smell like rotting meat.

Belkor took one step back, out of the cloud, but otherwise held his silence.

Nashi said something over his shoulder in Huttese and chuckled. Mors shared in the chuckle, and then said something in Huttese in return.

"I'm afraid I don't speak the language of this alien, ma'am," Belkor said stiffly, addressing Mors.

Mors waved a hand as though it didn't matter, as though nothing mattered. "Oh, he said you look as straight and rigid as the trees. I told him you were a young, ambitious officer, and that the Academy minted all of you that way these days. I told him he should hear you talk."

"Ma'am?"

Mors smiled. "Have you never heard yourself speak, Belkor? You speak as if all your words had a serif."

The Hutt said something in Huttese and the two shared another laugh.

Belkor did not relax his posture. "Of course, ma'am."

"Oh, don't be offended, Belkor." Mors stood on wobbly legs and bowed to the Hutt. "Safe journey, Nashi. I'll be in contact."

The Hutt bowed as best a slug could manage, nodded at Belkor, then slithered off in the company of the lieutenant.

Mors lowered her weight back onto the bench. "You dislike all this, don't you, Belkor?"

Belkor kept his face impassive. "Ma'am?"

"This," Mors said, gesturing expansively. "This

luxury. It offends you, doesn't it? It's all over your face."

Lies always came easy to Belkor. "That was the . . . appearance of the Hutt, ma'am. Luxury does not offend me. With rank come privileges."

Mors smiled and leaned back on the bench, nodding. "See? There's a serif on those words. Did you hear it? Ha! Well, indeed rank does have its privileges. We're both stationed at the ass end of the Empire, so I say we should make the most of it."

"Of course, ma'am."

"What about you, Belkor? You exercise few of those privileges. Will you have a wine with me?" She clapped her hands and a pale-green Twi'lek woman in a head wrap and tight-fitting tunic and trousers emerged from the nearby foliage with a ewer of wine and two goblets. Belkor had not noticed her before.

"I . . . need to stay clearheaded for my return trip, ma'am."

"Your loss," Mors said as the slave poured. "So, what brings you to my little moon, Belkor? Is all well on the planet?"

The woman truly was as stupid as she was indolent. "My quarterly report on Ryloth is due, ma'am."

"Is it?" Mors looked genuinely shocked. She fiddled with the tight bun of her hair for a moment. "My, time passes quickly."

"Particularly when one is as busy as you are," Belkor said, and managed not to smirk.

"Quite right," Mors said. She took a gulp of wine. "If we must, we must. Proceed, Colonel. What's happening on that arid rock underneath us?"

Standing throughout, Belkor went through a curated list of items that he wanted Mors to know—staff levels, troop movements, spice shipments, and on it went. Mors asked no questions during Belkor's recital, merely nodding absently from time to time.

"May I answer any questions?" Belkor asked, the words part of the exercise. Mors rarely asked anything, but Belkor needed to maintain the illusion of deference.

Mors drank the last of her wine and studied the empty goblet forlornly. "There is the one thing. How do matters fare with the terrorists?"

The question took Belkor aback, and he almost let his mask slip. "The Free Ryloth movement?"

"The terrorists," Mors reiterated.

"I, uh, have our best assets on it, ma'am," Belkor said. "Things have been quiet planetside. It's been over a month since the last attack."

Belkor had no intention of letting the quiet last another month. He'd need to feed some intel to Cham Syndulla to encourage an attack. Belkor needed violence from the movement to give him some of the ammunition he'd ultimately use to unseat Mors, but he didn't want the violence to escalate too far while he was in charge of quelling it. Controlled violence was what he needed. Channeled violence. And he'd been using Cham to that end for months.

Mors's eyes focused more than Belkor liked to see. The woman could hold her spice, apparently. "More than a month since an attack *here,* Belkor. But the movement attempted to hijack a shipment of weapons not long ago. They failed, of course, but . . ."

Belkor had heard nothing of it, from Cham or otherwise, and his ignorance alarmed him. "Where? When?"

Mors waved a delicate hand. "Doesn't matter. As I said, the attempt failed. All of the terrorists were killed." She chuckled as if she found that amusing.

Belkor treaded carefully. He hoped he hadn't lost

Cham, or he'd have to start over with another resistance leader. "Any, uh, familiar names among the dead?"

"Not that I've heard. The usual riffraff, no doubt."

"Well, I wish I'd known of this sooner. I would've doubled our efforts planetside, while we had the movement back on its heels."

"Do we have it on its heels?" Mors asked, looking pointedly at Belkor.

Belkor shifted on his feet. "As you know, ma'am, an insurgency is hard to fight. The resistance blends in with the nonmilitant populace, and killing innocents indiscriminately would only increase the number of otherwise neutral Twi'leks sympathetic to the resistance. We've made progress, but this will be a lengthy affair."

"Of course," Mors said. "Of course. I know you're doing all that can be done. And as for the failed hijacking, I only just learned of it. Oh, but as a result Senator Orn Free Taa will be returning to Ryloth in ten days. I only just learned that, too."

Belkor's mind immediately turned to Cham and possibilities. "Why is he returning, I wonder? It's been many months since he was here last."

"Who knows the minds of politicians, Belkor? But I think probably the Emperor has ordered him back to publicize the terrorists' failed hijacking, offer support for the occupation, that kind of thing."

"Reassure the nonmilitants," Belkor said. "Show them that the terrorists are doomed to failure."

"No doubt," said Mors. "In any event, now you know as much as me."

And Belkor would put it to good use. "Will you be arranging his welcome personally, ma'am? Or should I?"

"Oh, I trust you to handle it, Colonel. In my name, of course. Now, where's my wine girl?"

"I'll see to the preparations immediately," Belkor said. "Is that all?"

"That'll be all."

As Belkor walked away, Mors called after him. "Belkor!"

"Yes?"

"Lighten up some, Colonel! You must learn to enjoy yourself! Oh, and if you see my wine girl, please send her to me."

"Of course," Belkor said, and took his leave, his mind spinning with possibilities. By the time he reached the shuttle, he'd narrowed them down and already had a plan in mind. His opportunity had come. The assassination of Orn Free Taa on Mors's watch would be a fatal blow to the Moff. Taa was a powerless figurehead, of course, but he was a figurehead and mouthpiece the Emperor used as a tool when it came to quieting Ryloth. Belkor would simply need to take care to ensure that he himself wasn't caught in the backblast of Mors's fall.

Moff Belkor Dray sounded to him for the first time not merely aspirational but plausible, and soon.

The moment he reached his quarters planetside, he used a portable, personal comm to send an encrypted message to Cham.

We need to meet immediately.

Cham's answer came back within the hour, naming the time and place. The speed of Cham's reply surprised Belkor. It was almost as if the Twi'lek had been expecting the message.

Five hours after night fell, Belkor stripped out of his uniform, donned civilian clothes and a hooded jacket, and logged his location in the computer as "off-base, recreation," a euphemism officers used when visiting with their Twi'lek mistresses or frequenting cantinas. When a duty officer saw that entry in the log, out of consideration he asked no more questions.

"Safe travels, sir," said the duty officer over Belkor's comm. "It's breezy out there."

Belkor signed out an aircar from the vehicle bay, entered the code that lowered the bay's force field, and exited the Imperial compound.

Ryloth's capital city, Lessu, was built into and spiraled around a wind-carved stone spire as large as a mountain. The walls, villas, and more modest homesteads and businesses of the city clung like so much lichen to the face of the spire. Thousands of reinforced tunnels and natural caves also pockmarked the stone, and seen by day they reminded Belkor of the aftermath of an artillery barrage. The city had seen a lot of strife, as had the planet, and it showed.

Dozens of aircars, a few brave souls bent against the wind on speeder bikes, and the native Ryloth kinetic gliders, wings wide to harness the gusts, coasted over and around the spire, their nighttime lights blinking or flashing in the darkness. He spotted a couple of Imperial patrol craft hovering low over the city. Belkor used Imperial craft judiciously when enforcing Imperial rule. The sight of Imperial ships sometimes upset the natives. So he left the day-to-day policing of the city to a Twi'lek security force, made up of Twi'leks co-opted by better living conditions and pay to enforce Imperial rule against their own people.

He set his onboard comp to broadcast a high-level security code so he would be unbothered as he left the city's airspace.

Cooking fires burned here and there in the streets

and courtyards and caves below him. Even at the late hour, people and pack animals and vehicles thronged the streets, the heat and boredom bringing them outdoors.

Summer brought nighttime riots to Ryloth as surely as it brought high temperatures. The heat brought crowds into the streets and cantinas, and crowds brought anger, and anger brought riots. Belkor's policy, administered in Mors's name, was to contain the riots and, as best they could manage, prevent fatalities and extensive property damage, but never to squelch them. He considered them a useful venting mechanism. Most Twi'leks fell into the middle between the satisfied collaborators and the zealots of the resistance, but almost all were occasionally resentful of the Imperial occupation. They needed an outlet for their simmering anger.

"Give them their riots, or push them all into the Free Ryloth movement," Belkor had told Mors. "In time, we'll tame them and they'll welcome their bondage. Many already do."

Mors had seen the wisdom in it. As Belkor saw it, Cham Syndulla already had enough fighters and spies in his movement.

Belkor pulled back on the controls and took his aircar up to cruising altitude. The surrounding landscape came into view, pale in the light of Ryloth's largest moon, where Mors dwelled.

Scattered villages and towns, either walled or built mostly underground against the unrelenting winds and the planet's dangerous predators, dotted the broken, rocky ground within a few kilometers of Lessu. Tough, wind-resistant scrub and the thin-trunked, flexible whiptrees so common on Ryloth blanketed the jagged ground in dark patches.

Movement below caught his eye. He fixed the onboard cam on the activity and magnified: a trio of huge lyleks was dismembering another, smaller of their kind. The spiked pincers and powerful mandibles of the large insectoid predators moved up and down in a herky-jerky fashion, killing and cutting with a vicious efficiency that Belkor admired. No wasted effort in their slaughter. All business; very Imperial-like, he thought.

He turned westward into the face of Ryloth's winds, and the gusts fought him for control of the vehicle. Dirt and debris hit the windshield like shrapnel. He was not a good pilot, so he just white-knuckled the controls, sweating, and relied on the compensators while he flew toward the rendezvous point.

Once he was well clear of Lessu's airspace, he deactivated the transmission of his security code. Out of concern for leaving traces that could be tracked after the fact, he didn't enter the coordinates for the rendezvous into the nav computer. Instead, he simply put a live readout of coordinates on the comp screen and watched them scroll by as the aircar chewed up the klicks.

CHAPTER FOUR

Belkor flew over jagged canyons, salt plateaus, and rocky valleys dotted with vast towers of stone. Huge expanses of Ryloth were uninhabited, except for the occasional isolated village or settlement that had little contact with the outside world. Herds of predators and prey filled the wild country outside the cities. The planet would have been completely irrelevant except as a source of forced labor but for the presence of ryll, a miracle ore with military, recreational, and scientific applications.

In the distance to his right he saw the lights of a ryll-mining operation, but the scroll of coordinates told him to keep heading west. He slowed as he flew closer to his destination, watching the coordinates count down to the designated location.

He saw it ahead and below, a valley wooded in whiptrees and scrub, with boulders strewn about as though cast there by giants. Caves dotted the valley walls. Cham would be in one of them. Belkor circled the valley twice, looking for Cham's ship, but saw nothing. On his second pass, an infrared beacon pinged his aircar from one of the caves.

"Evening, Syndulla," he said, and headed down.

As he stepped out of his aircar, he was accosted by the omnipresent wind and the Twi'lek woman who always seemed to be at Cham's side—Isval, he thought her name was. She stepped out of the brush, turned him roughly around, and patted him down for weapons. The look on her face was more intimidating than the twin blasters and vibroblade she wore.

"Wait a minute," he said, but she didn't, and the strength in her hands left him no doubt that resistance would be useless. She removed his belt blaster, which was more ceremonial than anything: Belkor had fired a blaster only to qualify on the range, never in combat.

"Follow," she ordered him. "And don't speak to me."

"And who are you to—"

She whirled on him, lips twisted into a snarl, revealing teeth she'd sharpened to points, something typically done only by male Twi'leks. Her fists were bunched. "Was I unclear, Imperial? Do *not* speak to me."

She spun around and led him toward the cave where, presumably, Cham awaited. Having no desire to see those teeth again, he held his silence.

Cham stood at the mouth of a cave, holding the infrared light, his face grim and ghostly in the night air. The wind tore at Belkor's hair. Nervousness rooted in his stomach. He'd never trusted Cham, but he'd always figured Cham was not stupid. Cham knew Belkor was a traitor, to Mors if not to the Empire, but Cham also knew that Belkor had substantial information on Cham's operations. Names, places. Belkor could hamstring the resistance if he had to. And Cham wouldn't risk that. But . . . this meeting had a different feel to it than their previous encounters.

"Let's do this right here," Belkor said. "What I have to say won't take long."

"What I have to say will," Cham said, switching off the infrared. He turned and started heading into the cave. "Follow."

Layered between Isval and Cham, Belkor had little choice. He put a hand on the empty blaster holster he wore. Isval snickered.

"Eyes open," Cham said over his shoulder to her, and she stationed herself at the cave mouth.

Belkor scurried after Cham, and they headed deeper into the cave.

"I can't see, Syndulla," Belkor said, holding his hands out in front of him. Twi'leks, who spent much of their lives underground, saw quite well in the darkness. Belkor felt as vulnerable as he ever had. He was breathing too fast, sweating.

The infrared light came back on, revealing Cham directly before him, staring into his face.

"Blast!" Belkor said.

"These caves are old," Cham said. "The mountains are porous with them. My people retreated to them to form resistance bands. It's gone on cycle after cycle. The oppressor changes, but the caves remain the same."

He held the light up to the walls, which Belkor saw were covered in anti-occupation graffiti, some of it going back to the Clone Wars and earlier.

"Twi'leks disliked the Jedi and Separatists as much as the Empire," Belkor said.

"We dislike yokes of any kind," Cham said.

Behind them, a gust of wind howled across the mouth of the cave.

Belkor tried to recapture some of the conversational

ground he knew he'd lost. "I'm not here for a history lesson, Syndulla."

"No," Cham said, his tone different from any of their previous dealings, more self-assured. "You're here to learn a different kind of lesson."

"And how's that?" Belkor asked, hoping he sounded unconcerned. He glanced back over his shoulder, thinking that the female Twi'lek was back there in the darkness somewhere, watching him. He imagined her eyes locked onto him the way predators locked eyes on prey, and his mind flashed on the lyleks he'd seen on his flight there, dismembering the smaller, weaker one.

He cleared his throat and pushed the image out of his mind.

The tunnel snaked left. An orange glow lit an open space ahead.

Within the sand-floored chamber was a simple wooden table, with two chairs set beside it. Nothing else. Just the table.

"Are we playing holochess, Syndulla?"

"We've been playing holochess for years, Belkor. And you lost. You just didn't realize it. But you're about to. Sit. We're going to be honest with each other now. Completely honest."

"That sounds ill advised," Belkor said, an attempt to joke away his growing concern. The dry air pulled the moisture from his mouth. He slipped into the seat opposite Cham. The Twi'lek's orange skin was flushed, his lekku swaying slightly, his eyes on Belkor's.

Belkor had to work to answer Cham's gaze. "Are you on the spice, Syndulla? I think maybe you misunderstand our relationship, as does your girl out there. I'm not the one working for you. You're working for me. I can forgive a slip-up once, but—"

Cham held up a hand, his brow furrowed with anger, and Belkor stuttered into silence.

"Honesty, I said," Cham said. "I'll start. You're here to tell me that Orn Free Taa is returning to Ryloth on a state visit in ten days."

"I . . ." Belkor stopped himself and regathered his words. "You have excellent spies."

"More than you know. He'll be aboard a Star Destroyer, the *Perilous*."

Belkor sat back in his chair, sweating, studying Cham, affecting indifference but, he feared, doing a poor job of it. "And?"

Cham leaned forward in his chair, his hands gripping the edge of the table. He stared into Belkor's face. "And I see you, Belkor. Do you see me?"

"What? I don't . . . What?" Belkor felt off balance, and sure he must look ridiculous.

"I've always seen you," Cham said. "You thought I was dancing to your song this whole time, yes? You thought you were playing me? You're a *child*, Belkor."

Belkor blinked in the face of Cham's assuredness. He tried to summon words, found none, tried to summon his dignity, found it wanting. He stood on shaky legs. "Our relationship is over. I'm leaving."

"No, you're not. Sit down, Belkor Dray. Sit."

Belkor swallowed, felt his face color with anger and fear. "What are you going to do? Kill me? I've taken steps. If anything happens to me—"

"You have agents who'll kill me? A lie, Belkor. You'd trust no one enough to let them know about our relationship. Oh, I know you've got men loyal to you and not Mors all over the planet, but you wouldn't tell them about us or they wouldn't be loyal anymore, now would they? The fact that you have those forces is what makes you interesting to me. I have forces, too, Belkor. The two of us, we make quite a pair."

"A data disk," Belkor said, his tone high-pitched, his speech rapid. "In the event of my death. It identifies you, the location of many of your bases, your people. It'll go out to everyone who needs to know."

Cham smirked. "Now, that I believe, but it changes nothing. You don't know half of what there is to know about my network, Belkor. That disk would be a blow, but not a mortal one."

The Twi'lek said nothing for a moment, seemingly to allow Belkor to process his claims. Belkor didn't know what to make of them. Lies, truth. He couldn't say.

Cham's tone changed to somber. "Besides, I've been prepared to die for my principles for a very long time. Threats don't move me. But what about you? Do you have any principles, Belkor? Are you prepared to die for them? Are you prepared to die for the Empire? Here. Now."

He stood, drew his blaster, and pointed it at Belkor's head.

Belkor blinked, swallowed. "No."

Cham holstered his weapon and sat.

"I thought not. Why would you want to die? You're a creature of ambition, Belkor. That makes you easy to read and easy to play. And it means that between the two of us, you're the only one with anything to lose. Let me show you something."

Cham removed a portable holocrystal and palm-sized player from one of the pouches on his belt. He placed it on the table and activated it. Belkor watched images of his previous meetings with Cham played back at him, dozens of them. He heard his own voice telling Cham or one of Cham's agents about a shipment coming at this or that date, intelligence about the number of Imperial soldiers on guard at this or that spice-production plant, patrol schedules and how to avoid them, countless moments of incrimination, innumerable incidences of treason.

Belkor could feel himself deflating, feel the air going out of him. He looked around the cave for the imager, certain this meeting, too, was being recorded.

"You're recording this meeting, too," he said, his voice small.

"Of course," Cham said. "You're mine. You've always been mine. And now you know it. That's the honesty I promised you. Do we understand each other now?"

Belkor nodded, reeling. He felt dizzy. "We understand each other."

"Good. Now, I can be a kinder master to you than the Empire has been to Ryloth. No one has to lose here, Belkor. That's honesty, too. But I need more from you now than I've ever required before. I need more than information. I need commitment. I need collaboration."

Belkor was shaking his head. "I can't. I won't."

"You can, and you will. You must."

And despite his protests, Belkor knew he would. He had to. His thoughts were swirling and he saw no other out.

"Tell me what you want," he said softly.

"First, tell me everything about the *Perilous*. Is Taa bringing his full staff? Any other dignitaries aboard?"

"I only know about Taa," Belkor said. "I'm sure his staff will be there, but no one else of note."

Cham studied his face, as if searching his eyes for a lie. "Honesty, I said."

"That's the truth," Belkor said. "Just Taa."

Cham pursed his lips. "I believe you, Belkor. So, here is what I need from you . . ."

Cham leaned back in his chair and for the next half hour outlined what he required. Belkor listened to it in growing disbelief. He'd had no idea Cham had so many men and so much matériel at his disposal. He'd underestimated the Twi'lek, and it had cost him.

At last Cham finished and asked, "Do you understand?"

Belkor nodded. It felt like surrender.

"Good," Cham said. "Now for more honesty. If this fails, I'll expose you."

"What? I said I'll give you the assistance you want! But I can't give you a guarantee of success!"

Cham smiled, but without mirth. "I'm not trying to guarantee success. I'm trying to guarantee your very best efforts. No half measures, Belkor. You're in fully. We succeed together or die together, each in our way. Understood?"

Belkor could not even bring himself to speak. He just gave a brisk nod of his head.

"Good," Cham said. "Then let's get out of here."

They walked side by side, back through the tunnel, until they could see Isval's silhouette in the cave mouth. Something struck Belkor. He faced Cham.

"If I hadn't agreed to this? You'd have killed me, wouldn't you? Or she would have?"

Cham didn't hesitate. "I'd have done it, not her. That's why this cave. It goes back a way. No scavenging animals, and the dry air desiccates a corpse with surprising speed. So I would have just left you back there and saved myself the trouble and dirt of burying your body. No one would have ever found you."

Belkor stared into the darkness of the cavern behind them, imagining it as his tomb, then back at Cham.

"But it didn't come to that," Cham said. "Because

you're smart, Belkor. And now I'm going to tell you something important. You listening?"

Belkor nodded.

"The moment you get out of here, you're going to start having second thoughts. You're going to start thinking about how you can turn this around, save yourself, and throw me over. But you can't. I have people everywhere, Belkor. That's how I knew about Taa. All the information you've ever offered me in the past? I already knew it. I just wanted you to offer it so I could record you doing so, put you in my pocket so that I could take you back out and spend you when I needed to. So now I'm spending you. You slip up, try to flip this, and I'll know about it the moment it happens. And then I'll make everything known."

"You committed those crimes. Not me."

The words sounded stupid to Belkor even as he said them.

"Yes, but you abetted them. Dead Imperials, Belkor. Lots of them. The Empire will make those your responsibility, and no matter how you spin it, no one would forgive that. So when you walk out of here and the uncertainty sets in, you remember that I'm all you have. That if you betray me, there's nothing coming for you but an ugly death and more scandal for your family. But—*but*—if you do as I ask, this will work to both our benefits. Taa will be dead, Mors will be disgraced, and we'll arrange for you to look the hero somehow. Moff Dray. Sounds good, no?"

"I'll still be in your pocket," Belkor said.

"But you'll be alive. And a Moff. That's better than the alternative."

Belkor said nothing.

"Good-bye, Belkor. Start making arrangements. I'll be in touch soon. Oh, and welcome to the rebellion."

Belkor walked out of the cave, passed Isval without

really seeing her, and returned to his aircar. Once inside, he sat perfectly still for a moment before everything exploded out of him. He slammed his fist against the instrument panel again and again and again and again.

"Blast! Blast! Blast! Blast!"

He stopped only when he realized that he was bleeding. The pain helped refocus him. He cradled the hand against his shirt, fired up the engines, and headed back to Lessu in a haze. About halfway, the second thoughts Cham had anticipated started to bubble up. As best as his addled mind allowed, he turned the situation over in his mind, examining it from various angles. Other than collaborating with Cham or turning himself in, he saw only one other option: he could run, take up in some isolated location in the galaxy, and live out his life in obscurity. Cham could still expose him, of course, but he'd be long gone.

But by the time he saw Lessu's lights in the distance, he'd dismissed the idea of running. He'd always been compromised. So, he was in Cham's pocket. He could manage that; he could manage Cham. They'd need each other when he was Moff.

And all it would take was the murder of one Twi'lek senator.

Belkor could live with that.

Cham and Isval watched the dark and distance swallow Belkor's aircar.

"He didn't mention Vader or the Emperor?" Isval asked.

"He didn't. I gave him the opportunity and he was off balance. He'd have said something or I'd have seen it in his face. He doesn't know."

Isval exhaled. "Then the intel is good. Vader and Palpatine are coming with Taa."

Cham nodded. "It could still be a trap. Belkor just might not be in on it. They could suspect him of collaborating."

"No," Isval said. "We've been careful and so has he. And Mors is an idiot. She's sat up there on that moon for years and let Belkor run the show, undermining her at every turn. No, they just haven't told her that Vader and the Emperor are coming. They're replacing her, Cham, and making a big show of it. Probably bringing a garrison of stormtroopers, too. We're overdue for some heavier boots."

Cham nodded. "I think you're probably right."

"Then we're a go?" She was bouncing on the balls of her feet.

"We're a go," Cham answered. "And pity poor Belkor. When he learns what he's actually signed on for . . ."

Isval stiffened. "He's filth, Cham. Imperial filth. Don't be sentimental. Not about him. Not about them. Not ever."

Her vehemence didn't surprise him, given what she'd experienced in her youth. "It's not sentiment. It's principle. What am I without that?"

"On the winning side, I hope," Isval said. She changed the subject. "Now what?"

"Now we get everything ready," Cham said. "And I mean *everything*. This is the operation we've been waiting for. Mobilize everyone and get all the weapons and ships ready for use. We'll have full Imperial patrol schedules so we can move things into place. Let's find out if we're as good as we think we are."

"We are," she affirmed. "Consider it handled. But hear me, I'm heading back to Lessu for a day or two. I'll see to matters from there."

Cham turned to face her. Her beauty rarely registered with him, so often was it hidden behind the mask of her anger. But right then, in the dim light of the moons, she looked as vulnerable as she had the day he'd first met her. And as beautiful. He quieted the feelings for her that sometimes bubbled up. They were a complication he couldn't afford. She'd said not to be sentimental. He wouldn't be.

"What's in Lessu?" he asked, concerned.

The mask came back up. "It's just personal business. All right?"

He didn't pry. He had no right to pry. "All right. Just be careful."

"I'm always careful."

"Sure you are," Cham said, smiling.

Isval had rented another small garret in an underground housing complex in a poor part of Lessu. The thin walls allowed in noise from the adjacent rooms, shouting from one, shrill laughter from another. The smell of someone's dinner leaked through the shared ventilation system. Isval found she was hungry, but not for food.

The sight of Dray—with his impeccably combed hair, his unwrinkled, sharply creased clothes, his intolerably smug, self-assured expression—had made her need more acute. She'd felt it coming on days before, like one of Ryloth's sandstorms, brewing red and blurry on the horizon, until finally it exploded in violence.

She'd told Cham she'd be in Lessu two days, but she planned to use only the one. The need was too strong, the pressure, the agitation. She couldn't wait two days. She had to do it tonight. She had to. She'd be useless to Cham if she didn't, too sloppy, too angry. She needed release.

She knew how she appeared to others, with her pacing, her curtness, always on the verge of an explosion. Servitude had made her that way. If she was a monster, the Empire had spawned her.

Her reflection stared back her from the tiny mirror mounted on the wall. She'd donned a headband of the kind they loved, makeup to accent her high cheekbones, deep-set eyes, and full lips. It was the mask she wore when she hunted.

It wasn't her in the mask. It was the her she'd been, but made monstrous.

The pale-blue expanse of her skin looked like still water. How often had she heard those words out of the lips of some Imperial? Too often. She imagined them thinking that if they were nice, if they dressed oppression up in fine words, they were then somehow giving her a choice. But they weren't. They were just lying to themselves about what they took from her and why she was forced to give it. She'd never had a choice, not a real one, not until she'd strangled that corporal with a headband and fled to the resistance.

But she carried the scars; she'd always carry them, not on her skin but on her soul, and she picked them open when she needed a reminder of pain or needed to add fuel to her anger. Servitude and its degradations had broken her. She knew she'd never put herself back together, not completely, but she didn't care. The break had made her jagged, and now she used her edges and points to cut them. They'd made her into something—a slave, a possession, a *thing*—but after she'd escaped them, the making had continued. She'd gone on hammering the metal of her spirit until she'd made herself into something new: a warrior and, often enough, a killer. And Cham Syndulla had given her a place, and she loved him for that. For him it was a cause, but not for her. For her, it was just the vector she used to vent her anger against the Empire.

She tried out a smile in the mirror as she hung a necklace around her neck, found the smile serviceable, despite the sharpened eyeteeth. She wore fitted pants and a shirt that showed her bare midriff. She threw a sheer, shimmering robe over the whole, knowing the robe hugged her curves as she moved. She hid a blaster in a holster at the small of her back and her vibroblade in the leg wraps around her left calf.

She hesitated for a moment, recalling Cham's words about principles. She knew he would disapprove of what she did—of what she'd done a dozen times—and that his disapproval wouldn't be solely based in the risk she took, but also on principle. Principle. She paraphrased for herself her response to him, and it freed her to move.

"We do what we must to win, Cham. They're filth, and they deserve what they get."

She found she only half believed herself—Cham must have been influencing her more than she'd realized—but half was enough with the need on her.

She headed out and up the stairs, past a drunk sleeping in a heap against the wall, and onto the street. The thoroughfare filled her senses: the sounds of traffic and the hum of passersby; the smell of cooking fires, spice pipes, and the sweaty, dry stink of a typical Ryloth night. The wind painted her robe against her form and she felt eyes on her, gazes lingering on her sleek figure, but she ignored them.

She hailed a servicecar with a raised arm, and her curves and makeup drew one quickly. She told the driver to take her to the Octagon, one of the main plazas in Lessu, bordered on all eight sides by cantinas and clubs frequented by Imperials and working girls and men. She'd not hunted there before.

The Octagon sat about halfway up Lessu's spire, dug deeply into the stone. The bottom level of the plaza was thirty meters down, and a series of carved stone stairways, tunnels, and balconies, all torchlit, led up to ever higher tiers and more stairways, creating a mazelike warren that eventually descended back to street level.

Various cantinas and clubs were burrowed out of the stone, their interiors hidden from view. A steady stream of Imperial vehicles and smiling Imperial officers, often in the company of Twi'lek escorts, made their way to and from the Octagon's various levels. Pennons flapped in the wind, and lighted signs and paid hawkers advertised for this or that establishment. Isval eyed them from the window of her servicecar and hated them all.

"Level Seven, please," she said, and the driver set her down on one of the tiers of Level Seven, the second one down. The vehicle's door opened and the smells hit her instantly, the echoes of her previous life: smoke and perfume and spice. Laughter and music bounced up from the lower levels.

An older, paunchy officer in his dress grays eyed her as the servicecar flew off. He propositioned her with raised eyebrows and a knowing smirk, but she ignored him and headed down a nearby stairway.

"Stuck up," he called after her.

The maze was littered with dark corners, secret nooks, narrow tunnels, and blind alleys. Drunks and spice users and working girls lingered here and there, the castaways of Lessu's vice trade. As Isval descended the Octagon's tiers, the vices grew worse, the lighted signs more graphic. She'd spent her youth on Level

One, the Hole, as it was known. And the Hole was where she would hunt.

With a false smile and long-practiced skill, she avoided or extricated herself from the groping hands of drunk or spice-hazed Imperials on her way down. One of them removed himself too slowly, so she put a knee in his groin and left him moaning on a stairway. Laughter from above reminded her that she had to be careful about being seen.

She was sweating by the time she reached the bottom, and the stink of Level One brought it all back to her. The degradations, the hunger, the abuse, the constant unrelenting desperation.

Smoke and stink made a fog of the air. Torches were rare, signs were dim or unlit. Humans, Twi'leks, and other sentients moved through the dark stifling air like ghosts, too ashamed of their tastes to engage in them in anything other than near darkness. She moved among them, a ghost herself, looking for a likely spot and a likely target. She had both shortly.

She sat in a nook not far from a spice-and-vice club, cloaked in the darkness and her anger, and watched a junior officer walk out of the club with a young, underfed Twi'lek girl on his arm. The escort had seen maybe twenty summers, and she wore barely enough clothing to cover herself. The officer pawed at her as they walked through the night, his sweaty face flushed with the heat and his expectations of what was to come. He leaned over, stumbling, and murmured something in her ear. She smiled, the false smile that Isval knew well and had worn often.

She eyed him with contempt and growing rage. He was just some junior lieutenant, probably fresh off a transport from the Core, who thought wearing dress grays and carrying a weapon gave him a claim on Ryloth's resources and women.

Isval dug down to mine her resolve, found it, and stepped out of the nook. Her sudden appearance brought both the officer and the girl up short. But his surprised look quickly gave way to a leer as he looked Isval up and down. There was no one else in the immediate area.

The officer's drink-reddened face split in a sloppy smile and slurred words emerged. "Aren't you pretty? Why don't you join us—"

Isval sidled close, smiling, while she reached around to the small of her back. When she stood before him, she pulled the blaster and slammed its grip into his jaw. Teeth and blood spattered the street, and he fell in a groaning pile.

The girl gave a single startled exclamation and looked as though she might run.

"No, stay! Help me," Isval said. She disarmed the officer, grabbed him under the armpits, and dragged him back into the dark nook. The girl did not help her but followed tentatively, warily.

"What's your name?" Isval asked, standing over the officer.

The girl blinked and said nothing.

"I'm not going to hurt *you*," Isval said.

The officer moaned. His hand twitched. Isval stepped on it, felt a crunch, and the officer moaned again.

"Ryiin," the girl said softly. Her eyes darted between Isval and the officer. "What are you . . . are you robbing us?"

"You and this"—she kicked the officer—"aren't an 'us,' no matter what he told you."

"I don't . . . what?"

"Name your clan," Isval said.

Ryiin looked away in shame.

"You don't have one," Isval said, nodding. She said what she'd said many times before. "Not anymore. Listen to me, Ryiin. I used to stand where you're standing. I spent three years in the Hole before I escaped."

There was no hope in Ryiin's eyes. "Escape? There's no escape from this."

"There is if you want there to be."

Ryiin looked up. "How?"

"Come with me. I'll take you out of here. I have a place you can stay. Start again. Away from . . . this. I know, I know. You don't trust me. Why would you? But my offer is genuine."

Ryiin backed up a step, as if Isval had offered to harm her rather than help. Isval was not surprised. Hope and trust didn't appear much among the workers in the Octagon. "I can't."

"You can. You should. Look at me. Look. I'll help you."

She was shaking her head. "They'll come after me."

Isval didn't lie. "They might. But they probably won't. They don't even know your full name. And once you're gone, you're gone. And if you want to, you can stay gone."

"I . . . can't."

The officer groaned. Isval drew her vibroblade.

"What are you going to do?" Ryiin asked, horrified.

"What should be done to all of them," Isval answered, and knelt down, blade bare.

"Don't, don't!" Ryiin said. She hurried forward and knelt beside Isval, her eyes pleading. She placed her fingers on Isval's wrist. "Don't, all right? I'll go with you, but don't do this."

"I don't want you to come with me to save him," Isval snapped. "I want you to come with me to save you. What's he to you?"

Ryiin glanced at the officer, back at Isval. "He's nothing, but . . . he didn't do anything bad to me."

"He would have," Isval snapped. "And he's a soldier of the Empire. He's done something bad to all of us."

"I know that," Ryiin said. "But don't. All right? Just don't. I'll come with you. I want to. I'm just . . . afraid."

Voices from the walkway outside their nook froze them both into silence, but the sounds soon passed.

"This one owes you his life then," Isval said. She stood and kicked the officer in the head. He didn't even groan, just went limp. "Come on. You can't go back to get anything."

"There's nothing for me to go get."

Isval took Ryiin by the hand and walked her out of the pit, past the smoke and leers and spice and vice, ascending, ascending, and by the time she reached the top she felt as light as she had in months. The feeling wouldn't last, she knew, but she'd enjoy it while it did. She wondered what Cham would think of her if he knew what she did, what she had to do. She thought he wouldn't understand. Cham preached principle, but only those who'd never descended to Level One of the Octagon thought in terms of principle. Isval knew better; maybe Ryiin knew better. The real world didn't well accommodate principles.

When they reached the top of the Octagon, sweaty and out of breath, they fell in with the crowd there. Ryiin looked about wide-eyed, breathed deep the night's stink.

"How long's it been?" Isval asked.

"Weeks since I left the Hole," Ryiin answered.

"You still good?" Isval asked. This was the point when previous girls had turned back. Rarely, but it sometimes happened.

"I'm good," Ryiin said.

"Never go back," Isval said, and Ryiin nodded. "Now let's get you home. A new home."

A servicecar took the two of them back to the garret Isval had left earlier in the night. She led Ryiin up the stairs—the drunk was still there—and into the garret.

"It's not much," Isval said, showing the room to her. "But it's safe and it's yours."

"What do you mean? You're not staying? Isn't this your place?"

"No, it's yours. It's paid up through the year."

"The year!"

"There's food in the cabinets, and a few hundred credits in the drawer by the cooler. That ought to be enough to get you situated."

Hearing all that, Ryiin looked unsteady. She reached for a chair, slid into it. Her eyes welled. Isval stripped off her headdress, her clothing, and slipped back into her ordinary shirt, trousers, and weapons belt. Ryiin watched her throughout.

"I don't understand this, or you. What are you? Why are you doing this?"

"I told you," Isval said, looking in the small mirror. She took a rag, wet it from water in a jug, and wiped off the mask. "I used to be what you are. What you *were*. I just . . . want to help. I wish someone had helped me."

"That's not what I mean," Ryiin said. "Why me? I'm just a nobody."

"You're not nobody! You're not. I picked you . . . by chance. You were with an Imperial and you two were alone."

"So you . . . look for them? Imperials to kill? Why?"

Isval looked back at her by way of her reflection in the mirror. "You have to ask?"

Ryiin could not hold her reflected eyes. "Have you . . . done that before? Killed Imperials?"

This time Isval looked back at her own reflection. "You have to ask?"

Ryiin said nothing, but she shivered.

"I have a friend," Isval said. "He wants to save the whole planet. But that's . . . too big for me, too much. I just want to save someone, a few people. Maybe you."

Ryiin smiled.

Isval cleared her throat and gathered her things. "Take care of yourself, Ryiin. I don't normally check back. Dangerous for both of us."

"Normally? You've done this for other girls?"

"I have."

"Sounds like you've already saved a few someones. Can I ask how many?"

"Many. Doesn't matter."

"And each time you . . ."

Mentally, Isval finished the sentence. *Killed someone?*

"I'm going now," Isval said.

"Wait, I don't even know your name."

"You don't need to. Good-bye, Ryiin."

"Well, thank you. Thank you so much. Not just for saving me, but for not doing it."

Isval stopped in the doorway but didn't turn. Over her shoulder, she said, "Why do you care so much?"

Ryiin shook her head, shifted on her seat. "I don't know, but . . . it has to stop sometime, doesn't it? The violence. The killing. Someone has to stop, or it'll never end. Right? Maybe I'm saving you." She laughed.

Isval looked down at her hands but didn't reply.

"What is it?" Ryiin asked. "Did I say something wrong? I'm sorry."

"You didn't say anything wrong," Isval said. "You

probably didn't spend a lot of time in the Hole, though. Good fortune, Ryiin. Don't go back, all right?"

"That's it?" the girl asked.

"That's it." With that, Isval left the garret, another girl lifted out of bondage. Some of those she'd helped in the past had drifted back, but most didn't. Their new lives weren't easy, but at least they were no longer slaves.

She hailed a servicecar and, as the vehicle moved off, Ryiin's words replayed themselves for her.

It has to stop sometime, doesn't it?

Isval didn't see how it could stop, not for her. She had the driver take her back to the Octagon, Level Two.

"You don't look like a Level Two kind of lady," he said to her.

"You'd be surprised," she answered. She exited the car and headed down, into the deeper dark. She found the nook soon enough, the Imperial still lying there semiconscious, his hand broken, his face purpling from the blow she'd struck him. Spit and blood pooled on the ground near his mouth. She pulled her vibroblade and held it to his throat. His eyes blinked open. She imagined he could hardly see.

"Don't," he murmured.

She stared at his pain-clouded eyes a long while, the blade ready. She lifted it from his neck.

"Ryiin saved your life tonight," she said. "Remember that, because if you ever go looking for her, I'll come back. You hear me? You hear?"

He groaned assent.

She sheathed the knife. "So it's settled that you'll live. But you still owe me pain."

She kicked him in the ribs once, twice, felt them give way with an audible snap. He gasped in agony, moaned. She stepped over him, straddling him, grabbed his shirt in her fist, and punched him in the face again and again until he was as limp in her grasp as a child's doll. She dropped him to the ground and stared at him, her breath coming hard. She looked at her knuckles, raw and bleeding, just like the rest of her.

She was broken. And it would never stop. Not for her.

Eyes watched her as she stepped out of the alley and headed up a nearby flight of stairs. By the time she'd put a full level behind her, she heard the shouts from below. She'd been sloppy, hadn't covered her tracks, hadn't—as Cham always warned her to do— thought through her exit. But beatings happened often in the Octagon, and she appeared to be just another Twi'lek slave. She put three levels beneath her feet and still heard no pursuit.

By the time she'd retained another aircar, the need was gone. She could once more think clearly, and her mind was already turning to the preparations she needed to make to ready things for the attack on Taa and Vader. Cham's plan was elaborate, and extremely risky. But she loved the brazenness of it.

They had nine days to get everything ready.

CHAPTER FIVE

Cham paced the cracked stone of the crowded landing bay. He smiled to himself, thinking he was worse than Isval. All he needed to do was grumble some and the likeness would be perfect.

The underground base on Ryloth's third moon seethed with activity. A mishmash of technology, droid ships, and weapons sat arrayed on the launch bay's floor, with dozens of Twi'lek engineers and droid assistants hovering over them like worried mothers. Parts and tools lay in neat arrangements on the floors, the workers and droids plucking what they needed as they needed it.

No one even glanced up at him, so intensely were they focused on their work.

Cham and his agents had been buying and stealing and building ships and weapons for years. During that time he'd been filling weapons caches on Ryloth and Ryloth's moons, from crates of small arms to makeshift landing bays filled with droid tri-fighters and vulture droid fighters. He had a large force at his disposal, and he'd built it under the nose of the Empire, all with the compelled assistance of Belkor Dray.

Over the years his engineers—but particularly Kallon, who was a genius with artificial intelligence—had learned how to reprogram the brains in the droid fighters so they could operate without direction from a central droid control ship. They wouldn't be of much use in a dogfight with crewed ships, but dogfights were not part of Cham's plan.

He ran through the steps of the plan in his mind, doubts tugging at his resolve. He was committing everything—his people and his resources—to this one play. It would be worth it if he killed Vader and the Emperor. That could trigger a galaxy-wide rebellion, and in that chaos, with the Empire's resources spread thin, he could work to make Ryloth free. Otherwise . . .

He didn't dwell on the otherwise.

A free Ryloth; that was his goal. And if he had to bring down an Empire to do it, he was prepared to do so.

The tiny comlink implanted in his ear canal carried Isval's voice to him, as if she were speaking directly into his brain. She had a similar unit implanted, which allowed them to hear even each other's whispers but not be overheard by nearby listeners. Cham's communications engineers had created a comm subnet that rode on a group of old Clone Wars satellites orbiting Ryloth along with the rest of the war's detritus. The comsats gave the movement a secure, private network all over the planet and just beyond the orbit of the farthest moon.

"All's ready down here," she said. "All three teams are briefed."

He bit down twice to activate the implant. "You're on a decoy team, yes?"

She didn't hesitate before answering. "No, I'm leading the primary. I have to."

"Isval—"

"There's no discussion here, Cham. I'm the best chance we have. Besides . . . I have to. For Pok."

He couldn't argue with her thinking or her sentiment, but the thought of losing her made his legs go weak. He relied on her too much, cared for her too much. He remembered Pok's death, the sound of him choking, dying . . .

"I know what you're thinking," she said. "But if this goes wrong, you won't need me anymore, anyway. You won't even need you. There won't be much of a movement left to command."

She was right and he knew it. "Then let's make sure it doesn't go wrong."

"I've checked and double-checked," she said. "I see it in my sleep."

Cham did, too, and he'd triple-checked his thinking, and it all seemed solid, but they'd never planned anything on this large a scale, with so many moving parts and contingencies.

"If we don't bring down the shields, we abort," he said.

"If we don't short the shields, there'll be nothing to abort because we'll never even get started."

She was right about that, too, and her calm helped steady him. Normally she was agitated and restless, but she turned as calm as still water when action impended. Cham was the opposite, normally calm and controlled, but antsy in the face of imminent action. He worried for his people, probably too much for a revolutionary.

Once, he'd have led missions like this. Now he only planned them.

"I've become a bureaucrat," he muttered.

"Just don't let yourself get lazy," she joked, and he chuckled.

Her tone turned serious. "When do the last droid ships go?"

He glanced around at the three dozen or so vulture droids arranged on the landing bay. "Tonight, I think. When Belkor gives us the all-clear."

Belkor had provided them with information about Imperial patrols, incoming ships, and sensor scans. Cham had used the information to move the droid fighters and mines to the edge of the system unnoticed.

"And speaking of bureaucrats," she said, "how's our little Belkor handling this?"

"Oh, I think he's seeing things in his sleep, too."

"No indication he knows about Vader and the Emperor?"

"None." Cham paused, then said, "Two days, Isval. Our intel has the *Perilous* prepping."

"Two days," she agreed. "We're ready, Cham."

"We're ready," he echoed, saying it as though he could make it true by speaking with enough conviction.

Two days later Cham sat in the makeshift command center on Ryloth's third moon. Three of his comrades shared the room with him: Gobi at the subspace transmitter, his stubby fingers ready to transmit commands; Xira, monitoring the sensor readouts from the probe droids, her heavy-lidded eyes taking in the rapid stream of data displayed on the screen; and Kallon, the consulting engineer. Xira's data processing droid, D4L1, stood beside her chair, a hot link connecting him to the incoming data stream.

Nine viewscreens mounted on the wall showed the outer reaches of Ryloth's system, as seen from the half dozen probe droids they'd positioned in the system's

asteroid belt. The rest of the droid ships they'd prepared lurked in the asteroid belt, too, powered down
to almost zero, waiting for Gobi's remote command
to activate. A cloud of mines floated in space, orna-
ments hanging in the black, waiting for the *Perilous*
to emerge from hyperspace.

For the tenth time in the past ten minutes, Cham
wondered if Belkor had lost his nerve and betrayed
him, or given him bad information. And for the tenth
time he forced himself to stop thinking about it. If
Belkor had betrayed them, the movement would be
crippled with nothing to show for it.

But Belkor hadn't betrayed them; he couldn't, because Cham had made clear what the consequences
would be. No, things were going as planned. And if
they continued that way, then thousands of Imperials
would soon be dead, including the Emperor himself.

Not a terrorist, he reminded himself. *But a freedom
fighter.*

Everything he had worked to achieve for years was
about to fail or bear fruit, and all he could do was
watch it happen via instantaneous subspace transmission from over six hundred thousand kilometers
away.

A bureaucrat, indeed.

Vader and the Emperor strode onto the central tier of
the *Perilous*'s bridge. Royal Guards followed and
took flanking positions at the main lift behind them.
Crew members scurried around or sat at their stations, all of them about the business of preparing a
hyperspace jump for one of the Empire's most sophis-
ticated, powerful starships. Captain Luitt stood near
them, but kept a few paces of deck between them. He

avoided looking directly at Vader, his discomfort with Vader's presence palpable.

The captain turned to the Emperor, whose face was shrouded in the shadow of his hood. "I trust everything went well aboard the *Defiance,* my lord."

"Hyperdrive is online and course is set, sir," the helm called, and the information was echoed up to Luitt.

"I'd be honored if you'd give the order, my lord," said Luitt.

"Oh, no, Captain," the Emperor said, waving a hand. "I'm a political leader, not a military one. Proceed as you would normally."

"Engage the hyperdrive," the captain called, and the command caused a ripple of activity to flow along the bridge crew.

Vader felt the faint thrum in the deck as the *Perilous*'s powerful hyperdrive engaged. Stars and the black of space disappeared, replaced by the blue churn of hyperspace.

"En route to Ryloth," called the helm.

"Dim the view," Luitt ordered, and the transparisteel darkened until hyperspace was no longer visible. He turned to the Emperor. "My lord, if you and Lord Vader would prefer to retire to your quarters, I will let you know the instant we arrive in Ryloth's system."

"I think we will remain on the bridge for now, Captain," the Emperor said.

"Very good, sir," said Luitt, pursing his lips under his bristly gray mustache. "It won't be long."

The captain moved off, looking over the shoulders of his crew, issuing orders, and otherwise staying away from Vader. The bridge crew settled into its rhythm.

"I think you make him uncomfortable, Lord Vader," said the Emperor.

Vader made most of the naval officers he encountered uncomfortable. To them, he was a towering dark figure outside their chain of command who had emerged from nowhere and possessed powers they did not understand.

"His discomfort is useful to me," Vader said.

"Underlings should always be uncomfortable in the presence of their superiors," said the Emperor. "Don't you agree?"

Vader understood the question behind the question and answered accordingly. "Yes, my Master."

"Good."

The two surveyed the bridge in a silence broken only by the rasping of Vader's respirator while the *Perilous* crossed parsecs in a blink. After a time, the bridge crew broke into a different rhythm as they prepared to return the Star Destroyer to normal space.

"Coming out of hyperspace," called the helm.

"Coming out of hyperspace. Aye," the call echoed up the bridge.

"And the test begins," the Emperor said.

Vader looked at his Master, head tilted in a question, not taking his meaning until he, too, felt the disturbance in the Force.

"A ship is coming out of hyperspace," Xira said, her voice pitched high from excitement.

Cham realized he had been clenching his fists for the last thirty minutes. "Activate the mines. Let's pen them in. Shield bleeders on standby."

Kallon's head-tails bobbed with nervousness and his purple skin looked so pale as to be lavender. The bleeders were his brainchild. As always, he mumbled to himself under his breath.

Cham put a hand on Gobi's shoulder. "Be ready to transmit to the droid ships, Gobi."

"I'm more than ready, Cham," Gobi said, shaking with excitement or tension. "Let's force-feed these Imperials some fire."

"Let's do just that," said Cham.

Not a terrorist. But a freedom fighter.

As the *Perilous* emerged from hyperspace on the outer edge of Ryloth's system, the mammoth viewport undimmed, giving a view of several distant gas giants and the nearby belt of asteroids that divided the outer system from the inner. The system's star burned orange and bright in the distance. Ryloth itself was too far away to be visible.

"Maximum acceler—" began the captain, but before he finished an impact sounded from starboard and the huge starship vibrated.

Heads came up from stations and looked questions at one another. A second impact followed hard after, then a third, larger than the rest, caused the ship to list. Vader eyed the viewscreen, saw nothing. His Master stared at the floor, a strange half smile on his face.

"Situation!" the captain ordered, his voice calm.

"Sir, I'm . . ."

Another impact shook the ship, a fourth, another, another. The ship listed farther. Alarms blared.

"We have electrical shorts and a few fires all over the ship," the duty officer called.

"Injuries reported."

"What is happening, Captain?" Vader asked, stepping forward and grabbing Luitt by the arm hard enough to elicit a pained grimace.

Luitt looked at Vader, at the Emperor, and barked at his scan officer. "Situation, scan?"

"Mines, sir," the scan officer said. "Hundreds of them everywhere."

"Mines?" the captain repeated. "Full stop. Weapons online."

More explosions shook the ship, and a dozen mines floated into the viewscreen's field of view—they came in all shapes and sizes, some huge square cubes with magnetic sensors, others spiked spheres with kinetic detectors. Vader recognized a few as modern in design, others from the Clone Wars era, others from still earlier.

"The shields will prevent any real damage to the ship, my lord," Captain Luitt said to the Emperor. "My apologies for this inconvenience."

"Perform a deep scan on this area of the system," said Vader. "Particularly on the asteroid belt. I sense something . . ."

Captain Luitt pursed his lips in impatience. "My lord, this is probably just a grouping of mines left over from the Clone Wars and floating in the outer system. I've heard of it happening. They present no threat to us—"

Vader put a finger in the captain's face. "Do as I have instructed, Captain."

Luitt's brow furrowed, but he dared not disobey. "As you wish, Lord Vader. Scan, begin to . . ."

Another series of explosions boomed against the ship's shields, sending tremors through the deck.

"No damage," someone on the bridge crew called. "Shields holding."

"Sir, there are still over three hundred mines out there," said the scan officer.

Luitt couldn't bring himself to make eye contact with Vader. To the Emperor he said, "My lord, I think perhaps it would be best if you vacated the bridge."

"Quite the contrary," said the Emperor. "This is precisely where I belong."

The scan officer leaned over his instruments. "I'm getting unusual readings, sir. I think you should see this."

"What is it?" Luitt asked, irritable, though he hustled to the scan station. Vader followed hard after, looming over the captain and the crew member.

"This," the scan officer said, pointing at the readings on his screen.

Vader and Luitt took them in, and both understood their meaning. Luitt cursed and stood up straight. "Sound battle stations. Helm, full reverse!"

"There are mines on all sides of us, sir. If we reverse . . ."

"I don't care! Full reverse! Now!"

"It's too late for that, Captain," Vader said. He activated a remote on his armor to get his interceptor prepped for flight. "Alert your flight teams," he said to Luitt. "Be ready to scramble your V-wings."

"What? Why?" Luitt asked, looking from Vader to the Emperor. "The shields are still up."

"Likely not for much longer," Vader said.

"Do as Lord Vader commands," said the Emperor, putting just enough power in his tone to quail everyone on the bridge.

"Give the command," Luitt said to the duty officer. "And double the power to forward shields."

D4L1 beeped at Xira and she nodded in response. "*Perilous* is reversing."

"They detected the bleeders," Cham said.

They all watched the screens as the proximity mines to the rear of the *Perilous* blossomed into fire. One, five, a dozen, two score.

"Looks like very little damage from the mines so far."

"So far," Gobi said, nearly bouncing in his chair.

Kallon muttered under his breath, tapping the table at which he sat with a forefinger.

On the wall-mounted screens, Cham could see the enormous Star Destroyer from various angles, the image occasionally obscured by an asteroid spinning in front of one of the probe droids. Hundreds of un-exploded mines floated in space around the enormous ship, trailing after it as it moved into reverse.

The next step was the critical one. He could feel Kallon's eyes on him. He'd wanted the ship a bit closer to the asteroid belt, but there was nothing for it.

"Activate the shield bleeders, now," Cham said, and Gobi nodded.

"You can do it," Kallon said, and kept mumbling the phrase under his breath like an incantation. "You can do it."

They watched the screens, seeing through the eyes of the probes. Kallon had reengineered two dozen of the mines. When they contacted a ship's shields, they wouldn't explode but rather latch on to the shields' energy signature, set up a counter grid, and, in theory, weaken them enough for ships to get through.

Cham could not tell which mines were rigged to explode and which were programmed to bring down the shields, but he could tell when the bleeders hit the *Perilous*'s shields and activated.

The area of space around the huge ship grew a series of glowing lines, veins in the shield's protective field that extended out from each of the bleeders toward the others. The shields visibly flickered as the lines expanded. The *Perilous* looked like it was trapped in a glowing net.

"Caught a big fish!" Gobi said.

Maybe, Cham thought, still not quite willing to let himself believe.

"You can do it," Kallon mumbled to the bleeders. "You can."

"Talk to me, Kallon," said Cham.

Kallon studied the data coming over Xira's comp. D4L1 chirped something that Kallon must have disliked. He swatted the droid on his silver dome.

"I think it's working," Kallon said. He glanced up at the screen, at the net that surrounded the *Perilous*. "It *looks* like it's working."

"But is it?" Cham asked.

"Shields *are* weakening," Xira said, also studying the data.

"We go, then," Cham said. To Gobi: "Launch all the droid ships."

Gobi issued the signal. Through the eyes of the probes, they saw a fleet of several hundred vulture droids speed out of the asteroid field.

"This is it!" Gobi said.

"This is it," Cham softly echoed.

"What is that?" Luitt asked.

The viewscreen showed a dense matrix of glowing lines, like bolts of lightning, tracing jagged paths along the shields.

"Shields at fifty percent," the scan officer said, his tone going from puzzled to alarmed. "Seventeen! Back to twenty-five!"

"Get them back up to full!" Luitt commanded.

"Full stop," Vader ordered, and Luitt did not countermand.

With the shields weakening, they couldn't risk slamming into the mines all around them.

The helm put the *Perilous* into a stop, and the scan officer tapped his screen. "Captain, some of the mines aren't mines. They're devices creating some kind of feedback loop in the shield matrix. They're not bringing the shields down, but they're weakening them. Opening holes in places."

An uncomfortable rustle went through the bridge crew. Vader looked at his Master, but the Emperor seemed lost in thought, a faint smile raising the corners of his thin-lipped mouth.

Luitt stalked from station to station, studying readouts, and when he spoke his voice was tense. "Get it fixed. Weapons, get a lock on those devices and bring them down."

"There are hundreds of mines out there, sir," the weapons officer said. "A miss with the shields weakened could create a chain reaction of explosions."

"Then don't miss!" Luitt said.

"Sir," said the scan officer, "I can't be certain which is a regular mine and which isn't. There're too many and they're too small."

Luitt swallowed hard. No doubt he felt as trapped as the *Perilous*. He looked back at the Emperor, at Vader, back at his bridge crew.

Another crew member added, "The mines have proximity attractors. If the shields fall, they'll be drawn close and then explode."

Another uncomfortable rustle went through the crew. The *Perilous* couldn't move and yet had to move.

"I need options," Luitt said, and the crew buried themselves in data.

Vader gave him one. "Launch your fighter squadrons," he said. "I'll lead them."

Whatever discomfort Luitt had with Vader gave way in the face of the crisis. He nodded, relieved. "Of course. The fighters can take out the mines with precision."

"Sir," said the scan officer, his voice pitched high with controlled alarm. "There are several hundred vulture droids swarming out of the asteroid belt. They're heading directly for us."

"Battle stations," Luitt said, and alarms began to blare. Vader turned to the Emperor to speak, but before he could say anything, the Emperor said, "You intend to suggest that I remove myself to a safer location. To my shuttle perhaps, or to my quarters."

Vader nodded. His Master often knew his thoughts.

"I think I shall remain here and watch matters unfold," the Emperor said. "But you should do as you intended."

"Yes, Master," Vader said. He bowed and strode for the lift. As he approached, the doors opened to reveal a fretful Orn Free Taa. The Twi'lek waddled out of the lift, large ears sagging, jowls and belly bouncing, and stared at the viewscreen with alarm.

"Oh, my! What's happening?"

"Greetings, Senator," the Emperor said, and before Taa could reply, Vader gestured with his hand and used the Force to fling the senator out of his path. Taa hit the bulkhead with a gasp and sank to the ground at the feet of the one of the Emperor's Royal Guards.

"Lord Vader is in a hurry," the Emperor said. "Forgive him."

Vader entered the lift, turned, and stared at Taa as the doors closed.

He had little time. The moment the lift doors opened on the flight level, he hurried through the corridors of the *Perilous,* finally taking the lift down to the fighter bay.

Scores of V-wings sat in neat rows along the flight deck, engines already engaged. The blaring alarms had the flight deck buzzing. Pilots in their flight suits hurried to their ships and a dozen mech droids wheeled along, beeping and whirring. Eschewing the cockpit ladder, Vader used the Force to leap atop his interceptor and slide into his seat. As he strapped himself in and the canopy descended, the squadron commander's voice came over his helmet comm.

"What are we facing out there, sir?"

"Mines and vulture droids at a minimum, Commander."

"Vulture droids? Been a while since I've seen those, sir."

"Launch when ready," Vader said to the squadron as the antigravs lifted his ship off the deck. Dozens of V-wings followed suit.

The commander synced the fighters' identifications with the bridge comp, so they could be easily distinguished from the incoming vulture droids and mines.

"Clear to launch," said the bridge officer.

"Lord Vader," Luitt's voice said over the private channel. "The shields are at sixteen percent."

"Understood, Captain," Vader said, engaging his ion engines. His interceptor accelerated out into open space.

CHAPTER SIX

"Can you magnify on the launch bay?" Cham asked, and Kallon, still muttering, made it happen.

One of the screens on the wall gave a close-up of the Star Destroyer's belly launch bay, and, through the glowing net of the dying shields, they watched dozens of V-wings pour out of it. Cham had anticipated a fighter contingent. A third of the vulture droids would engage with the V-wings. The rest would continue on their mission.

"Status of the shields?" he asked Kallon.

Kallon shook his head. "Too far out for accurate readings, but . . ."

As they watched, the net of lines surrounding the *Perilous* flared and expired. The shields were down.

"Well," Kallon said, sitting back in his chair and grinning. "I think we have an accurate reading after all. They're down."

"Yes," Gobi exclaimed, and slammed his fist on the table, spilling his caf.

Even Cham couldn't contain a smile.

* * *

Vader saw the shields flare and fail even before Luitt's frantic call came over the comm.

"Shields are down, Lord Vader."

Scores of mines, drawn by their attractor arrays, floated toward the ship, gradually picking up speed, and hundreds of droid fighters chewed up the space behind them, swarming toward the vulnerable ship.

Vader wheeled his interceptor toward the mines and the oncoming vulture droids. He sensed a greater threat in the droids than he did the mines.

"Free all batteries to fire on the mines, Captain."

The V-wing squadron commander's voice carried over the comm. "Ten seconds before vultures are in range. Target the mines in the interim."

Vader fell into the deep well of anger that sat in his core, used it to center him in the Force, and flew entirely by feel. He targeted a mine, fired, watched it vaporize, and flew through the flames. Wheeling right, he targeted another, and another, destroying a mine with every shot. The explosions sometimes set off nearby mines, and space was soon filled with a network of concurrent detonations. Vader spun and whirled through the chaos.

"There are too many to get even half," said one of the pilots.

"Droids closing," the squadron commander said.

"Break off and engage the droids," Vader commanded.

Around him the Star Destroyer's formidable batteries of weapons scribed lines of ionized plasma on the velvet of space. Mines exploded to Vader's left and right. He circled wide and up, buzzing the *Perilous*'s bridge as he fired on another mine, another. And yet there were too many.

The first of the mines reached the hull of the Star Destroyer, latched on to the bulkhead, and blossomed into fire—two, eight, a dozen, a score. The explosions shot long tongues of flame into space. Debris and bodies flew out of the blast holes and into the vacuum. Vader could imagine the fires, the death, the blaring alarms.

Vader flew above the huge pyramid of the ship, hugging *Perilous*'s superstructure and destroying three mines before they could connect to the hull and focus their blast into the ship's bulkhead. Their explosions did superficial damage but didn't breach the ship.

"Droids in range," the squadron commander said. "Regroup and take attack formations."

Cham stared at the screens, his jaw clenched, his shoulders hunched, as the forces closed. The fighters looked tiny against the backdrop of the Star Destroyer, bloodflies to a lylek.

The dark of space around the *Perilous* was alight with weapons fire and explosions. Gobi hissed with glee each time a mine struck the Star Destroyer and birthed fire.

Cham knew that Kallon's reengineered vulture droids were not as maneuverable as they would be otherwise, not with their cargo and turgid brains. They would be no match for the V-wings, but Cham only needed a fraction of them to get through for the damage to the *Perilous* to be crippling.

"Fly, fly, little birds," he whispered.

The secure comm he wore in his ear pinged: Isval.

"Speak," he said softly.

"Preliminary word of the attack is arriving planetside. It's chaos down here."

"Intercepts?" he asked her.

"Not that I can tell, but I'm sitting in a repair ship. I'm sure it won't be long, though."

Cham looked up at the screen. "They'll be too late to stop this."

"How is it going?" she asked.

Cham stared at the screen. "Vultures are closing. You ready?"

"We're ready," she said.

"I'll be in touch," he said, and broke the connection.

On the screen, the fighters—vultures on the one hand, V-wings on the other—lit up space with weapons fire.

"And here we go!" Gobi said.

The approaching cloud of vulture droids opened fire as one, their repeating blasters spitting dashes of red energy through the void. Vader swung his interceptor away from the *Perilous,* burning from dozens of mine explosions, and flew directly toward the oncoming vultures. Lines of energy filled space around him, the solid green pulses from the *Perilous* and the intermittent red blasts of the droids.

Vader let the Force guide him, his hands smooth and rapid on the controls, and the ship danced unscathed in the matrix of blasts. The vulture droids dispersed in all directions as the interceptor and the trailing V-wings approached. Vader fixed on one of them, fired, destroyed it, swung hard right, fired again, and destroyed another.

Perhaps a third of the droids engaged with the V-wings, while the bulk of them continued on toward the *Perilous.* Vader's comm was filled with the chatter of the squadron's pilots, calling out to one another, picking targets, holding one another's flanks.

Vader picked one of the droids and locked on as it lurched left and right, attempting to shake his pursuit. The vultures were slow, awkward fliers, and something about them struck him as odd—and then he had it: They'd been modified. All of them had bulges on their bellies, an added compartment or weapon of some kind. It made them awkward in flight, far less maneuverable than usual.

Curious, he closed on one, targeted it with care, fired, and sheared off one of its wing pods. It spun out of control, and the centrifugal force started to tear it apart. Vader stayed on it as the belly compartment tore loose to reveal its contents.

Hundreds of metal spheres spilled out and into space. Vader slammed on his stick, driving the interceptor down, but he could not avoid the shrapnel altogether. The spheres slammed into his ship and clung there, and he saw that they weren't shrapnel but buzz droids. The magnetic balls sprouted legs and eyestalks and clambered along the wings and fuselage of his fighter, positioning themselves to do the most damage.

He dodged fire from a pursuing vulture droid by veering hard left, fired on another, destroying it, then drew on the Force and caused a wave of kinetic energy to repel the droids from his vessel. Unable to resist the sudden blast, they flew off in all directions and, to his surprise, exploded with enough force for the series of blast waves to rock his ship and temporarily send him spinning. A vulture got behind him while he was vulnerable, fired, and nicked his wing before he could right his ship and shake the pursuit.

"The vultures are carrying a payload of explosive buzz droids," Vader said over the comm. He glanced back toward the *Perilous* and saw scores of the vultures, fat with the explosive buzz droids, flying straight at the Star Destroyer.

"Try to keep them off the *Perilous*," the squadron

commander said to the rest of the pilots, understanding the implications right away.

Vader slammed on his stick, whirled his ship around, and headed back in the direction of the *Perilous,* but he could see he was already too late. Dozens of the droids had been vaporized in the withering fire from the Star Destroyer, and the more maneuverable V-wings locked on and destroyed many, too, but many would get through.

Meanwhile, clouds of buzz droids that had survived the destruction of the vulture droids carrying them floated free in space, legs and eyestalks waving. Vader saw several latch on to a V-wing as it flew through them. They scurried onto the wings and canopy and exploded, shearing a wing, shattering the canopy, and destroying the fighter.

Vader accelerated and flew directly toward a cloud of them, using his free hand to focus his use of the Force as he approached. A gesture, an exercise of will, and he slammed several of the free-floating buzz droids into one another, where they exploded, clearing his way. He locked on to another vulture droid before it could reach the *Perilous,* followed it as it veered left, then right, fired, and turned it to a cloud of flames.

As he'd expected, the vulture droids fired as they approached the Star Destroyer, but they did not reduce speed to increase maneuverability. Instead they stayed at maximum acceleration, obviously intending to crash into the ship and release their cargo. Vader destroyed another, then another. But he couldn't get them all, and the surviving vultures slammed into the ship at full speed.

Enormous towers of flame rose from the *Perilous*'s superstructure. Vader veered hard left and wheeled around, cutting down another vulture droid as he turned. He could imagine that the damage to the interior of the Star Destroyer was worse than he could see, as the vulture droids would have ejected their buzz droids into the corridors. The tiny bombs would run deeper into the ship and explode.

Two vultures headed directly for the shield generator. He destroyed one and then another, but the buzz droids they carried floated out of the fire of the vultures' destruction, glommed on to the shield generator, and there exploded into flame. Another vulture crashed into the flight deck; another hit adjacent to the bridge. Many crashed into or near the ship's gun turrets and destroyed them. Secondary explosions rocked the ship. The Star Destroyer was bleeding fire and debris and bodies from scores of wounds.

Vader flew under the ship, looking for more targets, and saw another wave of vultures streaking toward the *Perilous*.

Curses and exclamations of shock carried over the comm from the V-wing squadrons.

"Stay focused," the squadron commander barked. "And destroy as many as possible before they reach the ship."

Vader wheeled back around, accompanied by the bulk of the V-wing squadron, and opened fire on the vulture droids. He destroyed one, another. A V-wing to starboard caught droid fire and exploded.

Kallon had stopped muttering and even he was grinning as they watched the *Perilous* burn. Gobi could no longer sit, but paced the floor in excitement, eyes on the screens, a smile fixed on his face.

But Cham had a better understanding of the ship's ability to withstand damage than did his comrades. They'd wounded it, killed hundreds, maybe thousands of Imperials, but they were nowhere close to destroying it.

"Her guns are out of commission!" Gobi exclaimed. "She's defenseless! Let's finish her!"

"The second wave, Kallon," Cham ordered, and Kallon sent the command to the second wave of vulture droids Cham had held in reserve. He resumed muttering to himself the moment he sent the signal.

Another hundred or so vulture droids, all of them heavy with explosive buzz droids, powered up and accelerated out of the asteroid belt toward the ship. Cham watched them go, daring to let hope find a home in his chest. He bit down twice to activate the tiny comm implanted in his ear and spoke to Isval.

"We may not need you after all," he said. "Things are going well."

"I hope you're right," she returned, and he caught the disappointment in her tone. "But we're ready."

Isval sat in the copilot's chair of the boxy repair ship on the vast underground landing pad on Ryloth. Beside her in the pilot's seat, Eshgo fiddled with the comp.

The movement had been able to put teams aboard three of the repair shuttles, and now they were just waiting. She wanted to stand and pace, but there was no room. The antigrav tool pallet and the rest of her team—Eshgo, Drim, Crost, and Faylin, the lone human in their group—filled the cramped quarters of the shuttle.

Cham had said everything was going well. If all went according to plan—and things usually did when Cham made the plans—she expected a call to launch to go out shortly. If the *Perilous* was burning, and she hoped fervently that it was, it would need non-Imperial assistance.

Several dozen other repair ships sat on the pad. Maintenance droids and engineers holding datapads moved here and there, checking the status of the ships. The onboard comm was listening in on emergency Ryloth frequencies.

"Nothing," Eshgo said.

"They're not desperate enough yet to call for Twi'lek help," Isval said, staring out of the ship. "But they will be."

Meanwhile, there was nothing to do but wait, and Isval detested waiting.

Vader eyed the oncoming wave of vulture droids.

"Stay back, Commander," he said. "The entire squad. Destroy any ships that get past me."

"Sir, but . . ."

"Those are my orders, Commander."

"Yes, Lord Vader."

Captain Luitt's voice came over the comm, his tone stressed. Alarms blared in the background. "Lord Vader, I'm not sure we can survive another barrage from the vulture droids."

"You won't need to," Vader said, and cut the connection.

Vader fell entirely into the Force, let his anger flow through him, harnessed it for the weapon it was, and flew directly toward the vulture droids.

The mirth went out of the command center, replaced by the quiet of an unspoken question. Gobi gave it voice.

"Is that a single ship breaking off? Is that a V-wing or something else? What is it doing?"

Cham could not distinguish one fighter craft from another, but he had no doubt who sat at the controls of that single ship.

He's not a man, Isval had said, and Cham half believed it. He activated his comm and spoke to Isval. "I think we may need you after all."

"What's happening?" she asked, excitement in her tone.

He shook his head, uncertain. "Vader. I thought we might get lucky, but . . . just be ready."

When Vader got within weapons range of the vultures, the entire swarm broke in all directions and opened fire on him. Enmeshed in the Force, he intuitively calculated angles, velocities, and vectors, his interceptor rising, falling, spinning, wheeling, navigating the firestorm of blasterfire where the margin for error was millimeters. He didn't return fire. His weapon was not blasters. Instead, he fixed on the leading vulture droids and reached out with the Force.

With an effort of will and a slight gesture, he tore open the belly compartment of three vultures. The tiny, explosive buzz droids they held poured out into space. Many of the trailing vulture droids, unable to dodge, collided with the scattered buzz droids, and explosions turned dozens of vulture droids and buzz droids to debris.

Vader took hold of another vulture droid's belly and tore it open, then another. Clouds of buzz droids filled space with countless small explosions, wreaking havoc on the vulture droid swarm. Vader flew through and past them, still dodging blasterfire. He wheeled hard about and pursued them as the surviving vulture droids—perhaps only a score—made their way toward the *Perilous*.

"Allow none of the stragglers through, Commander," Vader called to the squadron commander as he accelerated in pursuit.

Vader had the vulture droids trapped between him and the rest of the squadron. He went high to avoid any crossfire and watched the V-wings trade fire with the droids. The droids hit and destroyed two V-wings, but the rest of the squad made short work of the remaining droids. Debris, fire, and clouds of buzz droids spun through space.

"Well done, Commander," Vader said. "Maintain a perimeter. I'm returning to the *Perilous*."

The Star Destroyer hung against the dark of space, the huge wedge of its superstructure burning in dozens of places along its length. Jagged holes in the hull yawned like mouths.

Vader entered through the smoke-filled landing bay and saw the destruction there. Flames were everywhere. Broken tubes vented gas and fluid. Crew scrambled everywhere, some in portable oxygen masks, others succumbing to smoke. Droids, automated suppression systems, and fire teams fought the fires here and there, but most went untended. The damage was more than the crew could deal with. They'd need assistance. Bodies and body parts lay scattered among the wreckage. Ships burned on the landing pad, including the Emperor's shuttle.

Seeing that, Vader suspected his Master had foreseen much of what had happened. But if so, he'd done little to stop it.

Vader set down his ship, popped his canopy, leapt out, and strode through the carnage and smoke. Wrecked mech droids, the ruins of fighters, and pieces of exploded vulture droids littered the landing bay, smoke curling up from the debris. Emergency alarms screamed. Vader hurried toward the bridge.

Throughout the ship, the scene was the same. Crew running about shouting commands, screams of pain, smoke and fire, chaos, disorder.

Vader's anger grew with every step he took.

Belkor stood in his quarters, heart racing, nervous sweat putting an uncomfortable sheen on his face. He took a deep breath when his comlink buzzed.

"This is Colonel Belkor."

"Sir, you should get to the comm center right away. The *Perilous* has been attacked."

Belkor had rehearsed his answer many times. "I'm on my way," he said, with just the right amount of alarm and urgency. "Status of the *Perilous*?"

"Unknown at this time, sir. We don't have details yet. Still awaiting word."

Belkor cut the connection, smoothed his uniform, adjusted his hat, donned his mask, and headed for the communications center. Men and women in uniform hurried through the halls of the installation. The ring of his boots off the uncarpeted floor sounded loud in his ears as he mentally replayed what he would say to Mors.

Ahead he saw the transparent doors of the communications hub. They slid open at his approach, leaking out a gust of frantic comm chatter. He caught snippets here and there. The lieutenant colonel in charge in his absence saw him enter and hurried toward him, nodding at something in his ear comm as he walked.

"Colonel Belkor," the lieutenant colonel said.

"Update," Belkor ordered. His legs felt weak.

"The *Perilous* was hit the moment she entered the system, sir."

Again, Belkor's rehearsed answer came quickly to his lips. "Hit? How? By whom?"

"Looks like the terrorists, sir, but we can't be certain."

"Status?"

He expected to hear that it had been destroyed, but he didn't.

"She's heavily damaged, sir."

Belkor's mask melted in the heat of his surprise. "What do you mean damaged? I thought—" He caught himself just in time, and said, "That's good news at least. Go on."

"She sounds *heavily* damaged, from what we can glean. Reports are still coming in. She's limping badly and on fire. Looks as though she was attacked by a whole swarm of mines and old droid fighters, if the reports are accurate. The attacking ships have been destroyed, but she needs help containing the fires and with repairs."

"Get me Moff Mors on the comm."

"Yes, sir."

Belkor felt the soft vibration of the encrypted comlink he kept in his pocket, Cham reaching out to him. He ignored it the first time, and the second, but on the third he looked around, stepped into a corner of the room, and put the comlink to his ear.

"Yes," he said, sounding as though he were speaking only to another Imperial officer. "I've heard, yes. It is unbelievable."

Cham's voice came over the connection. "Put out a call for all available repair ships, including non-Imperial ships, to get to the *Perilous* and offer aid."

Belkor swallowed his anger and adopted a fake half

smile. "I don't think that's possible. You didn't do what you were supposed to."

The lieutenant colonel was waving him over. He must have reached Moff Mors. Belkor signaled him to wait.

"Do it now, Belkor. Right now. She's burning and she'll go down. Do it."

Belkor's anger at being ordered around by Cham prevented him from speaking for a moment.

"I'll see what I can do," he finally said between gritted teeth, and cut the connection.

Belkor hustled to the lieutenant colonel.

"I have the Moff," the lieutenant colonel said.

"I'll take it in the conference room," Belkor said.

"Yes, sir."

Belkor composed himself before stepping into the quiet of the conference room. There, he activated the comm, and a hologram of Mors formed about the triangular conference table. She looked crisp in her uniform and clear eyed. Belkor did not like it at all.

"Moff Mors," Belkor began. "The *Perilous* was attacked the moment she—"

"I already heard!" Mors shouted. She was redfaced with anger. A lock of dark hair escaped the tight bun she wore it in and formed a hook across her brow. "What I want to know is how an entire fleet of rebel ships held position at the edge of the system and no one knew of it?"

"Our resources are limited, as you know. We don't normally patrol that far out in the system."

"That's not my question, Colonel! I want to know how they got there to begin with!"

In truth, Belkor had diverted patrol craft and flight clearances in a way that allowed Cham to move the ships into position, but he had been careful to do so using Mors's authorization code. The diversions themselves were not necessarily suspicious—changes to patrol routes happened all the time in response to intelligence. But if anyone grew suspicious, the investigation would point to Mors. It would be Belkor's word against Mors's, of course, but in that situation Belkor would come out the better. He could show that Mors was a spice addict, that she embezzled the proceeds of Imperial mining operations, that she fraternized with known criminal elements like the Hutts, and that she'd shirked her responsibility when she'd thrown the management of Ryloth into Belkor's lap. Meanwhile, Belkor, loyal to a fault, had tried his best to do his duty.

"I'll figure out what happened and hold those responsible to account," Belkor said. "Meanwhile, may I suggest that we send out an immediate call for all available repair ships to give aid to the *Perilous*?"

"Yes, yes," said Mors, and waved at him to go do it. "Do that. What?"

"What, ma'am?"

But Mors hadn't been speaking to him. She was speaking to someone on her staff that Belkor could not see. While Mors was occupied, Belkor opened the door and called out to the lieutenant colonel.

"All available repair ships, including non-Imperial ships, are to be ordered to assist the *Perilous*. Do it now."

"Yes, sir!" the lieutenant colonel said, and started issuing orders.

Belkor returned to the table and to Mors, who was still speaking to someone Belkor could not see. Something had changed. Mors looked shrunken, collapsing in on herself, her face crestfallen, her eyes fearful.

"I need that confirmed," Mors said to her staffer, a tremor in her voice. "I need it confirmed right now."

Something in Mors's tone alarmed Belkor.

"Moff?" he asked, his voice tentative.

Mors swallowed, cleared her throat, and sat down. "Belkor . . . the Emperor and Lord Vader are reportedly aboard the *Perilous*."

The words hit Belkor like a kick to the stomach. For a moment he could not speak or breathe. He put his palms on the table to support legs that seemed to have turned to cloth. "I . . . the Emperor?"

"This happened on your watch, Belkor," Mors said. She sounded small, timid, terrified.

"Our watch," Belkor said. "Our watch, ma'am."

To that, Mors said nothing.

Thoughts ricocheted around Belkor's mind, none of them making much sense.

Had Cham known? How could he have known?

He must have. Cham had known all along and he'd strung Belkor along and now Belkor was in too deep and he'd be responsible for—

"Colonel!" Mors said, bringing him back to himself.

"Ma'am?" Belkor said.

"Get escorts and repair ships up there, Belkor. And I'm coming down to Ryloth."

"Of course," Belkor said absently, and cut the hologram. "Of course you are."

He grabbed the holoprojector and slammed it against the table once, twice, until it shattered. He felt eyes on his back—everyone in the main room of the comm center was probably staring at him. He didn't care. For a long moment he simply sat there, breathing heavily, any attempt to think lost to the churn of his emotions. Vader. The Emperor.

He tried to think of how he could manage events, how he could extricate himself from the hole in which he'd buried himself.

He could run. He'd thought about it before. He

could do it, just get offplanet and find some hovel farther out on the Rim and . . .

He knew he couldn't. If Vader and the Emperor were dead and he was found to have fled, the Imperial Security Bureau would hound him to the universe's end and the ISB always found those they hunted. And if Vader and the Emperor weren't dead and he was found to have fled, Vader himself would hound him.

He had to see it through. He had no other choice.

He stood, took a deep breath, straightened his uniform, and turned back toward the main comm room. Eyes that had been on him found their duty stations. The lieutenant colonel, standing just outside the room, stood to attention when Belkor's eyes fell on him. Belkor walked through the door and said to him, "Ensure the repair ships have a fighter escort. Do it right now. I'll be . . . back. I need to check something."

"Yes, sir," the lieutenant colonel said, and almost sprinted to a nearby comm officer.

Belkor swallowed as he walked through comm central, out into the corridor and onto a lift, and finally into an officers-only restroom. He stood there, his back against the door. No one else was in the room, so he locked himself in. He consciously unclenched his jaw, his fists, his guts.

Vader and the Emperor. Vader and the Emperor.

His encrypted comm buzzed—Cham. He snatched it from his pocket, squeezing it so hard it slipped from his hand and fell to the floor. He picked it up, cursing, opened a channel, and held it to his ear.

"You bastard," he said. "Do you have any idea what you've done?"

"Calm down, Belkor."

"Calm down! You tried to kill—" He caught himself and reduced his tone to a whisper. "You tried to kill the Emperor and Vader."

"I'm *going to* kill the Emperor and Vader," Cham said. "And you're going to help me."

Belkor could not bring himself to agree. Cham must have read into his silence.

"You will, Belkor. You must. The attack already happened. You're implicated. There will be nowhere for you to run—"

Belkor cut the connection, his heart racing, sweating under his uniform, his mind filled anew with the static of stress. He paced back and forth in the restroom, back and forth, as the encrypted comm buzzed in his pocket.

"Blast, blast, blast, blast."

He answered the comm.

"Say nothing, *Colonel*," Cham snapped, pronouncing Belkor's rank as he would an insult. "And just listen. I told you I'd expose you if you didn't help, and I will. I will. But you're in this now. Did you order the rescue ships? Speak!"

"Yes," Belkor answered tightly.

"Good. Now listen to me. Vader and the Emperor and Taa die today. It's about to happen. You don't need to do anything more except supervise the repair and rescue just as you would otherwise. See, nothing suspicious? See? Do you hear me, Belkor?"

Belkor had to pull the answer up from the depths of his gut. "Yes. Mors is coming down to Ryloth."

Cham was quiet for a moment. "That changes nothing. Do as we just discussed. And keep this comm at hand in case I need anything else. Everything turns on the next hour."

CHAPTER SEVEN

CHAM POCKETED THE ENCRYPTED COMM AND stepped back into the command center. No one even turned to see him enter. All eyes were still on the screens, where the *Perilous* burned but still flew, moving at full speed through the system, racing toward Ryloth.

In truth Cham hadn't expected to bring the *Perilous* down with the vulture droids, though he'd started hoping for it before Vader had gotten in the way.

He bit down, activated the private comm, and addressed Isval, though he spoke loud enough for the others in the command center to hear him.

"Phase two is a go," he said, and the eyes in the room did turn to him then. "The alert's going out in moments. You're up, Isval. The *Perilous* is burning but flying, heading straight for Ryloth."

"Copy that," she responded.

"Good luck," he said to her.

Kallon, Xira, and Gobi all looked at him, brows furrowed in a question. D4 gave an interrogatory beep. Kallon voiced their shared thoughts: "There's a phase two?"

"There is," Cham said. He'd kept it need-to-know only.

"Yes!" Gobi said.

Cham stared at him until his glee wilted.

"What?" Gobi asked. "Did I say something wrong?"

"This isn't a game," Cham said, thinking of the danger Isval was about to put herself in. "You understand that? People are dying."

"Only their people," Gobi said weakly.

"So far," Cham said. "Let's hope it stays that way. But either way, it's no game."

"Right," Gobi said, his skin darkening with embarrassment. "Right."

Cham stared at the viewscreens. Matters were out of his hands, and the most dangerous part of the plan was just getting under way.

Isval shared a look with Eshgo, a nod, and they waited for the alert to come. They didn't have to wait long before it came over the comm: *All ships to aid an Imperial vessel in distress.*

"Repair Eighty-Three, copy that," she said.

On the landing pad all around her, Twi'lek repair teams hurried out of side caves and ran for their ships. Other vessels, already crewed, lurched into the air on their antigravs.

The onboard computer blinked as pertinent details, clearances, and assignments started emerging from central. She waited for theirs to come through, and when it did, Eshgo got them off the pad. In her secure wrist comlink Isval said to the two backup teams, "We are up. Status?"

"Up and out," came the first response.

"Off the pad and waiting for clearance," came the second.

"Comm silence between us from now on."

"Copy that," came the responses. "And good luck."

She cut the connection and said over her shoulder, "Copy that."

Drim, Faylin, and Crost all echoed her sentiment.

Eshgo piloted them out of the mouth of the landing bay and into Ryloth's winds. As soon as he hit open air, he accelerated to full in-atmo speed. Ryloth's dry, rocky terrain fell away below them. In moments the dying light of a planetside day gave way to the dark of outer space.

"We're clear of the outer atmosphere," Eshgo said, checking the instruments. "Accelerating to full. ETA in under an hour."

A fleet of repair ships, some Imperial, but most Rylothian, dotted space, heading in the direction of the wounded Star Destroyer. As they sped past Ryloth's moons, Isval's eyes lingered on the small rocky one where she knew Cham and many of the members of the movement were hiding in one of their long-standing underground bases. V-wings from the Imperial bases on the largest moon—the Moff's moon—fell in as escorts.

She bit down and activated the private comm with Cham. "Flying by you now. We'll soon clear the moons' orbits. I'm going to lose you after that."

"Get in and get out, Isval. As fast as you can. Speed is your ally."

She nodded. "Any Imperial chatter about Vader and the Emperor?"

"Frequencies are buzzing with the revelation that they were aboard, but no certain word on whether they're still alive. The *Perilous* is heading fast toward Ryloth. It's already past the asteroid belt."

"And Taa?"

Cham guffawed. "No one cares about Taa except us. But he's incidental at this point."

The communicator crackled in Isval's ear. She was losing the connection. Cham said something, but she couldn't make it out.

"Say again?"

"Think through your exits, Isval. You copy?"

She smiled. She should've known. "Got it, Cham."

The entire repair fleet streaked through the system.

"Got it," Eshgo said, pointing at a viewscreen, which showed a ship at the edge of the scanner's range. "That's her."

Isval watched as the *Perilous* took shape as a dot, then a larger blob, and finally a wedge. She leaned forward in her seat as they got closer and the ship got bigger. Faylin, Drim, and Crost edged up from their seats in the rear cargo area to look over her and Eshgo in the pilots' seats.

Drim whistled. Faylin swore. Crost exhaled, his breath turned bad from stress.

"You all right?" Isval asked him.

His lekku perked up. "Me? Yeah, fine."

"She's hurtin', all right," Eshgo said, meaning the ship.

"She is," Isval said. The sight of the heavily damaged *Perilous* buoyed her.

"Look at those fires," Drim observed, "Vultures did a job."

"Now we have to do ours," Isval said, to nods all around.

The *Perilous*'s forward landing bay was damaged, the edges made jagged and charred, ruining the ordinarily sleek wedge of the ship's lines, giving it a look like a huge mouth opened to swallow the stars. The Star Destroyer leaked flames from dozens of different onboard fires—large ones—and that was only what

Isval could see from her angle and distance. She imagined that Kallon's repurposed, explosive buzz droids had done a lot of additional damage deep inside the ship. Or at least she hoped so.

It pleased her to think of how many Imperials must have already died.

"More coming," she said to herself.

"How's that?" Eshgo said.

"Nothing," she said. "Talking to myself."

"You turning into Kallon?" Eshgo joked. "Muttering to yourself, now?"

She smiled.

Damage from vulture droids blackened the superstructure all along its length. An explosion had turned the forward sensor array into a jagged metal stub, rotating futilely on its mounts. The ship moved at velocity, sliding quickly through space despite the damage. A haphazard mix of fire suppression ships of all shapes and sizes, both Imperial and Twi'lek, already swarmed the huge ship, spraying suppression foam as directed. The smaller ships matched vectors with the Star Destroyer as they went, keeping pace.

"She's heading fast for Ryloth," Faylin said.

"I'm thinkin' she feels vulnerable," Eshgo said. Smiles answered his wry comment, but no laughter.

Isval had never been so close to a Star Destroyer, and as they neared it and it filled the cockpit's glass, its size took her aback. She didn't let it awe her, though. If the movement wanted to hit the Empire hard, they'd have to hit it at this scale. And they needed to kill enough Imperials for it to hurt. More important, they needed to kill Vader and the Emperor. Her gaze went to the bridge, where she imagined they were, if they were still alive.

"Stay sharp, people," she said to her team, and they

all nodded, though they, too, stared at the size of the Star Destroyer with eyes wide.

Orders and chatter carried over the comm channel, the Star Destroyer crew relaying orders to the incoming repair ships. Isval simply waited for the hail. It came within moments.

"This is Repair Eighty-Three from Ryloth," she responded.

"Port Forty-Five-A" came the call, along with instructions to the navcomp.

She ran a quick check, saw that Port 45A was far to stern, which was a long way from their target. She hailed them.

"Uh, this is Repair Eighty-Three. Sir, I have a crew of specialists aboard. We're supposed to assist in engine repair."

"Repair Eighty-Three, there's nothing here to indicate that."

"It's chaotic planetside, sir, as you can imagine. The call came and we launched. Orders and manifests are not exactly a priority at the moment. Keeping the *Perilous* flying is. My team can help best if we assist in the engine compartment."

"Understood Repair Eighty-Three. Uh . . . Port Two-Sixty-Six-R then."

Isval checked the location of 266R, saw that it was near the engine compartment and not too far from the hyperdrive chamber.

"Two-Sixty-Six-R," she said. "Thank you, bridge."

"Here we go," said Eshgo.

She felt the change come over her team. The nervous excitement, the quiet, shoulder-bunching tension. She felt it, too, so she gave them something to do.

"Double-check the gear, weapons, and explosives.

Everyone armed, but nothing visible. Deep breaths, people."

The team set to it without objection as Eshgo steered their ship to Bay 266R. Isval scanned the comp to see the docking assignments for ships bearing the two decoy teams. She committed their ports to memory.

Meanwhile the onboard comp matched velocity with the Star Destroyer while Eshgo spun them and backed up to the docking port for Bay 266R. The repair ship's port mated with the port on the *Perilous* and locked down. Green lights showed a clean seal.

"Work faces," she said to her team.

Nods around, bobbing lekku from the Twi'leks, serious expressions all around.

"Here we go," she said.

She took the steering column on the antigrav pallet, a large metal sled dotted with compartments—which were ordinarily stocked with tools and parts—and opened the bay to reveal the *Perilous*.

The sound hit her first: the blare of alarms, a constant stream of chatter over the ship's comm, the hustle and bustle of the crowded corridor. The smell hit her, too, the stink of burning plastic, charred flesh, and the acrid smell of electrical fires.

All along the wide hallway, comp terminals hung loose from their wall mounts, the wires dangling free and puking sparks. Uniformed Imperials hustled through the corridors, individually or in groups, all of them looking dazed, speaking urgently into their wrist comlinks. A few injured men and woman lay slouched against the wall, blood staining their uniforms and the otherwise clean white floors. Wheeled mouse droids darted through the chaos. A faint haze of smoke hung near the ceiling, stinging Isval's eyes. The venting hadn't been able to clear it all yet.

"You!" an officer shouted at her.

Her heart rate spiked, but she didn't let it reach her expression, which remained calm. The officer, a human man with red hair and freckles, held a datapad in one hand. He said something into a wrist comlink as she steered the antigrav pallet toward them. Her team followed.

A group of stormtroopers came out of a side hallway and rushed toward them. She froze for half a moment then reached for a weapon, but before she could draw her blaster, the stormtroopers rushed past them and on down the hall. She blinked and tried to recover herself, feigned patting herself for a tool.

"IDs," the officer said.

She stepped out from around the pallet and extended her datapad, which held their forged credentials. She hoped he wouldn't study them too closely. "Repair Eighty-Three. Engine repair. We—"

"Good, good." He glanced at her 'pad only in passing, then input some data into his own. He frowned at something and waved toward a junior officer standing across the corridor.

"Lieutenant Grolt, guide this repair team—"

"Sir, we know where we're going," Isval said.

The officer continued on as if she hadn't even spoken. "*Guide* this repair team to the engine access stations."

The whiptree-thin Lieutenant Grolt reminded Isval of the officer she'd beaten almost to death back in the Octagon. The expression on his ashen face showed that his world had been shaken by the attack on the *Perilous*. He, and everyone else aboard, had felt invulnerable on the Star Destroyer. She was glad they felt vulnerable now, felt some of the fear she and all Twi'leks lived with every day.

"Of course, sir." Grolt saluted. "Follow me," he

said to Isval and her team, and moved briskly through the chaos. Isval stared at the back of his head as they walked, considering ways to kill him if she had need.

The antigrav pallet helped part the way through the tumult of the busy corridor. All over the ship it was the same—heavy damage, fire, alarms, casualties, smoke, and everyone hurrying somewhere and paying little attention to anyone else.

As they moved along, Isval consulted the rough diagram of the Star Destroyer she kept in her head. They were nearing the target. They'd need to divert. She gave Eshgo a knowing look, and he gave a barely noticeable nod.

"You know, we know our way from here, Lieutenant," she said to Grolt. "I'm sure you have other things you'd rather be doing."

He didn't even turn to look at her.

"I have my assignment, Twi'lek," he said, and she realized that killing him had moved from possibility to certainty.

"Of course," she said, and shared a nod with Eshgo.

They came to a lift and piled in. She maneuvered the antigrav pallet so that it filled the lift, and Grolt pressed Level 29 on the lift's control pad.

When another Imperial tried to squeeze in, Eshgo put his body in the way.

"Sorry, sorry," he said, as if he were just trying to get out of the way.

Isval bumped them both with the antigrav pallet. "Apologies," she said. "I think we're filled, sir. This pallet . . ."

She gave a helpless shrug.

"Sorry," Grolt said to the officer.

"I'll wait," said the man, stepping back. He saluted Grolt, who returned the gesture.

The moment the doors closed, Isval drew the blaster

she kept in the holster in the small of her back and fired into the back of Grolt's head. He collapsed without a sound. The shot from the small blaster left his head intact, and the entry wound, cauterized by the blaster bolt, didn't even bleed.

Eshgo and Drim didn't need instructions. They threw open one of the pallet's larger compartments and started to stuff Grolt's body inside.

"Hurry," Isval said.

Isval watched the digital readout show their progress along the levels. Twenty-two, twenty-three.

"Come on!"

Faylin assisted, twisting Grolt's arms into impossible angles, tearing gristle, then pushing hard on Grolt's head, stuffing him all the way in.

Twenty-nine.

Eshgo closed up the compartment and the lift doors opened, revealing a pair of uniformed officers. Looks of surprise filled their faces. One of them wrinkled his nose, perhaps catching a whiff of blasterfire.

"Burning wires," Isval said.

"What level is this?" Eshgo said, looking at the pad. "This doesn't seem right. We should be one down. Coming?" he said to the waiting officers.

They eyed the full lift. "We'll wait," the taller of the two said.

Isval held off on a hard smile until the lift doors closed.

All of them exhaled as one but otherwise said nothing as the lift descended and opened on the level they'd passed moments before. Carrying the body of a dead Imperial officer, they moved through the bustling corridors toward the hyperdrive chamber.

As they approached that area of the ship, the corridors narrowed and became somewhat less filled with activity. Most of the bustle was in the main halls. Side passages were almost deserted.

"Could've saved a lot of time by putting a vulture and its payload right here," Faylin said.

"Too deep in the ship and too hardened," Isval said.

"And we'd have been bored with nothing to do back on Ryloth," Drim said.

Mindful of Cham's admonition, Isval took care to note the layout, in case their escape got hairy. She'd have been unconcerned about exit were she alone, but her team expected her to get them out, and so she would.

They came around a corner to see a group of four stormtroopers who stood at attention before a large, reinforced hatch that provided access to the hyperdrive chamber.

The stormtroopers tensed and put hands to blaster grips as Isval and her team approached.

"Easy," Isval said under her breath, though she felt lines of sweat drip down her sides from her armpits. She did her best to look harmless.

One of the troopers stepped forward and held up a gloved hand. "Stop there. This area is restricted." The amplifier in his helmet made his voice sound robotic.

Isval slowed but didn't stop. "We're with Repair Eighty-Three. Engine repair."

"Engine access stations are that way," the trooper said, pointing back the way they'd come.

"I know," Isval said, still coming toward him. "But the hyperdrive is damaged, too. We're authorized to repair it. See?"

She held out her datapad, but the stormtrooper would have none of it. "I don't care what that says, Twi'lek. Passage through this door isn't allowed without the presence of an authorized officer. Leave. Now." He stared at her, and she saw her reflected face in the black lenses of his helmet.

She felt her own team tense, but she decided to take a moment to regroup. "All right," she said. "We'll go get an officer then and come back."

She started to turn the antigrav pallet when a sound came from within the large compartment: a voice.

Someone was calling over Lieutenant Grolt's comm.

"Lieutenant Grolt," said the muffled voice. "You're needed in Weapons Bay Nineteen. Grolt, respond."

Isval felt her skin darken.

The stormtroopers looked at the pallet, then back at Isval, and grabbed for their blasters.

Vader's growing anger kept him company as the lift rose toward the bridge. The doors slid open to the sights and sounds of a ship in crisis. The ashen-faced crew went about their business professionally, the air filled with the hum of comm chatter and the occasional shouted order. Damage reports came in from all over the Star Destroyer and were relayed to appropriate duty stations in urgent voices, their recitations filling the air with tales of death and fire. Luitt moved among the stations, taking reports, issuing orders, trying to retake control of the situation. A member of the crew ran past Vader and hurried onto the lift.

The Emperor remained where he had been, standing on the central raised tier of the bridge. Orn Free Taa stood near him, staring down into the crew pits and tilting his head to see the various viewscreens there.

Eyes turned to Vader as he walked toward the central tier. Without breaking stride, he used the Force to take hold of Orn Free Taa. He lifted the obese Twi'lek from the floor and hung him in the air before the Emperor. Taa, wide-eyed, his many chins trembling, pawed at his throat and gasped for air. Vader took care not to kill him . . . yet.

"Lord Vader returns," the Emperor said. "You seem displeased, old friend."

Vader released his hold on Taa, and the Twi'lek fell hard to the deck. Vader stepped to the Emperor's side, looming over the prone Taa. He pointed a finger at the Twi'lek.

"There's a traitor on your staff, Senator. And that traitor is responsible for what has transpired here."

The words seemed to so shock Taa that he could muster no reply. He massaged his throat and scurried back a bit from Vader.

"What is this now?" Luitt asked, taking the corrugated stairs two at a time from a lower deck. "This alien scum is a traitor?"

Grunting, breathing heavily, Taa struggled to his feet. His eyes went from Luitt, to Vader, to the Emperor, pleading.

"Not him, no," the Emperor said. "But one or more members of his staff."

"My Emperor," Taa said, his voice rough from Vader's Force choke, "Lord Vader, I had no idea. If I had . . ." He sniffed, stood up straight. "I vow to find the traitors behind this foul attack and—"

"Oh, I believe you," the Emperor said dismissively. "But that hardly mitigates your fault, Senator. You had a traitor on your staff and were ignorant of it."

The Emperor signaled the Royal Guards, and they stepped to the senator's side.

Taa's chins quivered. He looked as though he might weep. His squinty eyes flicked from the guards to

Vader to the Emperor. "My Emperor, if only you could . . ."

To Luitt, the Emperor said, "Restrict all of the senator's staff to their quarters and deny them access to communications equipment or computer terminals. Present this as ordinary practice in situations of this kind. Lord Vader will interrogate them when we reach Ryloth."

Vader looked forward to the opportunity.

The Emperor turned back to Taa. "Senator, I trust I can count on your assistance in all things Ryloth for the foreseeable future? With the spice and slave trade, and the Free Ryloth movement? Harsher measures may be required to quell the difficulties on your planet. I think if my orders came out of your mouth, the people would accept them more readily. Do you agree?"

"Of . . . of course, my Emperor," Taa said.

"In the meantime, I trust you'll remain here with Lord Vader and me? It's fascinating to watch broken things get pieced back together."

Taa didn't bother to respond.

CHAPTER EIGHT

THE STORMTROOPERS DREW THEIR BLASTERS AT the same time as Isval's teammates. Isval did not bother to reach for her weapon, instead driving the antigrav pallet full-speed into the stormtroopers, slamming them into the walls and fouling their blaster shots, which went high and wide. Eshgo shot one of the troopers in the head, Drim shot another in the chest, and Faylin and Crost shot the other two in the face.

"We have minutes," she said to them, then broke comm silence to call over to the decoy teams elsewhere on the station. Cham had insisted on the decoys in case matters went badly and they needed distraction, and Cham, as usual, had been right.

Think through your exits, she reminded herself, though at the moment she cared less about an exit than bringing down the *Perilous.*

"You are go," she said to the decoy teams. "All teams. You are go. But we aren't hot yet. Repeat, we aren't yet hot."

Affirmative replies came. The two other teams who'd snuck into the Star Destroyer aboard the repair ships would set an explosive or three, even start a firefight if necessary.

Isval drew her twin blasters, Drim pulled a heavy blaster rifle from a compartment on the pallet, and Eshgo and the rest of the team readied weapons. Drim overrode the security protocol on the hyperdrive hatch, it slid open, and they rushed in after the pallet, leaving the dead stormtroopers behind them in the hallway.

"Captain," called the bridge communications officer, and something in his tone drew Vader's attention. "Sir, we're getting reports of a firefight on Deck Seventeen, and some explosions in Bay Twelve forward."

"A firefight?" Luitt asked. "How can we have a firefight?"

The comm officer put his hand to his earpiece, nodding, then said, "Sir, it's one of the repair crews. Twi'leks. The explosions, too, appear to be intentionally set. I have reports of multiple additional casualties. Security teams are en route."

Vader saw it then. The attack by the droid fighters, as bad as it had been, had been a ruse, or only half the plan. The Free Ryloth movement was more resourceful than either he or the Emperor had imagined.

"Tell your security teams to kill every Ryloth repair team on board," he said, the words silencing the bridge crew. He turned and strode for the lift.

Luitt called after him. "Lord Vader, there are almost a hundred teams aboard! My Emperor?"

"One hundred teams seems a manageable number," the Emperor said, his eyes not on the captain but on Vader.

"Give the order, Captain," Vader said. "Kill them all."

"Yes, Lord Vader."

The lift doors closed before Vader's face. He headed for Deck 17.

The huge, upright vertical slab of the Star Destroyer's hyperdrive sat at the bottom of a circular depression in the middle of the cavernous chamber that housed it. A corrugated metal walkway encircled the drive's bay. Computer stations and other hardware Isval didn't recognize or understand covered the walls. For a moment the layout reminded her of the Octagon in Lessu. The association summoned a grim smile. She'd leave dead Imperials here just as she had there.

Engineers and officers stood at intervals around the walkway, checking or monitoring comps and conduits. Apparently the thick hatch had prevented them from hearing the shots in the hallway beyond. The nearest one, a tech officer, turned to face them, lowering the datapad he held.

"You can't be in here unaccomp—" he began, but stopped, wide-eyed, when he registered the blasters she held. Isval shot him through the datapad and in the chest, and man and device fell to the floor. Beside her, Drim opened up with the blaster rifle, while Eshgo and Faylin and Crost, too, opened fire on the crew, sending them shouting and scrambling.

"Secure the hatch!" she said to Eshgo, and picked another target, fired, then a second, fired, and left both of them dead on the floor with smoking holes in their uniforms.

The Imperials scrambled, ducked, and tried to flee toward the hatch opposite. One, a short, stocky man in an engineer's uniform, ran for an alarm, but Drim shot him in the back. He slammed face-first into the bulkhead and fell to the floor, leaving a smear of blood on the wall.

None of the Imperials were armed—tech officers and engineers usually weren't—so she and her team put them all down quickly.

"Find a uniform," she said to Drim while she and the rest of the team moved the pallet to the base of a stairway. "No, two uniforms. Piecemeal them if you have to. No blaster holes."

"What? Why?"

"Just do it."

Eshgo, struggling with the locking mechanism on the hatch they'd entered through, finally just shot the control panel with his blaster. It exploded in sparks and smoke.

"Hatch is as secure as I can make it," he said.

It'd have to do. "Watch that other door, Drim," Isval said, pointing at it with her chin. "Don't blow the controls, though. We want a way out."

"Got it," Drim said, and darted around the walkway, bounding over the bodies, to the only other hatch that allowed ingress or egress into the chamber. Isval knew it led into a maintenance bay, which then led out, through a series of winding hallways, into one of the main corridors of the ship.

Faylin and Crost had already stripped one of the officers of his shirt and jacket, another of his trousers and hat.

She carefully lowered the antigrav pallet down the stairs that led down from the walkway until she stood before the huge slab of the hyperdrive. Eshgo assisted. It towered over her, more than twice her height. Proximity to it made her skin tingle, raised the hairs on her arms. Whorls and swirls scored the gray metal of the slab. She knew they helped channel the energy of the drive somehow, but to her they just looked like some indecipherable, mystical script. Arm-thick cables, large power relays, and other electronic equipment—most of it obscure to her—plugged into the slab at various places along its sides and disappeared into conduits that ran under the floor.

She opened the lower compartment in the pallet to reveal the dozen explosive charges they'd brought aboard. They looked like small missiles, each equipped with powerful magnetic pads and timers.

"Help me," she said to Eshgo, and they started lifting the explosives out.

The weapons somehow seemed heavier than when she'd loaded them back on Ryloth. She supposed the adrenaline dump of the last half hour had left her weakened.

A new alarm sounded over the ship's comm system, different in tone and cadence from the one they'd heard when they'd first boarded. She and Eshgo shared a look. Lines of concern furrowed his heavy brow.

"They know we're here," she said. "Let's hurry it up, laggards!" she shouted to Faylin and Crost.

"Yeah, yeah," Faylin said.

Isval opened the top of the pallet, pulled Grolt's already stiffening body out, and dropped him to the floor. She took out his comlink and smashed it under her heel.

"I've got one more job for you, Lieutenant Grolt," she said.

"What are you doing?" Eshgo asked.

"We're going to need the space," she said. "Let's get the charges set."

Vader stepped from the lift and used the Force to augment his speed, sprinting through the smoky, crowded corridors. He saw a Twi'lek repair crew ahead, four men and a woman. They navigated an antigrav tool-and-parts pallet through the corridor, and nothing about them looked suspicious. He didn't care. He ignited his lightsaber, and when he did, the Imperials in the corridor parted before him, wide-eyed, confused.

The Twi'leks had only a moment to register his approach before he cut them down in rapid succession. He left five corpses and a hall full of gawking troops behind him as he pelted onward.

Details about the location of the firefight carried over his comlink, and he headed directly for it. He heard the sound of blasterfire before he saw it. In the corridor ahead, a squad of stormtroopers crouched against the bulkhead, trading fire around the corner with unseen enemies. The corporal commanding the squad saw him approaching and turned to face him.

"Lord Vader, there are five sabot—"

Vader brushed past him and around the corner, enmeshed in the Force, lightsaber humming.

A Twi'lek male with green skin and a blaster rifle, making himself small against the bulkhead, opened fire at Vader. The red line of Vader's lightsaber flashed, deflecting the shots back at the Twi'lek, putting a dark hole in his chest and another in his face.

As Vader stalked down the corridor, a second Twi'lek darted out from around the corner, a blaster pistol spewing red bolts. Vader deflected them, extended his free hand, and used the Force to take hold of the Twi'lek's blaster. When he jerked the pistol from the alien's hand and into his own, the Twi'lek reached for a second blaster holstered on his thigh. Without breaking stride, Vader hurled his lightsaber, and the spinning blade cut the Twi'lek in two. Vader crushed the blaster he'd taken in his fist, dropped it to the floor, and, with his other hand, used the Force to recall his blade to his hand.

Boots thumped on the deck as the stormtroopers rushed around the corner and past him, blaster rifles firing. By the time Vader rounded the corner, three more Twi'leks lay dead.

"Lord Vader," said the voice of the bridge communications officer over his comlink. "We have reports of dead stormtroopers outside the hyperdrive chamber. The hatch is sealed from the inside."

Vader understood it then. The Twi'leks he'd just killed were decoys.

"I'm on my way there," he said. He stepped over the corpse of one of the Twi'leks and strode toward the aft section of the *Perilous*.

Eshgo and Isval put the charges in place, most around the hyperdrive slab but a few at the base of nearby system components, all of them exactly where Kallon had said to put them. They'd drilled on it dozens of times. The charges, when they blew, would destroy the hyperdrive. That explosion would start a series of secondary detonations that would end with the *Perilous*'s engines blowing the Star Destroyer out of space.

Isval saw that Eshgo's hands were shaking as he fiddled with the timers.

"I got it," she said. Her hands were steady, as they always were when she was killing Imperials.

He backed off and she set the timers on the charges, one after another. They'd blow in sequence, milliseconds apart. Kallon had told them the timing had to be precise or the chain reaction would not start.

"That's it," she said, wiping sweat from her brow.

She shared a look with her team, and all of them nodded. They might or might not get clear, but there was no stopping the destruction now. Once they armed the explosives and the timers started their countdown, nothing could save the *Perilous*. It would be a flying tomb.

They'd *try* to get clear, of course, but given that the entire ship was on alert, the odds were long.

Faylin, the only human on Isval's team, had already stripped and was putting on a piecemeal Imperial uniform. It was an ill fit and mismatched, but there were no blaster holes in it and it would withstand a superficial look.

"You look good, Corporal," Isval said to Faylin, whose pale face was even whiter than normal. "You good?"

Faylin pushed her long dark hair up under the Imperial hat. "I'm good. I'm good."

Isval squeezed Faylin's shoulder, stripped off her own clothes, and donned a makeshift Imperial uniform of her own, including boots and gloves. She couldn't do anything about her lekku or her blue skin, but she'd use Grolt's body to help her with that.

"Get to the door, people," she said, and her team drove the pallet up to the second hatch, where they waited for her.

She inhaled deeply and armed the charges. The timers started counting down immediately. They had forty-two standard minutes to get out of the blast zone.

A boom on the hatch they'd entered through indicated the use of some kind of ram, but the door did not give way. Another boom and still it held.

"Drim?" she called.

"I don't hear anything out here," he said, indicating the other hatch. "But then I'm not sure I would. The door's thick, Isval."

"All right, then," she said. "Let's go."

"And quickly," Eshgo added.

Isval slung Grolt's body over her shoulder, grunting under the burden, and hustled up the stairs to join her team.

Vader rushed through the ship, his anger going before him and parting the crew that otherwise choked the halls. He reached the hatch to the hyperdrive chamber. Four dead stormtroopers lay on the deck, and another group of stormtroopers and armed security personnel used a portable grav-ram in an attempt to force open the hatch. The control panel and door switch were dead, probably sabotaged from the other side.

The corporal in charge of the security team saw Vader approach and stepped out to meet him. Meanwhile, the ram powered up with a hum and slammed into the hatch, doing nothing.

"Lord Vader," the corporal said. "The door's been secured from the inside and the switch has been disabled. There's only one other way into the chamber and I've sent a team around—"

Vader ignited his lightsaber.

"Move," he said, not slowing, and the security personnel and stormtroopers nearly tripped over themselves as they scrambled out of his way.

He took his lightsaber in a two-handed grip, channeled the Force, channeled his rage, and slammed the blade into the hatch. It sank an arm's span into the metal. The heat from the weapon made a red-hot circle in the hatch around the blade. Vader held on to the hilt and poured in his power. The metal started to surrender to the heat of his weapon, the heat of his wrath.

He would cut through the hatch within a sixty count, and then the traitors would be his.

A sizzle from the direction of the hatch through which they'd first entered turned all their heads. The hatch was reddening with heat, at first a small circle, but expanding.

They were cutting their way in.

Isval cursed.

The circle expanded. Smoke poured off the door as whatever tool they were using to cut started to slag the metal.

"Nothing should be able to cut through that door," Eshgo said.

Isval consulted the map in her head and formulated a way back to their ship. It seemed a parsec away, given the challenges that stood between them and it. She wasn't sure they had enough time.

Behind them, the glowing red tip of a line of energy poked through the hatch. Isval recognized it: the blade of a lightsaber. Vader was out there, the Vader who'd wiped out Pok's entire crew single-handedly. The realization at once thrilled and terrified her. She thought of Pok's face, of vengeance, but Eshgo's voice brought her back.

"Isval, we need to leave!"

She blinked, nodded.

"Open it," she said to Drim, and everyone on the team took their positions, weapons ready, as the hatch parted along its seam.

Melted metal pooled on the floor near Vader's boots, bubbling and smoking, as his lightsaber bored through the hatch. He felt the fear of the traitors in the hyperdrive chamber. No doubt they'd seen his lightsaber, and they knew he was coming. They were right to fear. And their fear fed his anger. The steady rhythm of his respirator tolled the passage of time, the moments remaining to the traitors before he had them.

"Tell your team the traitors are to be taken alive," Vader said to the corporal. "Their final disposition is to be left to me."

"Yes, Lord Vader."

The hatch yawned open. There was no one there.

Isval realized she'd been holding her breath. Everyone else must have been, too, for they exhaled as one.

"Eshgo, Drim, Crost, you're in the pallet," she snapped. "Weapons hot."

"And try not to shoot each other," Eshgo said as Drim and Crost piled into two of the pallet's tool compartments. "Gonna be close," he added to Isval.

She knew. To Faylin, she said, "You're driving, Fay."

"And you?" Faylin asked while Eshgo contorted himself into the last compartment.

"I'm wounded or dead," Isval said. "I'll lie on top. Your backup if you need it. Cover me with Grolt."

Faylin wrinkled her nose but nodded.

Isval activated her comm and reached out to the decoy teams. "Ship is hot and set for half an hour. If you can, get off now."

She got no response.

"Anyone copy?"

Nothing. She didn't dwell on what it must mean. She had no time to dwell on anything. The opposite door was melting. Vader was coming.

She lay atop the pallet and Faylin covered her with Grolt's body, arranging him such that her head was hard to see. Faylin put Grolt's hat over Isval's head, also helping to hide her lekku.

"Anybody looks hard at us, they'll notice you," Faylin said. "Nix that. They won't even have to look hard, just look at all."

Isval knew, but the pallet couldn't hold her inside, too. Covering herself in a corpse was her only play.

"Just move fast," she said.

"Count on that," Faylin said.

Behind them, Isval could hear metal dripping from the door that Vader was cutting through, hitting the floor in sizzling dollops. She could hear voices through the small hole Vader had already cut. She resisted the urge to run across the chamber, stick the barrel of her blaster in the hole, and start firing blind. She needed to get her team out even more than she needed to kill Vader. The Imperials would be through in moments, and they'd see the explosive charges.

An idea struck her.

She was thinking through her exit. Cham would have smiled.

"Faylin, get us out of here, into a side hall, and wait."

"Wait? Isval, we only have half an hour."

"I know, but do it."

"Isval . . ."

"Just do it!"

"You sure?" Eshgo said, from inside the pallet.

"He asks that again and you can shoot him, Drim," Isval said.

Drim chuckled, and Faylin steered the pallet out into the network of halls that connected the hyperdrive chamber to one of the Star Destroyer's main corridors. Isval, covered in a corpse, breathed into Grolt's neck. She had to fight down a wave of sickness.

Before they'd gone ten meters, she realized she'd forgotten something and cursed.

"What?" Faylin asked, alarmed. "What is it?"

"Nothing. Nothing."

But it wasn't nothing. In the rush, she'd neglected to destroy the mechanism that would have sealed the hatch behind them. Once Vader cut his way through the first hatch, there was nothing to slow his pursuit.

"Which hall?" Faylin said.

"Just pick one!" Isval said.

But Faylin seemed paralyzed with indecision. From somewhere ahead they heard the heavy tread of boots—stormtrooper boots.

"That one," Isval hissed. "Right there. Just get us out of the hall."

The boots grew louder, the murmur of voices. Isval felt Eshgo, Drim, and Crost shifting their weight inside the pallet, no doubt trying to position themselves to fire should things go bad.

Faylin turned the pallet down a narrow maintenance hall. The overhead lights were flickering like strobes.

They waited there in silence as the voices and boots got louder. After a few seconds, a group of stormtroopers and security personnel ran past in the direction of the hyperdrive chamber.

When they were gone, Isval said, "Get us a little closer to the main corridor, then park it again."

"What are you waiting on?" Eshgo said, his voice muffled through the sides of the pallet. "This is our chance."

"No it's not," Isval said. "Not quite yet."

Careful not to dislodge Grolt's body, she twisted her head and moved her arm slightly to check the timepiece she wore on her wrist. Thirty-two minutes.

* * *

Vader's blade soon cut a large enough hole in the hatch. A circular portion of the door fell to the floor with a clang and he ducked through, the stormtroopers following him through the breach.

The traitors were gone, having fled out the door opposite. Dead Imperials lay all around the hyperdrive chamber, several of them missing pieces of their uniform, but the hyperdrive itself seemed intact.

The door opposite slid open, and the squad of Imperials the corporal had sent around to intercept the traitors rushed into the chamber and looked around at the bodies. Questions twisted the expressions of the faces not hidden by helmets.

"Sir," the corporal said, "we didn't see anyone. We—"

Vader ignored them. He sensed the danger and leapt down to the bottom of the hyperdrive well. Immediately he saw the dozen charges attached to the drive and its adjacent field amplifiers. The timers on each showed a mere twenty-seven minutes before they exploded.

He knelt and examined the charges more closely, saw the fail-safes. If engineers attempted to move or disarm the charges, they'd explode. If they did nothing they'd explode.

He stood, the sound of his respirator bouncing off the walls of the hyperdrive well. He activated his comlink.

"Captain Luitt, the hyperdrive is rigged to explode and it can't be stopped. Order an immediate evacuation."

A long pause, then, "What? No, I can send a team of engineers to—"

"You heard me, Captain. It's too late for that."

"You're . . . certain?"

"Give the order, Captain. The *Perilous* will explode in half an hour. And Captain, the Emperor is your priority. If he is not evacuated safely, I will hold you personally responsible."

"I . . . I understand, Lord Vader," said Luitt. "But . . . the Emperor has already left the bridge."

Vader considered that. "Thank you, Captain." He activated his private comm channel to the Emperor. "Master, the ship is going to explode in less than thirty minutes."

"Yes," the Emperor said. "I'm awaiting you aboard my shuttle."

"Your shuttle? But—"

"I had a second shuttle readied in the forward landing bay. You should hurry, my friend. There's little time."

"Yes, Master."

Vader hadn't known about the second shuttle, but he was unsurprised. His Master prepared for almost every contingency.

The evacuation alarm began to sound, shrill and prolonged. Countless drills had prepared the crew, and Vader imagined all of them scrambling for their assigned escape pods. The already chaotic state of affairs aboard the Star Destroyer would be still more chaotic now.

No doubt the traitors would try to make their escape in the tumult. Vader had no intention of letting them get off the ship.

The shrill sound of the evacuation alarm echoed down the halls, the death scream of a doomed ship. An automated voice gave a monotone recitation of the order to evacuate.

"Now we go," Isval said from under Grolt's corpse.

The corridors would be thronged. No one would look twice at the pallet. They might, *might* have a chance to get clear.

"That is well done," Eshgo said from inside the pallet.

She ignored him and said to Faylin, "Get to the main corridor. Fast. We don't have time to circle back to our repair ship. You see anything likely, any ship at all that we can use, a repair ship, fire suppression, whatever, you head for it. Understood? If we have to take it by force, we do that."

"Got it," Faylin said, and maneuvered the pallet back out into the corridors.

"Speed is your friend," Isval said, echoing Cham's words to her. "Move, Faylin."

Faylin propelled the pallet as fast as it would go— about jogging speed—out into the main corridor.

Crew members were everywhere, already rushing along the halls in a torrent, heading for their assigned escape pods and ships. Droids walked and rolled among the crew, likewise heading to their evacuation points. No one even slowed to look at the pallet or ask any questions.

Isval began to think they might actually be able to pull it off.

But if they escaped the ship, so, too, would many, probably most, Imperials. Vader and the Emperor would get clear, she had no doubt. She needed to reach Cham. They would need to improvise something. Taking down the *Perilous* was big, but not big enough. The still-experimental droid tri-fighters, maybe.

She bit down to activate the direct comm she had with Cham.

"Cham?" she whispered.

Static, then a syllable. ". . . val?"

"Can you hear me?"

More static, a garbled word.

They were still too far out to get much of a signal. "If you can hear me, I'll call you again in a moment."

Only white noise for an answer.

Vader used the Force to leap up to the walkway that surrounded the hyperdrive's well.

The stormtroopers and security personnel looked at one another in puzzlement, the evacuation order blaring.

"Go," Vader said to them. "The ship is lost."

Most of them nodded, turned, and headed off immediately, but three of the stormtroopers remained.

"Sir, we should accompany you to an escape pod."

"Unnecessary," Vader said. "I'll find my own way. Now go. That's my order."

The stormtroopers saluted and reluctantly headed off. Vader turned and looked at the hatch through which the traitors must have fled. At least one of them was wearing an Imperial uniform—maybe two. He didn't have much time, but he had enough to catch them and kill them and still get off the *Perilous*.

He drew on the Force and strode after them. They couldn't have gotten far. They'd be heading for the main corridor, to an escape ship or pod.

When he reached the main corridor, he found it bustling with pale-faced crew, officers, troops, and droids rushing along their designated evacuation routes. The dull repeated *thwump* of launching escape pods sounded loud in his ears.

He leapt up to a third-floor walkway, startling the crew hurrying past. They whispered his name in hushed tones as they moved away.

He perched there, a dark bird of prey looking down on the bustle for Twi'leks or anything else unusual.

Isval shifted her body a bit so she could see better and take her bearings. Crew rushed past the pallet in both directions, a blur of uniformed legs and tense voices. She tried to get a look at one of the location stamps on the bulkhead without moving much and finally saw one: 183B.

They weren't far from the bay where one of the decoy teams had docked. Possibly the team's repair ship was still there. Maybe the team hadn't evacuated yet or maybe—given the comm silence—they wouldn't evacuate.

"Make for One-Thirty-Seven-B," she said to Faylin, raising her voice to be heard over the hubbub in the corridor. "Decoy Team A docked there."

More legs hurried by, dark uniforms, the white armor of a group of stormtroopers.

"Got it," Faylin said, and steered them through the chaos.

Isval watched the location stamps disappear behind them. One Fifty-Seven. One Fifty-Three. One Forty-Seven. Almost there.

The low bass notes of launching escape pods sounded steadily, the sound like a drumbeat. The monotone voice of the computer announcing the time remaining—ten minutes—provided counterpoint.

One Forty-One.

A male voice sounded from right next to the pallet. Isval's face was turned the other way and she dared not move. She worried that Grolt's body was not covering her lekku.

"You all right?" the man asked. "Are they wounded? Do you need help?"

Faylin did not stop the pallet. "No, I've got them, sir. Thank you."

Isval's grip tightened on her blaster. If the officer examined Faylin's mismatched uniform or spotted Isval's blue skin . . .

The automated voice announced nine minutes.

The officer kept pace with the pallet. "Are you sure . . . Corporal?"

Isval imagined him puzzling over Faylin's uniform.

"Wait. What's your unit? Are you . . . what are you—"

Whatever question he planned to ask never got past his lips. Faylin's blaster sounded—a muffled discharge, as if she'd fired it while holding it against the man's stomach—and the man collapsed atop Grolt and Isval.

"Don't move!" Faylin said to her, and kept the pallet moving. "I don't know if anyone heard in all the noise."

A voice from behind rose above the tumult. "Hey! You there! Stop!"

Isval cursed.

"What's going on?" Eshgo asked from inside the pallet.

"Don't do anything," Faylin said. "Be still. All of you."

The voice calling out for them to stop faded, lost behind them in the ambient noise.

"He wasn't talking to us," Faylin explained.

Isval's heart hammered against her ribs. Between the stress of the situation and the weight of two dead Imperials lying on top of her, she could hardly breathe. She twisted her head to look out to the side and saw what she wanted to see: 137. Her hopes rose, but only for a flash.

"It's gone," Faylin said, sounding defeated.

"What?" Isval asked. "The ship?"

"Yes," Faylin said. "There's nothing here."

Isval cursed. She must have misremembered the bay number, or the Imperials had moved the ship, or the decoy team had already gotten off, or their docking bay assignment had changed after Isval had checked it.

"What else is there?" she asked.

"What do you mean?"

"Another ship, Faylin! Anything nearby? Focus."

"No, wait . . . yes. Stay put."

Faylin drove the pallet on, pushing through the tide of the crowd. The computer continued its inexorable countdown—eight minutes. Faylin moved the pallet toward the side of the corridor and stopped the cart.

"Hang on," she said. "Just hang on. The pallet won't fit through this hatch."

"What's the ship?" Isval asked.

"A ship's boat or shuttle or something. There's no one here."

The crew assigned to it could have been killed in the droid attack on the *Perilous*.

"You'll have to get out," Faylin said. "I'll let you know when."

Faylin circled the pallet, and Isval imagined her eyeing the Imperials hurrying past, waiting for the right moment. The computer announced seven minutes.

"Now," Faylin said, and heaved one of the dead Imperials off the pallet. Isval pushed Grolt off her and let him fall to the floor while Eshgo, Drim, and Crost threw open their compartments and clambered out of the pallet. Faylin helped Drim to his feet while Isval grabbed Crost under the armpits and pulled him up.

* * *

Vader saw them: Twi'leks crawling out of a tool pallet driven by a human in a stolen Imperial uniform.

He had them.

He activated his lightsaber, embraced his anger, and drew deeply on the Force.

CHAPTER NINE

Isval shoved her team toward the narrow hatch that led to the docked ship—an escort boat, she saw. Eshgo would be able to fly it.

"Go! Go!"

Drim stumbled and fell. Isval helped him up, and as she did she glanced back the way they'd come. She could not halt a gasp. Far down the corridor, she saw Vader leap down from a walkway ten meters above the deck. He hit the ground in a crouch, the red line of what could only be his lightsaber clutched in his fist.

"Come on, Isval!" Faylin said, tugging her shirt.

"That's him," Isval said, her voice robotic.

Faylin pulled her shirt. "Him who? It's time to go, Isval!"

But Isval thought of Pok, and had no intention of leaving. She'd gotten her team out. Her work was done.

"Get aboard and get it fired up," she said to Faylin. "Go now."

"Isval . . . ," Eshgo said.

"Get it fired up!" she said, and drew her blasters.

Vader was forty meters from her. He stood up straight, towering over the crew near him. He was looking right at her, his lightsaber held at his side, and she could feel the weight of his regard pressing against her like a punch. He exploded into motion, moving toward her at preternatural speed, his strides devouring the deck space between them. Crew scrambled out of the way at his approach, his dark form knifing through them.

She raised her blasters and took aim, shooting as fast as she could pull the triggers, scribing the air between them with lines of red energy. Vader didn't slow his sprint and his lightsaber was a blur as he came on, deflecting her shots in all directions. A few came back at her. One hit the pallet and sent tools skittering along the deck. Another scorched the bulkhead beside her, but still she fired.

The crew in the corridor panicked, scrambling in all directions. An officer got in Vader's way, slowing his approach for a moment, and Vader tossed him aside with his free hand as if the man weighed no more than a child.

"Isval!" Eshgo said from behind her.

Vader was twenty meters and closing.

She was shouting, firing, but her shots could not get past the line of his lightsaber. She didn't understand how it was possible, until her own words came back to her: Vader was not a man.

But she refused to stop, she couldn't.

"For Pok!" she shouted with each shot. "For Pok!"

Six minutes said the computer. Vader closed to ten meters. She fired again and again and again, screaming. Blaster shots from somewhere else in the corridor pinged off the bulkhead—stormtroopers, maybe.

Strong arms wrapped her from behind, picked her up off the deck—Eshgo.

"Stop!" she yelled, trying to twist her body in his grasp so she could keep firing. "What are you doing?"

"I'm saving your life!" he said, and carried her through the docking port door as blasterfire slammed into the jambs.

The moment he got her on the other side, he set her down, punched a button, and the huge hatch slid closed. She turned, teeth gritted, and caught a last glimpse of Vader before the door blocked her view— still rushing toward them, blade in hand, cape flowing out behind him.

She reached for the control panel, thinking to hit the button to reopen the hatch, but Eshgo shot the panel with a blaster.

She whirled on him, her fists clenched around her blasters, standing on her tiptoes to put her nose to his.

"You had no right—"

"You saw what I saw! He's not going down to blasterfire, Isval! He'd have cut you in half!"

As if to make the point, the energized blade of Vader's lightsaber burst through the hatch, just missing Eshgo's abdomen. They bounded back out of reach as the heat from the weapon started to redden the metal.

They stared at each other for a moment, breathing into each other's faces.

"You're right," she said, slumping. "I know you're right. But don't disobey an order again. Come on."

They piled into the escort boat. Drim already had the engines online. He gave way to Eshgo, who took the pilot's seat while Isval strapped into the copilot's chair.

"Who or what was that?" Faylin said.

"Vader," Isval said. "Vader."

Faylin cursed and Isval could only agree.

"Disengaging docking clamp," Eshgo said, and the boat floated free of the doomed Star Destroyer. "We're away. And there's Ryloth."

As the ship swung around, Isval looked out the viewport. Ryloth loomed large against the dark of space. The *Perilous* had covered an enormous amount of distance while they'd been aboard. The Star Destroyer would burn up overlooking the planet the Empire cruelly oppressed. Isval thought it appropriate.

Hundreds of escape pods and a mix of other ships, including a few dozen V-wings, dotted space around the *Perilous*. Some would land on the nearest moon. Some would land on Ryloth. And some would not get clear in time. The blast radius of the *Perilous* would be huge, given the detonation's provenance in the hyperdrive.

"Not too far," she said to Eshgo.

"What? We have to get far—"

"Do as I say," she said, and he didn't dare disobey her again.

She needed to get Cham on the comm.

Vader had lost the saboteurs.

The computer announced six minutes remaining.

Vader deactivated his lightsaber, drew on the Force, and hurried for the Emperor's shuttle in the forward landing bay. The corridors were emptying rapidly as the last of the crew evacuated. By the time he reached the shuttle bay, he was moving through a ghost ship.

Fires still burned here and there in the bay. The Emperor's shuttle sat on its pad, the engines already primed, and Vader sprinted up the gangplank to find his Master calm and seated in the passenger area of the ship, flanked by the red-robed and armored members of the Royal Guard. His Master touched a button on his chair.

"You may launch," the Emperor said to the pilot, and the shuttle immediately lifted off. "Sit down, old friend," he said to Vader.

"Senator Taa?" Vader asked.

The Emperor made a dismissive gesture. "Oh, I'm sure he's waddled himself to safety somehow. Rats always find their way off sinking ships."

Isval bit down to activate the comm she had with Cham.

"Cham, do you copy?"

"I do!"

"We're clear," she said.

"You're clear?" he echoed, and the relief in his voice touched her. "I'd been afraid to reach out to you even when you got within range. Didn't want to distract you. I show the *Perilous* midway between the inner moon and the planet. What's your status?"

"Charges are hot. She's going down, Cham."

"She's going down," Cham said, presumably repeating it not for her but for others in the room.

"I think the decoy teams are lost, and we have a problem."

His voice lowered. "What problem?"

She eyed the sea of smaller ships scattered across space, as thick as an asteroid field, as Eshgo put some distance between them and the *Perilous*. She held up a hand to stop Eshgo from going any farther. She didn't want to get too distant. He sighed to show his disapproval, but did as she commanded.

"They realized what we'd done and sounded an evacuation."

Cham was silent for a long moment. Finally he sighed and said, "Let's not call that a problem. An evac isn't ideal, but we can still say we took down a Star Destroyer and killed hundreds of Imperials in the process. That's a big blow."

She turned her head to the side, away from Eshgo, and whispered into the comm. "Big, but not big enough. It's not enough, Cham."

"It is, Isval. It has to be. We did what we—"

"It's not over! It can't be. The whole thing is pointless if we don't kill Vader and the Emperor. You wanted to start a fire and spread the Empire thin trying to put it out. This won't do it. They'll just lie, say something went wrong with the ship and it went down, but that the Emperor and Vader got off without harm. You want to kindle a blaze? Show the Empire to be vulnerable? Then we have to kill Vader and the Emperor."

She imagined him shaking his head. "I've only got two dozen droid tri-fighters left, Isval, and their brain overhauls are still in progress. They haven't been tested in a combat situation. Kallon said they—"

"You've got us, too, Cham. We're out here. Right now."

She looked out on the escaping ships. Time was slipping away.

"Cham, there's only one or two ships we'll need to destroy. The tri-fighters would act as a distraction to occupy the V-wings up here. We don't need them combat ready." She looked at the control panel, but the layout was foreign to her. To Eshgo, she asked, "Where are the weapons controls? Does this thing even have weapons?"

"It does," Eshgo said. "Here."

She nodded, said to Cham, "We just need to find

them. If we can locate them, I can kill them. Cham, you hear me?"

"What kind of ship are you in?"

"One with blasters. An escort boat. Get Belkor to tell us the ship ID of the Emperor and Vader. They'll have their own special ident."

She watched more pods shoot out from the *Perilous*'s sides, and a few more exited the front landing bay. The Star Destroyer had to be almost empty. There couldn't be more than two or three minutes before the charges blew.

"Cham?"

"All right, Isval. I'm going to launch the tri-fighters. I'll get back to you on the ship ident. Get ready."

She leaned back in her chair, relieved. "Get the weapons hot," she said to Eshgo. "As soon as those tri-fighters get up here, it's time to hunt."

Meanwhile she familiarized herself with the boat's instrumentation.

"To do what?" Kallon asked, in response to Cham's order to launch the tri-fighters. His lekku twitched with irritation. He detested putting anything in the field without first testing it thoroughly. "Their brains are still experimental. They'll be worthless in a fight."

"I know, but do it anyway. Just have them engage anything that's not Isval's ship."

Kallon sniffed. "And what's her ship?"

"It's an escort boat."

"That's it?" Kallon said. "An escort boat? No ident? How am I going to keep them from shooting at her?"

"By giving them the specs for an Imperial escort boat and telling them to shoot at everything else,"

Cham snapped. "The fighters are a distraction, and they're not going to last long anyway. I don't have time for this, Kallon. Just get them in the air. Now. Then we abandon this base for Ryloth."

With that, he left Kallon muttering, turned, and stepped out of the command center. He activated his encrypted comm to Belkor.

The Imperial answered quickly and irritably. "What?"

"The ship's going down, but an evacuation order went out—"

"I know," Belkor snapped. "We already got word and—"

"I need an ident for whatever ship Vader and the Emperor normally fly, and I need it right now."

Belkor held the line in silence for a few beats. Cham imagined him chewing on the request and balking at the taste.

"If those two don't die," Cham said, "this all falls down. I need that ident and I need it now."

"I'll be in contact," Belkor said, and disconnected.

Cham didn't know if he would be in contact. He thought Belkor might have just lost his nerve. He cursed as he watched the tri-fighters rise on their lifters and streak out of the landing bay. He activated his comm with Isval.

"Tri-fighters are launched. I don't know if I'm going to get the idents. See if you can see anything on your own."

Belkor stood in the midst of the busy communications center and tried to think through his course. Events were outrunning him. The air felt too close, the walls too near. He was breathing too hard. He needed room to move.

And he needed more than just Vader and the Emperor dead. Their deaths wouldn't be enough, not for him.

Before he knew what he was doing, he opened a comlink to Mors.

"What is it, Colonel?" Mors said, her voice tight with stress.

The fact that Mors was referring to him by rank instead of name did not bode well.

"Checking on your status, ma'am. Have you departed the moon?"

"Leaving now."

"Very good, ma'am. We'll ask the pilot for the ship's ident and prepare everything for your arrival."

He seemed to be operating outside himself, watching himself do things. He went to a comp station and retrieved the idents for the Emperor's shuttle and Mors's transport. He copied them into the encrypted comm he used to communicate with Cham, then stepped out of the center and raised the Twi'lek.

"You have them?" Cham said.

"I'm sending you two."

"Two?" Cham said.

"They're on one of them. Or maybe one of them is on each. That's the best I can do. Destroy them both to be sure."

He transmitted the idents. He was sweating.

"I've got them," Cham said. "Don't launch any more V-wings until this is done."

"I can delay only so long," Belkor said, failing to keep exasperation out of his tone. "Get this done, Twi'lek."

The Twi'lek disconnected without a reply and Belkor stood there, sweat gluing his uniform to his skin. If Mors joined Vader and the Emperor in death, Belkor could lay everything at the Moff's feet. That was his best play, his only play.

He looked through the glass at the hive of activity in the comm center and inhaled to steady himself. He straightened his uniform, smoothed his hair, and returned to his post.

His fate would be determined in the next few minutes.

Mors hustled onto her shuttle and Breehld, her personal pilot, got them airborne right away. The moon fell away beneath her, the blanket of the jungle's verdure coating the surface in green.

"Status," she said into her wrist comlink as she settled into the luxurious, cushioned passenger compartment of her shuttle.

Ryloth Imperial Control informed her that the *Perilous,* aflame and heavily damaged, with hundreds or thousands dead, was now between the planet and the orbit of the nearest moon, *Mors's* moon. The Star Destroyer was closer to Ryloth than she was.

"When she's in planetary orbit, I want all resources marshaled to assist with repairs and the wounded."

"Of course, ma'am."

The blue sky gave way to black space. She looked out a viewport as the shuttle left the moon in its wake and Ryloth grew larger.

She disliked Ryloth, its dirtiness, its dry air and howling winds, its endemic poverty. The food was bad, the people were angry, and she'd never seen a point in enduring either when she could, instead, live a life of comfort on the jungle moon and leave the dirty work to Belkor.

But that had been a mistake. Belkor had failed. Mors would have to do something about the young colonel. The thought displeased her, not because she liked Belkor, but because it would mean work for her, and she disliked work. She was too old for work.

The *Perilous* hung in the empty space about halfway between Ryloth and the orbit of its nearest moon when the first explosion of the chain reaction started. The ship's aft section burped several fireballs. Chunks and bits of the *Perilous*'s superstructure went spinning off into space, intermixing with the escape pods and V-wings.

"And here we go," Isval said softly.

"Deflectors at full," Eshgo said, his voice tense. "I'm not sure we're clear."

"Stay put," Isval said, scanning the hundreds of ships and pods that dotted space.

More explosions rocked the rear of the Star Destroyer, and tongues of flame hundreds of meters long lit up the darkness, licking the black.

"We should be farther out," Eshgo said, his voice tight.

Isval knew, but she also knew she needed them close enough for cleanup work afterward. She could not imagine that Vader and the Emperor hadn't escaped the ship.

The explosions spread rapidly then, one after another. The aft section blossomed into a single, huge ball of fire, vaporizing the engines, though inertia kept the Star Destroyer moving for Ryloth. Debris and flames flew in all directions. The blasts raced along the length of the ship, one section after another vanishing behind an orange curtain.

Isval's escort shipped bobbed on the blast waves. Even with her naked eye, she could see some of the escape pods hit by the waves starting to spin uncontrollably.

And that had been mere prelude, she knew. When the charges she'd placed on the hyperdrive went . . .

"Brace," she said over her shoulder to Drim, Faylin, and Crost. They had no way to strap themselves in, so they grabbed hold of any protuberance affixed to the cabin.

The vacuum killed the flames almost as quickly as they blossomed, and for a moment the Star Destroyer slid along in space, quiet, dark, and still, blackened by fire, torn by explosions. It looked almost peaceful, like a relic from a long-ago war. But the moment ended when the chain reaction set off by the dying hyperdrive turned the *Perilous* into a miniature star.

A white-hot explosion engulfed the entire remaining superstructure and shredded the ship. Isval squinted and shielded her eyes. Flaming, twisted debris flew in all directions.

"Brace! Brace!" Eshgo shouted, and clutched hard on the controls.

The blast wave, visible as a ripple in space, expanded out in all directions from the ragged corpse of the Star Destroyer. It tore through a few escape pods outright, turning them to scrap, and sent other pods and V-wings skipping along like pebbles in a torrent.

The wave hit the escort ship like a rock wall. The impact drove the ship backward and set it spinning. Metal groaned and whined. Alarms shrieked. Crost, Drim, and Faylin, with no straps, unable to keep their grip, were thrown around the rear area of the ship. The power failed abruptly, quieting the alarms and casting the interior in darkness.

Isval cursed. Crost, Drim, and Faylin groaned.

"You all right?" she called back to the three.

Ayes all around.

"I need us back up, Eshgo!" she said.

*   *   *

"Brace yourselves, my lords," came the shuttle pilot's voice over the comm. He tried to sound calm, but tension tightened his words.

The blast wave slammed into the side of the shuttle, knocking it sidewise, carrying it along for tens of kilometers, and causing it to list sharply. Vader and the Emperor, seated, used the Force to hold their position, but the four members of the Royal Guard were thrown hard against the bulkhead. A wall-mounted comp station spit sparks. An alarm rang. The cabin lights blinked, browned, and failed, casting the cabin in darkness and silencing the alarm. In the quiet, Vader's breathing was the only sound.

Backup power returned light to the cabin.

"One moment, my lords," the pilot said through a crackling comm.

The engines came back online and the pilot righted the ship. The Royal Guardsmen once more took their stations, never uttering a word.

Vader looked out one of the viewports, saw hundreds of pods and ships floating in space, many without power, and thousands if not millions of pieces of debris cast into space like so much flotsam by the explosion and subsequent blast wave.

Most of the ships spun or flew toward the brown ball of Ryloth, but some flew toward the planet's nearest moon. The rest just spiraled out into space.

"Deflectors are down, my lords, but engines are operable."

"Continue on to Ryloth," the Emperor said.

"We'll arrive shortly," the pilot answered.

"Very good, Captain," replied the Emperor.

*   *   *

Backup power came online a moment later, and Eshgo quickly steadied the spinning ship.

"We're back online," he said.

Isval looked out the viewport, saw thousands of ships and pieces of the Star Destroyer spinning or floating powerless in the wake of the blast wave. The first wave of pods started to hit Ryloth's atmosphere, lighting up the sky in orange lines as the friction of entry generated flames. Vader and the Emperor could be anywhere. She looked for something larger, a shuttle or something similar, but saw nothing within eyeshot. There was just too much real estate to cover and too many ships and pieces of debris.

"Give me a full scan," she said to Eshgo, and bit down on her comm with Cham. "I need those ship idents, Cham! Now or never!"

He replied right away. "Coming now," he said, and their onboard computer showed the idents.

"Scan for those," she said to Eshgo, but then performed the scan herself, staring at the comp screen, daring it not to find them.

"Incoming ships," Eshgo said, tapping the screen. "Looks like the tri-fighters. Some of the V-wings are still operational and have picked them up, too, I think. They're moving to intercept."

Isval knew the tri-fighters' experimental droid brains would leave them no match for the V-wings, which meant she had little time. If Vader and the Emperor had escaped the *Perilous*, she needed to find their ship and destroy it in the chaos.

"Come on! Come on!" she said to the comp.

A collective gasp came from everyone in the communications center as the readings showed the *Perilous* disintegrating into millions of small pieces. Many of them looked up at the ceiling for a moment, as if imagining the destruction occurring far above.

"Stations, people," Belkor said, his voice hollow.

Belkor had played sabacc only a few times, and he'd always played poorly, but he was about to bet everything he had. He dismissed the comm officer, ostensibly to let the junior officer gather himself, and raised Moff Mors's shuttle.

"This is Ryloth Imperial Control," he said.

"Go, control," said the pilot.

"The *Perilous* is gone. Escape pods are away, and there is a VIP ship in distress. You are the closest ship and are to proceed there immediately and offer assistance."

"How are we the closest?" said the pilot. Belkor remembered his name as Breehld.

"Planetside V-wings are launching now. *You're* the closest."

"Understood."

With that, he transmitted the ID of Vader and the Emperor's shuttle, together with the coordinates from the last reported location of the *Perilous*.

Mors's ship would have to swing around Ryloth, but that would take only a minute or two. And then, if all went well, Cham's droids would blow her from space.

"Alert search-and-rescue ships," he said. "We're going to have a lot of evacuees up in the black and on the ground. Track what you can as they fall."

Ryloth's harsh terrain and constant dust storms would make search and rescue difficult, but Belkor would need to make a good show of it. Most of the officers and men who'd be involved in search and rescue were loyal to him personally, so he could control things easily.

"No rescue is to launch yet," he ordered. "I want a full scan and detailed situation report first."

"Aye, sir."

The delay would allow Cham to get to Vader, the Emperor, and Mors.

CHAPTER TEN

THE COMM OVERHEAD CRACKLED AND BREEHLD, Mors's pilot, said, "Ma'am, uh, I've just received word." A long pause that Mors did not like. "The *Perilous* is gone."

Mors rose from her seat. "What do you mean 'gone'?"

A pause, then, "Apparently she's been destroyed, ma'am. Between the orbit of the first moon and Ryloth. That's the word I received from Ryloth Control."

Mors sagged back into her seat and swallowed hard. To her knowledge, an Imperial Star Destroyer had never before been destroyed. And now one had, above the planet she was administering, by a rebel movement that she was supposed to suppress.

Whatever had been left of her career before today had been blown to bits with the *Perilous*.

Though her shuttle was on the other side of the planet, she looked out the viewport half expecting to see parts of the Star Destroyer floating out there. She couldn't quite fathom how things had gotten to this point.

Yes, she could. She'd trusted Belkor too much. She'd relied on the man and been let down.

With her comlink she raised Belkor.

"Ma'am, I'm managing a lot down here at the moment." The colonel's voice sounded high-pitched and stressed over the connection.

Mors sputtered. "You're managing a lot? *You?*"

"The *Perilous* is gone, ma'am. But Vader and the Emperor escaped. There are many survivors, in fact. I've instructed your pilot to—"

"You *what?*"

"—to divert and assist in rescuing the Emperor and Lord Vader."

"Why isn't the area already filled with V-wings and rescue ships? What are you doing down there, Belkor?"

"Ma'am, we have limited ships, and getting them too close to the *Perilous* before her explosion seemed imprudent. I'm launching them now."

A headache began in Mors's left temple, a spike of pain she hadn't felt since the days she'd actually cared about her job. She held the comlink up to her mouth and spoke through gritted teeth.

"You are to do nothing more, Colonel, without first consulting me. Is that understood?"

A pause, then, "Yes, ma'am."

"You will answer to me for all of your failures the moment I set foot on Ryloth. Is that understood?"

A very long pause, then, "Yes, ma'am."

Mors cut the link, seething. She'd been too hands-off for years, letting Belkor run amok on Ryloth. She needed to at least give the appearance of running things. An investigation would be coming. Punishment would be coming.

Mors's sole chance at redeeming the situation, at least partially, was to find and bring the Emperor and Lord Vader safely to Ryloth's surface. If she did, perhaps she could maintain her station. She could put the blame for her inability to suppress the Free Ryloth movement on Belkor, blame the promising but underperforming officer for the missteps that had led to the destruction of a Star Destroyer. Mors would be held accountable for being a bad judge of character, a bit too willing to overlook the flaws in a subordinate, but perhaps she could skirt the worst of it.

She had no other course. To Breehld, she said, "Get us around the planet as fast you can, Breehld."

"Aye, ma'am."

The shuttle accelerated to full, speeding around Ryloth, chasing the ruins of the *Perilous*.

"Got one," Eshgo said, pointing at the scanner screen.

Isval saw it—a shuttle picking its way through the debris field toward Ryloth.

"Tri-fighters are closing, too," Eshgo said.

"Weapons hot," Isval said, activating the modest cannon array on the escort boat. "Let's go get him."

Eshgo accelerated through the debris, swinging the escort boat left and right to dodge pods and chunks of the *Perilous*. The scanner chirped, indicating that it had detected the ident of the second ship Cham had identified. They were tens of thousands of kilometers apart.

"Stay with the first," Isval said. "But keep a fix on the second. We'll come back around."

Mors looked out the viewport and gasped when she saw the scope of the destruction. Chunks of metal, some larger than her shuttle, floated everywhere. Escape pods and even V-wings without power floated free among the debris.

"Where are the rescue ships?" Mors asked herself. "Damn you, Belkor."

Debris spattered the ship's hull.

Breehld's voice came over the comm. "Ships incoming, ma'am."

"The rescue ships? How many?"

"No, ma'am. Scan is strange. I think they're old droid tri-fighters?"

"They're what? Never mind. Do you have the Emperor's shuttle?"

"Have it on the scanner, ma'am."

"Hail them."

"Very good— Wait . . . Ma'am, there's an escort boat coming at us on an attack vector."

Mors figured if the rebels had vultures and tri-fighters, they might also have repurposed Imperial escort ships.

"Take evasive action," she said. She threw herself in a seat but fumbled the straps.

Breehld, no doubt assuming she was strapped, slammed the ship hard to port. Mors was flung across the cabin and crashed hard into the bulkhead, knocking the wind from her.

Red lines lit up space as the tri-fighters' repeating blasters started firing at the surviving Imperial ships. Unable to dodge effectively, escape pods exploded in flames. The V-wings still flying answered the tri-fighters with cannon fire of their own.

"He's gone evasive," Eshgo said, swinging the escort left and right as he closed on the shuttle.

"Closer," Isval said to Eshgo, waiting for the targeting computer to lock on. "Just a bit closer."

The targeting computer beeped to indicate it had a lock.

Isval fired and the cannons loosed lines of hot plasma.

An impact rocked the shuttle, throwing Mors hard against the bulkhead, driving the breath from her lungs. Alarms wailed. She lifted herself to all fours, breathing hard.

"Breehld," she said, but he didn't respond. "Status."

Breehld was presumably too engaged in maneuvering the ship to answer. The shuttle swung hard down and up. Red lines streaked past the starboard portholes. Another impact struck the rear of the ship; a secondary explosion followed, larger than the impact, one or more engines going up. The lights died in the cabin and the ship bucked, flinging Mors around the cabin. She hit her head hard against one of the cabin's chairs. She gasped with pain and her vision blurred. Blood poured from her opened scalp and into her eyes.

"Breehld! Breehld!"

Smoke leaked into the cabin from somewhere, stinging her eyes. The alarms seemed to be growing fainter—either that or she was fading. She pawed at the chair, surprised to see blood on her hand, and tried to pull herself up. Whoever was shooting at them would be coming around for another pass. She didn't know if the deflectors were still operating. If not . . .

Dizziness allowed her to rise only partially before she sagged back to the deck.

"Breehld," she said, her voice sounding oddly distant.

The engines went offline and the ship went hard right and down. The smoke thickened. The lights went out entirely. Coughing, gagging, losing consciousness, she realized they were going down. She wondered what had happened to the backup power.

"Damn it," Isval said as the shuttle they'd been targeting veered right and down. Eshgo had to slam the escort boat hard left to avoid an escape pod, but he was a moment too slow. The escort boat nicked the pod, metal scraping metal, before he unpeeled from the ship.

"No damage, we're good," he said, breathing hard. "We're good."

"No we're not," Isval said, trying to keep her eye on the shuttle amid the debris and other ships and pods. She'd already lost weapons lock. "Come back around! Now, Eshgo! Now!"

"Trying," he said through clenched teeth, steering the ship through the debris. Despite his effort, bits of material peppered the escort boat's hull.

"I can't see him!" Isval said.

"I still have him on scan," Eshgo said. "Look! His power's out! Not even life support. He's floating dead, headed down."

"Where's the other one?" Isval said, and checked the scan herself. She saw the second ship heading straight for Ryloth. Worse, she saw incoming V-wings on the sensors, heading up from Ryloth.

"We're going to lose the second one, Isval," Eshgo said.

"I know!" she said, and raised Cham on their private comlink. "Cham? I need you to extrapolate a likely impact zone for—"

"I can't see anything, Isval. We're around the other

side of the planet, aboard ship and heading down for the base on Ryloth. What's happening there?"

"We hit one of the ships. Her power is down and she's falling into the atmosphere. I don't know if Vader and the Emperor were aboard. Even if they were, they may still be alive."

"We're losing him," Eshgo said, meaning the second shuttle.

"Just do what you can and get clear of there," Cham said to Isval. "Belkor's shaky. An exit, Isval. Think one through."

She nodded. "Meet you planetside, Cham." To Eshgo, she said, "Get after the second one. We'll find the first later."

She watched on the scanner as the first shuttle, powerless, fell into Ryloth's atmosphere. They'd crippled it, probably fatally, but there would be no way to be sure unless they found the ship or its wreckage later. Interference from the atmosphere would block further scanning, and she hated the uncertainty. But there was nothing for it.

"Attack vector on the second one," she said to Eshgo. "And we leave nothing to chance this time."

Vader stared out one of the small viewports at the millions of pieces of debris, the whole of it as dense as an asteroid field. Each bit of metal goaded his anger. The rebels would be made to pay.

"Treachery never goes unpunished, old friend," the Emperor said, as though reading his mind.

Vader heard an undertone of menace in his Master's tone. He turned, thinking to ask what his Master meant, but before he could, he felt something through the Force—impending danger. His Master, too, must have felt it, for he gave the concern a voice.

"They are coming," the Emperor said, his voice as soft and gelid as a cold breeze.

The pilot's voice came over the comm. "My lords, it appears an Imperial escort boat is heading toward us on an attack vector. She's not answering hails."

"She is hostile," his Master said over the comm. "Destroy her."

Vader would take no chances with his Master's safety. He stood and started for the cockpit.

The escort boat slashed the distance between it and the shuttle.

"She sees us," Eshgo said, adjusting his angle of approach. "Seeking a lock."

"And I see them," Isval said, watching as the targeting computer beeped to indicate a weapons lock. "And they're too late. Deflect this, bastards."

She fired as the Imperial shuttle went evasive. Her shots caught it low under the nose, destroying the shuttle's solitary gun port in a spray of fire and metal. The escort boat passed over and past the shuttle.

"Coming around!" Eshgo said, wheeling the boat around.

Vader threw open the cockpit hatch, and the wail of alarms poured out in a gush. The attacking ship was not visible through the viewport. In the distance, he saw the glow of V-wing fire.

"She's behind us," one of the pilots said, not to Vader but to the copilot.

"Guns are gone. The deflectors are holding."

Green beams passed over the ship, catching an escape pod in front of them and to starboard, vaporizing it. Vader clutched the sides of the hatch to maintain his balance. Another round of fire from the escort ship knifed over the shuttle. A second shot caught the shuttle's wing and caused it to buck. The pilot turned the ship hard to port, half turning, and the escort whizzed past them, passing close enough that Vader caught a glimpse of the escort's pilots: Twi'leks.

The Emperor's pilot cursed as he weaved at speed through the dispersing but still-dense debris field from the *Perilous*'s destruction. He pulled up hard on the stick, but he was too slow. A piece of stray super-structure slammed into the shuttle with a boom and put a web of cracks in the cockpit's large viewport.

Vader had seen enough. He took two strides forward and with one hand disconnected the pilot's seat straps, while with the other he lifted him from his seat and heaved him aside.

"Leave," Vader said, and took the pilot's seat. To the copilot he added, "You, too."

The copilot disconnected from his seat, wide-eyed, helped the pilot to his feet, and both hustled out of the cabin.

At a glance Vader took in the data provided by the instrument panel. The escort was closing for another round of fire. With the shuttle's weapons nonopera-tional, Vader focused on evasion for the moment. Using the debris to his advantage, he swung the shut-tle hard to port, then stern, then back again, changing altitude throughout, wheeling through the floating pieces of the *Perilous*. Cannon fire from the escort sprayed space with beams of green, but it went wide and high, striking debris and pods.

Vader let them close a bit, then slammed hard on the reverse thrusters, throwing him forward in his seat, and immediately reengaged the engines. The mo-mentary stop had been enough. The escort streaked past and over him. He gave chase instantly, inverting the shuttle as he did. The shuttle was not armed, true, but Vader was not without weapons.

Isval and Eshgo cursed as they sped over and past the shuttle.

"That pilot's good," Eshgo said tightly. "Very good."

"Where is he?" Faylin asked from the rear compartment. "What's he doing?"

Isval realigned their scan. "Got him! He's . . ."

She looked up through the canopy of the escort boat, eyes wide with disbelief, to see the shuttle, merely tens of meters distant and flying upside down. The ships' cockpit viewports faced each other. Isval could see Vader, and Vader could see them. Vader made a gesture with his gloved hand, as if he were pinching off a bleeding artery, and Isval felt her throat constrict. Instinctively she reached for her neck, but there was nothing there, just the pressure, just the squeezing. She couldn't breathe! She pawed at her neck, panicked now, legs kicking. Beside her, Eshgo was behaving the same way. She fought to draw breath, couldn't. She clawed at her collar, squirmed in her seat, made a tiny gasp. Whatever held her squeezed tighter, tighter.

"What's wrong?" Drim shouted from the back. "What is it? What is it?"

Her vision was darkening. Little bursts of light swam before her eyes. She remembered the sounds Pok had made over the comm when Vader had killed him—the long silence punctuated by the abortive gasps.

It was Vader choking her somehow. It had to be.

She glanced up and saw the Imperial shuttle, with Vader at the controls.

Someone was calling her name. Cham? Drim? Faylin?

She couldn't answer. Her mouth wouldn't work. She had no breath, no words. Her vision tunneled down to Vader, only Vader. She imagined herself reflected in the eyepieces of his helmet. Her world distilled down to his eyes and her anger, and that distillation gave her a moment of clarity.

She was failing, she knew, dying, but she wouldn't go alone.

She lowered her hands from her throat and seized the stick. She jerked it back, and the escort boat went nose-up for the shuttle. Everything went black.

Vader sensed the danger a fraction of a second before the dying Twi'lek flew the escort boat into the shuttle. He slammed on the stick hard right and back, but the shuttle was not as maneuverable as his Eta-interceptor and responded too slowly.

The escort slammed into the shuttle's belly and set it to spinning, aft over bow, the stars and planet in the viewport whirling past in a maddening spiral. Metal groaned and alarms screamed, but only for a moment before the shuttle lost all power. Vader sat in the pilot's seat, holding a dead stick in a dark cockpit. His armor compensated for the darkness by activating the light amplifiers in his helmet lenses. The sound of his respirator filled the quiet. Space through the viewport was a dizzying panorama of shifting images: Ryloth, debris from the *Perilous*, pods, Ryloth's distant moon, stars. Ryloth grew bigger with each rotation of the shuttle. The ship was falling toward the planet.

Motion flashed into Vader's field of view for a moment: the escort boat. It still had power but was heavily damaged from the collision. It spiraled toward

Ryloth, smoking, burning, coming in at too steep an angle; it would break up in the atmosphere.

He focused not on the churning perspective through the viewport, but on the fixed point of the instrument panel. Calm, immersed in the Force, he tried to reactivate emergency power, but without success. He rarely had to call on the mechanical talent he'd possessed since childhood, but it would serve him well now. He had only a short time before the ship hit the planet's atmosphere. And if it hit while spinning out of control, they'd burn up.

He set about redirecting all latent battery power in the ship to the thrusters. He needed only a few moments of thrust to straighten the ship, then rudder control for the reentry. His fingers moved quickly over the instrumentation. Ryloth grew larger with each passing moment.

A memory stabbed him, as sharp as a blade. He'd floated alone in an escape pod over Ryloth once, spinning high over its surface, after crashing a cruiser into a droid control ship. Another name bobbed up and broke the surface of the sea of memory.

Ahsoka.

He'd called her "Snips" sometimes.

He pushed the errant recollection aside and focused on his task. In moments he'd redirected enough power from backup batteries for at least a few seconds of thruster operation.

He did not hesitate. He fell into the Force, looked out the viewport, let himself feel the motion of the ship, and activated the thrusters.

The ship's spin slowed and its angle flattened. Another quick burn stopped the spin altogether, and the shuttle was on a path that would at least allow for reentry. And he still had a small amount of battery power left.

Behind him, the door to the cockpit slid open and he sensed the presence of his Master.

"The ship is nearly powerless," Vader said. "I will get us down, though."

"No doubt," his Master said, and sat in the co-pilot's seat. "We have been in situations like this before, you and I."

Vader said nothing, though his mind turned to a battle over Coruscant, shortly after he'd killed Darth Tyranus. As always, his Master seemed to fill all available space with his presence and push against Vader with his power.

"Over Coruscant," his Master said. "And . . . at other times."

Vader glanced over, but his Master's hooded eyes stared out through the nest of his wrinkled face and revealed nothing.

Ryloth filled the viewport as the ship descended. Seeing the mottled browns of its surface, the smears of green and tan, dredged memories of other times up from the sludge of his distant past, names he rarely thought of anymore. Anakin. Mace. Plo Koon . . .

The shuttle hit the atmosphere too sharply and skipped and bounced, the metal shrieking under the stress. He burned the thrusters for a fraction of a second, righted the angle of approach, and reduced the jarring bumps to mere vibrations. Flames from the friction of atmospheric entry sheathed the ship. Fire surrounded them. Fire.

Mustafar.

Obi-Wan.

He used his ever-present anger to burn away the memories, but the charred husks of the past clung to the forefront of his consciousness.

Padmé.

He rarely allowed himself to think her name.

His rage slipped his control and he squeezed the control stick so hard it cracked. His breath came hard, fast, loud.

He felt his Master's eyes on him, always on him, the weight of them, the questions they carried. He knew his Master could see into him, through him.

"You are troubled, my friend," his Master said, his voice calm while the ship screamed through Ryloth's stratosphere.

"No, Master," Vader said. He sank fully into the Force and used the focus it gave him to exorcise the past from his mind.

He focused on the now, on safely landing a shuttle that was almost entirely without power. His armor regulated his breathing, and instead of being overcome by his emotion, he harnessed it and fell even more deeply into the Force. He channeled the remaining battery power to the in-atmo emergency rudder and used it to make their angle of approach shallower. He realized that there must have been ships falling out of the sky all across the planet, hundreds of them.

The smears of brown and green and tan gained clarity as they fell. He could make out features of the terrain in the light of the setting sun: gorges, ridges, canyons, dry riverbeds, all of them streaked past, the surface everywhere broken and cracked. A huge forest of trees rose from the parched ground ahead. It looked out of place, a lesion on the otherwise dead surface of Ryloth, but he knew the planet featured several large expanses of woods.

The ship careened straight for it, held in gravity's unrelenting grip. The ground rose up at the ship as if the craft had been shot out of a blaster. He was still at too steep an angle, but the rudder controls barely responded, even to his strength. He managed to lower the in-atmo emergency flaps, and they helped flatten out the approach. The browns and tans disappeared. The forest filled the viewport entirely, under it, over it, like flying over an ocean of trees.

"Prepare for impact," he said, but of course his Master had already strapped himself in.

The shuttle skimmed the top of the tree line, and Vader tried to use the thin limbs at the crown of the forest's canopy as a makeshift brake. Limbs scraped the hull, some small, some large, and the ship lurched and bounced and slipped deeper into the canopy. The forward viewport was nothing but trees and leaves and the snap of thick branches. Metal screeched, scraped, the ship slamming into one tree after another.

They hit a large tree, the viewport cracked, and the shuttle careened to the right and down, hitting another tree as it fell, another, twisting upside down, righting, then hitting another tree and turning on its side. A limb twice as thick as Vader's arm jutted through the viewport, shattering it, splitting the space between Vader and his Master. And then it was gone as the ship continued to fall through the trees, the craft's speed and mass still cutting a swath through the flora. They struck another tree, another, before the ship finally slammed into the ground and buried itself on its side a meter into the soft loam of the forest floor. Soil exploded through the hole in the viewport and filled the cockpit to half a meter.

The sudden silence felt odd, a strange juxtaposition against the chaos of the preceding moments. Vader released his grip on the stick. The screech of one of Ryloth's fauna carried from somewhere out in the forest. The light of the setting sun filtered dimly through the forest canopy, casting the ruined cockpit in deep shadow. Through his armor's filters, Vader perceived the organic stink of the soil the ship had displaced in landing, the vegetable smell of the forest. Vader checked the instrumentation. Everything was dead, no power of any kind.

"Distress beacon is inoperable," he said, then released the straps on his seat and lowered himself to the bulkhead, which now served as the deck due to the ship lying on its side. His Master released his own chair straps, flipped as he fell, and landed gracefully beside Vader on the bulkhead.

"That landing was far beneath your capabilities," his Master said. "I've seen you do better in much more demanding circumstances. I fear your mind was not on the task."

Vader considered his response for a moment. When he spoke, he did not bother to lie. "I was . . . thinking of something else for a moment."

His Master nodded. "I guessed as much. And I'm pleased that you told me the truth, though I think it only a half-truth. In any event, your lapse has left four corpses in the rear compartment."

Vader didn't ask how his Master knew that four men had died. His Master simply knew things, many things, most things, and that was explanation enough. Of course his Master did not actually care about the dead men. He cared only about Vader's failure, and Vader's half-truth.

"It won't happen again, Master," Vader said, bowing his head.

"I should hope not," said his Master, perhaps meaning the mediocre piloting, perhaps meaning something else.

Vader turned and took a grip on the door that opened onto the passenger compartment, thinking to pry it open.

"You said you were thinking of something else,"

his Master said, using the tone he sometimes used when setting a verbal trap. "What was it?"

Vader left off the door and turned around. He stared into his Master's wrinkled face and this time offered no half-truth. "The past. My old life."

His Master stared back at Vader, his dark eyes like deep holes, and exhaled softly. "I see."

"It means nothing to me," Vader said, waving his gloved hand. "Stray thoughts, nothing more."

"Hmm," his Master said. "The past is a ghost that haunts us. Ghosts must be banished. Lingering on the past is weakness, Lord Vader."

"Yes, Master," Vader said.

Seeing his Master was done with the lesson, Vader turned back around, took a grip on the door, and heaved it open. He had to kneel to see into the passenger compartment. The bodies of the pilot and copilot lay not far from the door, eyes open, their limbs sticking out from their bodies at improbable angles. The landing had broken them.

The four Royal Guards lay strewn about the passenger cabin, two of them still strapped into dislodged seats.

"Lord Vader," the captain of the guards said, freeing himself of the straps. "Where is the Emperor? Is he—"

"He is here," the Emperor said from directly behind Vader, though Vader had neither heard nor felt him approach. "And unhurt."

"Get up," Vader said, and the two who'd been strapped into their seats rose to their feet, wobbly. The other two remained on the deck. To Vader's surprise, the leg of one of them twitched in his armor. He wasn't dead.

"There are only three dead here," he said to his Master.

"Are there?" his Master asked.

The leader of the guards knelt and checked his fellow. "He's unconscious, my Emperor. He didn't strap himself in and was thrown about during the landing."

The wounded guard groaned. His gloved hand opened and closed.

"Kill him," his Master said.

The leader of the Royal Guard, conditioned to obey any order of the Emperor instantly without question, did not hesitate. He stood, drew his heavy blaster, and shot his comrade once in the head, leaving a dark, smoking hole in his helmet.

"And now there are four," his Master said.

Vader did not miss the point. He turned to face his Master, his respirator loud and steady.

The Emperor shook his head with false regret. "He was stupid. And stupidity, like nostalgia, is weakness. I cannot abide weakness in those close to me. It's a shame, really. But sometimes we must make hard choices. Lead us out now, if you please, Lord Vader."

Vader activated his lightsaber. While it sizzled, his Master stared, expressionless, into Vader's face.

Vader drove his lightsaber through the bulkhead and used it to cut a door in the superstructure. He stepped through first, followed by the pair of Royal Guards, then his Master.

Dried leaves and fallen limbs covered the soft loam of the forest floor. Trees with smooth-barked trunks rose seventy meters toward the sky, blotting out the last of the day's light. The partially exposed root systems were so large they formed knotted tangles of twisted wood as tall as Vader. The canopy above rustled in Ryloth's constant winds, as if the entire forest were gossiping in whispered tones. Something large fluttered high above, disturbing leaves. In the distance, out in the dark, some native fauna howled as the day died.

"Check the survival kits," Vader said to the Royal Guards. "See what's salvageable."

They did not obey until Vader's Master gave them a nod. When they'd gone, Vader turned to his Master and tried to keep his tone deferential.

"Are you testing me, Master?"

"Testing you? Is that how you perceive things?"

"Am I wrong?"

His Master smiled and reached up to put a hand—a hand that could emit Force lightning—on Vader's shoulder, the gesture both a sign of affection and an assertion of power.

"We are, all of us, always being tested, my friend. Tests make us stronger, and strength is power, and power *is the point*. We must pass all the tests we face." A long pause, then, "Or die in the effort."

Vader could not read his Master's face or the meaning behind his words. But then again, he rarely could.

CHAPTER ELEVEN

THE COMMUNICATIONS CENTER BUZZED WITH THE sound of orders, but behind them was the low background murmur of collective disbelief. The air smelled of sweat, of distress.

"What is happening up there?" a lieutenant asked.

"Status on the Moff's shuttle?" asked another.

"Tri-fighters, now? How many?"

Belkor moved from station to station through the tumult, taking in facts, issuing orders, and doing his best to look as if he were trying to rescue the men he actually wanted dead, and in control of events that had long ago outrun him. He had no confirmation that the Moff's ship had been destroyed, only that it had disappeared from scans. The same was true of the Emperor's shuttle. Both were hopeful signs, but he dared not actually hope.

He realized he was breathing fast. His uniform felt too tight, the walls seemed too close, the ceiling too low.

"Sir, are you all right?"

"What? Of course, yes. Yes. Carry on, Lieutenant."

But he wasn't all right. He wouldn't be all right

until he knew the Emperor, Vader, and Mors were dead.

"Escape pods are landing all over the western hemisphere of the planet and the near moon, sir," said another lieutenant. "We're getting thousands of distress signals. Search and rescue is prioritizing rescue grids but, sir, this is overwhelming. They don't have enough personnel. They'll be at this for days."

"Disposition of the Emperor's shuttle or the Moff's ship?"

"Nothing yet, sir."

Belkor nodded, at once relieved and terrified. If he had somehow succeeded, his next challenge would be to concoct a believable enough cover story to exculpate himself.

But first he needed to ensure that the Emperor and Vader and the Moff were dead.

Isval heard someone screaming.

"Isval! Eshgo! One of you get up! I need help!"

It was Faylin's voice. Isval opened her eyes, groggy. She blinked, breathed deep through a throat that felt raw, and . . .

Ryloth filled the screen, huge and fulgent, and then it was gone, replaced by black, and then it was back, and then gone. They were spinning, bow over stern. Isval squeezed her eyes shut to quell a bout of nausea. She was muzzy-headed, but realized they were going to hit the atmosphere while the ship was spinning. They'd break up and burn all the way down.

"Faylin?" she said, her throat scratchy and pained. "Eshgo?"

Eshgo was slumped in his chair beside her, his chin on his chest. Faylin was blanketed awkwardly over him, trying to operate the shuttle's controls.

"He's dead, Isval!" she said. "And Crost and Drim are unconscious! I can't straighten the ship! I've flown sims, but . . ."

"Dead?" Isval repeated, her thoughts coming slow, but grief bubbling up through the sludge.

"Isval! You're a better pilot than me! You need to fly this ship or we'll be joining him! Grieve later! Isval!"

Faylin's tone helped her focus. She sat forward in the chair and tried to clear her head.

"First the spinning," Isval said, taking the stick in her hand. "Give me control."

"I don't know how to give you control!" Faylin said.

"Yes, you do," Isval said, finding the calm she always relied on in a crisis. "Remember your time in the sim. The blue button, near your left hand. Quickly."

"Right," Faylin said, calming down some. She pushed the button and Isval fired the boosters, compensating for the spin. The rotation slowed, slowed more, then stopped. Ryloth filled the screen. They were coming in day-side, and too steeply. Isval tried to correct.

"What can I do?" Faylin asked.

"Grab hold of something," Isval said. "Right now."

They hit the outer atmosphere, and it felt like running into a wall. The sudden loss of velocity threw them both forward. Faylin exclaimed but held on to Eshgo's chair. Thumps sounded from the rear compartment, and Isval tried not to think of what that meant for Drim and Crost. Flames sheathed the ship, painting the cockpit in orange light. The metal of the hull groaned and popped. The ship shook so badly that Isval's teeth ached.

"Flattening," she said, more to herself than to Faylin. "Flattening."

The vessel continued to vibrate, but it was the normal bouncing of reentry. "What happened to the other ship?" she asked Faylin. "The one we ran into?"

"What?"

"The other ship, Faylin! Did you see what happened to it?"

"I . . . yes, it went dark and spun toward Ryloth."

"Did it burn up? Did you see it burn up on reentry? This is important, Faylin."

"I didn't, no. We were spinning ourselves and I could barely . . . I was just trying to get you back. I thought we were going to crash."

Isval cursed. The rough vibration of reentry gave way to smooth flight as they entered normal atmosphere. She straightened the ship. Ryloth stretched out below them, bleak and brown and as desiccated by the sun as a dried fruit.

She checked the scanner, but it showed her nothing she could use. She looked out the cockpit and imagined a rain of pods and ships falling to the surface. Possibly one of them contained Vader and the Emperor, but she had no way to—

"Logs," she said, tapping the keys on the navcomp.

"Logs?" Faylin asked.

"Check Drim and Crost."

Faylin crawled back into the rear compartment. It took only a moment before she rendered her verdict. "They're gone. It's just us."

Isval nodded, intent on her task, refusing to allow herself to feel grief.

"Did you hear me?" Faylin insisted, her voice quaking. "I said they're gone."

"I heard you. Get back up here and sit. I may need you."

"Isval . . ."

"Sit, Faylin! This isn't over and I don't want them dying for nothing. Do you?"

"No," Faylin said softly. She gently removed Eshgo from his seat, laid him on the deck, and took his place. "Of course not."

Isval checked the scan logs and finally found what she was looking for. She jabbed a finger at the screen. "There!"

"What?"

"That's the shuttle's trajectory as it went down. You said it was dark, so it was just falling. It would've stayed on this path, at least roughly, as it descended. That narrows things down a bit." She bit down to activate her private comm with Cham.

Kallon piloted the transport, knifing through space toward Ryloth. Cham sat in the copilot's seat and tried to process how he felt: strange, outside himself, almost empty. He'd exhausted most of the resources available to the movement, but they'd brought down an Imperial Star Destroyer, and maybe, *maybe* killed the Emperor and Vader. He should've been exultant but instead he felt numb. He'd been filled with adrenaline for the last hour, and now he was deflating.

He tried again to hail Isval but received no response. He felt Kallon's eyes on him and kept the concern from his face, though his lekku twitched.

Their shuttle was coming in on the night side, opposite the face of the planet where the *Perilous* had been destroyed. A dozen more ships flew nearby, all of them packed with rebels and as much matériel as they'd been able to load rapidly and remove from the moon base. They flew at low power and low speed, the output of their engines diffused by bafflers, all in an effort to minimize their sensor profile.

"Scans are clean," Kallon said, eyeing the readout. "The Empire's occupied with rescue. Back door is open and no one's home."

"We get everyone planetside, then we regroup," Cham said. He needed status reports. He needed to know where Isval was, that she was all right.

"Sounds good," Kallon said. "Then what?"

The question took Cham aback momentarily. Then what, indeed? They'd accomplished more than he could've hoped, and he'd been so preoccupied with planning the destruction of the *Perilous* that he'd given only passing thought to what came next. Perhaps he hadn't believed they could do it. He had a movement to lead, a rebellion, but he wasn't sure where they were going after today. He needed to give them their next goal, something on which to focus. He needed that himself.

"I'm planning next steps now," he said to Kallon, just to put him off. When his private comlink with Isval pinged, he sighed with relief.

"Isval, you're all right! Thank the—"

"I'm sending you a last known trajectory," she said, speaking in the clipped, rapid tone she used when pursuing a task. "Use it to establish a likely crash zone. It'll be big, hundreds of kilometers square, but it's at least a start. I need you to confirm my findings."

"What? Slow down."

"No time to slow down, Cham. Vader and the Emperor went down in their shuttle, but they didn't burn up. They're alive. I'm sure of it. And what I'm sending you is their last known trajectory."

Cham processed her words as the data related to

the trajectory came through. He immediately fed the data into his navcomp and ran a subroutine.

"What's going on?" Kallon asked.

Cham didn't bother to answer. And he didn't question Isval's assertion that Vader and the Emperor were still alive. He trusted her implicitly, and he, like her, had seen Vader do too much, things no one should have been able to do. Cham could not imagine that a mere crash had killed him. He doubted they'd crashed at all.

And Cham wanted Vader dead, he realized. He *needed* him dead. Isval had been right. Striking a meaningful blow against the Empire meant cutting off its heads.

And so he had his next goal.

"What about the other ship you targeted? Who was on it? How do you know Vader was aboard this one and not that one?"

"The other went down, too, but Vader wasn't on it. I *saw* him on this one, Cham."

The subroutine completed its calculations, confirming Isval's conclusions. Cham transposed the result to an overlay of Ryloth's surface and sent it to Isval.

"Calculations confirmed. If that trajectory's right, we have a search zone," Cham said. "The Emperor could have been on the other ship, though. What do you mean you saw Vader?"

"Trust me that I did," Isval said. "So let's go with what we know. Vader was on that ship. Hard to imagine the Emperor was not with him. Hmm. That area's heavily forested."

No doubt Isval was staring at the same map overlay that Cham was looking at.

"Tough area to search," she said.

Cham was thinking the same thing. "It'll take too long to find anything in that region. And if they survived the crash, they'll have sent up a hail already. Rescue will be en route. I don't know how we get to them first."

Her response was immediate. "They were dark, Cham, no power. Faylin saw. It'll take them time to establish a portable communications array with enough reach to contact search and rescue. And there have to be hails and distress calls coming from everywhere on the surface by now. Their signal will be lost in it. We have some time."

"Not much. A fraction of an hour, maybe." An idea occurred to Cham. "Unless . . ."

"Say it. Unless?"

Cham was already working out details in his head. "Kallon can hack the Imperial satellites anytime he wants. He's been able to do it for years. We've just kept it in our pocket because it's useless alone. Unless we take out that communications station on the equator. We do that, then hack the sats to send out a jamming signal . . ."

"Communication will be reduced to line of sight," Isval said, and Cham imagined her slamming a fist on the instrumentation. "That's it, Cham. They'll be isolated. It'll buy us some time to hunt."

Cham warmed to the task. "We'll need Belkor. And he's going to ask about that second ship. I need the last known trajectory for it, too. Did it go down dark?"

"Yeah, even life support was down," Isval said. "Sending the data."

The moment it came through, Cham said, "Hold there and wait for me to call you back."

"Roger that." She hesitated, then, "Cham, it's just Faylin and me now. The rest are . . . gone."

Cham's lekku drooped. A ball formed in his throat, but he swallowed it down. They'd been good soldiers—

friends, even. He'd lost a lot of good people today. The weight of it made his head ache.

"Understood. I'm sorry, Isval. Stand by."

Before hailing Belkor, Cham ordered four of the ships flying with them to head to the search grid Isval had pinpointed and start looking for a downed Imperial shuttle. They accelerated and diverted at speed around the planet.

As soon as they were away, Cham hailed Belkor on their encrypted comlink.

Belkor felt the encrypted comlink vibrate against his chest, an irritating insect that wouldn't stop pestering him. He tried to ignore it, but the annoying hail continued. He stepped out of the communications center and into an adjacent office.

"This is Belkor," he said tightly.

"Listen carefully and do not interrupt," said Cham's voice. "Both ships are down, but I can't confirm that either is destroyed. I have a trajectory on Vader's ship—"

"What about the other one?"

"I told you not to interrupt, Belkor."

Belkor's jaw clenched so tightly around his anger that he wondered if he'd ever be able to open it again. Cham went on: "You're going to tell the Equatorial Communications Hub that an incoming Imperial escort ship is carrying wounded VIPs from the *Perilous*. They are to lower their shields and receive this ship. Do you understand?"

Belkor didn't even bother to ask how Cham knew about a classified installation hidden in the planet's equatorial verdure. Every time Belkor spoke to Cham, the Twi'lek said things that made his head swim. He seemed one or two steps ahead of Belkor's thinking at every turn.

"I can't do that."

"You must. That station's satellite relays need to be destroyed."

"To what end? It'll do nothing . . ."

"We'll hack the communications sats afterward, have them send a jamming signal."

The implications settled on Belkor. "You'll fog the whole net, disrupt communications for the whole planet."

"I know. Communication will be line of sight only. And that's what I need. We think Vader and the Emperor are alive but stranded."

Belkor's heart was a sledgehammer on his ribs. "We haven't received a distress call." He whispered, "Why do you think they're alive? If they crashed . . ."

"Because we've seen what Vader can do, Belkor, and a crash isn't going to kill him. We're going to have to stuff a blaster in his faceplate and pull the trigger to be sure. We bring down communications and they're isolated. That'll give us time, and we'll use it to hunt them down."

Belkor didn't miss the use of the collective pronoun, and he supposed it was warranted. Belkor was a traitor, the same as Cham. Given all he'd done, he might as well have been a member of Cham's Free Ryloth movement. He'd be treated the same way if he was caught.

He realized he was pacing, and his agitation was drawing eyes through the transparent glass that walled his office. He took a breath to steady himself, stopped pacing, and turned his back to the glass.

"How do you know where they are?"

"I don't know for certain," Cham admitted. "I have

a search zone. But it's large. That's why I need the extra time."

Belkor's mind turned to Mors. "The second ship. You said it was down. How do you know?"

"My people saw it. That's all I can say for certain."

Sweat ran in rivulets down Belkor's sides. "Well, I need you to say more, Syndulla." He dropped his voice to an even lower whisper. "The Moff was on it. I need her to stay on it. Do you understand?"

"I do," Cham said. "Odds are she's dead, Belkor. Her shuttle was dark and life support was down. We kill Vader and the Emperor, and this mess is clean. And you're the new Moff."

"I need to be sure," Belkor said. "I need the trajectory for the Moff's ship. Send it to me."

"I can't spare any resources to search another landing zone."

"I'll check on it myself!" Belkor snapped. "Just send me the damn data."

"Fine. Good," Cham said, in the tone one used when addressing an incensed child. Belkor found it infuriating. "Here it comes."

Belkor's comlink lit up as it received the data. "It's through," he said.

"Then do what I asked and do it now," Cham said.

Belkor smoothed his hair and gathered what he could of his composure. "I'll alert the base."

"Good hunting, Belkor," Cham said.

Belkor couldn't quite bring himself to wish Cham the same.

Kallon took them through reentry and into Ryloth's night sky. From there, he accelerated through the whipping winds and eventually piloted the ship into the yawning cave mouth that opened onto an old spice mine, the twisting shafts picked clean ten years or more before the Clone Wars. The ships accompanying theirs fell in behind. Kallon activated his vessel's external lights and flew into the maze of the mine. He knew the path by heart.

Looking out the cockpit glass at the rough, machine-scarred walls, Cham wondered how long it would be before they had to abandon this base, too. He was running out of hidey-holes and resources, consuming them all in a day. It would be fully worthwhile only if they killed Vader and the Emperor.

He raised Isval before the distance underground made communications iffy.

"Where are you?" she asked.

"We're safely to the Eastern Base," he said. "Heading down. Kallon's ready."

Beside him, Kallon nodded. "Very ready."

"What do you have for me?" Isval asked Cham.

She was all business, as usual. Cham smiled. "Belkor is informing the Equatorial Communications Hub of your approach. You're carrying wounded VIPs from the *Perilous*. You barely got clear before she went up."

"Damn rebels," she said.

He smiled. "Indeed. They appear to be having a good day."

Isval's tone turned serious again. "You trust Belkor to do this?"

Cham shook his head. "I don't trust him at all, but trust has nothing to do with it. He'll do it because he has to. He's too far in to turn back. He'll gripe, but he'll do whatever we need."

"All right," she said. "We're off to it, then."

"We're refueling and then I'll head back to the search area. Kallon will activate the hack as soon as you take down the station."

"Simple as the push of a button," Kallon said.

"How will he know when it's down? If you're underground I can't reach him."

"How will you know when it's down?" Cham asked Kallon.

"I'll know."

"He'll know," Cham said to Isval.

"Understood," Isval said to Cham. "See you at the search grid, then."

"Just limp in, Isval. You're supposed to be damaged."

"Right," she said.

"Good luck," he said. "I'll see you soon."

He sent her a set of coordinates within the search area where they thought Vader and the Emperor had gone down. They'd rendezvous there.

"Got it," she said. "Luck to you, too."

"Exits, Isval. Always think one through. Then think through another."

"Always," she said, and managed not to make it sound ironic.

The depth underground soon cut off communications.

Cham had neglected to tell her that he'd already diverted some of the rebel ships retreating from the moon base and sent them to the map grid to start the search for Vader and the Emperor's shuttle. Conceivably, they could get lucky and find their prey before Cham and Isval ever arrived.

"Hurry," he said to Kallon. "I want to get back out there."

CHAPTER TWELVE

Isval's comm buzzed on an open frequency, using her call sign. She and Faylin shared a look of surprise. They shouldn't be receiving any comm chatter. Still, she opened the channel.

"Go," she said.

"Isval, this is Nordon. We've found something in the search area. It looks like the ship Vader was supposed to be on—"

"Nordon! Wait, what are you doing in the search area already? Did Cham authorize that? And what are you doing on this frequency?"

Her tone was sharper than she intended, but only because she didn't want anyone else to find Vader. *She* wanted to find him, for Pok, for Eshgo, find him and see herself reflected in the lenses of his helmet as she pulled the trigger and put a blaster shot through his chest.

"The comm is encrypted, Isval. We're the first out here, and yes, Cham knows. He diverted us from the moon base withdrawal. Two more teams are en route."

"Three when we get there," she said.

"Right. Anyway, we found what looks like a downed ship in the forest at these coordinates."

Isval's shipboard comp took in the coordinates. They were at the northern edge of the search area.

"Send it out to the other teams en route," Isval said.

"Is it the Emperor's shuttle?" Faylin asked, eagerness in her tone.

"Have you confirmed the ID of the ship?" Isval asked Nordon, and held her breath in anticipation of the answer.

"The forest is too thick, but it looks like an Imperial shuttle. We could set down and have a look."

Isval was already shaking her head. "Negative, negative. Do not get on the ground, Nordon. If it's Vader . . . just don't get on the ground. Understood?"

"Understood. What then?"

Isval considered options. "Have you informed Cham?"

"Can't raise him."

Still in the underground base, then. She knew what Cham would advise: reconnoiter and wait for reinforcements.

"Eyeball it as best you can, Nordon. If you confirm it's the Emperor's shuttle, or if you get a visual on Vader or the Emperor, wipe them from the face of the planet."

"Copy that. What are you doing?"

"Blowing things up," she said.

"As usual," Nordon said. "See you soon, then."

"Here we go," Isval said to Faylin.

The generator hummed to life and the dish on the portable communications array started to turn as it sought an uplink.

"We'll have a connection in moments, Lord Vader," the captain of the Royal Guard said.

"Use the Emperor's personal frequency. Arrange for immediate—"

Vader sensed it before he could see it. He looked sharply at his Master, saw him staring up at the sky, at two rapidly approaching lights descending from altitude—ships, Vader knew. Perhaps they'd seen the fire.

"Ships incoming, my lords," said one of the Royal Guards. He held field magnifiers to his helmet's lenses. "Not Imperial. A pair of Twi'lek freighters, I think. Should I fire a flare, my lords?"

"I don't think that will be necessary," the Emperor said with a hard smile.

The ships closed the distance rapidly, their clunky, disk-shaped silhouettes coming into clear focus as they neared.

Vader activated his lightsaber and stepped in front of his Master.

Isval turned her mind from Nordon's discovery and piloted the escort ship in at a slow pace, heading toward Ryloth's equator. Below them, the planet's surface was a rocky, uneven sea of browns, tans, and blacks. Dry riverbeds veined the terrain. Thin forests dotted the landscape here and there. In the distance, one of the equatorial mountain ranges rose majestically into the sky, backlit by the reds and oranges of the setting sun. Isval rarely allowed herself the time to appreciate beauty, but she spent a moment doing just that.

"Something, eh?" Faylin asked. "I'm not even Twi'lek and it takes my breath away sometimes."

"Everything looks beautiful from far away," Isval said. "Harsh up close, though."

"Right," Faylin said, and tore her eyes away from the mountains. She leaned forward and stared out the viewscreen. "I don't see the base yet."

"We're three hundred klicks out," Isval said, eyeing the scanner readout. "No ships in the vicinity."

"They're all on rescue or patrol," Faylin said.

"Let's get this done and get to hunting."

Faylin nodded. "Copy that."

When they closed to within the communication distance typical for Imperial protocol, Isval hailed the base. "Equatorial Base Alpha, this is Imperial Escort Twenty-Nine, do you copy?"

The response came immediately. "Escort, you are loud and clear."

"I have wounded VIPs from the *Perilous* who are in need of immediate medical help. Please have a med team on standby and provide me with a landing pad number."

Isval watched the scanner, waiting to see the station's shields drop. Faylin sat in the seat beside her, fidgeting.

"Come on," Faylin muttered. "Show us your belly and we'll give you a scratch."

The shields remained up, however, and the comm crackled. "This is Major Steen Borkas. We received word you were en route. I apologize for this, but please forward your credentials, Escort Twenty-Nine. And who are the VIPs? I served on the *Perilous* way back when. I'm friends with many of the crew."

Isval shared a glance with Faylin and bit down on the comlink that connected her to Cham. "They want credentials, Cham. And names of the wounded. Apparently the base commander used to serve on the *Perilous*."

Nothing. Cham was still too deep underground.

"The captain's name was Luitt," Faylin said. "We could use his name."

"How do you know that?" Isval asked.

Faylin shrugged. "Picked it up somewhere. What are you going to tell them?"

Isval started composing lies in her mind.

Faylin leaned forward and pointed out the viewscreen. "There it is."

Ahead they could see the large installation, with its many concrete buildings, the shield generator, and the series of large satellite dishes that formed the hub of the Imperial communications network on Ryloth. The setting sun painted them all in orange. Isval thought she saw a couple of small transports out on the landing pads, but no fighter craft.

"Isval?" Faylin asked.

Isval activated the comm. "I have bridge crew aboard."

"Bridge crew?" came Borkas's reply. "I heard Luitt got off safely. Who do you have? The XO?"

Isval silently congratulated herself on not using Luitt's name and then started spinning the lies. "Sir, I honestly can't say. I'm just an escort pilot. The officers I have are in very bad shape, as is my boat. It was chaos up there and we barely got clear. I don't even have the ability to upload my credentials. The comp is a mess."

Beside her, Faylin screamed, as if she were wounded and in pain.

"Sir," Isval said, and feigned desperation. "We need help here."

"Escort Twenty-Nine, you are clear to land on Pad Nine," Major Borkas said. "Med team is en route."

Isval disconnected. "We don't go hot until we get closer," she said to Faylin.

Isval could not help but smile as the scanner showed the shields go down. As they drew nearer the base, they could make out more details: a group of troops and a med team with its droids hurrying toward Landing Pad 9; the observation and control deck, lit from within, which allowed them to see the officers and troops standing near the large windows and watching their approach.

"I see four dishes," Faylin said. "We can get them all on one pass."

"The dishes are the priority and I've got those. Your job is to kill every Imperial you can."

Faylin looked over at her, perhaps surprised at her bloodthirstiness, and nodded.

They closed, the escort's propulsion eating kilometers. The base grew larger and Isval started picking the order of her targets and gently maneuvering the escort into an attack run. They had to hit all the dishes on the first pass. She didn't think the escort boat had the firepower to take out a hardened shield generator, so they needed to get the dishes down before Borkas realized what was happening and reenergized the shields.

The comm crackled. "That was Landing Pad Nine," Borkas said. "*Nine*, Escort Twenty-Nine."

"Copy that," Isval said, but didn't change course. Instead she accelerated all at once. She activated the targeting computer, knowing the Imperials would pick up on it, and locked on.

"Fire at will," she said to Faylin.

She kept a mental count in her head, figuring they had thirty seconds at the most.

Faylin had the side-mounted cannons on manual and started firing. Plasma slammed into the base, scattering the medical team and leaving a few corpses on the pad. Isval fired on her locked target, and one of the dishes went up in a cloud of flame and smoke.

Three seconds in.

She didn't bother locking onto the second; she didn't have time. She switched the gun to manual and fired, connecting the space between the ship and the dish with lines of plasma. The second dish exploded, its base aflame, and the bulk of it toppled over into a nearby building, causing a secondary explosion that smothered the area in smoke.

Five seconds in.

Isval was unable to see, but she kept her eyes on her instrumentation as she slowed and wheeled the boat hard to port. She was down to twenty seconds. The targeting computer locked on the third dish and she fired. It disappeared into a column of flame and smoke and debris that rained against the escort's hull. She turned hard to get to the last, with Faylin firing blindly in the haze throughout.

They came out of the smoke and saw the fourth dish ahead. A burst of fire slammed into the side of the boat, causing alarms to scream and rocking them to starboard.

"Defensive emplacements," Isval said, down to ten seconds. "Going evasive. Target the dish, Faylin."

Green lines streaked in from the left and the right, bisecting the sky. Another slammed into the ship, but the escort boat's modest shields and hull held together.

"I can't hit anything with the ship moving like this!" Faylin said. "Hold it steady!"

Isval was going as slowly as she could so as not to overshoot the target, but the lack of speed cost them. She wheeled left and right, up and down, but the escort boat wasn't a fighter and evaded fire poorly.

Smoke started to fill the cabin. Alarms screamed, announcing failing systems.

"Take the stick," Isval said.

"We'll get hit!" Faylin said. "I'm half the pilot you are!"

"Do your best," Isval said calmly. She had to take out the dish. "You have the stick. I've got the guns . . . now."

Faylin spat a stream of expletives and took the stick. To her credit, she kept the ship moving, jerking the boat around more or less at random, nothing a seasoned pilot would do but effective enough to keep them from getting vaporized.

The comm rang on the movement's frequency. Nordon with an update, no doubt. Isval couldn't spare a moment to respond. Neither could Faylin, who white-knuckled the stick. Once they brought down the last dish, they wouldn't be able to respond until they were within line of sight.

The smoke blocked the targeting computer, so Isval went to manual and put the last dish in her sights. Faylin swung the ship left and right. Fire from the base crossed directly in front of the bow.

"Fire, Isval!" Faylin screamed.

They drew closer. Isval held her calm, then depressed the fire button. Plasma slammed into the dish, splintering it into a rain of metal shards and an expanding ball of flame.

"Get us clear," Isval said, exhaling, and Faylin pulled up and accelerated to full. They were out of range of blasterfire almost immediately. The sky filled the viewscreen as they climbed toward the outer atmosphere.

"No pursuit," Isval said, checking the scanner.

Faylin cursed softly, shaking her head.

Isval checked the comm, hoping Kallon was ready

with his hack. She tried her private comm just to make sure.

"Cham, do you copy?"

Nothing. She tried to open the channel on Nordon's frequency.

"Nordon, do you hear me?"

Again nothing, just dead air and bursts of static.

Faylin said, "Looks like it worked. They're jammed. Limited comm planetwide. Kallon is good."

"He is, but let's not get comfortable," Isval said. "Hardest part's yet to come."

She fed into the navcomp the coordinates of the location where they were supposed to meet Cham. They'd meet him there, then together head to the coordinates she'd received from Nordon. The hunt for Vader would soon be on.

The freighters completed a slow flyover, then turned and headed back toward the campsite. As they did, they accelerated and descended at a flat angle.

"I think perhaps they've seen what they wanted to see," the Emperor observed.

Noses down, the freighters began firing from blaster cannons mounted on the top and bottom of the ships, long red lines that exited the ship in superheated pulses. Trees one hundred meters from Vader and the Emperor exploded into splinters under the onslaught, and the lines cut a rapid path along the clearing toward them, putting a patchwork of smoking holes in the earth, closing in on Vader.

One with the Force, Vader held his ground and tensed for impact. Then he exploded into motion, his lightsaber humming as he spun it rapidly left and right, deflecting the powerful blaster shots off into the forest, shattering still more trees, destroying the tents, but sparing the communications array. The kinetic energy from the shots drove him backward, his boots putting furrows in the soft soil.

The Royal Guards, momentarily taken by surprise, recovered enough to plant blaster rifles against their shoulders. They fired at the freighters as the large ships sped over and past them, but the personal weapons did no harm to the shielded and armored ships.

"We should take cover in the trees, my lords!" said the captain.

"I think not," the Emperor said softly, watching the ships wheel about.

"They will come in lower this time," Vader said.

"I believe you're correct," the Emperor said. He removed his robe, took the elaborately crafted hilt of his lightsaber in hand, and ignited the blade.

Vader looked on in surprise. He seldom saw his Master so publicly demonstrate his power. And he understood what it meant, of course. There must be no survivors who could bear witness. Only the Royal Guards could be allowed to live—only they could be trusted never to reveal what they'd seen, or even to talk about it among themselves.

The freighters completed their turn and accelerated back toward the clearing, their engines screaming in the otherwise quiet air. The Royal Guards shifted position to stand before the Emperor, partially shielding him with their bodies, and fired as rapidly as they could at the oncoming ships. They hit the ships again and again, but the tiny bolts did no damage.

Vader sank more deeply into the Force. Beside him, he felt his Master's power gather. He reveled in the moment, in the combined pool of their collective, unadulterated might.

The freighters opened fire, writing thick lines of plasma onto the air. The shots churned the ground, destroyed trees, heated the air of the clearing; one slammed into the chest of a Royal Guard and vaporized all of him save for his helmet.

Lost in the Force, Vader anticipated the shots that would have hit him, saw the appropriate angles of impact and deflection, and used the rapid spinning of his lightsaber to turn first one, then a second, and then a third shot not into the tree line but back at the ships, the heat and energy of the blaster shots driving him backward, warming the hilt of his weapon, a heat he could feel even through his glove. His Master did the same with his lightsaber, the graceful arcs of its red line weaving a protective shield around him and turning the second ship's shots back at it. Both ships tried to turn out of the way of the redirected shots, one turning hard left, the other hard right, but they only exposed their underbellies and engines to the deflected bolts.

Engines exploded into flame and spit smoke. His Master raised his hands, forming one into a claw emitting jagged bolts of Force lightning that connected him for a moment to the ship. Vader imagined the interior of the craft lit up with the bolts of his Master's power, the pilots screaming and writhing in pain as the dark side seared their flesh. The Emperor clenched his other hand, taking a mental hold on the ship with the Force. Vader, too, lifted a hand and reached out with the Force toward the other ship.

Vader enmeshed himself in the Force, in his seething, ever-present wrath, and used it to take hold of the freighter and drive the entire ship toward the ground. He grunted with the effort, his respirator increasing his rate of breathing to account for the exertion.

The ship, its damaged engines unable to compensate enough against the downward push of Vader's power, went nose-down and streaked into the ground. Vader imagined the screams of the pilots as they watched the forest race toward them. The ship disappeared behind the tree line and exploded into a fireball that reached above the forest's canopy and caused the ground to vibrate. A cloud of black smoke rose into the darkening sky. A second boom sounded behind him, his Master having driven the second ship into the ground the same way. The forest went silent for a moment in the wake of the explosions, with only Vader's breathing to disrupt the quiet, before the howls and chirps and squeals of Ryloth's fauna returned. Vader, his Master, and the two Royal Guards stood untouched amid the smoking craters of blaster-fire that pockmarked the terrain. The Royal Guards gazed at Vader, at his Master, and Vader imagined the looks of wonder they must have under their helmets. They knew the Emperor had power, though Vader doubted they'd ever seen it so nakedly displayed.

"You," Vader said to the nearest.

"Sergeant Deez, my lord," said the guard, and bowed his head.

"Check the wreckage of those ships, Sergeant Deez. If there are any survivors, bring them to me."

"Yes, Lord Vader," Deez said. He slung his blaster rifle and sprinted off into the forest.

To the captain, Vader said, "Get on the communications array. Contact our forces."

His Master put a hand on Vader's armored shoulder, the power in his touch a palpable weight.

"It seems the traitors found us," the Emperor said. "It appears you were right, Lord Vader. We're being hunted."

"I offer again that I think we should move from this place," Vader said.

"I agree, my friend."

The captain of the Royal Guards, attempting to activate the communications array, called, "My lords, I can't get a signal. It doesn't make sense. The planet-wide network would have to be down for there to be dead air like this."

Vader strode over to the array, listened to the intermittent bursts of static, and understood the implications right away.

"It's jammed," he said. He turned to his Master. "More of them will be coming."

His Master chuckled. "It appears, then, that the hunt is just beginning."

Before long, Sergeant Deez returned and reported no survivors. Vader had expected as much. But he also expected he'd get another chance, and soon, to take one of the rebels alive.

The dull, repetitive beep of an alarm drove nails into Mors's temples. She opened her eyes and blinked in the antiseptic lighting of the shuttle's passenger cabin. Smoke and the acrid ionized stink of short circuits filled the air of the cabin. She lay on her back on the metal deck, staring up at a recessed light that blurred in and out of focus. Her muddled thoughts started to coalesce, to arrange themselves in an order that made sense of her surroundings.

Her ship had been shot at—no, shot *down*—and it had lost life support and the cabin had been filling with smoke and . . .

What was that damn alarm? How was she not dead? And where was Breehld?

"Breehld?" she said, and saying the word aloud made her head pound. She recognized it as the after-effect of partial hypoxia; recognized, too, that her ability to understand what had happened meant that she was coming back from it. She took stock of her body, thought nothing was broken, so she used her arm to lift herself from the deck. Her aged, over-weight frame ached, but she managed to sit upright. She blinked away a wave of dizziness.

Twilight leaked in through one of the viewports. She stood, wincing at the pain the effort caused her, moved to the viewport, and looked out on the beige, rocky terrain of Ryloth. Tors large and small rose from the cracked ground, and the ubiquitous wind whipped clouds of dry soil into the air.

Where on the planet was she? She didn't know the terrain well enough to even guess.

She activated her comlink. "Breehld?"

No response.

Who had shot them down? Breehld had said it was an Imperial escort. But why had it targeted Mors's shuttle? She started to change her comm frequency to hail Belkor but hesitated.

Belkor had sent her around the planet to help with rescuing someone.

Not someone. VIPs. Darth Vader and the Emperor.

She cursed, a wave of anxiety chasing away some of the bleariness.

What had happened to them? Had they survived the *Perilous*'s destruction? She had no idea what was going on. The autopilot must have engaged somehow as the shuttle descended, but she didn't even know how long she'd been unconscious.

Once more she reached to activate her comlink to hail Belkor—a habit. She always called Belkor when she had an issue, any issue. But again she hesitated.

What was making that damn beeping sound?

She looked around, finally traced the sound to a computer terminal stuck on reset. She powered it down and the beeping, mercifully, stopped. She stood there a moment, staring at her reflection in the darkened screen of the computer; she was bleeding from a head wound in her forehead, and her left eye was swollen. She feared she'd dislocated a shoulder, but after testing it realized that she must have just slammed into something during the descent. She'd probably hit something when she'd fallen. She tried again to piece together events.

As soon as her ship had reached the *Perilous*'s debris field, she'd been attacked. Of all the ships up there, hers had been targeted—and by an Imperial escort, no less. Obviously the escort ship had been hijacked by traitors, but . . .

Could Belkor have been involved?

She thought it unlikely, but then . . . was it really?

The Free Ryloth movement had, for years, managed to stay ahead of Belkor. Or had it?

The moment Darth Vader and the Emperor appeared in Ryloth's system, a visit that was not public knowledge, they were attacked by forces associated with the movement, forces that would have had to have been staged into position, given the sophistication and scale of the attack.

And then Mors herself was diverted to rescue operations—to prevent her from taking command from Belkor planetside?—and was immediately attacked.

She thought back on recent months, even years, recalling the successes of the Free Ryloth movement. Belkor had always had an explanation, something plausible. But now Mors was thinking of the kind of elaborate operation it must have taken to bring down an Imperial Star Destroyer, and the conviction started to come together in her mind. There was only one plausible explanation.

The movement had to have had Imperial help—*highly placed* Imperial help.

Belkor. Everything circled back to Belkor.

Mors cursed and staggered through the passenger compartment toward the cockpit. She opened the door to find Breehld slumped in his seat, his head hanging at an odd angle, his tongue lolling, his neck obviously broken. He'd probably died after the ship had first taken fire.

The man had served her for years. "Sorry, Breehld," Mors said.

She accessed the main computer and checked the ship's logs and status. The autopilot had, indeed, engaged at some point when the ship's power had come back on. Breehld had been unconscious or dead by then, of course. The ship had set down near Ryloth's equator. The shuttle had taken some damage from the firefight but was mostly intact, and certainly flyable.

It had been a while since Mors had flown anything herself, but she figured she could manage a shuttle. She unstrapped Breehld, took him under the armpits, and dragged him into the passenger compartment. Even that small effort left her gasping and covered in a sheen of sweat. She'd let herself go, she realized. She'd let everything go. And it had cost her.

Cursing her indolence, she laid Breehld on the deck with as much dignity as possible and returned to the cockpit. She sat in the pilot's seat, fired up the engines, and realized all of a sudden that she didn't know where to go. She certainly couldn't return to the communication center, at least not immediately, not given her suspicions about Belkor.

She checked the navcomp for nearby Imperial bases. She should've known which ones were nearby without needing the comp, but she'd been so disengaged from her duties in recent years that she had only a passing familiarity with planetary Imperial resources.

The Equatorial Communications Hub was closest, and Steen Borkas commanded there.

"Good," Mors muttered. She knew she could trust Steen. They'd served together as lieutenants. The man bled Imperial Gray. If Belkor was plotting, Steen would not be part of it. She activated the ship's communicator and hailed the hub.

No response, just bursts of static and dead air. Thinking something must have caused the comm system to malfunction, Mors ran a system check. It showed nothing wrong. She frowned. She could think of only a couple of reasons why an operational communications systems offered only dead air, and neither of them was good. Anxiety put a pit in her stomach. For a fleeting, hopefully foolish moment, she wondered if Belkor had arranged a coup and taken over the whole planet after killing Vader and the Emperor.

But that was absurd.

Wasn't it?

She told herself it was, but she needed to find out what exactly was going on. She engaged the engines and watched the planet's surface fall away beneath her. She felt a strange sense of being disembodied as the ship gained altitude and realized it was because she hadn't experienced flight from the cockpit in years. She soon had her bearings, however. The navcomp handled the headings, and she managed to fly with reasonable competence.

About fifty kilometers away from the communications hub, she saw the rising smoke, dark columns of black clouds that climbed from the terrain to diffuse into the darkening sky. She feared the entire base had been destroyed, but as she flew closer she saw that the communications dishes had taken most of the damage. The dead air on the comm suddenly made sense.

"What in the—"

All at once her computer blared an alarm, indicating that the hub's guns had a target-lock on her ship. Her comm line crackled to life and a voice came over it, the audio dulled and hollow due to the line-of-sight communication.

"Identify yourself, shuttle. And do not approach any closer."

Mors fumbled with the controls, trying to power down the engines while activating the comm.

"I'm not . . . I'm . . . This is Moff Delian Mors."

A pause, then a familiar voice spoke. "I'll need a visual, or I'll shoot you out of the sky," Steen Borkas said.

"Say again?" Mors said.

"A visual, ma'am. Now. Or I'll be forced to fire."

"What?"

"Now, please," Borkas said tightly.

Mors eyed the communications panel, looking for the button that would open a visual connection. Her unfamiliarity with the controls cost her time, the target-lock alarm screeching at her all the while.

"Hold on," she said. "Hold on. There, got it."

A visual came up on her viewscreen and Steen Borkas's thin, acne-scarred face filled most of it. Frantic activity went on behind Steen, junior officers and technicians moving rapidly among the comp stations. Borkas's eyes—set a bit too close together—widened when he saw Mors.

"Forgive me, Moff." He saluted briskly, his thin face reddening. "We . . . had reason to be skeptical. Where's your pilot, ma'am?"

"It's just me," Mors said. "Brief me when I land. Give me a landing pad."

"Yes, ma'am."

Mors set the shuttle down, unstrapped, and hurried to the gangplank. Borkas, two lieutenants, and a squad of stormtroopers awaited her outside. Borkas remained the rod-thin, bald, clean-shaven man he'd always been. As Mors debarked, the entourage saluted and Mors returned it as crisply as her wounded shoulder allowed.

"I need a medic for the Moff," Borkas ordered a lieutenant.

"Later," Mors said. "First we need to talk."

The landing pads were elevated ten meters relative to the rest of the base, so she could see the devastation clearly. Fires burned in several places. The air smelled of smoke and burning plastic. Small maintenance ships and fire suppression droids flew around the base, while teams of technicians and maintenance droids rolled or sprinted from here to there. Shouted orders carried through the still air. The remains of the communications dishes—ordinarily among the largest structures on the base—lay toppled, their bases smoking mountains of jagged metal crowned with the ruins of the huge concentric bowls.

"We're working on getting the network back up," Borkas said. "Dish Three is the least damaged. We're all-hands to get it partially operational."

"Good," Mors said, unable to stop staring at the destruction. Two score technicians and a dozen maintenance droids worked on what must have been Dish 3. Several maintenance ships hovered above, dropping cables that workmen were preparing to attach to the outer support ring of the dish. "How long?"

"Twelve hours, ma'am. Give or take. We got word of an incoming escort ship carrying Imperial VIPs."

Mors tensed, turned to face her old friend. "Word from whom?"

Borkas's brow furrowed. "The communication center. Or so we thought. Couldn't have been, though. The rebels must have hacked the communications system. Credentials seemed good, but . . . obviously they were not. As soon as we dropped our shields, that boat opened up. Took less than a minute to do all this."

"Less than a minute," Mors echoed stupidly, thinking of Belkor, of treachery.

Borkas drew himself up. "I'm sorry, ma'am. Once this is over, I will obviously offer my resignation."

Mors shook her head. "Absolutely not."

"Ma'am . . ."

"I won't hear of it, Steen," Mors said. "This isn't your fault."

Mors knew quite well whose fault it was, though she didn't say it: Hers. Belkor's. She continued, "I'm going to need every trusted worker I can find to get the situation back under control."

Borkas inclined his head in gratitude. "What is the situation, ma'am? We're in an informational vacuum here."

"Is there somewhere private we can talk?" Mors asked.

"Of course. Follow me."

"Before that, there's a body aboard my shuttle," Mors said. "A good man. See to him."

Steen ordered a couple of lieutenants to see to Breehld, then the two of them headed off. As they walked, Mors said, "It's good to see you, Steen."

"You as well, ma'am," said Borkas. "Wish the circumstances were better."

Years earlier, Mors had decided to delegate authority over Imperial operations to Belkor rather than Steen. Belkor had seemed more manageable, less a challenge to Mors's authority. She had regretted that decision a few times since, but never more than today.

They took a transport to the main building, a three-story, glass-walled hexagonal building situated in the center of the base. Mors rehearsed what she would say as they flew. Once they set down, Borkas led her through lifts and halls that buzzed with activity and finally into a private conference room. Mors lost track of the number of salutes she received. Steen ran a tight ship.

"Bring the Moff and myself some caf and something to eat," Borkas called out to someone in the hall.

"Pain reliever, too," Mors said, wincing at the aches in her shoulder, her head.

She sank into one of the cushioned chairs that surrounded the large conference table, suddenly exhausted. She exhaled and tapped her fingers on the table.

"So," Borkas said, turning and taking a seat as well. "We have an Imperial traitor."

Mors looked up sharply, eyebrows raised, feeling her face warm. "What? How did—"

A knock on the door announced the arrival of the meds, the caf, and the food. Borkas poured them each a caf, but Mors couldn't begin to imagine putting something in her unstable stomach other than the meds, which she swallowed right away.

The moment the junior officer left, Borkas continued: "How do I know that? It's not that hard to put together, ma'am. The *Perilous* is ambushed, the communications hub is attacked by an Imperial ship after a questionable order from the communications center. It *was* from the communications center, wasn't it, ma'am? Not a hack?"

"It wasn't a hack," Mors said.

"All of that took a lot of coordination," Borkas said. "A lot of looking the other way by Imperial authorities, if not outright collaboration. Is it a coup?"

Mors shook her head and stared into her cup.

"I can't say for sure," she said. She could not make eye contact with Borkas. "I've been . . . absent, Steen."

"Yes," Borkas said. "Things changed after you lost Murra. When was that, four years ago now?"

Mors nodded. She hadn't heard anyone else say her wife's name in a long time. She'd died in a transport accident on Coruscant. A fluke, a system malfunction had flown her and ten other civilians into the side of a building. For months afterward Mors had imagined what Murra must have felt as the transport accelerated. Terror? Resignation? The loss had eroded her, then broken her.

"Things didn't change," she said. "I did."

After Murra had died, she'd found herself purposeless and content in her purposelessness, just drifting. She'd turned hedonistic, grown lazy. Worse, she'd lost her ability or desire to discern a quality commander from a flatterer. So she'd promoted Belkor and those like him, while ignoring people like Steen Borkas. And now she'd lost a Star Destroyer, the Emperor, Lord Vader, and maybe a planet.

"I overlooked you, Steen. I'm sorry."

Steen's thin lips formed a still-thinner smile. "I don't feel unfairly treated, ma'am."

Mors knew it was a lie, but she took the words in the spirit they were offered. "Can I rely on you now, Steen? Despite everything?"

"As ever, ma'am."

Mors nodded and laid things out. "Belkor Dray is the traitor. I'm almost certain."

Borkas tensed as he sipped his caf. The contempt

in his eyes was more eloquent and cutting than any insult he might have hurled at Belkor.

"And," Mors went on, but she hesitated a moment before her dry mouth could utter the words. "Darth Vader and the Emperor were aboard the *Perilous*."

Borkas stared at her, looking dumbfounded. His hand started to tremble, sending caf over the cup's rim. He set it down on the table. "Were they . . . aboard when it exploded?"

Mors shook her head. "I don't know. My shuttle was diverted to assist in the rescue of VIPs. Could've been referring to them, but the diversion presumably came from Belkor and could have simply been a way to have me killed by the rebels while involved in rescue operations. We were attacked the moment we came within range."

"They had your ship ident," Borkas said.

"Yes," Mors agreed. "Which means that if Vader and the Emperor got off the *Perilous*, they had their ident, too."

Borkas looked up sharply. "Wait. That's it."

"What's it?"

"The intercept."

"I'm not following," Mors said.

Borkas spoke rapidly. "During the attack on the hub, we intercepted a communication to the shuttle on an open channel. Took us a while to decrypt it, and we still only got a partial. But it mentioned Vader. I assumed it was code or nonsense or . . ."

Mors was half out of her seat. "Mentioned him how?"

Borkas rose and started pacing, his eyes on the floor. "Coordinates, ma'am. If Vader and the Emperor escaped in a ship and it went down, then the rebels know where they landed. Or crashed."

Mors was standing now, too. "But so do we! What

do you have here, Borkas? In terms of combat-capable crew? Vehicles? I saw the stormtroopers. Anyone else? I need to get to those coordinates."

Borkas was nodding, warming to Mors's still-unspoken idea. "We have maintenance vehicles and transports, nothing armed. As for personnel, I've got mostly techs and a handful of untested officers. All in, I've got the twenty stormtroopers and maybe ten more bodies familiar enough with a blaster to serve. Eleven, counting me."

"That'll have to do," Mors said, placing her finger-tips on the tabletop. "But you're not coming, Steen."

"Ma'am—"

"Major, you're going to get the communications net back up, and when you do, you're going to reach out to officers we can trust. Only the ones we know are incapable of treachery. And you're going to have them round up every stormtrooper on Ryloth and bring them all to me. We can't count on anyone else. Whatever is going on here—a coup, an assassination attempt, both—hinges on killing me, the Emperor, and Vader. I'm going to make sure none of that happens. And then I'm going to put an end to Belkor and the Free Ryloth movement. They think today is their finest hour. I intend to make it their last."

Steen shook his head, his face flushed. "Ma'am, I've got someone I can leave in charge here. I'd rather accompany you. I don't have to tell him anything. He can supervise the repairs as well as me."

Mors looked Steen in the face, saw the desire there to do something, anything, and understood it quite well. "Very well, Steen. You're with me. One of your transports and my shuttle can carry the troops. Let's get everyone armed as quickly as possible and then move out."

"Yes, ma'am," Borkas said, and saluted.

CHAPTER THIRTEEN

Isval considered skipping the planned rendezvous with Cham and heading directly to the coordinates she'd received from Nordon, but with communications down, Cham wouldn't know how to find her. He didn't have those coordinates yet.

Faylin must have picked up on her tension. "You all right?" she asked.

"Fine," Isval said, shifting in her seat. "Just twitchy to get after Vader."

"We'll be at the rendezvous point shortly," Faylin said, checking the coordinates.

Below and before them, one of Ryloth's lush equatorial forests darkened the landscape. Most of the planet was dry and devoid of thick vegetation, but wind patterns and other meteorological phenomena that Isval didn't understand drew moisture to the equatorial region, giving Ryloth a belt of verdure. She rarely saw it up close, and now she couldn't stop staring down at the carpet of the forest's canopy. The last of the day's sunlight shaded it all in red.

"Keep an active scan," she said to Faylin. "Cham's never late."

Right on time, the scanner pinged a contact. Isval checked the details and saw it was Cham's transport. They'd need to be closer before she could hail him. Kallon's jamming signal was doing its work well. She found she was leaning forward in her seat, trying to spy Cham's ship. Movement in the distance caught her eye: the ship. At visual distance, their transmitters would cut through Kallon's jamming.

"Cham, do you copy?"

"Isval," he returned, and she heard the relief in his voice. "Put down in that clearing there. You see it?"

"Let's not waste the time, Cham. Nordon contacted me when we were attacking the communications hub. He had eyes on a downed Imperial shuttle. I have the coordinates."

She transmitted them to Cham's ship.

"Good," Cham said. "But I still want you to set down. I've got thirty of our people aboard—Goll and his troops. I want half of them on your ship."

Goll and his fighters were one of the strike teams the movement used when they needed to hit something and hit it hard. Pok's team had been the same way, until Pok had run into Vader.

"Good thought," she told him. No reason to put all their assets on one ship. To Faylin, she said, "You want to put us down?"

Faylin smiled and shook her head. "I've flown enough for today."

Isval set the escort boat down in a wide clearing, and Cham landed his converted transport. Isval opened the passenger compartment door on the escort and debarked. The passenger bay door on Cham's ship opened, and Goll and half his troops jogged out toward Isval's ship, all of them heavily laden with blasters and grenades. The men and women nodded at Isval as they passed—all but Goll, who stopped before her. He stood taller than any other Twi'lek she had ever met. Muscles bulged under his deep-green skin.

"It's good to see you, Isval. That was good work today."

"Good to see you, too, Goll. And the day's not done yet. Get your people aboard. We're leaving in five minutes."

"Got it," he said, and moved past her. "Seated and strapped in, ladies and gentlemen," he said to his team. "We're going right back up."

"Goll," Isval called, and the big Twi'lek turned. "Crost, Drim, and Eshgo are aboard. They . . . need to come off."

Goll's features fell and he nodded. He looked around the clearing. "This is good soil. We'll handle it, Isval."

While Goll pulled a few of his troops onto burial duty, Cham emerged from his ship, still wearing his headset, and the sight of him stalled her. He saw her and stopped, too, just for a moment, then covered the distance between them rapidly. For a moment Isval thought he might try to embrace her, and she didn't know how she felt about the warm rush the thought elicited.

But he merely took her by the shoulders and looked into her eyes, both of them saying nothing, yet—with their quiet—saying much. As ever, they walked up to the line but neither crossed. They couldn't do what they had to do for the movement if their relationship was anything more than it was.

Just another casualty of the conflict, Isval supposed.

"It's good to see you," he said, and his skin darkened.

She felt her skin darken in response. "And you, Cham."

"For a while I wasn't sure I would," he said. "And the thought didn't please me."

"I'm hard to get rid of," she said awkwardly.

He smiled, but she saw the openness of his expression disappear as he closed down his emotions. She took the cue and did the same, leaving everything unspoken.

"A Star Destroyer and an Imperial base in the span of hours?" he commented. "That has to be some kind of record. And damn good work."

His praise always pleased her. "We're not done yet, though. Now we get Vader and the Emperor."

"Now we get them," Cham agreed. "Engines are still hot. Let's get moving." He looked past her at Goll and his troops, rapidly digging graves. Pain animated his eyes. "Peaceful sleep, my friends."

When they'd interred their fallen, they boarded their respective ships and lifted off, flying low over the trees. Cham's transport ran ahead, with Isval's escort boat behind and slightly to starboard. They ran dark, no lights.

"Run every scan this boat has," Isval said to Faylin. "And keep your eyes sharp."

"Too dark to see anything," Faylin answered.

"Eyes sharp anyway," Isval snapped.

"Foliage is thick," Cham said over the comlink. "It's interfering with scans."

"A lot of life down there," Faylin said, checking on the infrared.

Clearings broke up the dense vegetation as they closed on the coordinates.

"Got something. Metal, large," Faylin said, and looked over at Isval. "Wreckage."

"You getting that, Cham?" Isval asked.

"I got it. These aren't the coordinates we were

given, but they're not too far out of the way. And there's no sign of Nordon."

"No," Isval said, and both of them knew what Cham meant. Nordon had run into Vader.

"We should check it out," Cham said.

"Agreed," she said. "Forest is too thick to tell anything from the air. We'll have to set down and go in on foot. I'll find somewhere to set down."

Faylin located a clearing on the scan, and Isval set the boat down. She kept the engines hot. She hailed Cham as he set down his transport near the escort boat.

"We should send the ships ahead to Nordon's coordinates," she suggested. "Just in case."

"Was thinking the same thing," he answered. "They can stagger the ships so we have a relay. Keep communication open between us."

"Right," Isval said.

Faylin would fly halfway to the coordinates Nordon had given them and hover there. Kallon would fly Cham's transport to the coordinates. He'd be close enough to have communications with Faylin, and she'd be close enough to have communications back to Cham and Isval.

"You get any sign of Nordon, you let us know right away," Isval told Faylin. "And don't worry about flying. The sim squared you away. You'll be fine."

"Right and right," Faylin answered weakly.

Isval debarked with Goll and the members of his team who had joined him on her ship, met Cham in the clearing, and headed out in the direction of the wreckage, four kilometers into the forest. The wind had picked up and now howled through the trees, causing a continuous rustle. The humid air smelled of loam and conifers. Howls, screeches, and growls rose above the sound of the wind to punctuate the darkness. Cham and Isval led, and Goll dispatched his crew into their usual scouting pattern to the left, right, and rear. The ships lifted off and darted away into the night.

"Heard all kinds of stories about the equatorial forests," Cham said to her.

"Me, too," she said.

"Lylek hordes, huge carnivorous primates, killer plants, you name it. But Vader's the worst thing we're going to find out here," he said.

She nodded.

Before long Faylin's voice came over the comlink. "I'm on station."

"Continuing on to Nordon's coordinates," Kallon said. "I'll be out of reach of all but Faylin in moments."

"Let us know what you see," Cham said.

Cham, Isval, and Goll and his team picked their way through the cages of exposed tree roots and the towering columns of tree trunks. The amount of movement in the canopy far above them caused a steady rain of sticks, leaves, and other debris.

Isval felt exposed, watched. The forest quieted as they closed on the wrecked ship. Goll pulled his men back in close. The group fell silent as they neared the site.

"You and two more with Isval and me," Cham said to Goll, who selected two of his team and ordered the rest to remain behind for support.

Cham and Isval quietly advanced the final two hundred meters to the crash site, weapons drawn. They could smell the stink of burned plastic as they approached, and they could see that a dozen or so trees had been sheared in half by a falling ship, the treetops crashing to the forest floor. Cham and Isval halted at the edge of the tree line.

The wreckage of a ship lay strewn about the clearing and nearby forest, mixed with tons of soil and trees displaced by the impact. Much of it still smoked, and the central fuselage was mostly intact.

Isval cursed. The ship wasn't Imperial. It was what she and Cham had feared: one of the movement's modified freighters. From the dispersal of the ship's wreckage, survivors seemed unlikely. She checked for markings, saw a partial number on part of the fuselage. It was enough.

"Nordon's ship," she said. "Cham?"

Cham was staring at the wreckage, a stricken look on his face. She took him by the arm.

"Cham, what's wrong with you?"

He turned to face her, his lekku twitching once, twice, and the mask came up. "Nothing. I'm fine. That's Nordon's ship."

"How'd it get brought down?" she asked, but knew the answer as soon as she asked the question.

"Vader," Cham said.

Isval nodded. Somehow Vader had done it. He'd single-handedly captured Pok's ship and killed everyone aboard, run through a storm of her blasterfire, somehow choked her unconscious from the cockpit of another ship, and now brought down an armed freighter.

"Can we do this?" she asked, her voice soft, the words escaping her before she could rein them in.

If Cham had heard her, he gave no sign. "We get their bodies," he said. "Goll."

"Understood," the huge Twi'lek said, gesturing to two of his men to search the wreckage.

Faylin's voice came over the comlink. "Kallon is at the coordinates. Scans show a downed ship, damaged but intact. It's an Imperial shuttle."

"Do not investigate," Cham ordered. "Get back here, both of you."

"Copy that," Faylin said.

Goll's team hadn't gone ten paces out of the tree line before a form crept out from behind the smoking fuselage, the arm of a Twi'lek in its jaws. The creature would have stood taller than a human or a Twi'lek, but its posture was hunched. Its insectoid-looking legs moved in a rapid, herky-jerky fashion, and its thin arms ended in curved claws as large as meat hooks. A humped, spiked carapace bulged on its back, and its misshapen head was mostly tooth-filled mouth and overlarge eyes.

The men froze. Isval and Cham cursed as one, lifting their weapons to take aim.

"Gutkurr," Cham whispered, and Isval nodded.

"Ease back," she said to Goll's two men, and they started to slowly walk backward.

On Ryloth, only lyleks were more dangerous than the predatory gutkurrs. Isval had seen blaster shots bounce off a gutkurr's hide more than once.

"Slow," Cham said to the men. "Slow and quiet."

Another gutkurr darted out of the wreckage, took the other end of the arm in its jaws, and tried to pull the prize away from its fellow, both of them hissing and growling. A third, fourth, and fifth emerged from the wreckage, and more growls and hisses from within suggested the presence of more gutkurrs, many more.

"We are leaving," Cham said softly. "Quietly now."

Isval hated leaving Nordon's body to the gutkurrs, but there was nothing for it. She wished him a peaceful sleep.

The wind picked up, blowing at their back, showering them in needles and leaves and twigs. Isval cursed again, knowing what it meant.

As one, the gutkurrs whirled around to face in their direction, rising up on their legs, fanged mouths open as if tasting the wind.

"If they have our scent," Cham said, "we use suppressing fire and retreat to the clearing. A retreat, not a rout."

The gutkurrs lowered themselves back into a crouch, and several of them uttered a sound like a harsh bark. One of them turned a circle in excitement. Four more bounded out of the wreckage, including the largest of the pack, a female. She thumped into the smaller gutkurrs near her, asserting dominance, and growled loudly. The pack encircled her, hissing excitedly. She reared up to her full height, mouth open.

"She's got us," Isval whispered.

"Maybe not," Cham said, but the words lacked conviction.

Goll's team reached the tree line.

The pack leader fell back into a hunched crouch, roared, and bounded toward them. The entire pack fell in behind her, their claws throwing up divots of dirt.

Cham and Isval fired their blasters, and Goll's team followed their lead. Red lines slammed into the leading gutkurrs, sending them tumbling to the ground. Their fellows leapt over them or thudded into them, but those that were shot rolled back onto their feet and continued to run.

"Back to the clearing!" Cham ordered. "Run, but don't get separated!"

They turned and sprinted back through the forest, turning every few moments to fire into the pack. The gutkurrs hissed and roared, crashing through the deadwood and underbrush in their eagerness to feed. In moments Isval, Cham, and the rest reached the support team they'd left behind them. Goll shouted at them.

"Gutkurrs! Suppressing fire and an organized retreat back to the clearing!"

A grenade explosion to the right splintered a tree and sent pieces of a gutkurr flying into the air.

Isval called Faylin over the comlink. "Faylin, we need you back at the clearing right now, and set down with the doors open!"

"What? What's happening down there? Are you under attack?"

"Yes," Isval said. "Hurry!"

"On my way!"

Isval vaulted over roots, ducked under tree limbs. She and Cham and three of Goll's people turned, took position at the base of a large tree, and fired back into the onrushing pack. Shots bounced off the creatures' hides, but the impact, at least, sent them careening backward.

"They're spreading out!" Goll shouted, firing left. "Trying to encircle us. Grenades!"

More explosions to the right and left, angry hisses from the gutkurrs.

"Keep moving!" Isval said, standing and running back in the direction of the clearing. "Just keep moving!"

From the right, a gutkurr leapt high over a fallen tree and landed on the back of one of Goll's people. She rolled over, shouting, and tried to bring her blaster rifle to bear, but too slowly. The gutkurr's hooked claws tore through her clothes and unzipped her abdomen, spilling gore. Isval cursed and shot it through the head once, twice, and it collapsed atop its victim, dead.

"Gotta leave her," Cham said, pulling at Isval's arm.

She backed off, firing at anything moving in the trees, then turned and ran.

"ETA, Faylin?" Isval called over the comlink.

"Thirty seconds!"

"There's too many of them!" one of Goll's crew shouted.

From her right, Isval heard someone scream in pain. Blaster shots rang out, along with curses, growls, and hisses.

"Keep firing and keep moving!" Cham yelled, his blaster rifle painting the air with lines of energy.

Above, Isval heard the hum of the escort boat as it flew low over the trees.

"Can you see us on scan?" Isval called to Faylin. She spotted a gutkurr in the underbrush and fired a series of shots at it, but she couldn't tell if she'd hit it.

"Yes! What are those things? There're dozens of them!"

"Gutkurrs, a whole pack," Isval said, and fired into the trees. She hit a gutkurr in the side and sent it sprawling. The pack had spread out and slowed their pursuit, forming an arc. She had no doubt some of them were circling wide to get behind them and cut off their retreat. "Can you put down some fire?"

"Fire? But I'm not—"

"You can do it, Faylin! We need it! Our blasters aren't getting it done!"

"All right, got it."

"Hold the line here!" Cham shouted to the team. "Incoming fire. Close ranks! Close ranks!"

Cham, Isval, Goll, and his surviving people clustered at the top of a low rise, behind a tree, everyone gasping. They took aim at anything that moved, and filled the forest with fire. Gutkurrs hissed and growled out in the darkness.

Blasterfire from the escort boat rained out of the

sky, thick bolts of plasma that tore through the trees and slammed into the ground. Trees splintered, cracked, and toppled. Clouds of soil exploded around them. Gutkurrs screamed and howled. Acrid smoke filled the air.

"Hold fire, Faylin!" Cham ordered. "We're moving . . . now."

The group stood, turned, and sprinted for the clearing, leaping over roots and deadwood. The gutkurrs must have seen them, for they roared and shrieked and bounded through the trees. One of Goll's men stumbled and fell in front of Isval. She heaved him up by his armpits, fired blindly back over her shoulder, and they ran on together.

"The boat's blasters dispersed the pack, but they're still coming after you," Faylin said over the comlink. "Circling wide on both sides. Hurry!"

"Get to the clearing, Faylin," Isval ordered. To the rest of the group, she shouted, "Run!"

They didn't bother firing anymore. They just ran as fast as they could, the sound of the pursuing gutkurrs hard on their heels. The boat buzzed overhead, audible through the forest canopy, and set down not far ahead. Isval caught movement out of her peripheral vision from time to time, and she thought the trees would never end.

But then they did, opening into the clearing. Faylin already had the passenger compartment doors open.

"Move! Move!" Cham said, waving everyone past. Isval fell in with him and Goll, and the three of them blanketed the tree line with blasterfire. She couldn't tell if they hit anything.

"Let's go!" Cham said, and they turned and ran.

The moment they did, they saw several gutkurrs break from the trees to their left, pelting over the clearing toward the rest of the group, which hadn't yet reached the ship. Isval took aim with both blasters as she ran. She fired once, twice, hitting the two leading creatures in the sides of their heads, causing both to tumble to the ground, dead. Cham and Goll sprayed the last two with so much blasterfire that it blackened their carapaces and knocked them down and five meters back.

Gutkurrs broke from the tree line behind and to the right. The rest of Goll's crew took position just outside the ship's open door and fired in teams at the creatures, but that didn't stop them. They dashed across the clearing, a dozen or more, closing on the ship. Isval, Goll, and Cham ran, Cham shouting, "Get aboard! Get aboard!"

Goll's people ceased firing and ran up the gangplank and into the compartment, Isval, Cham, and Goll just behind. The moment they were inside, Isval slammed her hand on the button to close the door. It started to rise . . . and just then two gutkurrs grabbed it and tried to scramble inside. Cham and Goll shared a look, raised their weapons as one, and fired. The blaster shots drove both creatures off the ramp, and the hatch closed fully. Goll did a quick head count and took stock of injuries.

"Four lost," he said softly to Cham. "The rest are good."

Cham's expression fell for a moment, but only Isval could have noticed. He nodded and put a hand on Goll's shoulder. After Goll moved back to debrief his surviving crew, Cham said to Faylin over the comlink, "Get us to Nordon's coordinates."

"On the way," Faylin said. "Everything all right back there?"

Cham shook his head but said, "As well as can be."

Isval stepped to Cham's side. She almost touched

him but held back. "What is it? And don't you dare tell me nothing is wrong."

He didn't look at her, but he answered in a quiet monotone. "Been a long day, is all."

"A lie," she said. "Tell me."

"You really want to know?"

She wasn't sure she did, but she nodded anyway.

"We've thrown everything we had at this," he said. "In one day, I've spent almost the entirety of the resources I built up over years."

She let her voice fall to an angry whisper. "We've lost less than thirty of our people. And we brought down a Star Destroyer. That's not a bad trade."

He looked at her then, and his eyes were pained. "Thirty is a lot, Isval."

She recoiled at the implication of her own words. "I know. Of course it is. I know."

"I know you know," he said. "But it's not just that. Almost every ship we had is gone. And when the Empire does a post-action analysis of today, they'll bring everything to bear—they'll have to. They'll track down our bases and they'll track us down. We'll have to disperse after today, at least most of us. That's best case."

She was shaking her head. "Why didn't you say this before? We could have—"

"We could've what? Done nothing? Let this opportunity pass?"

Isval's stomach hollowed out. "No, but . . . I didn't realize . . ."

"You didn't realize there'd be nothing left afterward? I know. I'm not sure I did, either, but I've been thinking about it since the *Perilous* went down and it's becoming clear to me now. It's a hard truth, but we might as well square up to it. After today, the movement as it exists is done."

She still refused to believe it. "No, wait. Listen, the Empire's not good enough to track our bases or us. We've dodged them for years."

"We've dodged them with Belkor as our puppet. He's done after this. We both know that."

Isval didn't deny it. Belkor had perhaps convinced himself that he could survive the day's events, but Isval knew better. No story Belkor could craft would keep him away from Imperial security investigators.

"We can rebuild the movement," she said. "The same way we built it in the first place."

He smiled, and it looked forced. "I don't have it in me, Isval."

The hole in her stomach grew larger. "There is no movement without you," she whispered.

He shook his head. "It's bigger than me. And if we start a galaxy-wide rebellion, Ryloth will have a chance at freedom. No, the movement's an idea, not a person."

She knew it wasn't. She knew Ryloth needed him. She knew she needed him.

"You're wrong," she said.

"I'm right, and the fight will go on, Isval, but after this it'll have to fall to someone else to lead." He grimaced. "I'll do what I can even after today, but we don't have enough tools left to do much more than what we've done. We'll start the fire by killing Vader and the Emperor. It's just that someone else is going to have to fan the flames and burn the Empire down."

"Closing in," Faylin said over the comlink.

Vader, the Emperor, and the two surviving Royal Guards put kilometers behind them as night ate the last of the day. The darkness deepened as they picked their way through the uneven ground, the tangle of roots, the columns of tree trunks. The darkness seemed to amplify sound, isolate it, echo it back until Vader's breathing filled the forest. The moons hadn't risen and it would be hours before they did. The forest canopy hid the meager light of the stars, leaving them in a sea of ink. Vader's armor allowed him to see in infrared and several other spectrums, and the Royal Guards' armor, too, could compensate for low light, but the Emperor . . .

Vader spared a glance to his left, at his Master, who walked confidently through the darkness.

The Emperor saw clearly, saw everything, as ever.

Creatures large and small moved through the foliage at the edge of Vader's vision, slinking, crawling, loping. Animals prowled the forest's canopy high above, predators hunting prey. From time to time, the abortive squeal of something dying punctuated the quiet.

"It's instructive, isn't it, this place?" his Master asked.

"It is unforgiving of weakness," Vader said.

"It is," his Master said. "The weak are found out and killed by the strong."

"As it must be," Vader said.

"As it must be, indeed," his Master echoed.

"But sometimes the strong mistake their strength," Vader dared to add. "And so demonstrate weakness."

"Do they?" his Master commented, and Vader said nothing more.

Long into the hours of night Vader walked beside his Master, silent but for the respirator. He would stop, or not, as his Master commanded. Before long, the breathing of the guardsmen sounded not unlike Vader's. They were taxed, but still his Master pressed on. Eventually his Master stopped and held up a hand.

"You can rest here for a time, Captain. But not long. We will press on again soon."

"Thank you, my Emperor," said the captain, and he and Deez set about making a hurried camp. In moments they had a small chem fire going. Vader stood near it, staring down into the flames. His Master sat cross-legged in a pose of meditation. Tension hung between Vader and his Master, tension whose provenance Vader could not quite place.

"Master?"

"Do you think treachery begins in the deed, my friend?"

"No. It begins in the thoughts."

His Master showed teeth: perhaps a smile, perhaps a snarl. "And yet we can't know the thoughts of another, especially those of a traitor, who guards his thoughts closely so as not to reveal his treachery. And so we must draw out the thoughts to have them manifest in deeds, and thus reveal the truth. Do you agree?"

Vader stared into the flames. "I hear nothing with which to disagree."

Again the smile or snarl from his Master. "You were a traitor, were you not, Lord Vader?"

Vader's breathing caught on the hook of sudden anger. "What did you say?"

"To the Jedi. To Padmé. To Obi-Wan. To all those you loved."

His Master turned to look at him, his eyes reflecting the flames.

Vader didn't know the answer his Master wanted to hear, so he simply answered with the truth. "Yes."

His Master turned his eyes back to the fire.

The captain of the Royal Guard sat on the ground across from them.

"You should remove your helmet, Captain," the

Emperor said. "It must wear on you to have it on all the time."

"Thank you, my Emperor," the captain said. He removed his helmet to reveal a mien familiar to Vader, the scarred face of a clone, the features an echo of so many faces from Vader's past. Rex. Cody. Sixes. Echo. The roster of names moved through Vader's mind, each of them a trigger for a memory, each of them a ghost from his past.

"Is there an Imperial installation nearby, my lords?" the captain asked. Sergeant Deez removed his helmet, too, showing a face that wasn't that of a clone: a clean-shaven, ax-jawed human with short-cropped blond hair and tattoos of abstract patterns inked on his cheeks.

If Deez had been a clone, Vader imagined they'd have called him Ink.

"What are we looking for, my lords?" Deez asked.

Vader's Master stared into the glow of the fire. "Oh, I think we'll know when we find it, Sergeant."

"Of course, my lord," said the captain. He broke out premade meals for himself and his comrade. Neither the Emperor nor Vader ate. Instead, both meditated, communing with the Force, Vader standing, his Master seated.

Vader, still pondering his Master's words, drifted into the Force, let its rough currents pull him where it willed. As was so often the case, he saw moments from his past, a series of inchoate, violent, pain-filled images and sounds.

His decapitation of Darth Tyranus, the first kill his Master had asked of him.

Padmé's screams.

His murder of the younglings in the Jedi Temple, their eyes wide with a fear that only fed his righteous wrath.

Padmé's screams, her pain.

Treachery.

Mace Windu's shouts of rage as he'd realized the truth.

Padmé's screams.

Traitor.

The fires of Mustafar, his hatred for Obi-Wan, who'd feared him and tried to keep him from his destiny, who'd tried to take Padmé from him, who'd put him in the armor.

Padmé's screams, her despair.

"No, Anakin! No!"

Vader opened his eyes, his fists clenched, his anger overflowing, to see his Master standing across the fire from him, staring at him. His Master's expression was unreadable, his features partially hidden within the depths of his hood.

Vader sensed the anger in his Master, sensed, too, the threat that lived in that anger. Vader did not fear it, not at that moment.

"Where are the guards?" he asked. The Royal Guards were nowhere to be seen. "How long was I . . ."

"I sent them away. They will return soon." A long silence, then, "What did you see as you meditated?"

"I saw . . . deaths, and faces from my past, the events that led me to this moment. I see them frequently when I consider the destiny the Force has for me."

His Master's anger grew, though his expression did not change. His voice was the low murmur of a predator. "Your destiny, yes. I have seen hints of it, as well."

For a moment, caught up in the aftereffects of his vision, Vader wondered what it would be like to face his Master in battle, to take his small, frail body in his hands, lift it from the ground, and . . .

He cut off the thoughts, but his Master had sensed them, for his face split in a dark smile.

"I see you, apprentice."

"And I see you, Master. You think I *long* for the past when I see it in visions, but you're wrong. I don't long for it. I think of it and the man I was then and regard it all with contempt. And the only thing that makes it tolerable to ponder is that it ends with me here, in this armor, with you. I feel no longing. I feel no regret. My memories feed my anger and my anger feeds my strength and so am I able to serve you, and the Force, better. Your doubt . . ."

"Continue," said his Master.

Vader did, heedless of what might come next. "Your doubt is unwarranted and . . . angers me."

Several moments passed, each Sith Lord staring across the flames at the other. Finally Vader stepped around the fire and fell to one knee before his Master. He felt his Master's eyes on him, the eyes that saw deeply into everything. He imagined his Master considering options.

"The guards are returning," his Master said. "And they are not alone. Rise, Lord Vader."

CHAPTER FOURTEEN

BELKOR SAT IN THE COPILOT'S SEAT OF THE small, maneuverable search-and-rescue craft. They were scouring Ryloth's surface near the equator, the search location based on the data Cham had provided about Mors's descent trajectory.

"Hard to run a search in the dark with comm down to line of sight," Ophim, the pilot flying with him, complained.

"It is," Belkor said.

Belkor had assembled a team of men who owed him favors, men who wore the uniform but had no particular loyalty to the Empire, men who'd do what he asked without too many questions. He'd given them a cover story, of course: The rebels who'd brought down the *Perilous* had done so in the guise of Imperial troops with the apparent aid of Moff Delian Mors. Belkor had a general location for the Moff's ship, which loyal Imperial troops had almost brought down. Belkor told the men that they were among a select group to whom he'd confided, because he didn't know how deep the conspiracy might run.

If anyone suspected him of concocting a story, none

of them had spoken up. They owed Belkor their positions and the perks of power; they owed Mors nothing.

"Run through the search grid again," he transmitted to the four V-wings flying beside his search-and-rescue craft. "Fly a comm ladder. I need to know what you see."

They acknowledged his order and veered off to search again. They'd staggered their formation so that one was always in contact with another, and that one with yet another, and so on all the way back to Belkor's ship. Maintaining the formation required constant attention and limited their ability to search.

"Anything from the three V-wings to the south?" he asked Ophim.

"Nothing, sir."

Belkor looked out the glass bubble cockpit of the craft. Much of the bubble was lit with the heads-up display of the craft's elaborate sensor array. The bubble itself provided light amplification, so he could look out and down on the terrain as if it were dusk. Ryloth's forests stretched out below, banded to the south by a desert dotted with tors.

He clenched his jaw in frustration.

"I take that back, sir," Ophim said, holding a finger up to the headset he wore. "One of the V-wings is reporting smoke."

"Where?"

Ophim put a finger on the screen to show the location—close to the Equatorial Communications Hub. The smoke was probably the result of the attack on the hub that Belkor had enabled.

Still, he had nothing else. Mors could have gone down near the hub; the smoke could be from her ship.

"Go," he said to Ophim. "Send the V-wings the coordinates. They're to continue their check of the grid. Then we rendezvous at the communications hub."

Ophim nodded, accelerating, and the nimble S&R craft darted through the cutting winds.

"Anything from the V-wing on station near the smoke?" Belkor asked.

Ophim shook his head. "Dead air, sir. They broke up the comm ladder when you ordered the rendezvous at the hub."

Belkor cursed. He wouldn't know anything more until he was close enough to see for himself. Within a few minutes he'd convinced himself that it was Mors's shuttle, that it had gone down near the hub, and that the Moff had died on impact, but his fantasy broke on the rocks of reality as the lights of the hub came into view in the distance.

"Incoming from the V-wing on station," said Ophim. "Smoke is from the Equatorial Communications Hub. But . . ."

"But?"

"The hub suffered an attack, which explains the success of the jamming signal, and I think you should contact the commander of the station."

"What? Why?"

"Sir, the V-wing pilot reports that Moff Mors was here."

Belkor wasn't sure he'd heard correctly. "What did you say?"

Ophim looked skeptical. "According to one of our men, the Moff was here."

"When? How? Is she still here?"

"I don't know, though I gather she is not here now."

Belkor's mind started working through possibilities. The Moff had survived the downing of her shuttle and had ended up at the communications hub. "Before or after the attack?" he murmured.

"What's that, sir?"

Belkor felt the sweat forming under his shirt anew. "Nothing, Ophim, speaking to myself. Get Major Borkas on the line."

Through the bubble of the recon craft he stared down at the distant, smoking ruins of the communications hub. Cham's team had done a thorough job on the dishes, which lay in jagged, bent piles. Dozens of droids and men and ships, working in the glow of portable lights, buzzed around one of the fallen dishes, working to get it repaired.

Belkor wasn't thinking clearly, he realized. He had not been prepared for Mors to have made it away from her ship, much less into the hands of an officer like Steen Borkas. Mors could already have deduced Belkor's involvement in the day's events. She hadn't attempted to contact Belkor after the crash, after all. She could have shared her suspicions with Borkas, could be on her way back to the communication center at that moment. Belkor could return to find a security team waiting for him.

All at once he felt weak, like he was nothing but liquid, like he would drain away.

Ophim nodded when communications were established. Belkor cleared his throat and gathered himself.

"This is Colonel Belkor Dray. Am I speaking to Major Borkas?"

"Colonel Dray?" The voice did not sound like Borkas's. "Major Borkas isn't here. I'm Captain Narrin. The major left with Moff Mors over an hour ago."

Belkor looked over at Ophim and cut off the comm for a moment. "Did anyone tell them anything about the Moff's . . . betrayal?"

"No, sir," Ophim said. "Need to know, you said."

"Good." Belkor reactivated the comm. "Left for where, Narrin?"

"She, Borkas, and a squad of stormtroopers took two ships on a rescue mission. VIPs who escaped the *Perilous,* as I understand things. You're here to assist? Those must be some VIPs, sir, to bring the whole High Command down the equator."

You've no idea, Belkor thought but didn't say. He tried to process what he'd heard. The Moff was still attempting to find Vader and the Emperor, which meant she knew or at least believed that they'd survived the explosion of the *Perilous* and its immediate aftermath. That made sense. The Moff could perhaps save her office, or at least her life, if she was the hero leading the team that found Vader and the Emperor. But she hadn't tried to contact Belkor.

"Did the Moff arrive before or after the attack on the station?"

"Afterward, sir."

That might explain it. "Did she dispatch anyone to send word to the communication center that she was alive? Or that she was searching for Va—the VIPs?"

"Uh, let me check, sir," said Narrin. After a lengthy silence, the captain returned. "No, sir, she did not. But she and the major were in a hurry."

"No doubt," Belkor said, feeling certain that the Moff had deduced his treachery.

"Sir, I don't have the coordinates the Moff and the major are searching, and with comm being line of sight, we've no way to raise them and alert them that you're en route."

"That's quite all right, Captain. I know the search coordinates."

"Sir, if you don't mind my asking, what in the hell is going on out there?"

"I don't have time to brief you fully, Narrin. Terrorists have struck the Empire. That's all you need to know for now. How long before normal communication is possible?"

"We're focusing our efforts on Dish Three. Nine hours, sir. Maybe a bit less."

Nine hours. Belkor had nine hours to find the Moff and arrange for her demise.

"What else can we do for you, sir?" Narrin asked. "If we can help with these terrorists . . ."

"Nothing," Belkor replied. "You've been most helpful already. We'll be on our way immediately."

"Good luck, sir."

The moment they cut the comm, Belkor said to Ophim, "So, we know that Borkas is in league with the Moff."

"They aren't rescuing any VIPs from the *Perilous,*" Ophim said.

"Agreed," Belkor said, running with it. "Probably meeting other collaborators, or rendezvousing with the terrorists."

"We'll get them, sir," Ophim said.

"Yes, we will," said Belkor.

The Moff had two ships and some stormtroopers. Belkor had the search-and-rescue recon craft and half a dozen V-wings. If he could catch the Moff in the air, it would be over in moments.

"Here are the coordinates," he said, feeding Ophim the site where Cham thought Vader and the Emperor had gone down. "Alert the V-wings and let's get on our way."

"Yes, sir."

Vader sensed it, a hostile, hungry wave coursing toward them through the thick forest. The Royal Guards broke through the tree line at a full run, blaster rifles hanging from their hands. The sergeant had lost his helmet, and his eyes were wide and white in the mask of his tattoos. The ground vibrated slightly, and the foliage behind them shook as whatever was in pursuit charged hard after them. The captain stumbled as he ran but managed to keep his feet. He waved for Vader and the Emperor to retreat.

"Run, my lords!" the captain shouted, his voice muffled by his helmet. "We need a more defensible position!"

"Defensible from what?" Vader asked, igniting his lightsaber.

"Lyleks, my lord! More than—"

Vader heard them then, the insectoid clicking and hissing of Ryloth's apex predator carried on the wind. From the sound he judged there to be a dozen or so of the huge creatures, all tearing through the forest and closing fast.

"Lyleks," the Emperor said. "Interesting."

"My lords!" the captain said as he reached them, gasping. "They'll be on us in moments! We should move!"

Deez aimed his blaster rifle back at the trees. "Seconds only, Captain," he said tensely.

Vader activated his saber and took position beside the Emperor. Seeing this, the sergeant and the captain stood near the Emperor, too, rifles ready. They didn't have long to wait.

The lyleks burst through the trees, huge insectoid creatures bounding over logs, the pair of tentacles near their mandibles squirming. Seeing Vader, the Emperor, and the guards, they hissed and rushed forward.

The guards fired, their rifles writing red streaks in the air. The bolts struck the lyleks but bounced off their carapaces, deflecting into the trees.

Vader raised his hand, seized one of the leading

lyleks with the Force, and flung it sideways into the trees. It struck a tree trunk as thick around as a man, and its ridged, spiked carapace cracked open, leaving it squirming helplessly at the base of the tree.

Beside Vader, his Master gestured with both hands and jagged lines of Force lightning shot forth, striking two of the foremost lyleks, lifting the creatures from the ground and driving them backward, tumbling, hissing, screaming in agony, dying.

When his Master ended the lightning, he drew his lightsaber and he and Vader moved forward as one, each protecting the other as they twisted and spun out of the way of the lyleks' tentacles and snapping mandibles, slashing and severing legs, tentacles, heads. In moments the forest was still and Vader and his Master stood back-to-back in the midst of the carnage. Both deactivated their weapons. The sergeant and the captain simply stared at them, their blaster rifles hanging uselessly from their gloved hands.

The Emperor cocked his head, as though hearing something from far away. "There are more."

Alerted, Vader attuned himself to the Force. He felt them coming.

"Many more," his Master said.

"This terrain is poor for a stand against so many, Master," Vader said, feeling the lylek horde draw closer. A rushing sound came from the forest, like an incoming tide. "There are hundreds," he added, hearing the snapping of limbs, the hisses of the lyleks, the insectoid chittering. "At least."

"Agreed," the Emperor said absently, his voice as calm as still water. "Let's find a more suitable spot to face these creatures, Captain."

The captain sagged with relief. "Yes, my lord. Follow me." To Deez, he said, "Take the rear, Sergeant."

With that the captain turned and bolted through

the forest, leaping logs and skirting tree trunks. Vader deactivated his lightsaber, and he and his Master kept pace. Vader noticed that the forest had quieted around them. There was only his breathing and the distant clicking and chittering of the pursuing horde, the snapping of wood, the low rumble of the lyleks' collective tread. They were gaining.

"I don't see any of them yet," Deez said.

"They're still coming," Vader said. He presumed the lyleks could smell them somehow, or had a keen sense of hearing, or used some other sense to hunt.

The four men broke into a clearing covered in low grass and brush and dashed across it. The exhausted breathing of the Royal Guards now sounded as loud to Vader as his respirator. He still felt the lyleks behind them, their numbers growing as their bloodlust drew more of their kind. He imagined a horde could clear the fauna from a few square miles of forest.

"Hurry, my lords!" the captain said.

They'd almost crossed the clearing by the time the lyleks broke through the tree line behind them.

"There they are!" Deez said.

Vader spared a glance back to see that two score lyleks at least had burst out of the trees, a clicking wall of spiked exoskeletons, tentacles, and mammoth jaws. More followed, more, the horde boiling out of the trees. They clambered over one another in their hunger, a tangle of limbs and claws and clicks.

The creatures saw them right away, of course, and uttered a collective hiss and eager clicking. Their thick limbs and great weight threw up chunks of soil and dirt as they lumbered across the clearing. The four men reached the tree line on the opposite side of the clearing and plunged once more into the tangle of trunks and roots.

"Look for a cliff or a tunnel," Vader said calmly. "A place where we can channel their attack."

"They're closing!" Deez cried, looking back. He fired behind him with his blaster rifle. "Shots bounce off the carapaces!"

The Emperor gestured with a free hand, using the Force to topple trees. They fell into the horde, crushing lyleks, knocking down other trees that crushed still more. The survivors clambered over the dead without pausing, continuing their frenetic pursuit.

The captain drew one of the grenades he carried, activated it, and tossed it behind them at the horde. It exploded a couple of seconds later, the boom reverberating through the forest, toppling another tree, and causing shrieks of pain among the lyleks.

"Go right, Captain," the Emperor said. "One hundred meters from here there is a tunnel."

The captain did not question, though Vader wondered how his Master knew. The captain angled right as the lyleks closed from behind, their huge bodies snapping trees as they came. The distance between the four men and the horde shrank, and both guards fired their rifles one-handed as they ran, the shots blowing off parts of tree trunks and striking lyleks but not slowing the overall advance of the horde.

They reached a steep ravine and the guards started down the side, stumbling and grabbing at roots to stay upright as they descended. Vader and the Emperor leapt down from the top. A creek bisected the ravine; the opposite side was a steep wall of rocks and tree roots and soil that extended as far as they could see to the left and right. The lyleks were still coming.

"Where, my Emperor?" the captain asked. "I don't see a tunnel anywhere."

The lead lyleks from the horde poured over the side of the ravine, long limbs digging into the soil, tentacles grabbing at branches and roots as they scrambled down.

Vader activated his lightsaber and stood beside the Emperor, eyeing the side of the ravine for the tunnel. Meanwhile the captain and Deez shot at everything that moved, their blasterfire lighting up the darkness. Lyleks hissed and chittered.

"Heads!" Deez exclaimed as he fired. "A head shot puts them down!"

More lyleks came over the side, more, until they looked like a seething avalanche tumbling down the hill.

"There!" Vader said, finally spotting the opening, a dark oval low on the face of the valley wall, perhaps two meters tall, and partially blocked by exposed tree roots as thick as an arm.

"Go, Sergeant," the captain said to Deez as they all backpedaled quickly toward the tunnel entrance. "Then the Emperor, then Lord Vader. I bring up the rear. Go!"

The lyleks rolled toward them, clambering over one another as they came, the pedipalps at either side of their large mouths waving spasmodically, as if already shoveling flesh into their jaws. Half a dozen lylek carcasses hung in the roots along the side of the ravine, but the rest kept coming.

The captain's blaster rifle dropped one with a shot to the head, then another, but the creatures just kept pounding forward. Ten or more had reached the ravine's bottom and clambered wildly toward the men, tentacles squirming, jaws working.

Vader raised a hand, fell into the Force, and loosed a blast of power that slammed into the lyleks on the ravine's floor, driving them backward, partially back up the ravine's side, and into those that came behind, turning the creatures' advance into a chaotic scramble of limbs and agitated clicking. They tore at one another in their frustrated frenzy.

Deez ducked into the darkness of the tunnel, followed by the Emperor, followed by Vader, who deactivated his lightsaber, and finally by the captain, who backed in, still firing as he retreated. The tunnel, as black as pitch, went back only a meter before opening into a large cavern that had openings to the left and right and center.

"The hillside must be honeycombed with these!" Deez said.

"Keep going!" the captain said over his shoulder, still firing out through the mouth of the tunnel. "Move, move!"

"No," Vader said, reigniting his lightsaber. "This is where we stand."

There was movement in the growth at the tunnel's mouth, and then a lylek lurched through, snapping roots, all teeth and hisses, only half a meter from the captain. Vader pushed the captain aside, bounded forward, and drove the blade of his lightsaber into the creature's mouth and out the top of its head. The huge carcass collapsed. Behind it, dozens more lyleks scrambled to get in around their fallen fellow. Vader bowed his head, raised his hand, and loosed a blast of power, eliciting squeals of pain and sending the lyleks flying backward.

"Back away," the Emperor commanded, and Vader and the captain fell back.

The Emperor gestured casually, and the tunnel's ceiling came down in a shower of rock and dirt. The sound of frustrated hisses and roars carried through the rubble. The four men stood in the light of Vader's lightsaber. He deactivated it, casting them in darkness. The captain turned on his helmet lights.

"Listen," Deez said, cocking his head. "I think

something is down there." He nodded at the left-hand tunnel.

Vader reached out with the Force, felt the lyleks coming at them down the side tunnel.

"You're correct, Sergeant," he said.

"We shouldn't make our stand here, my lords," said the captain. "They'll be coming at us from both directions."

The lyleks were getting closer, their clicks and hisses growing louder. Deez pulled one of the grenades he carried. Vader grabbed him by the wrist to stop him.

"You could collapse the tunnels," he said.

Deez looked embarrassed. "Right. Of course, Lord Vader."

"Please, my Emperor," said the captain, gesturing down the central tunnel.

"He's right, Master," said Vader. "We should continue."

"Agreed," the Emperor said, and they turned and hurried into the winding central tunnel, which sloped downward, widening as they went. They'd covered maybe two hundred meters, moving ever deeper underground, when they heard the first sounds of the lyleks' pursuit coming from behind them. Rock formations dotted the floor and thick clumps of crystal hung from the ceiling of the tunnel, but there was nothing that would have made for a defensible pocket. The chitters and hisses bounced off the stone, seeming to race ahead of them.

"They're faster than us in this terrain," Deez said. "We're going to have to turn and fight."

As the lyleks closed on them, the tunnel seemed to hum under the force of their tread. Soon Vader could hear the clatter of their exoskeletons as they ran over the stone.

"They are almost upon us," he said. The captain

fell back, taking station with Deez at the rear, between the Emperor and the horde. Vader ignited his lightsaber to provide at least some additional light.

"Here they come!" the captain said, and started firing wild one-handed shots over his shoulder.

"I see them!" said Deez, and started firing, too.

Lyleks squealed and hissed.

"You may use your grenades," Vader said. The cavern was wide enough to endure the blast without collapsing.

Both guards immediately activated and tossed grenades; five seconds later the tunnel behind them reverberated with the sound of the explosions, lylek screams, and the rumble of falling stone. The blast wave roared from the confines of the tunnel. Vader and the Emperor used the Force to deflect the bulk of the wave from them, but the power of it drove the two Royal Guards face-first into the floor, their armor scraping along the stone.

Vader turned and used the Force to lift both guards to their feet. Deez was bleeding from the nose and looked stunned.

"We won't slow for you again," Vader said. "The horde is still coming."

As if to make his point, the sounds of the pursuing lyleks rose up from behind, clicking, hisses, and squeals.

Vader took position beside his Master as the four of them continued down the tunnel. He sought a place where they could stop and hold their ground, but the tunnel went on and on, not narrowing, with its downward slope diving ever deeper into the planet.

Drawing on the Force as he ran, he gestured at the ceiling and took hold of several large chunks of crystal stalactites. He rocked them loose with his power, then let them dangle there, waiting for the vibration of the passing horde to cause them to fall.

The tunnel wound left and right as they descended, but Vader saw no side tunnels. Just the single tube continuing to burrow into Ryloth's crust.

From behind came the boom of falling rock—the crystals Vader had loosened—and the squeals of crushed lyleks. Yet still they came, the horde seemingly unbreakable. And they were still closing.

At the end of a long, sloped straightaway, Vader let the rest of the group run on while he stopped to look back. His helmet reflected the meager light projected by his lightsaber and he saw the horde enter the far end of the tunnel, an ocean of legs, tentacles, and mandibles, saw them scrabble over and around the stalagmites that dotted the floor. The beat of their armored, pointed legs put small pits in the stone. Some of them clambered along the walls like giant arachnids, coating the surface of the tunnel behind them. Their tentacles waved as they scurried, jaws working as if already masticating flesh. Vader could not escape the feeling that he was being steered, perhaps by the lyleks, or perhaps by his Master.

He fell deeply into the Force and loosed a wave of power from his outstretched hand that filled the circumference of the tunnel. The blast slammed into the charging horde, cracking exoskeletons, shattering stalagmites, and driving a score or more of the lyleks in the lead backward in a shower of broken bodies and broken stone. They squealed and chittered and flailed, and the lyleks following after scrambled over the fallen and wounded, their eyes fixed on Vader.

Vader was prepared to meet them all, slaughter every one of them then and there, but his Master's voice from up the tunnel pulled him around.

"Come, Lord Vader!"

He deactivated his lightsaber, turned, and hurried forward, using the Force to augment his speed and catch up with the other three.

"What happened?" Deez asked, but Vader ignored him. When he reached his Master's side, he voiced his thoughts.

"Yes," the Emperor agreed. "The beasts are herding us—unintentionally, I think."

"Herding us to where?" Vader asked.

"We'll soon know," the Emperor said. "I think we should prepare ourselves."

They hustled through the tunnel, which had finally started to narrow.

"There's light ahead," the captain said. "Look!"

Vader saw it, a dim, green glow coming through a circular opening about a meter and a half in diameter. Soon the tunnel gave way to a large cavern thirty meters across, a hemispherical cyst in the planet. They stood in the opening, five meters up on the wall of the cyst. Clusters of glowing crystal sprouted from the walls and floor—the source of the ambient light.

Hundreds of lyleks milled about on the floor of the cyst, all of them tending what Vader assumed to be the queen of the colony, a lylek with a bloated abdomen three times the size of the rest. Large, gray, leathery-looking sacs adhered to the walls in clumps of ten or twenty here and there—egg sacs. A dozen or more tunnel openings dotted the walls and ceiling, all of them about the same size as that in which the four men stood. For a moment no one spoke, and the only sound in the tunnel was the labored breathing of the guards and Vader's respirator.

The queen lylek noticed them then. She swung her huge head in their direction, fixed her eyes on them, and hissed in alarm, the sound bouncing off the walls of the cavern, echoing. The rest of the lyleks in the cavern turned toward them, too, their movement causing a collective clicking. They hissed as one, their tentacles squirming in agitation. Down the tunnel behind the men, the pursuing lyleks continued to close.

"And now we know to where we were being herded," the Emperor said.

Vader turned to Deez and the captain. "You two are to hold as long as you can here."

The captain stiffened. "We will stay with our Emperor."

"Do as Lord Vader commands," the Emperor said.

"What are you going to do then?" Deez asked while he and the captain took grenades in hand, activated them, and waited for the pursuing lyleks to appear.

"We're going kill them all," Vader said, igniting his lightsaber.

The Emperor cackled, drew his own lightsaber, and activated the red blade.

CHAPTER FIFTEEN

Faylin called back from the cockpit. "Kallon's almost in range. And . . . got him."

Kallon's voice sounded over Cham's and Isval's comm. "Cham, I've found the Emperor's shuttle."

"Where are you?" Cham asked, instinctively looking out the viewport of the escort boat, though he could see nothing but night.

A pause, then, "I'm on the ground near it. Listen, I know—"

Cham cursed. "I told you surveillance only, Kallon!"

"Scans showed no life so—"

"No life? Bodies?" After too long a pause, Cham added, "I can't see you, Kallon, so if you're nodding or shaking your head . . ."

"Right, right. Yes, there are three bodies, and one of them is a Royal Guard, which means they were here, Cham. The remains of a camp are here, too."

"A camp? Kallon, they could come back. I want you to get on your ship and—"

"The *remains* of a camp, I said. And if they were anywhere near here, they'd have heard my ship and come back already. They're gone, Cham, and I think you need to get Goll down here."

Cham felt his skin warm and his lekku perk up. "You think they're on foot in the forest?"

"Goll will have to confirm, but I think so," Kallon said. "If a ship had picked them up, they'd have taken the guard's body, wouldn't they? And I don't see a sign of anything big landing nearby, anyway. I'm not the tracker, of course, but . . ."

"But you think they're on foot. Remember that I can't see you nodding."

"Yes, I think they're on foot."

Cham barely managed to hold in a grin. Isval did not. She grinned fiercely and nodded.

"We're coming down, Kallon," Cham said. "Stay put. I mean it."

Isval reached out and squeezed his shoulder. "They're on foot, Cham. We'll catch them. We will." The narrow confines of the boat did not allow her room for her habitual pacing, so she just shifted from foot to foot. "They can't have gone far. They don't know the terrain. They could be wounded from the crash. Slow."

"Or not," Cham said, trying to curb her eagerness, though he felt it himself. "Set us down near Kallon, Faylin."

Isval stopped fidgeting and looked Cham in the eyes, an expression of concern on her face. She put a hand on his shoulder. "Are you all right? Really all right?"

He nodded to reassure her. "I'm fine. Let's do what we came to do."

She looked skeptical but nodded in return and left him to take a seat next to Goll.

Cham watched her go, regretting his earlier words to her. He'd changed her with them. Unlike him, she had never had much of a life outside of the movement. He hadn't appreciated how much she needed it, how much she needed him. He'd vented his own concerns and, in doing so, had undermined her foundation.

He should've kept his damn mouth shut.

Isval sat beside Goll, tiny beside his bulk. He smelled of sweat and oiled metal.

"How much of that did you hear?" she asked softly.

"I heard they're on foot."

"That's not what I mean."

"I make it a point not to listen," he said, staring straight ahead.

She put a hand on his forearm; his flesh was lined with veins. "How much?"

He shrugged the mountains of his shoulders. "Enough."

She nodded, sat quietly for a moment, then said, "He's wrong. The movement isn't just an idea. It's also him."

"I know," Goll said.

She put out a fist. "Nothing happens to him, then. Agreed? We're going to need to rebuild after today, and for that we'll need him."

He sniffed, then tapped her tiny fist with the callused boulder of his own. "Agreed. And how about nothing happens to any of us?"

"You think you can track them?" she asked. "Vader, I mean?"

"I can," he said.

"Even in the dark?"

He turned and looked at her with an expression that told her to stop asking stupid questions.

"Good," she said. "Good."

Faylin's voice came over the ship's communicator. "We're here. Setting down."

Faylin lowered the escort boat through the forest's canopy, tree limbs scraping the hull, and set it down on the surface.

"Stay here," Cham said to Faylin. "Keep a scan live. Let me know if you pick up anything."

Goll ordered his crew to stay aboard the escort for the moment, to minimize foot traffic near the campsite while he did his initial tracking. Then he, Cham, and Isval debarked into the humidity of the equatorial forest. Insects buzzed and clicked. Animals in the trees squeaked, bellowed, and squealed.

Kallon was waiting for them in the clearing, hands crossed over his ample belly, a grin on his face. The wreckage of an Imperial shuttle, still intact, lay in the clearing.

"Camp is there," he said to Goll, jerking a thumb over his shoulder at some debris, the remains of a fire, and the shredded material of an all-climate tent. "I haven't walked near it."

"Good," Goll said. "Bodies?"

"Inside the ship. Haven't touched them, either. Just looked inside but didn't enter."

"Good," Goll repeated, all business.

Isval walked over to the wreck with Cham, Goll, and Kallon. Goll was looking at the ground, the ship, the trees, and Isval could only imagine that he was drawing conclusions she couldn't.

The shuttle lay on its side, sunk half a meter into the churned-up loam of the forest floor. A splintered tree limb had speared the cockpit glass. The hull was blackened from blasterfire and blistered from the heat of what Isval assumed to be a barely controlled reentry. Pieces of destroyed equipment lay scattered on the ground near the ship. Goll picked up a few fragments, walked a bit, picked up a few more.

"A generator and a portable comm array," he said, dropping a piece of metal.

"Destroyed in the crash?" Cham asked.

Goll looked up at the night sky, then at the ground of the clearing. Slowly he walked toward the edge of the forest, stopping now and again to examine one of the holes in the turf. At last he turned to answer Cham's question. "I don't think so. These holes are from a ship's blasters. Nordon?"

"Could be," Cham said. "Nordon caught Vader and the Emperor in the clearing and fired on them. Makes sense."

"Except the part about how Vader and the Emperor brought them down," Isval said, to which Cham didn't respond.

"Let me check the bodies," Goll said.

"We need to be quick," Cham reminded him. "They have a sizable head start."

"Right."

Cham, Kallon, and Isval watched as Goll climbed up the side of the ship and disappeared through a hole that appeared to have been cut through the bulkhead. While they waited, Isval looked out at the dark wall of the forest, knowing that Vader was out there somewhere, hoping that she could get to him before Imperial troops did. Finally Goll lifted himself out of the wreckage.

"Bodies are two pilots and a Royal Guard. Pilots died from blunt injuries, probably in the crash. The guard died from a blaster shot to the head. Let me see if I can find a trail."

* * *

"I've got two vessels on scan," Belkor said, checking the recon ship's sensors. "No, make that three, though they're all grounded." The recon ship had such a keen sensor array compared with other ships that Belkor knew the vessels he'd picked up could not have seen him on their own scans.

"Mors could have picked up another ship," Ophim said in an excited voice. "Sir, I can get two of the V-wings here quickly. We take Mors out now, maybe we end this whole thing quickly."

"Hang on," Belkor said, eyeing the readout in the heads-up display. He frowned.

Ophim was gazing at the data, too. "That's an Imperial escort and some kind of native transport. The third ship is an Imperial shuttle, heavily damaged." He frowned. "That doesn't make sense."

It made sense to Belkor, of course. It was Cham or Cham's people; it had to be.

Ophim looked over at him, eyes wide. "Sir, that could be Mors with the Free Ryloth traitors she conspired with. I'll get the V-wings en route."

He reached for the comm button, but Belkor stayed his hand. "Let's get a better look first, Lieutenant."

"But, sir, if they pick us up on their scans—"

"A better look, Ophim," Belkor said firmly. "We . . . have to be sure."

"Aye, sir."

Ophim flew the recon craft at low altitude, virtually scraping the forest canopy below. As they closed, Belkor felt his skin warm. Sweat leaked down his sides, damp and clammy. He could smell his own stink. His heart was pounding. He knew what he might have to do, but the doing would come hard.

"Staying low, sir. That ought to keep us off their scans for a bit."

Belkor nodded but couldn't bring himself to speak.

He waited until his craft was close enough to the group on the ground to overcome the jamming signal polluting the airwaves.

"I don't think they can see us yet, sir," Ophim said, unnecessarily—but no doubt instinctively—speaking in a whisper. "They're on the ground. They may not even have an active scan going."

Belkor took the encrypted comlink from his pocket and hailed Cham, half hoping he'd get no answer.

Goll started near the camp, using a dim red light that wouldn't destroy his night vision while he studied the ground for signs. He carefully walked the area around and near the camp, sometimes looking off into the trees. Finally he stood, nodded, and looked over at Cham.

"I have them," he said, and gestured with the block of his chin. "That way. Four of them."

"You're sure?" Isval asked, and received a withering glare in response.

"He's sure," Cham said. He gave a start when he felt the buzz of the encrypted comlink he carried in his pocket. He took it in hand, stared at it as if it were a foreign thing.

"What is it?" Isval asked. "Isn't that . . ."

"Belkor."

"How?"

He shrugged, then raised Faylin on his normal comlink. "Anything on scan?"

"All's quiet, Cham."

Not so much, Cham thought, and answered Belkor's hail.

*   *   *

Cham's voice carried out of the encrypted comlink.

"Belkor? Where are you? I don't have anything on scan."

Belkor ignored the Twi'lek and put on a show for Ophim, who could hear only Belkor's half of the conversation. "This is Colonel Belkor Dray. You are to power down your ships immediately and surrender all aboard."

"What are you talking about? If this is—"

"A wise decision," Belkor said, and cut the connection. He put the comlink back in his pocket. To Ophim, he said, "I'll take the stick."

"Sir? Of course, sir."

Ophim transferred control of the ship to Belkor.

"What is that?" Belkor asked, gesturing to nothing at all outside the bubble of the cockpit.

"What is what, sir?" Ophim turned to look out on Ryloth's night. "I don't see anything. There's nothing on scan."

Belkor drew his blaster pistol in a sweaty fist and shot Ophim in the back of the head. Gore splattered the glass of the bubble. For a moment Belkor felt dizzy and thought he might vomit, but he held it down.

He looked away from the blood, cursing, rationalizing, apologizing. His encrypted comlink buzzed in his pocket. He gathered himself before answering the hail.

"I'm in the air, Syndulla. Ten klicks south of your position."

"How'd you find us? Why can't I see you on scan?"

"Too long a story. You can't see me because I'm in a recon bubble. That's the Emperor's shuttle? Tell me there are bodies aboard."

"There are, but not Vader or the Emperor. They struck out on foot."

"How do you know that?"

"We know."

Belkor quieted the connection and cursed loud and long as he looked down on the unending expanse of equatorial forest stretching out in all directions. If Vader and the Emperor were on foot, finding them would be nearly impossible.

"We're tracking them," Cham added.

Belkor pressed the button on the comlink so hard it made his finger hurt. "How?"

"I have people who can do it. We're *from* this planet, Belkor. We know it. Now, what do you have out here with you?"

"Nothing you can use. You're on your own. Mors is out here, and I think she knows everything. I need to find her quickly." Belkor looked over at Ophim, and his anger boiled over. "You should've killed her in space, Syndulla! You should've killed them all! I gave you the damn idents! This could all be over!"

Cham was silent for a beat, then said, "But it's not, not yet. Is Mors on foot? Why do you think she knows everything?"

Belkor ground his teeth, blinked away a blurriness of vision. He was losing control of himself, he realized, the same way he'd lost control of events.

"Mors is on a ship with twenty stormtroopers from the Equatorial Comm Hub. And I think she knows because she came here instead of the communication center. She's looking for Vader and the Emperor, too."

"All right," Cham said. "All right. Let me think a moment. Stand by."

Belkor, strapped into his seat and unable to pace, instead fidgeted with his uniform, his hat, his hair. He imagined Cham consulting with his people, figuring out the best way to back Belkor into a corner. Finally Cham came back on the comlink.

"Listen to me, Belkor. You're going to help us get Vader. Then I'm going to help you get Mors. *Then* this will all be over."

Belkor was breathing hard, trying not to look at Ophim's corpse.

"Do you hear me, Belkor? Now, what do you have out here with you?"

"I'm . . . alone in the recon ship, but I've got six V-wings checking the map grid for Mors. We're set up in a communication ladder."

"Can you trust the crew in the V-wings?"

A laugh slipped through Belkor's teeth, and he heard the hysteria in it. "To kill Mors? Yes. I've made her out as the traitor who brought down the *Perilous*. But to kill Vader and the Emperor? No. To help Twi'lek terrorists? No, I can't trust them to do that, Syndulla. No."

"Right, so here's what we're going to do," Cham said. "Keep your V-wings in the air looking for Mors. If you or your men see her ship, shoot her down. But keep them in the comm ladder in case you—we— need them. Throughout, keep within comm distance of me as we track Vader and the Emperor. Keep your communication ladder intact, because when I call for support, I'll want those V-wings to come in hot."

"They won't help you! Did you not hear me? And they won't fire on the Emperor!"

Cham's voice finally lost its calm. "They won't know, Belkor! Not in the dark! Not in this foliage." The Twi'lek lowered his voice. "I'll give you coordinates, and you'll give them coordinates, and they'll come in firing. And only if I need them. Only if."

Belkor couldn't keep a sneer out of his tone. "Always planning for every contingency. One day you'll come up short, Syndulla."

"Maybe, but not today, Belkor. Neither of us will. Not today."

"I'm not putting my ships at your disposal, Twi'lek," Belkor said. "Mors could leave the area and head back to the communication center. I could return there and find a security team waiting."

"You're not thinking it through," Cham said. "She doesn't know how deep the conspiracy goes, so she came after the only people she can be sure aren't involved. Vader and the Emperor. She won't go anywhere until she has them. Trust me, Belkor. Help me get the Emperor, then I'll make sure you get Mors."

Belkor heard the words, understood them even, but had no capacity to analyze them. He was exhausted, he knew. Too stressed to think clearly. He *wasn't* thinking things through. He wanted to pull back, start the day over, make different decisions. He didn't want to be responsible for the deaths of hundreds or thousands of Imperials aboard the *Perilous*. He didn't want a corpse in the seat next to him. He should eat a blaster shot. He knew he should, but he knew he didn't have it in him. Instead he stared out the cockpit bubble, drew in a deep breath, and screamed until his voice was hoarse and he was out of breath.

"Let's just get his over with, Syndulla."

Cham pocketed the encrypted comlink, frowning. He felt a measure of pity for Belkor. Cham had maneuvered him into a box and there was no way out. There was no other end for Belkor but death. The only question was whether he faced an Imperial Inquisitor first. He shook his head, his lekku waving.

"Faylin, you and Kallon are to hop along at half-hour intervals behind us. I'll give you heading and distance. Don't lose us. We may need you for an extraction."

"Understood," they both said.

"Belkor?" Isval asked him.

"He's unstable," Cham said.

"Yes," Isval agreed. She checked the power packs on her blasters.

"He'll trail us in the recon ship, and if we need the V-wings for a bombardment, we can call them in."

"Vader downed two of our armed freighters and did it from the ground. I don't know if—"

Cham interrupted her, his voice a bit sharper than he wished. "Do you have a better idea, Isval? I'm just doing what I can, using what resources I have. We're better off with the V-wings than without, aren't we?"

At first she recoiled from his tone, but her skin darkened and she stuck out her chin. "Yeah, we are." She turned and walked away, and Cham watched her go. He seemed always to be watching her go.

"Goll, you ready?" Isval asked, holstering her blasters.

"Ready," the big Twi'lek said.

"Cham and I are with you in the lead. The rest of your team in standard formation twenty meters behind. Let's move, people."

"You heard her," Goll called to his crew, and they nodded.

"We stay quiet, people," Cham said. To have their best chance, they'd need to catch Vader and the Emperor unawares.

Isval, Goll, and Cham strode into the forest, Goll moving them along as quickly as he could while following Vader and the Emperor's path. Only after they were deep among the trees did Cham wonder if catching Vader unawares was actually possible.

* * *

Mors flew the transport, with one of Steen's officers copiloting. Half of the stormtroopers and four more of Steen's men from the communications hub sat in the passenger compartment of the shuttle. Mors looked out on Ryloth's night. Two of the planet's moons had risen, ghostly crescents casting pale light on the carpet of treetops that swayed below. The dark expanse of the equatorial forest extended as far as Mors could see in all directions, broken often by clearings and deep ravines.

The terrain intimidated Mors. She flew a desk; she had no experience in search operations. Neither did Steen. Neither did any of them. With the aid of the navcomp, one of Steen's young officers had put together a search grid as well as he could, but the search area was vast and Mors wasn't even entirely sure what she was looking for: a downed but mostly intact ship? A debris field? Survivors on foot? Bodies? So they searched slowly, with extra care, poring over the scan results and hoping to get lucky.

"Is that something?" the copilot asked, pointing at signs of life on the scan. The middle-aged officer had a paunch and ears so large they stuck out like sails from under his cap.

"Fauna," Mors said, checking the scan. "Big one. A lylek probably. They're everywhere in the forests, I've heard."

The copilot sighed with impatience. "More than a thousand ships and pods went down from the *Perilous*. We haven't seen *any*. And we haven't seen any other search ships, either. You'd think we wouldn't be able to fly ten kilometers without bumping into one or the other, even if just by accident."

"You'd think wrong," Mors said. "It's a big planet

and the blast wave from the explosion would have dispersed the pods widely. They're scattered all over the western hemisphere. With communications down to line of sight, it's like being in a boat and trying to find a thousand floating buoys scattered across an ocean. You could go days without finding anything or seeing another boat and probably would. Frankly, we're just lucky to have a starting point."

"I suppose," said the copilot. He nodded out the cockpit. "Starting point or not, that's a lot of space down there, ma'am."

Mors could only nod—she knew she was looking at several thousand square kilometers of rough terrain that made scans slow and iffy.

For the tenth time since leaving the communications hub behind, she wondered if she'd made a mistake in going after Vader and the Emperor. She wondered if she should have taken Steen and the stormtroopers and flown to the communication center, arrested Belkor, retaken control of operations, and *then* gone after Vader and the Emperor.

Except that if Belkor's conspiracy ran deep among the command personnel, Mors would be killed on some pretext long before she ever reached the communication center. Or she would retake command, but in the time it took her to do so, Vader and the Emperor would be killed by the rebels, who were also looking for them. No, her only course was to find Lord Vader and the Emperor first, then gather loyalist forces before attempting to move on Belkor.

But to find them, she was going to have be more lucky than skilled.

She rubbed her tired eyes, stared out at the moon for a moment, and returned to the work of studying the scan results.

* * *

Cham and Isval kept several paces behind Goll, letting the big Twi'lek do his work uninterrupted and without distraction. Goll worked fast and in silence, save for grunting to himself from time to time as he examined the ground, a tree, leaves, the underbrush. He wore a perpetual frown throughout, the crease in his forehead as deep as one of the forest's ravines. He stopped with his hands on his hips, as though to think or study something on the wind, then moved on. Cham hailed Faylin and Isval and Belkor regularly so they could keep pace in their ships. He had one comm or another in his hand at all times.

"You might as well start juggling those things," Isval said.

Cham smiled as he raised Faylin and Kallon again to give them his location. He'd ordered them not to stay in the air any longer than they had to, as it would make them easier to pick up on the scans of any Imperial ships that might be in the area. He just needed them to stay within communication distance.

Goll suddenly stood upright, big head cocked to the side. He ran a hand down his right lekku. He looked left, then right.

"What is—" Isval began, but Goll silenced her with a raised hand.

Signaling for them to wait, he walked ahead, his dim red light held close to the ground as he moved through the trees and underbrush. Isval had no idea what he was looking at, but his tension was obvious from the hunch of his shoulders. Isval was bunching her own shoulders, on edge, holding her blasters too tightly. She took a deep breath.

A soft whistle from Goll gave them the all-clear to proceed. Cham and Isval found him standing at the edge of a clearing with his hands on his hips, staring ahead.

"See it?" he asked when they stood at his side.

The clearing extended on past the limits of Isval's night vision.

"I'm looking at a clearing," she said. "What am I supposed to see?"

"It wasn't a clearing a short time ago. See all the broken limbs? The churned soil? The toppled trees?"

Once Goll pointed them out, the features were obvious.

"A horde," Cham said.

"Yes, it was," Goll said softly. "And I'd wager they were after the Emperor's group. Timing's right."

"Lyleks?" Isval said, awed by the number of them it must have taken to cut such a large swath out of the forest. They'd have trampled everything along their way. "How can we follow Vader now?"

"The horde obliterated the human tracks," Goll said, "but once a horde is after you, it almost always catches you. So we just follow the horde."

"And . . . what if we find it?" Isval asked. She'd never seen a lylek up close and had no desire to change that.

"Better question is, *What if we don't?*" Cham said, leaving the implication dangling there.

Isval took his meaning. If Vader and the Emperor could handle a lylek horde, it was difficult to imagine a group of Twi'lek freedom fighters presenting much trouble.

"We're in too far to stop now," she said.

"Yeah, and that's what I keep saying about Belkor," Cham reminded her, and that brought her up short. "If we run into a horde, we're all dead."

Goll grunted agreement.

"Even so," Isval said, thinking of Pok and Eshgo

and Drim and everyone else who'd died at the hands of Vader and the Empire. "Even so."

She stared at Cham, trying to will him to make the right call.

A long moment passed before Goll spoke again: "So what are we doing, Cham?"

"Following the horde," Cham said, and gestured at the trail the lyleks had made through the forest floor. "We're in too far to stop now."

CHAPTER SIXTEEN

VADER ENVELOPED HIMSELF IN THE FORCE, LET it saturate him, and through it magnified and channeled his omnipresent rage and hate. Beside him the Emperor, too, unbridled his power and sank into the Force. As one they leapt down from the mouth of the tunnel.

The moment they hit the floor the lyleks swarmed forward, hundreds of them, a wave of spiked limbs and clicking mandibles. They raised their upper bodies as they charged, freeing themselves to use their spiked front legs like spears. They climbed over one another in their eagerness to kill and feed.

Vader extended a gloved hand and loosed a blast of power that blew apart two of the lyleks rushing toward him, showering those behind with gore and chunks of carapace. At the same time, his Master unleashed a destructive wave of power that cast three of the huge creatures backward and into the wall, cracking exoskeletons and leaving them broken, twitching, dying.

Vader rushed forward, blade held high. He ducked a tentacle, sidestepped the stab of a spiked leg, and with a crosscut severed the head from a lylek as it lunged at him. Crushing the skull under his boot, he used the Force to propel the headless carcass into a trio of the creatures behind it, turning them into a knot of legs and tentacles and chittering.

Feeling danger behind, he spun and lopped off the two front legs of another lylek that was poised to impale him through the back. He leapt atop its flailing, skittering body, riding it for a time while his blade slashed and stabbed at its fellows. He ended the creature's squeals of pain by driving his blade down and through its abdomen.

Bounding off its back, he rushed among the seething mass of lyleks, heedless now of their stabbing limbs and biting teeth, his lightsaber severing legs, tentacles, heads, mandibles, covering the floor in ichor-soaked body parts. Impacts from the tentacles and legs and hulking bodies barely moved him. None penetrated his armor, and what little pain they managed to inflict could not surpass the pain he carried always within him.

A spiked leg caught him squarely, slammed hard into his side, and drove him sideways into the tentacles of another lylek, which immediately wrapped around his legs and lifted him upside down from the floor.

While he hung there, another lylek lunged forward, mouth open wide as though to snap off his head. He drove his lightsaber into its open mouth and out the back of its head, and it fell dead to the floor. The creature holding him drew him toward its own mouth, but he simply bent at the waist and severed the tentacle holding him. He flipped in midair as he fell, landed on his feet, spun, and severed the forelegs from a lylek before him. It collapsed, screeching and spraying ichor from the stumps, its huge body thumping into him in its pained spasms. The impact of its bulk knocked him backward, but he rode the motion into a spinning crosscut that bisected another lylek's head. He'd killed dozens, a score or more, yet still they kept coming, the press of them restricting his movement, buffeting him, spiked legs slamming into the floor all around him.

Roaring, he dodged and jumped and spun through them, his blade slashing and stabbing, until a blow from a tentacle caught him flush in the chest and sent him careening backward. The creature that had struck him followed up, tentacles grasping, jaws clicking, the spears of its forelegs raised high. Meanwhile the spiked leg from another lylek slammed into his back. His armor prevented the limb from skewering him, but the impact drove him back toward the charging lylek.

Stumbling, Vader nevertheless held out a hand, channeled the Force, and loosed a blast of power that slammed the charging creature five meters backward into the wall. Wanting a moment to gather himself and check on his Master, he jumped high above the teeming mass of lyleks to a ledge five meters up on the wall, using the Force to augment his leap. The creatures he had just escaped gnashed their mandibles, waved their tentacles, and tried to climb over one another in their frustration as they scrabbled at the side of the wall.

From above, back near the tunnel mouth, Vader heard the shouts of the guards and the rapid whumps of repeated blasterfire. An explosion boomed—a grenade—causing the walls to vibrate.

Vader called on the Force, leapt, and propelled himself up to the mouth of the tunnel. Deez and the captain had both taken a knee, blaster rifles planted on their shoulders as they fired into the lyleks trying to

advance down the tunnel toward them. Vader casually loosed a blast of power down the tunnel mouth,
destroying the leading lyleks and pushing half a dozen
more backward.

Seeing Vader, the captain shouted, "Where is the
Emperor?" Deez just kept firing.

Vader turned and looked down to the floor below,
where his Master, surrounded by a dozen or more
lyleks, was spinning, whirling, leaping, his lightsaber
moving so fast it blurred. He looked tiny amid their
bulk but moved with preternatural speed, his blade
stabbing and slashing and severing. He was laughing,
the familiar cackle somehow audible above the sounds
of the horde.

But then a score or more of lyleks lurched at him at
once from all sides, leaping and climbing over one
another, their tentacles a squirming net, their claws
slashing, their massive chitinous bodies blocking him
from Vader's view.

A thought flashed through Vader's mind, a stray
thought, just for a moment: his Master dead, Vader
ruling the Empire, the galaxy, unconstrained by the
leash of an old man . . .

He killed the thought, leapt from the mouth of the
tunnel, flipped in midair, and landed hard atop one of
the lyleks. It bucked, tentacles squirming. He drove
his blade down through its back and out its abdomen,
killing it.

Tentacles reached for him from the left and right,
and a third lylek reared up over its dead kin to get
at him, but he vaulted from the carcass on which
he stood and onto the back of another lylek a
meter away. Again he drove his lightsaber down and
through it.

"Master!" he shouted, still unable to see the Emperor in the press of the creatures.

A blast of power from somewhere under the throng of creatures drove four lyleks ten meters into the air, their bodies shattered by the force of the impact, limbs and tentacles showering down in a macabre rain. His Master stood in the center of the circle of surviving lyleks, his hair mussed, his robe torn, his lightsaber in hand, but otherwise seemingly unharmed.

Vader leapt down to his Master's side. They took position back-to-back.

"Master," Vader said.

"Lord Vader," his Master responded, and chuckled. "Enjoyable, no? Did you consider allowing me to die to realize your own ambitions?"

Vader didn't even attempt to lie. "I did, but only for a moment."

"Good," his Master said. "Very good."

As if on command, the lyleks surged toward them from all sides. As one, Vader and his Master channeled the Force and unleashed blasts of power that slammed into the advancing creatures, shattering several and casting six or seven hard against the walls. Still the lyleks came on, chittering and grasping and slashing.

Vader and his Master stood back-to-back in the center of the press, their lightsabers murderous red lines that lylek limbs and tentacles and bodies could not pass. The carcasses piled up around them, a mountain of the dead, and still they came on. Soon both of them were covered in gore, lost in the Force, in their unbridled ability to kill.

Vader sensed a new danger a moment before it materialized: a lylek from somewhere in the rear of the surviving mass sprang high over the others toward him and his Master, chittering, the spikes of its legs aimed forward as though to impale. Vader answered the creature's leap with a Force-augmented leap of his own, wielding his lightsaber in a two-handed grip, intercepting the creature in midair, and cutting it in two with the red streak of his blade.

He landed atop a dead lylek and immediately bounded back to his Master's side. He hit the floor in a crouch, expecting to be swarmed by the remaining lyleks, but instead found them backing away from him. He soon saw why—they were making way for the approach of the queen.

"You perceived the smaller danger but not the larger," his Master said. "Here it is now."

The quiet of the forest unnerved Isval. It seemed the lylek horde had stripped it of life, or that all the creatures in it were waiting in pensive silence for whatever terrible thing might come next. The swath the lyleks had cut through the terrain would have struck her as impossible had she not seen it for herself. Uprooted trees, shattered trunks, undergrowth pounded into the dirt. And yet she knew that within a month it would be overgrown and gone, as if nothing had ever happened.

There were lessons in that, she thought.

She and Cham hustled along beside Goll, who covered ground rapidly with the path so easy to follow. Goll's team trailed them, the sound of their bouncing gear and equipment loud in the quiet. Chewing up the kilometers gave Isval time to consider the endgame.

"What do we expect to find here?" Isval asked Cham. "Bodies?"

Cham shrugged, looked to Goll.

"If the lyleks caught them, there won't be anything left of the bodies," Goll said. "But there will be signs of a feeding frenzy. That'll tell us all we need to know."

The thought of Vader and the Emperor being torn apart by a hungry pack of Ryloth's chief predatory animal seemed fitting somehow. Still, Isval had seen the things Vader could do—things that no one should have been able to do.

"And if there was no feeding frenzy?" she asked. "If they escaped?"

"No one escapes on foot," Goll said.

Isval was not so sure.

Within the half hour they found the first of the lylek carcasses. The huge body lay in the undergrowth, its head missing. Isval eyed the body, which seemed all edges and spikes and points, covered in a dry, chitinous exoskeleton that looked like weathered stone and was probably sturdier than armor. Its tentacles were rubbery lengths thicker around than her arm.

"Blaster shot," Goll said, examining the stump of the lylek's neck. "See the charring? 'Bout the only way a blaster brings one of these down."

"If they killed the entire horde, could you pick the trail back up?" Cham asked.

Goll looked at him in disbelief. "Cham, killing one lylek is one thing. Maybe just a lucky shot. But wiping out a horde with a blaster while on foot? That's like trying to kill a sandstorm. It's a force of nature. It'll consume you and barely know you're there."

"Could you pick the trail back up, Goll?"

"I . . . yes, I think. Lot of variables, of course, but—"

"Good," Cham said.

Soon they found more carcasses, all of them headshot.

"Getting closer," Goll said softly. "Stay sharp."

They came to the edge of a ravine, and all three of them stopped cold. They looked down into it for a long time, staring in shocked silence. Goll broke the quiet with a soft curse.

Dozens of lylek carcasses lay scattered about the bottom and walls of the ravine. A number of them headshot, but some other force had destroyed the rest. Legs were broken and twisted, exoskeletons shattered and cracked. One carcass lay half buried in the hillside on the opposite side of the ravine. Goll surveyed the scene, the usual furrow back in his brow.

"The horde didn't come out of the ravine," he said. "Lyleks nest underground. This must be an entry point." He didn't sound certain to Isval. "Probably a lot of holes leading down to the nest all along that side of the ravine. But I don't . . ."

"Was there a feeding frenzy here?" Cham asked.

Isval knew the answer before Goll said it.

"I don't . . . no, I don't think so," he said. "Come on."

Isval hesitated a moment as a mental image formed in her brain of lyleks bubbling up out of holes in the ground, trapping them in the bottom of the ravine.

"Stay up here and cover the approaches," she said to Goll's people, who lined the edge of the ravine, staring down in wonder.

"Stay sharp," Goll ordered them, and started down the side of the ravine, using what remained of the undergrowth to keep his footing as he descended. Cham and Isval followed.

The creek that once ran through the ravine had been churned into a paste of mud ichor by the lylek horde. Eyeing the carcasses of the dead, Isval could not imagine what Vader and the Emperor had done to break apart the lyleks so thoroughly.

"Grenades?" Goll asked, though Isval saw no sign of charring or burning.

"Must be something we haven't seen," Cham said.

"These are apex predators," Goll said in disbelief. "We fortify our cities out of fear of facing a handful of these. And this group of four, facing a horde on foot? These are apex predators," he repeated.

Vader is the apex predator, Isval thought but didn't dare say aloud.

Goll studied the churned dirt around what appeared to be a collapsed tunnel entrance. A massive tangle of tree roots and the hind end of a lylek stuck out of the rubble, the rest of it buried under the collapse.

"A lot of activity around this tunnel," Goll said, studying the ground. "Like they were trying to get at something in there. Probably Vader and his group retreated into this tunnel, then collapsed it behind them to cut off pursuit." He backed off, looking up, left, and right. "There will be a lot of other tunnels nearby that lead down into the nest. The whole hill is probably riddled with them, going down a long way. They wouldn't have escaped by collapsing this tunnel. The lyleks would have come at them from another tunnel."

"You're telling us Vader is underground?" Cham said.

"I'm telling you he went underground," Goll said. "Probably the rest of the horde did, too."

"What remains of it," Isval said, looking at the carcasses.

"If they come out," Cham asked, "will they have to come out here?"

"That's a big if, Cham."

"But if they do?" Isval persisted.

Goll shook his head. "I've seen computer models of lylek nests. They're labyrinthine. There are scores of entry and exit points. If the Emperor and Vader somehow manage to stay alive down there, they could come out anywhere within, say, a ten-kilometer radius of here. Sorry, Cham. I think we just lost them."

Cham's skin darkened, a sign of his frustration. Isval was clenching a fist.

Cham activated his comlink. "Kallon, Faylin, we think Vader and the Emperor are underground. They may come up anywhere within a fifteen-kilometer radius of our current location. Get up in the air and start a scan. You find anything at all, sound off immediately."

"If there are any ships out here, they could detect us," Kallon told him.

"I know," Cham said. "But do it."

After Kallon and Faylin acknowledged the order, Cham took the encrypted comlink he used with Belkor and repeated the same thing. Isval could only hear Cham's half of the conversation.

"They could be, Belkor, but I doubt it." Cham looked at the many dead lyleks, the collapsed tunnel. "You're not seeing what I'm seeing here. Just get up in the air and scan. I know. Just do it." He cut the connection.

"They could already be out and on the move, Cham," Goll pointed out. "That ten-klick estimate is just an estimate."

"I realize that," Cham said, and cleared his throat. "Options? What else do we have?"

Goll shrugged.

"We could go down after them," Isval offered.

"That is *not* an option," Goll said.

"We don't have gear for that, and it's too dangerous," Cham said.

"None of us would come out," Goll said. "I guarantee that."

Isval's irritation with the situation boiled over into anger at Goll. "Are you also guaranteeing that Vader won't come out, then? That they're dead down there?"

Goll put his hands on his hips, looked around at all the dead lyleks, and shook his head. "Not after seeing this, no. I don't know what could kill them, if not this."

His admission deflated the bubble of Isval's anger.

Goll looked up at the sky through the openings in the forest's thick canopy. "Wind's bringing rain. Smell it?"

As if on cue, thunder rumbled.

"What kind of men are we after here, Cham?" Goll asked. "This is like nothing I've ever seen, or even heard of."

Cham just shook his head, lekku waving. Isval had only the one answer, and she still wouldn't say it out loud.

Apex predators. That's what kind of men they were after.

Vader and the Emperor stood in the shadow of the queen's towering form. Her respiration was audible in the sudden lull, loud and wet. Each of her six legs was a meter and a half in circumference, and the spikes they ended in looked like sword blades. Her squirming tentacles—four instead of two—were ten meters long, as thick as a man's waist, and ended in glistening points of chitin that leaked some kind of ichor, or perhaps poison. Her mouth could easily bite a person in half.

She advanced slowly, tentacles squirming, the ends of her legs striking the ground with a clipped, staccato rhythm. She lowered her head and hissed as she came on. Her mandibles worked the empty air.

Vader's Master wore the same knowing half smile

he seemed always to wear. "Shall we begin, Lord Vader?"

Vader answered only with the sound of his breathing.

The queen exploded into motion and so, too, did Vader and the Emperor. A tentacle lashed at Vader and he leapt over it, sidestepping a second tentacle, and chopped down with his blade. He missed as the queen snapped the tentacle back, his blade putting a charred furrow in the stone of the floor. He leapt high over her, flipping at the apex of his trajectory, and as he descended he took his blade in a two-handed grip and pointed it downward to impale her.

She lurched sidewise and lashed out with a tentacle, which struck him squarely and knocked him to the floor. She turned as though to advance on him, but his Master sprang before her, jumping, twirling, and ducking under the rapid swings of her tentacles and the spikes of her legs. His lightsaber slashed rapidly at every opening, striking the tentacles but scarring them only, not severing them.

The queen lunged toward his Master and he flipped backward, landing a few paces away. Vader jumped to his feet, spinning out of the way of her attempt to stab him with the chitinous spike at the end of one of her tentacles. He found himself face-to-face with five lyleks, all of them hissing, tentacles squirming. He stabbed one through the head, backflipped high over another, hit the ground, and severed its rear legs.

To his right his Master gestured and, with the Force, lifted two of the lyleks from the floor. Vader and his Master exchanged no words, but each knew precisely what the other intended. With a casual throwing motion, the Emperor flung the two lyleks in Vader's direction, their legs and tentacles squirming, bellies exposed. Slashing and turning a rapid spin, Vader bisected both of them; the four gory pieces that remained fell to the floor in a heap.

From above, blaster shots slammed into the lylek that remained before him, with several shots bouncing off its carapace before one finally caught it in the head and put it down. Vader glanced up to see Deez kneeling in the tunnel's mouth, blaster rifle lowered, firing down into the melee.

Vader reflexively slashed with his lightsaber as another lylek scrabbled toward him. The blade took off the legs and left the creature squealing and spasming. He saw his Master dodging the rapid, repeated strikes of the queen's tentacles. The Emperor twisted and spun and leapt, slashing with his lightsaber where he could, and where the blade bit into the thick tentacles it opened black gashes that leaked a thick ichor. The pain seemed only to make her angrier.

Vader leapt high and landed at his Master's side. The queen roared and loosed a flurry of strikes. Working in tandem, they parried her blows, counterstruck, opened dozens of holes in her tentacles, their blades spinning blurs before them. Her very bulk slowly pushed them backward, and from time to time they had to turn their attention to a lylek that rushed them or tried to jump them from the side. Moving almost as one, the two Sith Lords turned and spun around an unspoken central point, parrying, slashing, killing. Frustrated, the queen rushed toward them with surprising speed. Her huge body slammed into them both, knocking them backward. Quick as a lightning strike, she struck with snapping mandibles . . .

The Emperor fell flat to the floor to avoid the bite and she slammed her legs down at him like so many pikes, each blow chipping the stone of the floor. He rolled and spun underneath the mountain of her body while Vader slashed at her tentacles, the ichor from her many wounds spraying in all directions. She was trying simply to smash his Master with her mass, but Vader perceived her intent, raised a hand, and held her up, straining, grunting for the fraction of a moment that it took for his Master to roll out from under her. And then they were at her again, their blades humming and cutting. She hissed, wounded tentacles flailing, legs stomping, and bounded backward in a crouch.

"Emperor!" Deez shouted from above, and fired at the queen as rapidly as he could pull the trigger.

The shots bounced off her carapace and ricocheted wildly around the chamber. Vader used his lightsaber to deflect one into the face of the lylek nearest him, killing it. Beside him, his Master split the head of a lylek that lunged at him. Vader decided to finish matters.

"Master," he said, and nothing more.

"Go," the Emperor said.

Vader sprinted forward and leapt high. The moment he reached the apex of his jump, his Master seized him with the Force and flung him the rest of the way so that he landed atop the queen's back.

Immediately she bucked, tentacles flailing, and he drove his lightsaber down into her back. To his surprise, the blade only bit partially and then slipped to the side. She screamed and hissed with agony. He grasped it two-handed again, preparing another blow, but she reared up hard, bucking, and flung him to the floor. He landed near his Master, who grabbed him by the arm and heaved him to his feet with uncanny strength.

She whirled around at them and whipped her tentacles at Vader and his Master, following with a lunge forward and a vicious bite at Vader. They sidestepped her attacks, once more falling into their usual rhythm, and crosscut at her head with their lightsabers. Both blades struck home. The Emperor tore a long gash in the armored exoskeleton of her head, and Vader destroyed one eye. She shrieked and reared backward, eye socket leaking gore, tentacles whipping wildly. Deez continued to pour down fire at her, but the shots appeared to do her little or no harm. Still, the distress of their queen drove the remaining lyleks into a frenzy, and they charged from all sides.

Vader bounded backward, leapt high up on the wall, and hung with one hand from a narrow ledge, his boots planted on the stone. He'd assumed his Master would do the same, but he hadn't. Instead, his Master stood in the center of a crowd of the creatures, spinning, whirling, slashing, killing. Deez diverted his fire from the wounded queen to the lyleks attacking the Emperor, but the frenetic motion of the combat prevented him from aiming accurately, and his shots bounced off their carapaces in all directions.

The queen recovered enough to survey the scene and her eye fell on Vader, perched as he was on the wall, seemingly vulnerable, and she lurched toward him, shrieking. She pushed through the lyleks around her, her tentacles squirming wildly, grasping for him. Her remaining eye fixed on him and her mouth opened wide in a prolonged hiss.

Below, an explosion of Force lightning shredded a handful of lyleks and left his Master standing in the center of a circle of charred, dead creatures. He made eye contact with Vader, nodding, and Vader knew to hold his position as the queen closed.

His Master raised both hands and sent a storm of Force lightning into the queen, enmeshing her in sizzling blue lines. She screamed and spasmed in agony, her mandibles parting wide to reveal the rows of her teeth as the lightning tore at her carapace and the organs underneath, burning her inside and out.

Vader acted quickly. Drawing on the Force, he leapt off the wall straight at her head. Despite her pain, she managed to snatch him out of midair with a tentacle, seizing him around the waist and squeezing. His armor creaked under the strain and he shouted with pain but, as ever, let the pain draw him deeper into the Force.

She lifted him high and jerked him toward her slashed face, the ruin of her eye, her mouth opened wide to hiss, exactly as he'd anticipated.

"Finish her!" his Master shouted.

He threw his lightsaber at her open mouth, guiding it with the Force, causing it to spin as rapidly as a rotor as it flew into her gullet. She gagged, recoiled, one good eye wide with pain and confusion, as Vader maintained his mental hold on his spinning blade, cutting her apart from the inside out. Desperately, instinctively, she drove the spiked, poisoned tip of another tentacle at his chest.

Enmeshed in the Force, he caught the spike in his gauntleted fist and stopped it before it reached his armor. He grunted with pain, with exertion, the thick, muscular appendage of the giant creature straining against his Force-fueled strength. He was the stronger, and stared into her face as his lightsaber tore through her innards and his Master's lightning charred her flesh.

She screamed again in a final burst of agony, and the hulking remains of her body collapsed to the floor, taking Vader, clutched now in a limp tentacle, with her. He hit the floor in a crouch along with the bulk of her carcass, shook off the tentacle, and recalled his lightsaber to his hand. The blade cut through her carcass and returned to his hand, slick with fluid.

The remaining lyleks shrieked and chittered, tentacles and legs jerking wildly. Deez continued to blast at them.

Vader met the eyes of his Master, standing five meters away, and both nodded. Immersed in the Force, they set about slaughtering the remaining lyleks. The lines of their lightsabers rose and fell, rose and fell, and the confused, stunned beasts barely defended themselves. Soon the floor was carpeted in carcasses, and Vader and his Master were the only living things standing amid the carnage.

His Master's cackle filled the silence. Both deactivated their blades.

"Well done, my friend," the Emperor said.

Back up in the tunnel, Deez used the high-tensile cable integrated into his belt to rappel down the wall. He picked his way through the slaughter, obviously trying and failing to control the expression of awe on his face, until he stood before Vader and the Emperor. He took a knee, his fist to his chest.

"My Emperor."

"The captain?" Vader asked.

"Killed by one of the creatures, Lord Vader," Deez said as he stood. "His body is . . . not recoverable."

To Vader, the Emperor's mind seemed to be elsewhere. He may have heard Deez or not; Vader could not tell.

"I think we should leave this place before it starts to stink," the Emperor said finally. "This is the way to the surface, I'm quite sure."

Together, Vader, the Emperor, and Deez moved quickly through the tunnels, ever upward, back toward the surface. They stayed alert for lyleks, but the tunnels were empty. The entire nest must have been annihilated.

"The creatures struggled when the queen died. When the head is removed, the body must soon die," the Emperor commented.

Vader said nothing, merely looked at his Master.

"Do you not see? That's why we're hunted, Lord Vader. The rebels hope to cut the head from the Empire."

"Of course," Vader said. It was unlike his Master to state something so obvious except with a purpose. "And?"

His Master adorned his face with his usual half smile. "Many things are that way, even some relationships. If the head is removed, the body cannot exist alone. The relationship is complementary, almost symbiotic."

Vader understood his point then. "Yes, Master."

The roll of thunder reverberating through the stone told them they were nearing the surface. The tunnel they traversed gradually narrowed until they could move only single-file. Deez led, and Vader came last.

Ahead, Vader saw that the tunnel was blocked. He could hear the sound of dripping water and falling rain from behind the blockage. Deez climbed amid the rubble, trying to peer through it.

"We're right at the end," he said. "I can see the outside through a crack in this rockfall. Probably a rockslide caused by the rain. We'll need to clear it, my lords."

Vader and the Emperor stepped around Deez, faced the tons of rock and dirt, and both felt deeply into the Force. As one, they raised their hands, summoned their collective power, and loosed a sudden blast that was more powerful than a grenade. Rock and dirt exploded outward, no doubt traveling high into the night sky.

Beyond, they could see the trunks of trees and falling rain.

"It's clear, Sergeant," said the Emperor with a smile.

Concerned that the lylek carcasses would eventually attract scavengers, maybe gutkurrs again, Goll led Isval and Cham a few kilometers away from the ravine and into the forest. Thunder rumbled; lightning veined the sky. The rain eventually worked its way through the canopy and turned the forest floor sodden. The air smelled of loam.

"The weather is going to make scanning for Vader from the ships even more difficult," Isval said.

Cham only nodded, preoccupied with endgames and exits. He didn't see one and he very much wanted to.

"What's on your mind?" Isval asked.

Cham forced a false smile. "Tomorrow."

Now it was Isval's turn to nod and say nothing.

Cham had called a halt here, figuring there was little point in wandering aimlessly through the forest. They'd lost the Emperor's trail. It would have to be found by air—or not at all. Meanwhile, they'd wait. Isval, of course, tried to pace away her impatience. Goll's team sat on logs and tended their gear.

"We should keep moving," Isval said, pausing in front of Cham.

"To where?" Cham asked her.

She grunted and continued pacing.

Cham allowed himself to consider the possibility that Vader and the Emperor were dead, devoured by the lyleks deep underground. He doubted it—but the uncertainty gnawed at him. He was running out of time to bring events to a close. Eventually the Equatorial Communications Hub would get a dish back up and override Kallon's jamming signal. At that point, a coordinated search and rescue would begin in earnest. He'd have no room to maneuver, then. Too, he figured that word of the destruction of the *Perilous* had reached Coruscant, and that, at that very moment, Imperial ships and soldiers were being prepped to come to Ryloth, if they weren't already en route. Once they arrived, they'd try to blockade the whole system, and then . . .

And then they'd scour it for Cham's people.

Exits. Endgames.

He had hours, at best, if he wanted to give his people a chance to get clear. He felt the day and events slipping out of his grasp. And he was tired, damn tired.

His comlink with Kallon and Faylin pinged.

"Go," he said into it.

Isval stopped pacing and stared at him, as tense as a drawn bowstring.

"Cham," Kallon's voice called over the comm, "I just had an explosion on scan."

Cham's heartbeat accelerated. His lekku flicked with excitement. "You're sure? How far?"

"Five klicks from your location. Precise coordinates incoming."

"What is it?" Isval asked, having heard only Cham's half of the conversation. "What is it?"

Cham held up a finger for her to be patient. "Kallon, just note the location. Do not approach on your own. Acknowledge."

"Not even a little peek?"

"Kallon, if that's Vader, he took two ships down while he was on the ground, and he survived the attack of a lylek horde. Do not approach. We have to play this just right. Acknowledge."

"Acknowledged. You want a ride?"

"We can cover five klicks on foot faster than if you

come back here to pick us up. Just set down and stay on comm. Faylin, get in the vicinity, but not too close."

"Got it," Faylin said.

Cham cut the communication and explained to Isval what he'd heard from Kallon. "Could be something unrelated," he cautioned, seeing her flush with excitement.

She nodded, her fidgeting stilled by the prospect of action. "But it might be them. It probably is. And we've got nothing else. Goll, get your people up. We're moving."

Goll and his troops readied their gear and formed up.

"Belkor?" Isval asked Cham.

"Right," he said to Isval, and raised Belkor on the encrypted comm. "Put yourself down. We have something we're checking out. Just be ready if I call."

"Wait, Syndulla, I—"

Cham cut the connection and imagined Belkor shouting at him from the cockpit. But Belkor was unstable, and Cham didn't trust him not to foul things. The Imperial might make a run at Vader and the Emperor before Cham was ready, or he might compromise their position early. Cham just needed Belkor in reserve with his V-wings, ready for a call.

At this point, Cham regarded Belkor as a hammer. He decided he wouldn't get the Imperial involved until he had a nail he wanted struck.

"Let's go," he said to Goll and Isval. "Quickly, now."

Vader, the Emperor, and Deez walked out of the tunnel and into the forest. Thunder boomed and a hard rain fell, causing the leaves above them to rustle.

"Which direction, my lords?" Deez asked.

Before either of them could answer, a green-skinned

Twi'lek girl, perhaps in late adolescence, emerged from the underbrush. She wore a weathered rain parka and had a long-barreled, Clone Wars–era blaster pistol on her hip. Field gear stuck out of her backpack. The end of a carved wooden tube, almost like a musical instrument, stuck out of the pack, too. Seeing Vader and the Emperor and Deez, her big eyes widened and her lekku twitched, but to her credit she didn't run.

Deez started to level his rifle but Vader grabbed the guard's arm, halting him. That seemed to put the girl a bit less on edge, though she looked ready to bolt if she needed to. Vader sensed more curiosity in the girl than fear.

"Who are you?" Deez asked.

"Who are *you*?" the girl responded, her accent so thick that Vader found it hard to understand her at first. "What are you doing out here? Are you lost?"

The girl apparently did not recognize the Emperor or his companions. She must have been from one of the remote settlements that were known to dot Ryloth's wilderness.

"Come here, girl," the Emperor said, putting the power of the Force into his command.

Unable to resist, the girl walked out of the tree line until she stood, small and vulnerable, before him.

With preternatural speed the Emperor drew, ignited, and slashed at the girl with his lightsaber, but Vader had sensed his Master's intent and moved with greater speed, igniting his own blade and intercepting his Master's blow before it could land.

The girl, under the sway of the Emperor's power, seemed scarcely to notice the danger. She simply stood there, staring vacantly, her face aglow in the red light of the crossed blades.

The Emperor's mouth twisted in a snarl, and Vader felt his power gathering.

Behind Vader, Deez raised his rifle and aimed it at Vader's back, but Vader stretched his free hand back and unleashed a blast of power that lifted the guardsman from his feet and flung him into the trees. Branches cracked audibly under the impact of Deez's body.

Vader and his Master stared at each other across the sizzling glow of their crossed blades.

"Has it come to this?" his Master said. He sounded calm, almost resigned, but not at all surprised.

The tone surprised Vader. "Forgive me, Master," he said, and deactivated his blade. "I think the girl can be of use to us."

"Do you?" the Emperor asked softly.

"There must be a village nearby," Vader said. "If they have a ship . . ."

Deez climbed to his feet and staggered out of the brush, groaning. He leveled his blaster rifle uncertainly at Vader, looking to the Emperor for a directive.

His Master's scowl lingered for a moment before twisting into a half smile that didn't reach his eyes. He gestured at Deez to stand down, his eyes never leaving Vader's faceplate.

"I agree. She can be of use to us."

The Emperor looked at his blade, at Vader, pursed his lips, and deactivated the weapon. To the girl he said, "Is your village nearby?"

The Twi'lek, still under the influence of the Emperor's power and with an unblinking, faraway look in her eye, nodded. "It's not far. I was out checking hunting traps and heard a boom. I thought it was a rockslide and came to look. I saw you from the trees."

"And what did you think when you saw us?" the Emperor asked.

The girl's brow creased, as if she didn't understand. "Think? I assumed you were lost, that maybe you'd crashed. Strangers are uncommon out here. You'll be welcomed at the village, though. It's custom."

His Master smiled. "That's nice to hear. How many of you are there?"

"Thirty-seven," the girl said. "But Naria's with child, so it will soon be thirty-eight."

"Indeed," said the Emperor. He looked at Vader curiously.

"Master?" Vader asked, but the Emperor ignored him.

"Maybe you have some news of what's happening in the cities?" the girl asked.

"Maybe we do," the Emperor said. "Do you have a ship in your village?"

The girl shook her head. "No, no ship. Not even a working communicator. We lost it last year and haven't been able to get another in trade. But we have food and warmth and songs."

The Emperor smiled. "Very good. Take us to your village."

Without another word, the girl turned and led them through the forest.

Vader figured the girl's village must have been founded by slaves who'd escaped from one of Ryloth's mines, or by refugees displaced long ago during the Clone Wars. Many such villages existed on Ryloth, and many of those had little or no contact with the outside world. The Empire knew of the settlements, of course, sometimes disbanding them and "relocating" the people to labor camps if slave labor was needed somewhere, but generally the Empire left them alone. The girl's village had no ship and no communicator, though, so it would be of little use to

Vader and his Master except as a way-stop. Still, there might be something there they could use.

"What's your name, girl?" the Emperor asked her as they picked their way through the trees.

"Drua," the girl said. She looked at Deez. "What's your name? And why do you wear that . . . suit?"

Deez seemed momentarily taken aback by the question before saying, "My name is Sergeant, and it's my honor to wear this armor."

The Emperor diverted the conversation. "So you're out here on your own, Drua?"

"Of course! I know the forest as well as any." She looked up through a hole in the forest's canopy. "The rain is going to end within the hour."

"Where are your parents?" the Emperor asked, and Vader thought it an odd question to come from his Master.

The girl did not turn back to face them, and her voice fell a bit when she said, "My mother died two winters back. I didn't know my father."

"Not unlike you, apprentice," the Emperor said quietly.

The words dredged Vader's memory. He flashed for a moment on his mother, a slave; flashed, too, on the Tusken Raiders who'd killed her, on the satisfying moments when he killed them, all of them, every one of them.

"You live alone, then?" the Emperor asked.

"Of course not! I live with my grandfather," Drua said.

"Well," said the Emperor. "We will try not to be too much of an imposition."

Cham checked their location against the coordinates on his comp.

"Getting close," he said to Goll and Isval, who walked on either side of him.

Goll signaled to his people, who had sorted themselves into their usual skirmish line formation, to fall back some and move in silence.

"Let me check the area first," Goll said to Cham, and Cham nodded.

Goll disappeared ahead into the trees and rain. Cham marveled at Goll's woodcraft as he and Isval stood there under Ryloth's trees, waiting in the rain, saying nothing.

Finally, Cham decided to repair the damage he'd caused earlier. "I'm sorry about what I said before."

"About what?" she asked, not looking at him.

"You know what. About the movement. About being tired. About the fight going on without me."

She looked at him then, her skin wet and flushed. "So . . ."

"So we keep on after today. No matter what happens. We can rebuild the movement."

Her eyes narrowed and she studied his face. "You're a bad liar, Syndulla. You meant what you said."

He held up his hands in protest.

"No," she said. "Hear me. I thought about what you said. If we kill Vader and the—"

"When," he corrected her. "When we kill Vader."

She blinked. "Right. *When* we kill Vader and the Emperor, the Empire won't just fall down overnight. But we'll have started something, a rebellion maybe, but the rebellion will need leaders. You."

He wasn't sure what she wanted to hear so he said nothing.

"I'm not making myself clear," she said. "You were right, at least in part. I see that. The movement *is* done after today, but that's not because it's going to die. It's because it's going to change and it's going to spread. What we did today, what we *do* today, is going to ripple through the whole Empire. And whatever grows out of those ripples will need leaders. You, Cham."

"And you," Cham said.

She shook her head, her lekku waving. "I'm a fighter, not a leader, not a planner. That's you, and that's why I don't want to hear any more talk about letting someone else carry the fight. After today we fight on different ground, and we maybe aren't the Free Ryloth movement, but we still fight."

Cham had always fought for Ryloth, and only for Ryloth, but he found Isval's thinking contagious. Maybe a bigger picture was what he needed to consider. Earlier he thought he'd lost his purpose, but maybe in losing it he'd found another one, a bigger one. Maybe.

"I hear your words, Isval."

"Then heed them," she said.

At that moment Goll returned from the woods. Isval didn't wait for him to speak. "What'd you find?" she asked.

"An old lylek tunnel leading down. Looks like it had been blocked by a rockslide, and then cleared by an explosive."

"A grenade," Cham said.

"Yeah," Goll said. "Cleared so someone could get through from underneath."

"Had to be them," Isval said, grinning fiercely.

Goll smiled, too. "I agree, unless lots of people are wandering around in lylek nests. I found a trail leading away from the tunnel. There's more than one left in their group, but the rain makes it hard to distinguish numbers. Gonna make it hard to stay on their trail, too, so we should get moving."

It occurred to Cham all of a sudden that they were

as close as they'd been all day to their quarry—half an hour, maybe an hour, behind finally getting another shot at the Emperor and his right hand. He looked at Isval, at Goll, back at Goll's team.

"I know what you're thinking," Isval said.

"Good, because I don't," Goll said, looking from Isval to Cham and back again. "You look like you've swallowed a rock, Cham."

"We can do this," Isval said, putting a hand on his forearm. "*Think through an exit* is all we need to do, right?"

"Right," Cham agreed, and then he said the words that he always said to Belkor, words that felt uncomfortably like a rationalization. "We've come too far to stop now. Let's go finish this."

The wind carried a soft, irritating buzz from somewhere ahead. To Vader it sounded vaguely insectoid. The buzzing rose and fell with the velocity of the wind.

The sound seemed to put Deez on alarm. He held his rifle at the ready, looking hard at the trees around them, as if anticipating an attack.

Drua looked puzzled, then amused by his reaction. "There's nothing to fear. Those are lylek tubes. The sound keeps them away. Irritates their brains. My grandfather says its gives them a headache so they don't come around."

"A sound keeps lyleks away?" the Emperor said. "How very interesting."

"Oh, it wouldn't keep one of them away if it was determined," Drua said. "Grandpa says it just steers them in another direction. Why walk into a headache, right?"

The ground rose as Drua led them through the

trees. Large boulders and rock piles dotted the landscape here and there, getting more frequent as they went. The buzzing sound grew louder and they soon saw the cause. Curved wooden tubes about as long as a human man's arm hung from the trees, swaying in the wind. Holes of various sizes and at various places had been bored into them. When the wind blew through the holes, the tubes emitted the irritating buzz. Looking at them all hanging there, Vader was reminded of gallows.

"Puts one's teeth on edge," the Emperor said. "What if the wind dies down, Drua? Won't lyleks come then?"

Drua looked at him as if he were ridiculous. "There's always wind. And if we have to, we can run. We have a fortified place we can hide."

"I see," the Emperor said.

Soon the forest gave way to jagged hills of piled earth and rock. They picked their way through those until the ground fell away before them and they found themselves looking down on an enormous, steep-walled rock quarry. Two large tunnels opened near the base of the quarry on the side opposite them, dark holes, like the planet opening its mouth in a scream. Vader assumed them to be old mine shafts, and probably one of them was the fortified place Drua had mentioned.

Drua's village clustered near one of the tunnels: thirty to forty single-story structures made of stacked stone and tree-limb beams, with roofs of stretched hide and bark. Raised gardens covered a sizable area of the quarry's bottom near the village. Vader saw no livestock.

Torches burned along the walls of the quarry in two places, the flames dancing in the rain, marking a serpentine path along the steep walls. Torches burned at the bottom of the quarry, too, at the edges of the village. Vader could see Twi'leks moving about among the buildings. From a distance they looked like shadows, or ghosts.

As he watched, a fire sprang to life in a common area and half a dozen Twi'leks gathered around it, ordinary people doing ordinary things. Music carried up from the quarry, the sounds of a woodwind and then a lilting, haunting female voice.

"That's Mala singing the Dirge of Valaunt," Drua said.

"A dirge?" the Emperor said. "How very quaint. Drua, does the village have computers? Any vehicles at all?"

Drua smiled and shook her head. "No, nothing like that. We live simply." She patted the blaster at her hip. "We make exception for some things, of course, but the Elders say that too much technology makes us slaves all over again. We have our ways and they serve us well."

She led them along the lip of the quarry until they reached the torchlit path that snaked down to the bottom. "Mind your steps," she said. "The way is treacherous."

The Emperor chuckled softly at that.

They picked their way down the side of the quarry, Vader and the Emperor as sure-footed as Drua, Deez nearly slipping from time to time.

At the bottom, a Twi'lek man, muscular, green-skinned, and armed with a blaster pistol, met them. A carved wooden whistle hung from a lanyard around his neck. He looked with mild suspicion on Vader, the Emperor, and Deez.

"Narmn, it's all right," Drua said. "I found these lost souls in the forest. This is Sergeant and . . ." She trailed off, perhaps realizing for the first time that she'd never gotten the names of the other two.

The Emperor said, "My name is Krataa, and this"—he gestured at Vader—"is Irluuk."

Narmn's eyes narrowed but he bowed, his lekku shifting slightly, and said, "Krataa and Irluuk and Sergeant, you are here, and because you are here, you are welcome."

"That is most gracious of you," the Emperor said.

Narmn and Drua led them along the quarry's floor toward the warmth and light of the village. Narmn put the whistle to his lips as they walked and blew a series of notes that Vader assumed indicated the arrival of strangers. The Dirge of Valaunt trailed off.

"I'm going to run ahead and gather Grandfather," Drua said, and, after a nod from Narmn, she sprinted off.

"Gather everyone," the Emperor called after her. "I look forward to meeting them."

Meanwhile, more and more Twi'leks emerged from the buildings and congregated at the village's edge, more shadows, more ghosts, all of them apparently waiting to greet the strangers, Krataa and Irluuk and Sergeant.

Other than the Emperor, only Vader knew the false names were ancient Sith words that meant "death" and "fate."

Goll moved ten meters ahead of Cham and Isval, who walked ten meters ahead of Goll's people. All of them were tense, and all but Goll had their weapons drawn and ready. Isval reminded herself that Goll was too good to allow them to simply stumble upon Vader and the Emperor; reminded herself, too, that Vader and the Emperor did not know they were being hunted.

Goll picked his way through the forest ahead of

them, studying leaves and branches but mostly the ground, grunting and nodding to himself, moving them confidently through the woods.

"There's four of them, but not the same four," he said softly, returning to them for a brief update. "They lost one of the Royal Guards, and there's an adolescent with them now, or a small-boned female. Possibly Twi'lek, but there's no way to know for sure."

"How far ahead are they?" Isval asked.

"Not far," Goll said. "I can scout ahead alone if—"

Cham cut him off. "No. We stick together. We just stay staggered. When you see them, we stop to evaluate the situation and plan the attack. We'll get one chance only, and we have to do it exactly right. We all know what Vader can do. We need surprise if we can get it."

Isval nodded, Goll nodded, and they set off, Goll taking position well out in front.

"Some people hunt lyleks," Cham whispered to Isval. "Did you know that?"

"I've heard that, yes. What are you getting at?"

"Why do you suppose they do that?" Cham asked. "Risk their lives that way?"

"The thrill, maybe," she said. "Or to prove they can."

"Maybe they think it's important somehow," Cham said, and Isval realized he wasn't talking about lyleks, and neither was she.

"They must," she said. "Otherwise it would be foolish."

CHAPTER SEVENTEEN

Smiles and looks of wonder greeted Vader, the Emperor, and Deez as Narmn led them into the village proper. The modest homes recalled to Vader the kind of home he'd had on Tatooine, long ago.

The Emperor smiled and nodded, returning greetings and thanking the Twi'leks for their hospitality. Vader said nothing, though he was aware that both his suit and Deez's armor were the subject of many whispered questions and pointed fingers. The Twi'leks crowded around them, interested in the strangers. Deez interposed himself as best he could between the Emperor and the villagers.

"Keep some distance," he said to the Twi'leks, a bit harshly.

"It's fine, Sergeant," the Emperor said. "It doesn't matter. Does it, Irluuk?"

Vader answered with a question of his own, speaking in an old Sith tongue, so only the Emperor would understand him. "You plan to kill them, Master?"

"I plan no such thing, apprentice," the Emperor returned in the same language, never losing his smile.

"But they will die anyway. You killed them all the moment you spared that girl."

"I don't understand," Vader said.

"You will. Patience, my friend."

Drua emerged from the small crowd and stood before them, her smile bright in the light of the torches. A frail, wrinkled, tan-skinned Twi'lek accompanied her, one hand on the girl's shoulder. His milky-white eyes announced his blindness.

"My grandfather," Drua announced.

Her grandfather bowed his head in the same fashion Narmn had. Probably his lekku were signing a greeting that Vader could not discern.

"Our custom is to welcome all strangers," the grandfather said in a thin, broken voice. "But my granddaughter has shared your names and so you are strangers no longer. Welcome, Sergeant, Krataa, and Irluuk. The village is here and they have seen you."

Head nods around, waving lekku, smiles. Grandfather raised his hands for quiet and continued: "The rain has stopped and we have new friends. It is late, but it is not so late. We should celebrate and have music."

Cheers and whoops answered his words. Music started from somewhere ahead, the woodwinds they'd heard earlier, accompanied by a drum. Many of the villagers started to sing or hum in Ryl, their native tongue, the rising and falling melody like pouring rain and booming thunder.

Drua took the Emperor by the hand and led him toward the village center. The villagers patted Vader and Deez on the shoulders as they followed, uttering words of welcome. Vader allowed himself to be led, looking into the colorful smiling faces, knowing that he was looking at ghosts.

A large fire was already burning in the village cen-

ter. Two Twi'leks playing carved woodwinds stood
near it, swaying to the music they made. A drummer
sat between them, keeping time.

Carved stumps were arranged in a circle around the
fire. Vader and Deez and the Emperor were seated on
them. The rest of the villagers milled around, talking
and smiling; one couple even danced. Others sat on
the stumps and chatted with one another. Drua's
grandfather sat near Vader and the Emperor. Before
Drua sat, the Emperor said to her, "Drua, perhaps
you could bring Irluuk the broken communications
unit you spoke of. He has skill in that regard."

Vader looked a question at his Master.

"Indulge me," the Emperor said to him. "Drua, can
you get it?"

"Of course," Drua said, and sped off. She returned
quickly, bringing Vader a small, decades-old communicator and a box of hand tools, the kind of equipment Vader had used as a boy, when he'd made things
of metal, rather than being encased in it. He opened
the box and took a tool in hand, finding that it felt as
right as the hilt of his lightsaber. He quickly disas-
sembled the communicator and set to work fixing it.
He saw the problem right away. He'd have it operational quickly. Drua watched in wide-eyed wonder.

His Master leaned over and said, "I see you've retained the skills of your youth."

"But nothing else from that time," Vader said.

"We will see," the Emperor replied.

The wind carried a faint but irritating buzzing sound
from somewhere ahead.

"What is that?" Isval asked Cham.

Cham shrugged, brow furrowed. "Let's see what
Goll says."

He signaled a halt to Goll's team, who trailed Isval and Cham. They didn't have long to wait before Goll returned from his position scouting ahead.

"What's that sound?" Cham asked.

"A signaling device, I think, or art or something," Goll said. "Or maybe it keeps animals away. I'm not sure, but it seems harmless. And it doesn't matter, because we found them. Vader and the Emperor. We found them."

Isval's heart beat against her ribs. She felt herself flush, felt the calm of action settle on her.

Cham took Goll by the shoulders. "Where, man?"

"There's a gorge half a klick that way." He nodded to indicate the direction. "Looks like an old quarry. I saw them in it."

"Saw them!" Isval said, unable to contain herself. "Why are we waiting? Let's go. Cham, call in Belkor's V-wings, we can—"

"No, no," Goll said, shaking his huge head, and the seriousness of his expression deflated Isval. "Don't call in anything yet, least of all Belkor."

"What is it?" Cham said warily.

"There's a village there, Cham. Isolated settlement. All rustics. All Twi'leks. I didn't see so much as a comm array. They—"

"What did Vader do to them?" Isval snapped.

"Nothing," Goll said. "They—"

"Nothing?" Isval repeated. "What do you mean nothing?"

"Let me finish a sentence, Isval!" Goll said, and Isval clamped her mouth shut. "They're all gathered in the village center. It's like a . . . celebration or something."

Isval understood. Goll had said they were rustics. "The villagers don't know who they are. To them, they're just guests."

The harshness of life on Ryloth had established certain norms in Twi'lek settlements—among them, hospitality to strangers. That didn't extend to Imperial forces, of course, but some settlements had been isolated for so long they knew almost nothing of the Empire. It appeared Vader and the Emperor had stumbled into one of those, and the Twi'leks there had taken them in.

"Show us," Cham said.

Syndulla had told him to set down because he had found something, but Belkor didn't answer to Syndulla. He needed to keep looking, not just for Vader and the Emperor, but for Mors. He wouldn't fly out of comm distance from Cham, but he'd darn well keep looking.

"Up, down, up, down," he said to Ophim's corpse, which was already beginning to stink. "He thinks I'm a fishing lure. I'm not, Ophim. I'm not!"

He realized he was sweating, maybe feverish, and talking to a corpse. The sound of the rain beating down on the bubble for the last half hour had given him a headache, and his thoughts flowed like mud.

"Just get through the next few hours, right? Right, Ophim?"

Belkor flew the recon bubble at the height of the forest canopy, moving slowly, the elaborate scanners on the ship poring over the landscape below and the sky all around.

Nothing, nothing, and nothing.

He checked his clock, seeing how much time he had before the comm hub got a dish operational and overrode the jamming signal. Time was running out. His head would not stop hurting. And they had found nothing! Well, not nothing. Cham had found something, but Cham hadn't told him what it was.

"He doesn't trust me," Belkor said to Ophim.

He tried to raise Cham on the encrypted comm, but Cham wasn't acknowledging.

Belkor slammed the comm against the palm of his hand and shouted, "Pick up! Pick up! Pick up!"

In frustration he threw the comm against the inside of the cockpit's bubble. It bounced off the clear plastic and slammed to the deck. He immediately regretted his action, fearing he'd broken his only connection to Cham.

He cursed and giggled and cursed more.

He realized he was having some kind of fit, an attack of anxiety or stress or something. His heart was racing and it felt like someone was driving nails into his skull. He took some breaths, tried to gather himself, managed to at least get himself under some kind of control.

And when he did, he decided that he'd had enough orders from Cham. The Twi'lek was too slow to act, too methodical, and he wasn't keeping Belkor informed. He said he had a lead on Vader and the Emperor? Good enough. Belkor would see what that lead was.

He already had the recon bubble running dark. From the outside, in the night and rain, it would be invisible to the naked eye.

Still hugging the treetops, he sent his location, speed, and direction to his V-wings so they could keep pace with him and stay in contact. Then he set off in the direction he knew Cham to be.

"Let's go see what he's found, Ophim."

* * *

Mors operated the scan in the transport. The officer flying it stayed close to the top of the trees, but not too close. The transport was not an agile craft. If they caught a thick limb . . .

A ship showed at the outside range of Mors's scanner, bringing her to full attention. She activated the comm and hailed Steen.

"You seeing that, Steen?" Mors looked in the direction of Steen's transport, even though the dark and rain prevented her from seeing it except on scan.

Steen's voice carried over the comm. "It's a V-wing, ma'am. No doubt one of Belkor's. And here it comes."

"Moving fast," said the officer flying the transport. Mors really should have tried to memorize his name.

"Hail him," Mors said, trying to keep her voice calm. Neither Mors's shuttle nor Steen's transport was capable of winning a fight against even a single V-wing. They had to talk their way out of this, or their attempt to rescue Lord Vader and the Emperor was about to end in fire.

"You do it, Steen. Belkor's men may not respond to me." To the pilot, Mors said, "Do not go evasive."

"Uh, you're sure, ma'am?"

"Yes," Mors said, though she clenched a fist as the V-wing closed. Its weapons locked on to Mors's shuttle. Alarms started to wail.

"He has weapons locked," the pilot said, unnecessarily.

"This is Major Steen Borkas of the Equatorial Communications Hub," Steen said over the comm, his voice calm and commanding. "Power down those weapons and identify yourself immediately, V-wing."

The V-wing's in-atmo lights came into view, closing fast. The agile fighter slew straight toward the shuttle and transport.

"I say again, power down and identify yourself, V-wing."

The weapons lock stayed hot, so Mors played the cards she held. She could not imagine Belkor had told the V-wing pilots the whole truth.

"V-wing," Mors said, "are you assisting with search operations for Lord Vader and the Emperor? That's our purpose here. Acknowledge."

The V-wing buzzed over and past the shuttle and transport, the telltale hum of its engines audible even through the shuttle's bulkhead. Mors let herself exhale.

"Say again, transport?" the V-wing pilot said.

Mors decided to dive in altogether. "Son, this is Moff Delian Mors and I asked if you were assisting in the search for Lord Vader and the Emperor, both of whom are on the ground somewhere near here. And they are on the ground because their Star Destroyer and then their shuttle were destroyed as a direct result of action by Imperial traitors, specifically Colonel Belkor Dray. Do you hear me?"

Quiet over the comm.

"Son, I hope you understand me, and I hope you realize that this is all going to come out eventually. Belkor didn't tell you about Vader and the Emperor?"

A long silence, then, "No, ma'am."

"Son, there will be an investigation like we've never seen, the Imperial Security Bureau, stormtrooper garrisons, all of it. Listen, I don't know all of what Belkor told you, but you should believe none of it. And unless you're also a traitor, power down your weapons now, and communicate with no one other than us. Acknowledge."

The next moments turned a few more of Mors's hairs gray, but finally the V-wing released its weapons lock.

"Acknowledged. Ma'am, this is Wing Leader Arim Meensa, and Belkor told us *you* were the traitor. And I guess I was willing to believe that. Maybe a bit too willing, as I owe Belkor. But I know Major Borkas's reputation, and there's no way he's involved in treachery against the Emperor. What's going on here, ma'am?"

"A slow-motion assassination attempt," Mors said. "But we're going to stop it. Tell me what you know, who's out here, where Belkor is—everything."

The V-wing pulled into formation beside the transport and the shuttle. "Yes, ma'am," said the pilot.

Soon Mors and Steen knew that Belkor was in a recon bubble and had a total of six V-wings flying a comm ladder as they looked both for Mors and for Vader and Palpatine's crashed shuttle. She learned, too, that Belkor had told the pilots that they would probably end up having to attack a ground target based only on coordinates, and that when he gave the order to attack, they needed to move fast and ask no questions. Finally, she learned that Belkor had abruptly changed the search area a short time earlier. From that, Mors drew the obvious conclusion.

"Belkor has assets on the ground," she told Steen over the comm. "More traitors, or maybe a rebel group. But either way, they have a lead on the Emperor and Lord Vader."

"Could be," Steen said, though he sounded skeptical.

"We need to get to Belkor," Mors said, but knew the recon bubble scanners would pick up their approach long before they picked up Belkor on their own scans. Belkor could easily evade them. Besides, they didn't know exactly where he was. All they had were his last known coordinates, and they knew that he was still within comm range of Meensa's V-wing.

"Send the V-wing," Steen said abruptly. "Shoot him down."

"Maybe," Mors said, thinking. "But I'm thinking not. We need to get to the Emperor. If Belkor is working with a group on the ground who are trailing the Emperor and Vader and we shoot down Belkor, the group on the ground may still get to him. He's just an elderly man, Steen. They can't be moving very fast."

"Right," Steen said. "I see your point."

Mors raised the wing leader, trying out another idea. "Meensa, will your men take your orders even over Belkor's?"

"Ma'am, we all owe the colonel in one way or another but . . . yes, they'll obey whatever I tell them."

"Good. Then listen to me. You're going to keep doing as he's ordered, but we're going to stay with you and you're going to keep us apprised of what's happening as it's happening. And then when he calls in the attack, you're going to give me the coordinates and delay your arrival."

"Delay, ma'am?"

"I need to get there first, get the stormtroopers on the ground. Then you fly in. Tell your men whatever you have to, tell them to take a recon pass at first. They'll see the stormtroopers, they'll see Lord Vader, and then you tell them that it's Belkor who's the traitor. Can you do all that?"

"Easily, ma'am."

A mist started to rise from the warm, wet ground. Crouched low, Cham looked down at the village nestled in the quarry below. The scene struck him as surreal. Vader and the Emperor and a helmetless Royal Guard sat near a fire amid a circle of Twi'leks, passing around fruits and drinking gourds. Vader was working on something he held in his hands. Music carried up from the bottom of the quarry, a lilting melody played by woodwinds and drums.

"You won't believe this," he said, and handed the macrobinoculars to Isval, who came away with the same baffled expression that Cham knew he must have worn. Goll took the macrobinoculars from Isval, surveyed the scene, grunted, and handed them back to Cham.

"Even with sniper rifles that would be a difficult shot," Goll said. "And we don't have sniper rifles."

"What do we do?" Isval asked Cham.

Cham looked at Goll, then nodded at the torchlit path that led down one side of the quarry. "Can your troops get down the side without alerting anyone?"

"Those paths are half cut into the quarry wall," Goll replied, eyeing the path. "Between that and this mist, I think we could get down the path unseen, yes, assuming no one comes along for a nighttime stroll. But unless the mist thickens, as soon as my people hit the bottom of that quarry and start heading for the village, they'll be there for all to see."

"Right," Cham agreed. "One thing at a time, though. One thing at a time."

"What are you thinking?" Isval asked.

Cham could hear the edge in her voice, her need to do something now that they had Vader and the Emperor in their sights.

"I'm thinking we get Goll's people in position and then we wait," he said.

She bit down hard, as if trying to wall off words she knew she shouldn't say. Finally, she burst out, "Wait for what? They're right there!"

"And so are three dozen innocent people," Cham snapped. "*Our* people, backward or not. I send Goll's

team, what do you think happens? I call for Belkor's
V-wings to hit these coordinates and what happens?"

Isval just stared at him, her fists clenching and un-
clenching.

"It's late," Cham said soothingly. "The villagers
will return to their homes soon. We watch where
Vader and the Emperor go. Everyone has to sleep,
even them. Then we move in. Quick. Precise. No one
gets hurt but them. Then this is over."

Goll looked from Cham to Isval, back to Cham.

Isval finally gave a nod. "If this mist gets too thick,
we won't be able to see the bottom of the quarry from
here."

"One thing at a time," Cham repeated.

"I'll have my troops start moving down," Goll said.
His words were half question, half statement, and
Cham nodded.

After he'd gone, Isval held out her hand for the
macrobinoculars. "I'll watch."

"Figured," Cham said. "I need to talk to Kallon
anyway."

"About what?" she asked.

"About exits," Cham said.

He watched for a moment as Goll's fighters
crouched low and started crawling single-file down
the cut-out path that led down to the bottom of the
quarry. Then he moved off into the trees and raised
Kallon on the comm.

"Cham," Kallon acknowledged.

"Don't argue with what I'm about to say. Understand?"

"Uh, yes, all right."

Cham exhaled, then said it: "I need you to leave
now, fly back, and start an organized retreat of our
forces into the mountains. See to the dispersal of the
people and matériel we have left."

"I don't—"

"You're interrupting."

"Right. Go on."

"The Empire will have troops on the way to Ryloth already, and they will lock down this system and scan every millimeter of the planet's surface. Like nothing we've ever seen before, Kallon. And you know they'll find every hidden base we have. And they will turn Twi'leks over to the Imperial Security Bureau by the hundreds. Our people need to start getting clear now, break up into their constituent cells. They know the process. You know it, too. Go start it."

A long pause, then, "All right. I will. See you on the other side, Cham. What's happening there?"

"We found them. Now we just have to kill them."

Cham cut the connection and hailed Faylin.

"Go, Cham," she said.

"Stay where you are and stay on this frequency. You're our ride out if something goes sideways. We'll have to pack in double. I sent Kallon on another mission."

"Understood."

Cham returned to Isval's side. She was standing beside Goll, staring through the macrobinoculars down at the village, at their prey. Goll's people had worked their way well down the path.

"There's no one from the village anywhere near the path's bottom," Isval said. "They're all in the village center."

"Good," Cham said.

"Did you see what Vader's working on?"

"No," Cham said. "Can you tell?"

"It's a communicator," Isval said. "An old one, but no mistaking it."

"An old comm isn't going to cut through Kallon's jamming signal."

"Agreed," Isval said.

"Incongruous to think of him working on a communicator, though," Cham said. "Makes me wonder who he was before he put on that suit."

Isval put down the magnifiers. "Let's peel it off his corpse and find out."

Belkor realized that he was humming to himself as he flew along in the recon bubble, some song or other from when he'd been a lieutenant.

Somewhere throughout the course of the day he'd come to the conclusion that he was going to die, and nothing he could do would stop that now. He accepted that. But he'd also concluded that he wanted to take Vader and the Emperor and Syndulla and his foolish group of followers out first. Everyone would remember his name for generations to come.

"And why not, Ophim?" he said to the corpse still strapped into the seat beside him.

He wondered if he'd completely lost his mind, but then figured that people who'd gone insane never wondered if they'd gone insane.

Still humming, he pored over scans, knowing the general area where Syndulla had to be. In short order he'd found them, a large group of life-forms grouped around some kind of small canyon.

"There you are," he said, and accelerated toward it.

Vader barely heard the music of the Twi'leks and couldn't touch the food. He was among them but apart from them. His armor and his power and his understanding put him as far away from these people as a distant star. They were ephemeral, passing, and unable to touch him. He focused on the communicator, his hands, working the tools, cleaning the circuits, connecting the fibers, the whole of it a meditation.

"That is amazing," Drua said, watching him work.

Vader pieced it back together and handed it to the young Twi'lek. "It's done."

"You fixed it?" Drua asked. "Just like that?"

"That isn't what I said," Vader answered, though Drua didn't take his meaning. He hadn't fixed it to make the device function. He'd fixed it to ensure he'd feel nothing while doing so. He'd fixed it to exorcise his own ghosts. No doubt his Master had told the Twi'lek to bring him the communicator for just that reason, too.

The young Twi'lek powered up the communicator, not knowing, as Vader did, that the jamming signal would prevent it from picking up any communications. She spun it through several frequencies.

Suddenly the device squawked to life, and the girl grinned. "Hey, listen to this!" She had the communicator tuned to an unsecured Imperial frequency used to direct commercial shipping, and Vader heard a droning voice giving instructions to an inbound freighter. He sat up straight, surprised, realizing right away what it meant.

"It appears communication is back up," the Emperor said, then to Deez, "Sergeant, if you wouldn't mind, please transmit a hail on the Moff's secure frequency."

"And if the Moff is the traitor?" Vader asked.

The Emperor chuckled. "Delian Mors is many things, Lord Vader, lazy, hedonistic, nihilistic, but she is and never will be a traitor to the Empire. And after today's events, I suspect that she will begin correcting her weaknesses. Proceed, Sergeant."

The Emperor told Deez the code for the frequency;

Deez turned the old communicator to the secure channel available only to Moffs and transmitted a hail.

The Emperor said to Vader, "This will all be over soon."

Vader looked around at the Twi'leks, all of them smiling, eating, singing.

Ghosts. All of them ghosts.

The sudden crackle of comm static almost startled Mors out of her seat.

"Comm is back up, ma'am!" said the pilot.

"Yes, I hear that!" Mors exclaimed, and raised Steen. "Steen, send my thanks to your people back at the hub. They're hours early."

"Will do, ma'am."

"Incoming message, ma'am," the pilot said. "The channel is . . . locked, ma'am. I can't respond."

Mors checked it and saw that the transmission was on the secure channel reserved for Moffs. "I'll take it," she said, and input the code that allowed access. "This is Moff Delian Mors. To whom am I speaking?"

"This is Sergeant Erstin Deez of the Royal Guard, and I am hailing you on behalf of Emperor Palpatine." Mors did not recognize the voice. "The Emperor and Lord Vader are at the following coordinates and require immediate extraction."

Mors could hardly believe what she was hearing.

"You get those coordinates?" she asked the pilot.

"Have them, ma'am," said the pilot.

"Sergeant Deez," Mors returned, "we believe the Emperor and Lord Vader are in danger. If possible, remove them from their current location and hail me again on this channel with the new coordinates."

"Understood, Moff Mors."

"We're on our way," Mors said.

* * *

Belkor flew high above what he now realized was an old mining quarry. A few small fires and one large one burned on the quarry's floor. Many life-forms, humanoid, congregated around the large fire. He zeroed in on the scan, magnified, magnified, magnified, until he could see . . .

Vader and the Emperor, seated among a throng of Twi'leks.

He tried to contain a giggle, but it burst out. The scene struck him as ridiculous. The *day* struck him as ridiculous.

Another group of Twi'leks crept down the side of the quarry, while a handful more remained at the lip, overlooking the village.

"Hello, Syndulla," Belkor said.

He had them now, all of them in one place, and he was going to kill them.

"They deserve it," he said—to Ophim, or perhaps to himself, he wasn't sure anymore and didn't think it mattered.

He started to reach for the comm—it would be enjoyable to taunt Syndulla—but it exploded with a burst of static that elicited a little yelp from him. At first he wondered if he was imagining it. The communications hub couldn't have repaired the third dish that quickly, could they?

He stared at the squelching comm set for a few breaths, his chest rising and falling, sweat beading his forehead. If the comm was back up, then what?

"What does it mean, Ophim?" he asked.

He reached slowly for the communicator, stared at it a moment, activated it, and then hailed the hub. "Do you . . . copy?"

Static, then, "This is the Equatorial Communications Hub. We copy. Identify—"

Belkor dropped the communicator as if it were on fire, then hurriedly grabbed it again. He transmitted the coordinates of the Twi'lek village to the V-wing leader. "The traitors are on the ground there. There's a Twi'lek village at the bottom of an old quarry, and many Twi'leks along the side and lip of the quarry. Kill everything. No one is to escape. Acknowledge."

A long moment passed before the wing commander said, "Acknowledged . . . sir."

Belkor wanted to see it all for himself, so he decreased his altitude and waited for the V-wings to start the slaughter. He would've joined them if the recon ship had any weapons. Unarmed as it was, all he could do was enjoy the show. And he could still taunt Syndulla.

Cham's encrypted comm buzzed. He activated it. "Go," he said to Belkor.

"Guess what, Syndulla?" Belkor said, his tone vaguely frantic. "Comm is back up!"

Cham felt his skin flush. "What? How do you know that?"

"Try it!" Belkor said. "Go ahead. It's all crashing down, now, Syndulla. Not just for me, though. Get ready."

Cham activated his comm and hailed Kallon, who by then would be far too distant to hail if the jamming signal was still working. "Kallon, do you copy? Kallon?"

"I copy," came Kallon's startled reply. "Cham—"

Cham cursed, cut the connection, and looked to Isval, beside him. She looked stricken. Goll stood next to her, his thick arms crossed over his chest.

"Comm is back up," Cham told them.

"We have to go, then," she said, and nodded at the village.

"My people are in position," Goll said.

Cham nodded. Goll's fighters lined the path leading down to the quarry's bottom, ready to move in on the village. Goll remained with Cham and Isval to provide fire support and coordination from up top.

"He has a comm, Cham," Isval said. "Vader does. We saw it. They'll send for rescue. We're out of time."

Cham shook his head, trying to assess things clearly, though his thoughts were jumbled. "No, we have a little time. No one is close."

"We don't know that," Isval said. "What if someone is? This is our one chance. This is the whole point of everything."

Cham looked down on the village, the Twi'leks, the women and children. He shook his head.

"Not yet," he said.

CHAPTER EIGHTEEN

"You have to do it," Isval said, but she could hear the lack of conviction in her voice. "It's now or not."

Cham looked down on the village for several beats, his eyes pained.

"Cham?" Goll asked gently. "Go or no go?"

Cham didn't turn his gaze from the villagers. "We go. But we fire warning shots."

"What?" Goll asked.

"Cham . . ." Isval said.

"I'm not firing on Twi'leks," Cham said. "They'll flee into that mine shaft when the warning shots come. That's why it's there. It's a safe-hole. Probably lets out somewhere in the forest."

"We won't have surprise," Goll said, leaving the implication unspoken.

Isval spoke it, though: "You'll get some of our people killed. You've seen what Vader can do."

She hated herself for saying it but knew it needed to be said.

Cham's face twisted in an expression she'd never seen him show before: pain, rage, despair, all of them lived in his eyes. He was weary, she saw. "Don't you think I know that, Isval? But our people signed up to fight and maybe die. Those villagers didn't. We're freedom fighters, not . . ." He trailed off, shaking his head.

"Not what?" Isval asked.

"Think about what we're considering here," Cham said. "Having V-wings strafe a village of Twi'leks. Imperial pilots killing Twi'leks on our orders. That's what we're talking about. Think about that."

Isval didn't have to think about it. Cham's words hit her like a punch. She thought of Ryiin, the other girls she'd saved over the years. She imagined girls like them in the village, just stuck in a bad situation, in the wrong place at the wrong time.

She'd been convinced that strafing the village was the right thing to do. That killing Twi'leks was worth it to get at Vader.

Her skin warmed with shame and she bowed her head.

"It's all right," Cham said to her.

She looked up at him. "No it's not."

"We all lose ourselves sometimes, Isval," he said. "We just have to find our way back."

And all at once she was reminded why Cham was so important to the movement and to whatever came after. He'd fought the Empire for years, hated what the Empire stood for no less than she did, but always his hate and his methods were informed by his principles.

She loved him. She admitted it to herself. He *was* a freedom fighter. Nothing more, perhaps, but assuredly nothing less.

"We could still walk away," she said, though the words came hard.

He shook his head immediately. "Pok," he said.

"Crost, Drim, Veraul, Eshgo, Div, Mirsil, Nordon, Krev . . ."

He went on for a time, naming every member of the movement who'd died that day, and once more Isval understood the weight he carried and labored under.

"For them we can't walk away," he said. "This can't just be worthwhile. A Star Destroyer is worthwhile. This has to be worth *them*. And that means Darth Vader and the Emperor. You were right about that all along, Isval."

She searched for words, found none, and instead put her hand on his.

Goll cleared his throat. "We can put some fire behind the villagers, give them time to get into the tunnel. But what if Vader and the Emperor run, too? Then where are we? They could take the whole village hostage, or just flee through that tunnel. What if they run, Cham? Do we let them go, or do we take the chance we hit some villagers?"

"We won't have to take a chance," Cham said, then he and Isval spoke as one. "Vader won't run."

Goll looked them in the face, nodded, and raised his wrist comlink to his mouth to issue orders to his men.

"Sometimes it's possible for a decision to be right and wrong at the same time," Cham said.

"Yeah" was all Isval said, all she *could* say.

When Goll gave Cham the nod that his men were ready, Cham pulled out the encrypted comlink and raised Belkor. "Belkor, have your V-wings hit these coordinates on my mark."

"I think I will," Belkor answered, sounding almost giddy. "But I think I'll do it now."

"No. On my mark, Belkor. Not before."

"I can see you, Syndulla!" Belkor said. Now he was giggling. "I can see you, and you're going to burn

with the rest of them! I don't answer to you anymore!"

Cham heard the telltale sound of V-wings knifing
through the atmosphere. They were already close,
and closing. Cham cursed.

"Warning shots!" he shouted to Goll. "Now! Right
now!"

Belkor watched his scan as his ships flew in toward
the village. He saw them come into scanner range,
flying low and fast over the trees. In a few seconds
they'd scorch the earth. He couldn't stop grinning.
He felt like he should caper, but the cockpit had no
room for it. Instead he danced a little in his seat.

And then he noticed something odd on the scan:
two additional ships, a transport and a shuttle.

"What are those?" he asked. "Those shouldn't be
there, Ophim."

He hailed the wing leader. "Meensa, I'm seeing two
ships accompanying your wing. Identify them."

No response.

"Meensa, identify those ships."

A hole opened in Belkor's stomach, a hollow space
that started to expand and fill with doubt. "What's
going on here?"

He hailed the transport and received no response,
so he tried the shuttle. That vessel responded, and
when he heard the voice on the other end he had trouble breathing for a moment.

"Hello, Belkor," said Mors.

Cham stared down at the quarry, hoping he was
doing the right thing, as Goll raised his wrist comlink
to his mouth and called down to his crew.

"Warning shots to scatter the villagers west. Then move in on Vader and the Emperor. Not too close. Air support is incoming."

Goll's team filed down the path in a crouch and darted along the quarry's floor, using old rockpiles as cover, shooting as they went. They fired at buildings or aimed high, the red lines of their blasters writing lines in the mist.

Cham heard the surprised shouts of the villagers carrying up from the floor of the quarry. Several of the rough-hewn structures caught fire from the blaster shots, the flames spreading quickly. One of Goll's fighters must have flung a grenade toward the village—not close enough to harm anyone, Cham presumed, but close enough to rattle the walls of the quarry and panic the villagers.

At first the Twi'leks milled around in the village center. There was shouting, there were some screams, and a few braver villagers climbed to the roofs of nearby buildings to get a look out into the quarry. Some of those fired wildly at the oncoming soldiers, but none came close to hitting anyone.

Cham watched it all unfold through the macrobinoculars, hoping that the villagers wouldn't stand and fight, hoping that he wouldn't have to call off the V-wing's strafing run. He watched, encouraged, as several of the Twi'leks started to sprint toward the mine tunnel. The adults herded children and assisted a few elderly.

"Keep going," he whispered.

Soon the other villagers started urging their friends and families to flee. Cham could see them gesturing at the tunnel. A few pulled at Vader and the Emperor, and Cham froze, fearing they might run into the tunnel, too.

He held his breath.

*   *   *

Drua tugged at Vader's cape. All around them, the Twi'lek villagers were shouting, screaming, fleeing. A few fired off into the darkness at the unseen attackers. Flames rose into the sky from two burning homes.

"Our hunters have finally caught up with us," the Emperor said, standing and straightening his clothing. Deez stood before him, shielding him, rifle readied.

"Come on!" Drua said. "Both of you. There's a safe place."

"We should retreat to the tunnel, my lords," Deez said. "Reinforcements are en route."

"Oh, I think not," the Emperor said.

Vader pushed Drua away.

"Go," the Emperor commanded her.

Drua looked surprised, then angry.

"Go, girl," the Emperor said again, and she ran away along with the rest of the remaining villagers.

"You'll have to do this yourself, my friend," the Emperor said to Vader. "I can't be seen using the Force before so many witnesses."

"I will stay at your side, my Emperor," Deez said.

Vader ignited his lightsaber.

"That's it!" Isval said, looking through the macrobinoculars.

Darth Vader and the Emperor and the lone Royal Guard stood alone in the village center, the firelight turning their shadowed forms into dark ghosts. A thin red beam extended from Vader's fist: his lightsaber.

Isval could hear the V-wings streaking in.

"Cham, the villagers are clear. Tell Belkor to have

the V-wings level the place! It's just Vader and the Emperor. We have them."

Belkor opened his mouth, closed it, opened it again, but words seemed unwilling to abandon his teeth. He was flushed, sweating. Finally he stammered, "Moff?"

"You tried to kill me, Belkor. And you killed hundreds of your fellows."

"No, no," Belkor said. "This is all a misunderstanding. I was—"

"Do *not* insult me further, Colonel," Mors snapped. "And don't do yourself any more dishonor by pleading your innocence. I know everything that you did. You have to pay."

Emotions boiled over in Belkor, anger, despair, hatred—he wasn't even sure he had a name for the rush of feeling. Instead he screamed into the comm, spraying it with spittle. "Pay? What about you? You should pay, too, you fraud! You should pay for your negligence, your laziness, for your drug use, for your slaves, for your own treachery against the Empire! I was a traitor today! You have been a traitor your entire career! You should pay, too, Mors!"

"I *will* pay," Mors said. "I *am* paying. But I'm not covered in blood, Belkor. You are."

Belkor looked over at Ophim's bruise-colored corpse, the gaping head wound he'd put there. He nodded in resignation. He *was* covered in blood. Realizing it, acknowledging it, he suddenly felt boneless, like he was made only of liquid. He sagged in his seat, the weight of the day too much.

"Because of that," Mors said, "you have to pay more than me."

To his enormous surprise, Belkor felt more relieved than anything. He did need to pay. He did.

"What are you going to do, then, Moff?" he asked, his voice little more than a whisper. "Turn me over to the ISB? To Vader?"

"No, Belkor. I'm not going to turn you over to the Security Bureau or Vader."

One of the V-wings diverted slightly from the rest of the group and blazed toward the recon ship on an attack vector.

Belkor nodded and sighed. He didn't even think of running. It would have been pointless anyway. A recon ship had no chance of evading a V-wing.

"No, you couldn't turn me over to them, could you?" he said. "I might tell them things you don't want them to know."

"It's all over, Colonel," Mors said.

Thank goodness, Belkor thought.

"Good-bye," Mors said.

The V-wing closed. Belkor's comp blared an alarm when the V-wing gained a weapons lock.

He took his hands off the stick and sat back in his seat. He looked over at Ophim's corpse. "I'm sorry, Ophim."

His computer screeched a warning that the V-wing's weapons were active. Belkor closed his eyes. His world exploded in fire.

Isval, Cham, and Goll ducked instinctively as a ship exploded overhead into an orange fireball. Cham already had the encrypted comm to Belkor in his fist. He activated it.

"What was that, Belkor? Belkor?"

No response.

A V-wing knifed through the sky overhead, cutting through the cloud left in the sky by the explosion. Several more were swooping in behind it.

"Have them strafe the village, Belkor. Just tell them . . ."

"That was a recon bubble," Goll said, causing Cham to trail off.

"What?" Cham asked him.

"The ship that exploded was a recon bubble."

"No," Isval said, despair creeping into her voice. "It wasn't. Was it?"

Cham squeezed the communicator so tightly his knuckles hurt. "Belkor, do you read? Belkor?"

Nothing.

And Cham knew that it was all coming undone.

Mors was well within visual range when Belkor's ship exploded above the quarry, shooting orange and red streamers across the sky. Mors felt ambivalent as she watched the V-wing knife through the fire and smoke. In some ways, Mors had made Belkor. She supposed it was right that she was also the one to unmake him. She sighed and turned her mind from the colonel and his treachery back to events at hand.

"We land to either side of the Twi'lek forces in the quarry," she said to Steen. "None escape. Send a contingent of stormtroopers to secure the Emperor."

"Aye, ma'am."

"Attack wing," Mors said to the V-wings. "Take a visual pass of the quarry rim and surrounding forest. Weapons are loose for anything you see there. Do not fire into the quarry, however."

She figured anything outside the quarry was either Imperial traitors, Twi'lek forces of the Free Ryloth movement, or Twi'lek natives. She didn't distinguish among those groups for purposes of targeting.

"Setting down," said the pilot, wheeling the shuttle down in front of the Twi'leks who'd descended the side of the quarry and were advancing toward the native village.

Behind them, cutting off their retreat, Steen's transport landed. Before the transport even hit the ground, the passenger doors were thrown open and the stormtroopers started leaping out, blaster rifles spitting plasma. Half of them sprinted back toward the village to find the Emperor.

The Twi'leks turned to face them as the doors to the shuttle opened and the stormtroopers on Mors's ship rushed out, rifles hot. The Twi'leks were caught in a crossfire. Lines of energy lit up the bottom of the quarry. A handful of shots came from somewhere above and to Mors's right, presumably from along the lip of the quarry.

The V-wings screamed through the sky overhead without firing a shot at the village.

"Where did those other ships come from?" Isval asked, firing down at the transport and shuttle that had landed to either side of Goll's team and puked stormtroopers.

The quarry's floor was alight with blasterfire. Shouts carried up through the night air. Goll's people were trapped, pinned down.

She saw Vader bound out of the village at a run, lightsaber in hand.

"See him?" she said.

"See him," Goll and Cham said.

They fired by turns at Vader, at the stormtroopers. Someone from the quarry's bottom returned fire, the shots pinging off the stone and sending Isval and Goll back from the edge for a moment. Cham just kept firing, his jaw set, his eyes fixed.

"They're cut off!" Goll shouted, returning to the lip

to fire. "We have to get down there or extract them. Get Faylin and the shuttle over here."

"She'll never make it through the V-wings," Isval said, and Cham knew she was right.

The men on the quarry's floor were dead, or soon would be.

Cham resolved to hurt the Empire as best he could before he died.

"Everything on Vader," he said. "Focus on him."

The three of them poured fire down on the dark shadow and the glowing red line he carried.

Mors watched through the cockpit viewport—impervious to small-arms fire—as soldiers on both sides shouted orders, fired their blasters, and died. The Twi'leks dropped to their bellies or knees and divided into two groups, each firing in a different direction, while the stormtroopers ran toward them in a crouch, firing as they came. Twi'leks screamed and died. Stormtroopers hit by blaster bolts flew backward or spun to the ground, their armor blackened by fire. Mors sat in her seat and watched it all unfold. It could—and would—end only one way. The Twi'leks were surrounded.

She looked up, saw the V-wings turning sharply to come back in on an attack vector. They must have found something along the top of the quarry at which to shoot.

Movement outside the ship caught her eye, and when she saw the source, it caught her breath.

Lord Vader strode heedlessly through the crossfire, cape flowing out behind him, his lightsaber cutting the air before him, deflecting dozens of blaster shots back at the Twi'leks, killing one, another, another. He did it all almost casually, as though his mind was on other things. The black lenses of his helmet were fixed upward, at the rim of the quarry.

As Mors watched, Vader exploded into motion, moving at a preternatural speed that left her mouth hanging open stupidly. Vader was heading directly for the side of the quarry, which was too steep for an ordinary man to scale. But Mors knew she wasn't looking at an ordinary man.

"Who is that?" the pilot asked softly as both of them leaned in their seats to follow Vader's progress. "Is that . . ."

Mors nodded. "Darth Vader," she said, and pitied the person or persons upon whom Vader had fixed his gaze.

"Those V-wings are coming back around," Goll said, firing down into the quarry at Vader, who was sprinting across the quarry's floor, coming on so fast that Cham would not have believed it had he not seen it. Isval had both pistols out and aimed, firing red lines at Vader. Cham was shooting as fast as he could, too, but Vader's blade was faster, deflecting every shot, sending fully half of them back at Isval and Cham and Goll, causing them to duck and cover.

When Vader reached the steep-walled side of the quarry he bounded up, caught a hold on some protuberance or other, crouched, and bounded up again.

"That's impossible," Goll muttered, but he kept firing.

Isval knew better. She'd seen what Vader could do. Nothing he did surprised her.

And now he was coming for them.

They kept firing, leaning out over the lip of the quarry to fire down the steep side, but Vader's lightsaber turned the air red before him and none of their shots so much as touched him. He leapt from one spot to the next, ascending, pausing only for a moment upon landing to tense before leaping again and ascending farther.

"How is he doing this?" Goll shouted.

Vader's cape flowed out behind him as he came, and he looked to Isval like some kind of mythological being, some dark spirit of death come to take a tithe of lives. She couldn't let him take Cham's. The movement needed him. And he had a daughter. She wouldn't.

"Get out of here," she said to Goll and Cham.

She looked down past Vader to the floor of the quarry. The firefight was already slowing. Goll's fighters were dying or dead. She could hear the V-wings streaking back toward them.

"Get out of here!" she said. "Now!"

Cham seemed not to hear her. He was firing rapidly at Vader, his teeth clenched, his skin flushed.

"Goll, get him out of here!"

She turned and looked back to see the V-wings bearing down on them. Goll followed her gaze, turned, and saw the ships incoming.

"Come on, Cham!" Goll said, grabbing him by the shoulder.

"I'm not leaving! You go!"

Vader leapt up again, again. His eyes were fixed upward, on Isval, on Cham.

"Go, damn it!" Isval shouted. "You have a daughter, Cham! Think of Hera! Take him, Goll! Remember our deal! Go!"

She stood up, making herself plain to Vader.

"What are you doing?" Cham exclaimed. "Get down, Isval!"

She turned and smiled at him, not a half smile, a full one. "I'm thinking through an exit. I love you, Cham. Now get out of here!"

And with that, before Cham could say anything, she ran along the lip of the quarry away from them, firing at Vader with both blasters as she went.

"Isval!" Cham called after her, but she ignored him. He loved her, too. He had for years.

"Do you remember me?" Isval shouted down to Vader, still firing at him. "Do you? I saw you on the *Perilous* before I blew it to hell!"

The sound of the V-wings streaking in sounded like a scream.

"Come on, Cham!" Goll said, and pulled him up by his collar. "Now! Right now!"

"I'm . . . not . . . leaving her!" Cham said, looking at Isval, trying to shake himself loose from Goll.

Above, the V-wings were roaring down on them.

Goll finally heaved him up, flung him over his back like a knapsack, and started running for the tree line. Cham cursed him, tried to shake himself free, but Goll was even stronger than he looked and Cham might as well have been a child.

"Isval!" he shouted.

Blasterfire sounded from above them, the V-wings opening fire. Trees splintered and cracked, huge chunks of dirt and stone exploded, and the concussive blast of the V-wings' firepower caused Goll to stumble. Rocks pelted Cham, most of them small, until a large one caught him in the temple. He saw sparks and turned dizzy. Goll seemed to be moving in slow motion. Distinct sounds disappeared, replaced by a dull roar. Everything went black.

Vader bounded over the side of the quarry, standing in the smoky aftermath of the V-wings' strafing run.

The wind billowed his cape, and Isval could hear the rhythmic work of his respirator. She was eight meters from him, the man or god or whatever he was who'd done repeatedly what no one should have been able to do.

"You should be dead," she said, her voice hoarse. She holstered her blasters.

"As should you," he said, and his voice was as deep as the quarry. He deactivated his lightsaber.

She thought of Pok, of Eshgo, of Nordon, and everything in her boiled over at once. She shouted and rushed him, drawing a knife as she came, knowing even as she did that she'd never get close enough to use it but hoping somehow to take him by surprise.

Of course she didn't.

No one took Vader by surprise. How could they?

He raised a hand and somehow stopped her altogether. Her body would not respond to her mind. It was as though he held her in a giant fist. She felt her body rise, lifted off the ground, felt the knife fall from her grasp. Vader turned his head slightly sideways, eyeing her, and made a pinching gesture with thumb and forefinger.

Her windpipe closed and she could not breathe, could not even gag. She stared at him as her body screamed for oxygen, hoping to pierce him with her eyes, with her rage, with her hate.

Her vision went dark, narrowing down into a tunnel, at the end of which stood a dark figure in dark armor with his hand raised. In seconds she couldn't see. She could hear the slow, steady beat of Vader's respiration but could draw no breath herself. The world went dark.

* * *

Cham opened his eyes. He was in a ship, Faylin's ship. He felt it go airborne as he left Isval behind, as he left everything behind.

"No," he muttered, but it was done. She was gone. Everything was gone.

He stared at the bulkhead, not really seeing it, not really seeing anything.

"What happened?" Faylin called back from the cockpit. "Where is everyone? What happened, Goll?"

"Just fly the damn ship, Faylin," Goll said. "Cham? You all right? Are you hit?"

"Are they dead?" Faylin asked. "Is everyone dead?"

"Fly the ship, human!" Goll snapped.

"They *are* dead," Cham said, his voice dull and gray. "Everyone is dead. The movement is dead."

Isval was dead.

"Don't say that," Faylin said, shaking her head. "Don't. That's not right. We're still here. We're still here."

"Stay on top of the trees, Faylin," Goll said. "With the comm back up, this area will be crawling with Imperial ships soon."

She didn't say anything but did as Goll asked.

"What are we?" Cham said. "*What* are we, Faylin? A swarm of insects trying to sting a rancor."

"You're not thinking clearly," Goll said. "That's grief talking. I've seen it before."

"Have you?" Cham snapped at him. "Have you really?"

"She was my friend, too, Cham," Goll said.

But she'd been more to Cham than a friend, and all of it had gone unsaid until the end. "You shouldn't have listened to her," he said to Goll.

"Of course I should've. And you know it. You have to carry this forward, Cham. You're the only one who can. She knew that. That's why she delayed Vader. You know that."

Cham did know it. On some level, in some way, he knew she was right.

"What do we do now, Goll?" Faylin asked. "Where am I even going?"

Goll stared at Cham. "Cham? What are we doing next?"

Cham thought of all he'd lost that day—not just Isval, but the many others. He thought of the men and women he'd lose in the coming days, when the Empire put Ryloth under its heel and questioned every suspected rebel they could find. He knew it would never end. Ryloth was just another obstacle to the Emperor and his plans. Tomorrow another world would be ground to dust. Then another. The Empire was a machine, and its gears would just keep turning, grinding away at freedom until there was none left in the galaxy.

Someone had to keep fighting against that. Someone had to make them pay for that, for Isval, for every life they took in their fixation on order and control.

Cham could not quit. He could never quit. He'd just paid the dearest price he could imagine. The Empire could do nothing more to him. He'd fight, fight them forever and without remorse and without pity and without quitting. Ever.

"We get as many of our people clear of the system as quickly as we can," he said. "Then we get out of here. Kallon should've already started the withdrawal. Then . . ."

He paused, and Isval's face appeared in his mind's eye, her fierce eyes, her smile, not a half smile but a full smile, the one he'd keep close to him forever. His eyes welled, but his conviction didn't waver.

"Then what?" asked Faylin.

"Then we fight, Faylin. We damn well keep fighting."

Plans would come later. For now, the resolve to carry on the fight was enough.

Goll grinned and thumped him on his shoulder hard enough to hurt. "You heard the man! We fight!"

Isval came back to consciousness on her knees, her wrists behind her, bound with some kind of restraint. Stormtroopers called out orders to one another; they moved through the quarry shooting any of the Free Ryloth troops that still survived. She was the only one they were taking prisoner, it seemed. She imagined herself being subjected to interrogation by Vader and tried not to think too hard about it. The fact that she didn't see Cham anywhere gave her hope. She told herself he'd gotten away. She'd thought through an exit—his.

The Emperor stood before her, an old man in dark robes, his jaw hard, his eyes as sharp as knives. Beside him stood Darth Vader, looming and dark. Stormtroopers stood in a loose ring behind him, their white armor ghostly in the dark. A Royal Guard stood just behind the Emperor, his helmet gone, his face inked with tattoos, the whole of him covered in grime.

"She fears I will turn her over to the ISB," the Emperor said to Vader, his voice surprisingly gentle. "There are far worse things than that, my dear."

"I don't fear you at all," she said.

"I think that's true," he said. "I should've expected nothing else. But you also understand very little."

Isval stuck out her chin. "I understand the Empire lost a Star Destroyer and hundreds of troops today. *You* lost them. To us."

"True," he said, the frustrating hint of a smile lurking in his words. "Very true. You know what I've lost, but do you know what I've gained? Have you considered that?"

"You've gained nothing!" she said contemptuously. "You barely escaped with your life."

"Oh, my life was never in danger, dear girl. But since you seem unable to understand what actually happened here, I will tell you. Everything that happened today happened only because I allowed it to. True, your sorry little movement struck its blow, but it did so too soon, before the time was ripe and before it was mature enough to pose a serious threat. And now it's exhausted itself and will grow into nothing. What's left of it after today, do you think?"

Hearing an echo of Cham's words come from the mouth of the Emperor was too much.

"Shut up," she said, looking away and hating herself for the tears that welled in her eyes. "You don't know what you're talking about."

Cham was left, she told herself. He, at least, was left.

"Ah, she begins to see now," the Emperor said. "Perhaps you thought the events today would spark a rebellion? Ah, you did." He laughed contemptuously, the sound gouging itself into Isval's brain. "That was never going to happen, my dear. Your little movement was a candle that I encouraged you to light and now . . . it has gone out, igniting nothing." He knelt and looked her in the face. His eyes were as empty as a corpse's. "Nothing." He stood, looking down on her. "Lord Vader."

Behind him, towering and dark, Vader ignited his lightsaber. Isval heard her death in the sizzle of its blade. The tears in her eyes dried, replaced by defiance, by anger, by hope kindled in the knowledge that

Cham, at least, had escaped, that the fire of rebellion had not gone out because he carried it.

She stared up at Vader, unafraid. "I hate you and everything you stand for," she said. "But when I murdered, I murdered out of love."

Vader raised his blade, his breathing loud and steady. When he spoke, his voice was as deep and hollow as a funeral gong.

"I know precisely what you mean," he said, and slashed.

Her decapitated body fell at Vader's feet. He deactivated his blade.

"There's work for that yet, my friend," the Emperor said, nodding at the hilt of Vader's blade.

"Master?"

"The villagers, Lord Vader. Drua and her people. We can't allow so many witnesses to live. I'll wait for you here."

Vader looked from his Master to the dark mouth of the mine inside of which Drua and the rest of the villagers had fled. He felt the Emperor's eyes on him, the intensity of the gaze, the weight of his expectations, and Vader knew that the day's events had been only half about depleting a rebel movement before it could grow. They had also, as Vader had suspected, been about testing him, forcing him to face the ghosts of his past and exorcise them forever and fully. He saw that more clearly now; saw, too, that his Master was right to administer the test. It also explained why his Master had shown so little of his true power throughout the day. Perhaps he'd wanted Vader to rely on himself to overcome the challenges they'd faced. Or perhaps he'd wanted to seem weaker than he was, to draw out any treacherous ambitions Vader may have held.

"I hear and I obey, Master," Vader said.

He ignited his lightsaber and strode toward the cave, his mind drifting back to another day, a day when he strode into the Jedi Temple filled with nothing but younglings. He'd slaughtered them then, and he would slaughter the Twi'leks now.

His Master's laughter followed him into the cave, and it lingered in his mind, louder even than the screams of the Twi'leks as they began to die by his blade.

When it was done, he returned to his Master's side.

"Well done, old friend," Darth Sidious said. He wiped his hands, as if to clean them of dirt. "And now let's move on to more important things."

Read on for the short story

ORIENTATION

by John Jackson Miller

This story was originally published
in *Star Wars Insider Magazine* #157.

"BATTLE STATIONS! HOSTILES OFF THE STAR-
board bow!"

In the command well of the Imperial cruiser *Defi-ance,* twenty members of the skeleton crew hastily turned to their terminals, ready to defend against attack. Every mind was attuned to the situation—save the one belonging to the figure looming dark and large above them on the catwalk. Darth Vader looked on with utter disinterest.

There was nothing in this "battle" to engage the Dark Lord's attention. It wasn't real. There was no one to challenge the Empire. He and his Master Darth Sidious, who now ruled the galaxy as the Emperor, had brought the Clone Wars to a conclusion not long before; and while the two were on their way to Ryloth now to root out insurgency, the "hostiles" outside were pure fiction, part of a training exercise.

"Hard about, my cretins," shouted Commandant Baylo, passing Vader as he stalked along the catwalk. "While I've been waiting for your picnic to end, you've lost your forward shields!" He clapped his hands on the railing and leaned over to bellow, "We have an observer today. Are you trying to make me look bad?"

Vader thought he already did. Well past seventy and with a nose too long for his face, Pell Baylo walked with an exaggerated limp that caused the stumpy man to bob up and down like a flying thing. He nonetheless commanded the attention of the cadets in the pits on either side of the catwalk, all of whom were now scrambling to correct their errors.

Vader thought his own presence here was a mistake, too. But Sidious had brought him to *Defiance*'s bridge and left him. It was his duty to remain, even if he saw no other reason for being there.

Crossing the vast swath of cosmos between Coruscant and Ryloth, Darth Sidious had ordered a stop in the Denon system so he could consult with several chiefs of the navy, visiting there to discuss how the jumble of affiliated military schools that had existed under the Republic might be better integrated into the Imperial Academy. His livelihood under review, Baylo had suggested a time-saving solution: The meeting could take place aboard *Defiance,* the cruiser he'd operated as a flight training school for nearly fifty standard years. The commandant could show his students in action while they conveyed His Imperial Highness on one leg of his trip.

The Emperor had praised Baylo for his suggestion. Vader saw through the offer. *A futile effort to save his school.* The Clone Wars had brought the *Defiance* Flight Training Institute—known to most spacers as the Baylo School—directly under the umbrella of the

Republic Navy, with Baylo receiving a rank as a line officer. Yet the commandant treated the institute as his personal property, ignoring schedules and asserting he knew best when recruits were ready for service. Even now, with the Empire in charge, naval leaders were loath to rein Baylo in; he'd trained many of them aboard *Defiance,* after all. Vader expected that resistance would wilt now that the Emperor was on the scene. Baylo was just another fossil, married to archaic practices.

But his Master had spent half a minute on the bridge before departing for his meetings with the naval chiefs who were Baylo's superiors—leaving Vader behind to observe Baylo's silly pantomime show. Vader had objected, as strenuously as he dared: "I would serve you better elsewhere, Master." The Emperor had not been amused. "I decide where you are needed. You will remain and be my eyes."

That was hours ago, and Vader hadn't seen anything worth his attention. Baylo had run his cadets through their paces, dressing down one after another and spewing aphorisms. The first mock attack concluded, he unleashed another one.

"—it's all about attitude, in more ways than one," Baylo was saying to someone, mid-rant. "Think about your direction, your facing. Don't you know where you're going, cadet? Because if *you* don't, your ship certainly won't . . ."

The trainees—humans in their early twenties, some on their first orientation flights—seemed almost happy to absorb the platitudes and abuse. Vader knew Baylo had a mythic status in naval circles, and not just for his exploits. *Defiance* had fought pirates when it was in patrol service, yes—but Baylo's spine had been injured, and now his daily battle was with near-constant pain. Twice since he had been aboard,

Vader had heard cadets whispering of Baylo's bravery in working despite the agony.

Ridiculous. Baylo knew nothing of pain.

A voice came from behind. "Shuttle arriving from Denon, Commandant. Vice Admiral Tallatz aboard."

Baylo stood back from the railing. "That'll be the last of Palpatine's—of the *Emperor's* guests for his meeting." He checked the time. "Navigator, plot our hyperspace route to—"

"I already have it, sir," called out a female voice from the pit.

"I'll be the judge of that." Forcing one atrophied foot in front of the other, Baylo fought his way down the steps into the command well. A woman with deep-brown skin, dressed in sharp cadet grays, slid her chair from her terminal, allowing the old man to approach. She wore the trace of a knowing smile as Baylo read the monitor.

"I'm impressed, cadet," he said. "You'll go far—and so will this ship. Or did you *not* intend to plot a course into Wild Space?"

The cadet's grin vanished. The young woman looked past him at her calculations, suddenly puzzled. "It is a course to Christophsis, sir, where the *Perilous* will meet us."

"You've failed to account for a singularity along our route, which will reshape our hyperspace passage in a most startling way. We now know who our next admiral will be," he added with a snort. The young woman stepped away in humiliation as Baylo began to work the console. After a moment's effort, he stepped back. "There. Small repair, major difference." He looked around and about. "Details matter, everyone. A navy isn't built on captains—but on crews that watch their work."

"Aye, Commandant," came the response from the cadets.

Aware of Vader's gaze, Baylo looked up at the Dark Lord. "They don't learn right away, but they do learn. I get results. You can tell your Emperor that."

"He is your Emperor, as well." They were the first words Vader had spoken before the trainees, and several shifted in their seats on hearing his powerful voice.

But if Baylo was shaken, he didn't show it. "I'm sorry. I forget—what are you to the Emperor, again?"

"You would do well never to learn."

That time, Vader got a reaction. Baylo straightened— a strenuous feat for him—and he slapped the back of the chair of the woman he had corrected. "Well, I can still teach my people a few things. Extra courier detail for you, Sloane, once you're done here. You can think about navigation while you're finding your way around ship."

"Aye, Commandant." The cadet returned to her station and stared blankly at the screen before her, trying to understand her mistake.

Baylo hobbled back toward the staircase. "You have the settings. Take us to hyperspace as soon as the admiral's docking is complete. I must prepare in case they need me." He struggled up the steps and made his way past Vader. "Carry on, cadets."

Vader watched the aged commandant exit—and then thought about the exchange. The man Vader had been would have bristled at such treatment. His Jedi teachers all thought they knew better than he did. And they were so smug, always pretending they knew some secret about the universe he was unworthy to learn. It was all a lie, a false front to hide their weaknesses. Darth Sidious, now the Emperor, had the

346 JOHN JACKSON MILLER

secrets, not them. It had been a delight to prove them all wrong.

But Sidious was now in that same role as teacher, and he was doing many of the same things: acting as though he knew better, and doling out information only as he chose. Vader had traded all the Masters on the Jedi Council for one. A better one, he knew: The secrets of power Sidious shared were real. And yet, as different as their Master–apprentice relationship was, he had served Sidious long enough to get that familiar feeling. The Emperor had something else to do—and he had given Vader busywork.

No. That concept fundamentally clashed with something Vader had long known about himself. *Every job I do is important—because I am the one doing it.*

His cape trailing behind him, Vader descended the stairs into the command well. There, at the end, sat the chastened cadet from earlier.

"Tallatz has debarked," called out her neighbor. "His shuttle's clear."

Sloane looked hard at the numbers before her again and sighed. "Commandant's coordinates locked in the navicomputer. Stand by for hyperspace jump on my mark."

"*Hold.*"

Vader's voice startled her, and she turned her chair. Brown eyes widened as she looked up at him. "Yes, my lord?"

"What do you see?"

"N-nothing."

"You fear to contradict your master."

She shuffled in her seat. "My lord, I don't wish to say the admiral is wrong about—"

"No. That is *exactly* what you wish to do." The woman had hidden her emotions from her companions, but she could not fool Vader. He had felt her anger at being embarrassed—and it had bubbled up since, finally breaking through his own preoccupied thoughts. "Speak, cadet—?"

"Sloane." She swallowed hard. "Rae Sloane, of Ganthel." She gestured to the panel behind her. "I've studied our orientation and done the math, with the computer and without. Something isn't right . . ."

Baylo was waiting in the anteroom as Vader stepped onto the administrative deck. Wearing an antique greatcoat, dress attire for the era during which he trained, Baylo leaned near a large viewport looking out upon the streaming stars of hyperspace. He was using the window frame for support, Vader saw. He looked old, even for Baylo.

He straightened as he saw Vader. "Told you we'd get under way on time."

Vader said nothing.

"Hmph." Baylo looked back at the closed door. "Not used to waiting outside my own office."

"It is not your office."

Baylo looked at Vader—and chuckled lightly. "Whatever you say," he said. Before the old man could return his gaze outside, the door to the office opened. Three women and one man emerged, admirals all: chiefs of various branches of the Imperial Navy. Each glanced briefly at Baylo and silently headed for the lift.

That evoked a frown from the commandant, but only for a moment. "The Emperor will see us now," Vader said.

"Who told you that?"

Vader simply pointed to the door. Shrugging, Baylo

took a breath and started for it, shadowed by the Dark Lord.

The master of *Defiance* stood in his own office, hands clasped and eyes directly forward. The room was windowless save for a single viewport—and the walls were covered with plaques and pictures depicting the names and faces of cadet classes from the past. Vader thought the room somber, a pathetic shrine to a soon-to-be-forgotten past. An appropriate setting, too: Seated at Baylo's desk, the black-robed Emperor began to describe his just-settled plans for the Imperial Academy. They included several modifications to streamline operations, making the body more responsive to him. And one other change: "*Defiance* is approaching obsolescence—and we will employ no one who is unresponsive to command. The 'Baylo School,' as you call it, will be folded into the existing training center at Corellia. And you will take a chair at the navigation institute planetside."

"No."

The Emperor was more surprised by Baylo's response than Vader was. "Repeat yourself," his Master said, in a voice nearing a hiss.

"No, I will not transfer this vessel to your new command." Still standing as erect as his gnarled frame would allow, Baylo nodded toward the great seal on the wall to the right of his desk. "*Defiance* was commissioned by the Galactic Republic—and detached to me so those who trained here might serve that Republic. I do not recognize your order as legitimate."

The Emperor frowned. "Don't play games, Commandant. Whether you've had time to redecorate or not, the Republic is no more. The Senate decided—"

"—to dissolve its pact with the people," Baylo said, voice rising in volume. "What I owed allegiance to no longer exists. I consider the Galactic Empire a hostile power—and I can't fulfill these orders." He reached inside his waistcoat, an act that drew Vader's immediate attention. But before he reached through the Force to summon his lightsaber, Vader saw Baylo produce a datapad. "This is my resignation." He offered it to the Emperor.

The Emperor simply stared. Then he chuckled. "A republican, Baylo? I was told you were more intelligent."

Finding no takers, Baylo returned the datapad to his pocket. "I am, of course, willing to report to the brig until we reach our destination. I understand the need to keep an orderly ship." He fixed his eyes on the Emperor. "But order's place is in the military. Not in civilian life." Baylo looked back toward Vader. Seeing no response, the commandant shrugged. He looked up to the viewport, and the stars streaking by. "Enjoy the rest of your journey. I figure I'm dismissed."

Vader took a step toward Baylo. He, too, had been watching the stars flying past outside while listening to the man's little speech—and waiting to see how the Emperor reacted. Baylo turned to discover Vader barring his way. "This guy again." Baylo spoke through clenched teeth, trying not to betray any fear. "I don't care if you kill me."

"No," Vader said. *That much is true.* "Because you think you are already dead."

The Emperor looked keenly at Vader. "His ailments?"

"No. He plotted a course that will cause *Defiance* to emerge from hyperspace at Christophsis—and plunge into its sun."

The Emperor's eyes widened a little.

"I countermanded the orders."

Now they narrowed. His Master asked, "And?"

And as if in answer, *Defiance* returned to realspace at that moment—with millions of safe kilometers between it and the aforementioned star. Vader could see it shining outside the viewport, along with something else: *Perilous* was there, waiting as instructed.

Seeing them, Baylo mouthed an obscenity. The Emperor saw them, too. "Very good, my old friend." He looked kindly on Vader. "This is part of what I expect from you—to manage the petty problems so that I can focus on larger matters."

Vader felt a surge of pride. He had suspected it was a test the Emperor had placed in his path; instead, he'd caught something his Master had missed. Even so, the word *petty* didn't sit well with Vader, and he could feel it bothered Baylo more. "You have something to say?" Vader asked.

"You bet," Baylo said, throwing caution away. He'd sagged on learning of his plot's failure, but in focusing his pain and anger on the Emperor he seemed to gain strength. "I've watched you and your cronies, Palpatine. Corrupting the navy, bit by bit during the Clone Wars. Turning something noble, something meant as a shield, into a weapon. Something *oppressive*. A service it's taken generations to build, that students of mine have given their lives to!" He thrust his finger at the images on the far wall. "I'm older than you, 'Emperor'—no matter what you look like now. I remember when this was an honorable calling!"

Vader had been waiting for his Master's angry reprisal ever since Baylo opened his disrespectful mouth, but instead the Emperor seemed amused. "You would have killed several of your own colleagues."

"Traitors, trying to save their posts."

"And a crew of your cadets, for vengeance?"

"A better fate than turning them into droids. Because that's what you want, isn't it? Mindless slaves, just robots in your—"

The words caught in Baylo's throat—as did his breath. Vader clutched the fingers of his right hand together, summoning the dark side of the Force to snap the commandant's windpipe. He fell to the deck like a Toydarian whose wings had been clipped; a not unpleasant comparison, Vader thought.

But the Emperor's smile vanished. "Lord Vader!" he said, rising from his seat. "I did not instruct you to kill him."

Vader looked at the Emperor and said nothing. Alone again, they were Master and apprentice, Sidious and Vader; and the elder Sith Lord spoke freely and angrily. "I would have kept the wretch alive, to take pleasure from his pain as I transformed his navy—while I broke down his precious ship into cafeteria trays." He mused as he looked on the corpse. "And a teacher who could so easily kill his students might be molded into something I could use."

"He was a threat," Vader said. "He is finished."

Sidious scowled. "Still, I did not command it."

"He is a petty thing, one of those you expect *me* to deal with. My way is faster," Vader said, before catching himself, and adding: "—Master."

Sidious looked at him. But before more words could pass between them, a chime came from the door. "Enter," the Emperor said.

The door slid open, and Sloane stepped forward. "Captain Luitt of *Perilous* has hailed," she said. Reluctant to look directly at the Emperor and his ominous servant, she sought for something else to focus on. "He's ready to resume your journey to Ryloth as soon as you . . ." The proper cadet trailed off as her eyes discovered the body on the floor. She gasped.

"Commandant Baylo succumbed to his injuries at last," the Emperor said, indifferent.

Sloane looked startled. Baylo had been all right the last time she'd seen him. But she could not be unhappy, Vader thought: Baylo had belittled her in public. Sloane would probably realize that later, once she remembered where her priorities lay. She was smart, and smart people could figure that out.

But now the Emperor claimed her attention as he stepped past the fallen commandant en route to the exit. "I have an additional instruction for you to convey to your superiors at the Academy."

"Y-yes, my lord?"

"This training vessel's name is to be changed," the Emperor said, looking back purposefully at Vader. "From *Defiance*—to *Obedience*."

"Of—of course." She bowed and prepared to follow.

And Vader did, as well.